D1311060

Foreword

This book was written several years ago and I have only now garnered enough confidence—and this is mostly a lie, as I am still incredibly nervous—to publish it. My greatest fear is that it will be misunderstood or misinterpreted, that certain oddments of the narrative might be seen as debut amateurisms. Worse, I fear that such amateurisms are actually present, hiding between the many layers of revision (it took me about a week before I noticed I wrote "forward" just above, for instance).

Anyway, I hope you enjoy the story. And I hope any unanswered questions you might have are addressed in the Appendix at the end of the text.

Acknowledgements

There are droves of people who have helped me with this book, most of whom have no idea they have helped. Be it a one-on-one conversation that influenced a scene's dialogue or a technical insight revealed in a podcast (hey, Alzabo Soup), every little tidbit has been invaluable.

I'd first like to thank my family, especially my parents for not warding me away (that much) from a writing career.

I wish to thank the earliest readers: Julia, Victoria, Fox, Imola, Benny, Foyinsi, Devon, Amber, Kehan, and Scott; and additional shoutout to Ash and Sophie for their support and community efforts.

Further thanks to my writing teachers and mentors—no matter how brief our acquaintance—for their encouragement. To name a few: Ed Pierce, Kathryn Howd-Machan, Eleanor Henderson, Antonio DiRenzo, Joan Marcus, Tyrell Stewart-Harris, and Martha McPhee.

Special thanks to Kelly McMasters for guiding my latest revisions and providing me with all manner of wisdom.

Also special thanks to the artists: the cartographer Dominique Strange of Domino44maps, the cover illustrator Zhongxiu He, and the moonblood illustrator Shuqi Gao.

I would lastly like to thank my inspirations, my holy trinity, though they will never hear it: Gene Wolfe, Ursula K. LeGuin, and Jean "Moebius" Giraud.

*Dedicated to
both Winifreds*

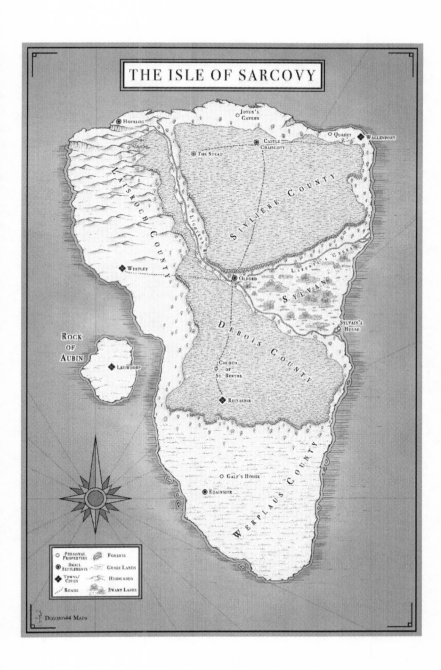

THE ISLE OF SARCOVY

FITZMORLEY

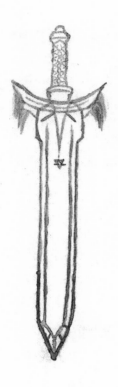

Part I

Chapter I – The Rudiment

Fitzmorley stood out in Rolle's Channel, waiting for more salmon to swim unwarily with the current into his net. He had caught two already: they floated dead in their private sections of the trap, each tied shut with thin ropes. When he glanced down at them again, his thoughts were invaded by a vision. A memory. The most persistent one he knew.

It often came to him with slow aggression, preceded by the smell of wet grass and the salt breeze carried over acres of flat accented green. It began with the house cutting into the hill. Gale stood atop it, leaning against his five-pace-long sword just above the cracked triangle of the ashlar gable. Any memory of the hill-house placed that man there unfalteringly, now that he was gone.

Then Fitzmorley was there where the man stood, alone at the crown of the highest hillock in all of Werplaus, the island's southernmost quarter. All about him was the long weedy plain, punctuated by the sea's bold blue line. Northward: a hairy bump of rising land and forestry. And the dark stranger approaching. By this point, and like a rabbit frightened into its burrow, Fitzmorley did what he could to shirk the memory.

At present, out in the channel, he stared down at the dead salmon. Once they'd been sealed and trapped, Fitzmorley—or simply 'Morley' now—had to clutch them and smash their heads with the mallet he kept strapped against his hip. He stared at them and they did not stare back, their eyes flat and unreal. He realized that he hated fishing.

"—course, the sprats round here are easiest to catch if ye go down closer to Gaeshena's Rock," Serryl spoke beside him. "Ye hafta take a boat out fer that job, like with any sprat catch. Bit harder over there 'cause of the sea stacks—goes without sayin', that. But over there, a few o' them barely peek above the water. One rough current, one scraped hull and yer swimmin' home. No sprats, no salmon, no eels. Just a load o' soggy clothes and a long walk back." The fisherwoman twaddled on, as was her unobstructed habit. And Morley was lulled back into his past.

His memory then placed him down below the hill-house's gable, where he sat against the earth-burdened wall of flat stones. Beside him was the first anthill of the new year, so nearly stomped earlier in his absentminded pacing. The little mound, garrisoned by an army of biting specks, was

8

raised strategically beside Gale's alphabet stone. The large tile, graphed with charcoal characters both old-form and miniscule, leaned upright aside the house's curtained entry. He'd had only one duty that day, as he remembered: cutting leeks and carrots for the night's stew.

The stranger beyond, the killer, was still there and getting closer. Morley tried now to replace the memory with another, tried to supplant the man's figure with that of the silver wolf's, his and Gale's only other visitor over their many years together—sixteen years up to that point. This didn't work either. The stranger was still there, arms swaying with his bipedal gait, his mantle of many rings glinting, his yellow hair tossing every speck of the day's grey light. And yet in this memory, his boots marched in time with a walking stave—not a sword—in his right hand.

Morley was again parted from his thoughts as the channel's waves tried to lift him. He tightened his grip on the fish-trap. Every Hetta season when it was warm enough to go fishing without clothes on, Serryl made daily ventures out to gather more of the week's supper. She brought Morley with her when it was time to use the haaf, a massive frame of gorse wood with a net fixed into the inner grooves of each beam. Another plank went down the middle, dividing the net into two sections—hence Serryl's insistence of Morley's help.

Serryl's husband and son, Tommas and Robi, both incapable of lending a hand, either remained back at Egainshir—their home and hamlet—or hiked up north to the edge of the Crouxwood to split logs. Tommas, though strong of body, could not swim and had no intention to start learning; Serryl proposed it was more out of fear than casual reluctance. Robi, meanwhile, was only a small boy. Here, where the water of Rolle's Channel was nearly five paces deep, his feet wouldn't even touch the bottom unless he were wholly submerged.

The task was thus assigned to Morley. Though he lacked strength, he was of perfect height for the job. Even better, he was patient and had a fine knack for remaining perfectly still and silent for long periods. Serryl was his opposite in this regard.

"Ye ever climb around Michel's Rock here?" the woman asked, gesturing with her head to the elongated sea stack nearby, the outermost parameter of their narrow channel. "I'd gone up there a few times when I first started livin' here. The others used to have me go on up there to get eggs—this was back before we had the chickens, o' course. I did the same with my brothers back in Olford, only it was trees we climbed, not rocks.

"Y'know, I still wonder if I should ever make the ole climb again. Seabird eggs are much, much, much bigger than the wee chickee eggs. But aye, dangerous climb it is. Don't wanna risk the fall anymore, not with Robi back home. And Tommas as well, but he knows what I get up to." As usual, Morley said nothing and kept on watching the water flow around him, churning against the beams, swishing through the languid horsehair net.

Once more, the memory beckoned him back. Watching through the eyes of the past, he clambered over the verdant slope wrapped about the hill-house's gable. On the other side was the garden, the goat pen, its five denizens, and Gale. He was seated in the grass and bundled to the chin in his shepherd's cloak. It seemed then that, in retrospect, as Fitzmorley sat himself beside his greying guardian, the man had already gotten up and surmounted the hill without a word. He had gone to meet the stranger. He had left the boy behind.

This time, as was becoming more frequent, the memory didn't end there. Fitzmorley saw himself crawl back up the sod-draped mound of their home, close enough to the top to heed the words of the older men on the other side. These words came as dull mutterings, clear as a puddle yet disconsonant as a sheep's bleating.

Soon, there came the only set of words that stayed with him.

"He isn't my son," said Gale to the unnamed outsider. "Whatever you planned for me today…need not be spoiled on his account."

And in an instant, as another spray of seawater glazed his lips and wetted his clumped brown hair, Morley lost his reverie. He looked again at the dead salmon floating next to him, then at Serryl. He had never told her about the memory, about its reality. He had never told anyone. Not even when asked.

"—and once Istain can get those lemons he's been raving on over, we can act like nobles with our fancy feasts, *hah*! Think on that. I didn't believe him when he talked about fish with lemon but, aye, the more I think about it, the more I wanna lather the stuff on a hot bit o' sprat. What d'ye think, eh?" The young man was barely listening.

"I think it's time to head in," he said. "What d'you think?" Serryl raised an eyebrow, then flicked back some of the black hair wetted against her brow.

"With only two salmons?" she wondered aloud. "Don't think we could give it another hour, mayhaps two? Still plenty and plenty of sunlight, lad."

Though Serryl was the fisherwoman, the one in charge, Morley had been the only one to make the day's catch: this gave him a fair sliver of authority for the time being. The day previous, they had caught four—though one was oddly emaciated—and the rest of the season saw an average of three catches a day whenever they lugged out the haaf.

"I didn't eat last night," he admitted. "That means we have three. Arrin doesn't want fish tonight anyway, he kinda hates the taste. And Amarta is trying out a maslin bread today. Even if that doesn't turn out too well, it'll still be a large loaf."

Serryl puckered her lips, then wiped her mouth. Morley avoided her eyes as she searched his expressionless face.

"Right, then," she soon said, "we'll head in early."

They waded back to shore with the net beams across their backs. Despite the seasonal warmth, a chill passed over them as they stepped through the tide. They were both near-naked, adorned in nothing more than loincloths. Once they reached the first dry stretch of sand, they placed down the haaf. Morley then tended to the fish he'd caught, untying their sections in the mesh, pinching their limp tailfins as he took them up. Serryl dragged the haaf to the open shed closer to the dune grass, rambling the whole way there.

"Yeah, I could settle fer a boiled egg tonight, eh?" she said. "Robi hasn't been feeling all too well lately—probably some Hetta ill. Those're common round here. Have to talk to Reffen about it, much as I'd not like to. He's an odd one, I've always thought so. Course, we're in a place where most others might'n find us odd—think of all those Reineshir folk. With their color clothes and their big houses. Only been there once on the way down from Olford. I'll never plan to head back that way again. They found me too strange and I them." She took up her tunic by the shed and slipped it on.

"Are you going out fishing tomorrow?" Morley quietly asked. He had been feeling rather unmotivated of late—he thought this was at least partly descriptive of how he felt.

"Was thinkin' I'd head out again, yeah," she replied. Ninety out of the hundred of the Hetta season, Serryl went fishing. Otherwise, she went crabbing.

"You think you can get either of the watcher-women to go with you?" he suggested. Serryl threw him his bundle of clothes. "They get bored often, as anyone can tell." He punctuated the request and statement with the invocation he'd learned from Gale: "Please?"

"Ye gonna be elsewhere, then?" she asked. Morley nodded and stepped into his threadbare trousers, tossing on his shirt deftly with his other hand. "Where ye gonna be? Semhren want another day-long gib-gab?" He shook his head. "Yeva wants to take ye out fer a walk and some sweet kissin'?" The lad said nothing. "Ceridwen wants to show ye how to do the weavin', *heh*, while she goes off and flirts with Arrin? Eh?"

"I'm going to Gale's house tomorrow," he mumbled. "Our old hillhouse."

Serryl paused, her trousers halfway up her thighs. She continued pulling them on before her sudden dolor was obvious. More obvious.

"It's been long enough, I think," Morley continued. "Istain's coming with me. There are some things I left behind. Afterwards, we're going to Reineshir to sell them, see if we can make at least a silver piece from the trade."

"Really?" She seemed surprised. "That's resourcey, I'd say."

Morley had long been unable to walk up to that mound, let alone step inside the potent house. In fact, whenever he took a day to hike out there, he could only get as far as the foot of the hill before recalling that horrid morning about three years earlier. The day he was adequately introduced to Death and, worse yet, Dying.

Serryl uncovered a pair of hooks from within the shed and stuck them into the lips of the salmon, holding them up in admiration.

"Even fer such a frugal pair, they're still pretty pretty, eh?" she said. Morley nodded and allowed a smile.

He liked Serryl very much. More so than most of the other folk in Egainshir, he had a peculiar feeling about her, an expectation of the unexpected. She enjoyed being around other people. To her, silence was a foul omen, a sign of deceitful change. Having spent his whole life with Gale, the lonesome ridder, there had been few opportunities for Morley to speak with women. He often wondered about their integral differences, what set them apart as *women* as opposed to *men*.

Serryl had a comely and hairless face, wide hips, and breasts. Hers was the only female body he'd seen bared in all his life. He had seen Gale's when they went swimming together during the hot season, but he'd thought little of it: it was only an exaggeration of his own, after all, nothing of intrigue.

After moving to Egainshir, however, Morley found that nearly everyone else on the Werplaus plain seemed to guard their bodies with special care. Indeed, Morley would've embraced this strange sentiment as well if Serryl hadn't, on their first ever outing, recommended he don a loincloth to keep the rest of his clothes dry when fishing. And as she called no attention to the sheer strangeness of the occasion, Morley couldn't help but imbibe an air of normality—of liberation, even. It persisted through their further outings until he was utterly comfortable with the little custom.

Still, these feelings did naught in informing him of the meaning behind physical difference. Apart from all the key distinctions, Serryl's body was nondescript in comparison to, say, Istain's or Tommas'. This wasn't so for some of the other women in Egainshir, however. He reckoned the watcher sisters, Gertruda and Lunferda, were the largest people in all of Werplaus. The only other women—Amarta, Ceridwen, and Yeva—were noticeably smaller, only slightly larger than Morley himself. But something still set him apart from all the rest, something curious.

As had been said of him before, the young man was the 'analogue of slender'—a common jest between the hamlet's elders—a matter of his constitution as a 'halfelev,' whatever that really meant. It had something to do with his features, as far as he could tell: the shape of his eyes and ears, and how they seemed much sharper than everyone else's.

He'd been told what it all meant before but could never understand fully. For all he knew 'halfelev' was another sex, another meaningless difference.

"Shall we get on, then?" Serryl spoke as she clambered with some effort up the dunes. Morley followed and, in five beats, the bumpy expanse of Werplaus was all before him. It was the only part of the world he knew—it *was* the world, at that. He'd only been as far as the south edge of the Crouxwood, back when Tommas brought him up to help collect wood.

Morley understood though could not well conceive that most of the island—which he knew to be called Sarcovy—was covered over with those massive, lightly swaying trunks. The Werplaus plain, the fields that had fostered him, had only sparse gorse bushes amidst all the knee-high grasses. The air was fresher near the woodlands, he felt, as if the leaves licked all the salt out of it. Even the winds were different between the two places: here, it was hollow, cold, and somewhat haunting; there, it hissed and sang, churned the branches and agitated the murmuring bark. A part of him—very, very small though impossible to ignore—wanted to step further in, abandon comfort for curiosity, perhaps even get lost.

He realized, well over halfway into their long walk from the shore back to the hamlet, that his wish would be humored the following morning. He shuddered. Then he lost himself again in Serryl's ramblings.

"Course, it's a slight past season fer the khalfrey crabs and too early fer dove-catchin'. Ye ever have crayfish? Those were our specialty up in Olford. Me and my brothers did all sorts to try and catch them—nets, bare hands, hook and bait. Seth was best at catchin' with his hands, but Sieger knew the best means o' cookin' them. Stuck 'em in a hot pan with basil and chive and onion. Whatever we had round. Might hafta take a trip up there just fer them, eh? The crayfish, I mean. And sure, my brothers too."

They approached Egainshir from the north an hour before sundown, their two fish dangling between them. They were greeted by Gertruda, who sat alone outside her house. Her chair was carved out of a four-pace-high section of a red oak trunk. As usual, she gripped her quarterstaff and puffed on a long deep pipe filled with brownleaf.

"The fishers return early," she bellowed. Like her sister—who was seated in a chair of dry wicker at the south end—Gertruda was thick and brawny, with coal-black hair and bushy eyebrows. They both spoke very loudly at all times. "And yet, half'n hour too late!"

"Too late fer what?" Serryl asked.

"Lunferda spotted the old silver wolf." The woman punctuated her claim by drawing on her pipe. She spouted the smoke through the other side of her mouth. It wafted in Morley's direction and he inhaled.

"The beast was south," she continued. "Pacing. Watching the sheep. And the goats."

"Lies," Morley blurted. The word sounded harsh as it left him. He gave a disarming smile.

"If I was lying," she said, taking a long pull from her pipe, "I'd have said *I* was the one who spotted it. Not Lunferda." Serryl and Morley exchanged a glance. The young man wondered if the wolf had seen them, armed only with fishing hooks, as they passed over the plain.

"We scared it off, though," Gertruda added. "Can't wait to tell Tommas when he gets back, *heh*. Still thinks Lun and I are as useless as Semhren."

"You *are* as useless as me!" came the old scholar's voice, shouted from the other side of the watchwomen's house. Gertruda waved haughtily as if Semhren were right in front of her.

"Right. I need to go put these away fer later," Serryl said to herself, continuing onward. Morley followed close behind. The watchwoman sucked away at her pipe.

Once within the hamlet's circle of houses—of which there were twelve including the varken-ox, cow, and sheep pens—Morley halted and sighed, casually relieved by his arrival and the total regularity in everything around him.

Semhren was groggily fetching water from the well; Ceridwen and Amarta were patching up clothes on a bench by the latter's kiln, a fat clay dome hugging the side of her house; Arrin was strolling in the distance over a tide of white wool; Robi was trying to chop up kindling beside his parents' house.

Everything was in perfect order. Like the day before, like the week before, like the year before.

Morley sat down on the turf and stretched his legs—Tommas always recommended a stretch before and after a long walk. The young man let his thoughts wander again. He still didn't quite believe Gertruda's claim that a wolf had circled the hamlet earlier that day. And yet, he prayed it was true. And he wished, above all, that he had been there to see it.

He remembered the morning when Gale himself spotted the clear figure drawing near to their hill-house: the man took up his greatsword and strode to the top of the mound, waited for the monster to move on. Such excitement, such danger, he'd thought as he dashed up to Gale's side, up to the crown of the hill. Though he had stood latched to the man's leg, he had stood nonetheless. He would not dare retreat into their home. The wolf soon left them in peace. And for years after, Morley yearned for another encounter, another opportunity to be brave.

Then the stranger came. The killer came. And he failed to be brave. And now…

Morley felt a foot jab into the small of his back. Still seated in the grass, he peered up into the sky, an effort to see who was behind him, and saw an upside-down face towering over him. Yeva.

"Hey," she said as Morley pushed himself up. Her short black hair was a knotted mess, as if she'd tried braiding it earlier and failed. Relatedly, she wore a tunic over trousers. No effort in being a proper lass today, as Ceridwen would've said of her.

"No weaving?" Morley asked her, nodding to Amarta's house.

"Was just making us chamomile—you're back early," she said with her typical speed. "Catch a load quick today?"

"Just two salmons, nothing much." He sagged, strangely exasperated. "I'm not feeling well. I feel healthy. But I'm just not feeling right."

He stood and, silently inviting Yeva along, he started for the goats' enclosure, just past the little room beside the pens that he shared with Arrin and Ceridwen—the two young lovers from the nearby Rock of Aubin. Yeva joined him as he walked on. Like Serryl, Yeva was one of Morley's closest friends in the hamlet, if only because she too stood out from everyone else: her hair and skin were far darker than the common peach and cream hue in the others.

"Do you dread something?" she asked. "Like, maybe, going back to Gale's tomorrow?" Morley eyed her, surprised by her insight. When he made no quick reply, she continued, "By the way, do you and Istain plan to come back here from Gale's before leaving for Reineshir?"

"Probably not." he said. "The house is northeast from here and Reineshir is due north, I think. Istain says it's at least five kalcubits away and a kalcubit takes almost an hour to walk. We'd waste too much time if we came back here from the house, then left again. Why?" Yeva grunted.

"I wanted to come along. I've never been to Gale's house, only heard about it from you—and I didn't want to have to walk back on my own, specially not with wolves around."

"I see," Morley said. In his head, he drew up a quick image of a life spent with Yeva in the hill-house. "Well, it's not much. It used to be comfortable, but I'm sure it's now in disrepair. Not much is inside and there'll be even less after tomorrow. But maybe you and I can walk there together one of these days." He imagined the two of them laying together on the house's slope. "Why not come with us to Reineshir?"

Yeva gave him a conspicuous look. "Because it's Reineshir. Filthy, charmless, filled with drunkards—haven't you ever been there yourself?" She caught herself quick. "No, I guess you haven't."

They were by the goats' fence. Morley clambered up onto his usual post and Yeva joined him. Minny and Geat, the only two goats left from Gale's little herd, milled about nearby. The rest of the goats he'd inherited from Gale had been sold off to the Reineshir folk, but Geat was vaguely

16

special. He was dull grey with a large spot of black fur around each eye and a long curling tuft of brownish hair at his chin. Six curving horns also clung to his head like an ornate helmet.

Beyond these curious features, he had a bizarre tendency of coddling his owner—if he could be said to truly have one. And he often showed exuberant appreciation for those who treated him as more than he was. A remarkable animal, as many agreed.

"So, what's troubling you, really?" the girl pressed.

"It's not so much the return to the hill-house," he began, "and it's not the thought of going to Reineshir for the first time. Yes, I'm both excited and nervous. And I'm sure the two feelings put together could be enough to make anyone unwell, but there's—it's—" The wind picked up. The grass hissed.

"I don't know," he concluded. "I really don't know."

"What are you thinking?" Yeva asked. "Right now, what are you thinking?" Morley didn't want to say.

The wolf, its snarling bright face—the sword under the hill, sheathed and cobwebbed—the wolf in the distance, a black speck, now a man. His mind whirred.

Tell her, go on—she asked, so tell her, go on.

"I'm hungry," he said. It was only half a lie.

"There you are," the girl said. "That was an easy one. Amarta's bread is almost ready—she made one maslin loaf earlier and it worked out well, so now she's making a second. Bread and fish for supper. And plenty of beer, since you and Istain are resupplying tomorrow." Morley nodded to his friend. "Want a tear of the first loaf? I can go get you a piece."

"Yes," he answered, clasping his hands together. Yeva rotated on the wooden bars and squeezed Morley's bony shoulder before hopping down. He didn't watch her go. He simply fell back into his imaginings. After a matter of minutes his thoughts coalesced, pulled him into a lucid fantasy.

The stranger, now pale and dead, came to Egainshir. He walked with his blade at hand. Morley, the only one left in the hamlet, unsheathed Gale's sword, the one yet waiting for him in the loft of the hill-house. Morley stepped forward to meet the man. They exchanged words, meaningless, senseless words—like the babblings of an infant. The words weren't what mattered, of course. The stranger's head was shining like a ridder's helm, like a skinless skull, like an apparition. And Morley was taller, bulkier—like everyone else he knew. The undead man attacked first: his weapon swept through the open air, only a finger's length from Morley's head. The boy—now a strong-bodied ridder, the analogue of might—attacked next: he knocked the stranger away with one swipe of his free hand.

When his enemy stirred and leapt back up to his feet, Morley saw that it was no longer the stranger. It was Gale, or Serryl, or Arrin, or Gertruda, or Yeva—it was anyone from the past and present, ever-changing as they charged closer. And Morley shrank, receded into his cryptic body, his torment. He was a slender halfelev again, a terrified child.

Geat, his favorite of the two goats, was standing in close proximity, staring.

"Still nice and warm," Yeva said delightedly behind him. She nudged Morley's arm with a hunk of bread then climbed back up onto the fence, holding her own cut in her mouth. She watched him devour it. Once he had swallowed the last scrap of crust, she leaned toward him.

"What's on your mind now?" This time, he decided to tell the truth.

"That was good bread."

*　　　*　　　*

Morley woke in the early morning, long before dawn. The time had come.

Arrin and Ceridwen, the young shepherd and the young weaver, were cuddled up in their furs and quilts beside him. The former lay with his messy dark hair spilling over his eyes while the latter—whose long hair was the color of cut wheat—rested her head over his chest, the smattering of freckles across her face observable even in the low light.

They slept in the wicker shack that Morley and Arrin had built themselves, with help from Tommas, when the halfelev first began living at the hamlet. Despite its general convenience, the shack's interior space was so small that at least one person had to sleep on their side through the night, else everyone would be cramped against the brambly walls and each other. Luckily, both Arrin and Ceridwen were wrapped cozily in each other's arms. Morley was able to escape their nest without waking either.

Outside, the twin moons still shone: the bronze one hovered straight overhead while its silver sister—bound to crawl closer through the year's second half—remained low and distant just over the horizon. The resident tradesman, Istain, was loading his oxcart with empty baskets, bags, and casks. He'd already burdened its bed with trading wares—clothes, combed wool, medicaments, and so on—the evening prior. They together led Nudd the Varken-Ox out of his pen. He shook his great-horned head and huffed through his flat snout as they yoked him to the cart. After that, Istain offered a length of rope and pointed to the goats' enclosure.

"Geat's comin' along as well," he said. "He has to be reminded what it means to be a goat, so to speak. I'll explain along the way. This can be his leash." He waved the rope faintly.

"Geat won't need that," said Morley. "He'll follow me anywhere." With that, Morley went to fetch his favorite goat.

By the time they returned and closed up the cart with Geat in its bed, the hamlet's trio of elders was awake, together observing the ready travelers. They lit their pipes with a shared taper, then approached.

"You watch for that wolf, Morley," said Elmaen, the proprietor and first settler of Egainshir. "And hope it hasn't moved into the hill-house. Gale and I spent too long in digging that heap out and building it up and all. If it's irreparable, don't tell me about it." Morley only nodded. His thoughts were too scattered and sleep-worn to permit a reply.

Reffen the Apothecarist was trying to reach over the side of the cart to reacquire his medicine box. Upon giving up, he said, "I have three more sheaves of poultice for you to sell." He handed them to Istain, who tossed them carelessly next to the medicine box.

"They'll get bought up," the tradesman assured. "They always sell."

"And mind that you get me the right quantities of somniferum, if they have it this time. And chamomile."

"They'll get bought up too," said Istain. "I don't forget easy."

"And see that you—"

Morley failed to hear the third request, as Semhren had sidled up to him. The elder, dressed in the worn old robe of his expired office, looked as though he meant to speak privately.

"I imparted a gift unto your old companion," he said with a low voice, "good Sir Gale. He'd helped me build my house when I first fled for this part of the land, as you know. Might you reason what this gift may have been?" Morley, who was no more wakened than he was a moment before, knew immediately what the old scholar referred to.

"*Chevaliers of Bienvale*," he said with impulsive discretion. "I can get it for you. And *The Divine Conjecture*, if you want."

Semhren nodded with a pleased expression. "Mind that you hide those books when you're in Reineshir," he mentioned. "Never mind the cost of the full text, *Chevaliers* has blank pages near the end, as you know. A few leaves of unsoiled parchment alone are worth more than a few barrels of beer." He checked on the other men nearby for a beat. "I have other uses for them." With that, he headed for the well.

Istain climbed up onto the driver's bench after an exchange with Elmaen. Before Morley could join him in the seat, a softer shape came into his periphery, unpreceded by words or gentle footfalls. It was Amarta, the resident weaver and baker. She wore the shepherd cloak that once belonged to Gale. Morley noticed that she didn't carry along her infant boy, yet unnamed, as she usually did during the darker hours.

"You're going now?" she said, her voice a sleepless rasp. Morley launched himself up onto the driver's bench.

"We are," the lad said gravely. "We'll be back at nightfall. Or else tomorrow morning if the weather is brutish." Amarta stepped closer.

"Could you bring me something?" she asked, touching Morley's knee.

"Whatever you need," he said.

"No needs. I only want something from the hill. Anything. A cup, a spade, a fistful of earth-clay, anything." Morley nodded at this. "And if you remember…if you find the time, could you get it blessed at the chapel in Reineshir?"

Istain, overhearing her plea, chuckled. "You'd be better off getting it blessed by Elmaen, dear," he suggested, whipping the reins. Nudd the Varken-Ox gingerly moved forward; Amarta gingerly moved back.

"I'll find something for you," Morley promised her. As the varken-ox lumbered by Serryl's house and veered north, Morley glanced back at Amarta. She had receded into her house but continued watching from the door. Though all was washed in shadow, Morley thought he could see Yeva peer around the corner beside Amarta.

"Bit o' ceremony in our leaving, eh?" said Istain once they were many strides away from the ringed hamlet. He then added, "Ah, that's right. It's your first time to Reineshir."

"Yes," said Morley, electing not to bring up the hill-house now that it loomed so close. Though it was yet a few hours away, Morley felt there could be no turning back, no leaping down from the driver's bench, no charging on back to the hamlet. To do so would be to sacrifice years of hard-earned adulthood. And yet, would his inevitable reactions to the hill-

20

house not dispense with that persona all the same? He did all he could to weigh these matters as Istain rambled on beside him, unacknowledged and Serryl-like. Soon enough, it truly was too late to turn back.

Morley's innards quaked and perspired. He felt for a time as though he needed to vomit all the tremulous bile throughout his body. These feelings were only abated by faint comforting images of his recent days: Serryl redressing after their outing the previous afternoon; Yeva trying not to laugh after watching him fall from the goats' fence; the glowing faces of Egainshir, all around the first warming bonfire of the Hetta season.

He then saw Gale through the murk of his memory. He slept in their bed under the hill as Morley crept up to read beside the gleam of their firepit. The older man's mouth was open, sighing softly. And for a time, little Fitzmorley wondered what dreams flooded his aging soul, what ephemera carried him to distant shores. Perhaps, in his cold bed beneath the soil...

"He's dead," Morley said. "Gale is dead." Istain looked at him, but said nothing for a moment.

"What's that?" he soon inquired. The youth felt as though a wad of cotton was lodged in his throat.

"A stranger came to our hill-house," he went on. "Gale called him Darry. They spoke of things I didn't understand. Then they fought and killed each other. Now they're both dead." Istain shifted in his seat.

"That's what I thought you said," he muttered, "just didn't get why you'd say it. Elmaen told us all long ago, of course. And I helped him bury the—"

"Gale told me to flee and run to Egainshir," Morley went on absently, "more than once. But I didn't move. I don't know why I didn't move. I stood there on the hill, watching them. I thought I was being brave." The cartwheels churned on over the sharp stalks of grass. "The brave don't run. Not even when told to." His voice faltered. He stared out over the black fields, turning his face from Istain.

"Not sure 'bout that," said the tradesman after a silence. "I never knew that part. You're not blamin' yourself for his death, are you?" Morley swayed his head.

"If I made for Egainshir quicker," he said, "the fight would've ended during my run probably. Maybe they still would've killed each other, maybe not. But I just think if I hadn't been standing there...Gale kept yelling at me to go. I might as well have done something, even tried to help in the fight. It'd make no difference if I was killed too."

"Oh, don't you think that way," Istain said. "No good thinkin' that way, boy. Egainshir'd be a lesser place without you. And anyway, I thought—well, I assumed you had run off at the first sign o' trouble. Not 'cause you're not brave or——"

"I assume that's what everyone thinks," Morley replied. "Elmaen stopped asking me what happened after a week. And I didn't speak one word for a while after, as you know. Not to anyone about anything."

Morley felt a tickle under his eyes. He craned his neck back and gazed up into the sky. It was brightening into blue-grey, dull as the loops around a barrel.

"These are the first words I've spoken about it," he said. "Aloud. The first ever. After three years. And now they've been spoken."

"And now they've been spoken," Istain remarked. "How do you feel about that?"

Morley didn't hear him, as he was staring onward at a rise of earth much further ahead. He thought it looked very much like the hill-house. But this couldn't be possible, he thought, as so little time had passed since they'd left Egainshir. Then again, the sky suggested otherwise. The clouds above were now turning to gold as the sun poked up from the south. They had to have been riding for nearly two hours already.

It didn't matter, he realized. He'd done something new, something so profoundly simple he almost felt ashamed for not doing it sooner. As he had once been with his sorrows, he was now muted in his joy. The sickness was gone from him. The dead were at peace. The air was clear and the ground was firm and the day seemed promising. The cart clattered and its driver chewed the lip of a pipe. And old treasures, precious though mundane, waited ahead. Waited in the barrow of Sir Gale.

I'm ready, Morley thought.

Though what he was ready for, he could not know. Of this alone he was certain.

The feeling did not leave him. Not even after he reluctantly entered the mound. Not even as he marched out with two books, a greatsword, and a stew ladle in hand. Not even as they rode on northward. The feeling did not leave him.

Chapter II – Reineshir

Anae Dammedottir Bertriss walked between the high wall of her family's manor and the lines of ugly thatch-roofed houses. She carried along her favorite of the town's stray cats, Ama, a grey and white beast with tufted ears. The Bertriss girl was herself flaxen-haired, wide-eyed, and bearing as always her smirk.

They took the first turn before the flat-roofed brewery and idled down Reineshir's central street toward the vendors' green. Along the way, she surveyed the waste-filled alleys and stationary carts; she also eyed the wooden porches protruding from the middlemost height of each squarish daubed building. All she could see and hear—and smell—were the worn-out coopers and lumbermen, sharing their afternoon ales outside the town warehouse.

Other bystanders along the road, meanwhile, most of whom were men and all of whom were sipping from their own mugs, either leered at or avoided her. Their faces were leathery though untanned; their garments were squalid and torn, though perfectly suitable for their environ. She paid little mind to these loiterers. She was far too busy searching for the other local cats.

She had long ago taken to naming them: Emfred was black and had only one eye, Sunflash was striped with orange and cream colors, Hecaton had a stubby tail and proved to be the best mouser in town. Ama, still draped in Anae's arms, was yet her favorite. She was the largest feline Anae had ever seen. The cat was grey and white with a fluffy round head and tufted ears. Anae could do anything with her and she wouldn't resist.

They stopped at the corner of the atelier—the edge of that little town, as Anae saw it—and looked across the quiet vendors' green before them. To continue eastward past the trading stalls—some packed to the brim with goods, some miserably dilapidated—was to continue unto the lumberyard, an uninteresting clearing of stumps and sawdust. According to Gerry, one of the younger timbermen, it used to sustain a plentiful orchard and vineyard. He'd told Anae this during one of their brief liaisons, adding that all of it was withered by the time Rien Debois, the first earl of the town, began his settlement.

Though she didn't care much about the truth, Anae tried to argue that nobody lived on the island before the Biens showed up, despite what her book said. Gerry only nodded dumbly. They then went for a stroll over the remnants of his fabled garden.

The chapel bell pealed once, as it did every four hours. Sometimes. If Chaplain Wyer were awake. The bell was supplemented today with the sound of Russe the Smith cursing in the name of the All-Being as he dropped his hammer. Elsewhere, Meggs screeched at her husband. This was the song of Reineshir.

Before Anae could make much progress down the outermost street, she stopped again and peered south: a familiar ox-driven wagon was approaching from the tree line. It was the only vehicle on the island that made the regular trip between Reineshir and barren Werplaus.

Istain van Egainshir was the driver's name. She knew him well enough. She often asked about the odd folk who lived with him beyond the Crouxwood. Sir Elmaen the Forgotten, Old Reffen, the Watching Sisters, and all the rest. Though Istain always had much to share, Anae continued imagining Werplaus as a land where old hags sat about a pile of embers, sharing tales of youth as they knitted their beautiful scarves.

However, Istain wasn't alone today—this was a first, as far as she knew. There were two others accompanying him: a young man and an animal, likely a goat or a recently sheared sheep. Or a really fat ugly dog wearing a helmet. Probably a goat, she decided.

Curious, Anae dodged into the closest alleyway, a cluttered space between the atelier and the butcher-tanners' workshop. She waited with Ama in her arms. After an interval, the creaking and clunking of the wagon came into earshot. She moved further into the alley, turned along the corner of the atelier, and ascended its steps onto a shaded balcony over the main road. She raced to its furthest end, the best vantage point. From there, she could see all that Istain had for sale without having to approach and ask—and inevitably evoke his piteous tradesman routine, once so effective.

But when Istain and his cart came into view, when she saw his new cargo, something inside her fluttered. And Ama's tail swayed.

She could not ascertain the feeling: was it that long-forgotten sense of nervousness that first followed her into Reineshir five years prior? Was it enthusiasm, the similarly rare emotion that dressed her before holiday celebrations and hid in her stomach whenever she sneaked out at night? Or was it just an extremely potent form of attraction, one which was so often clouded over by Gerry's simple ruggedness? She settled with this third option and held Ama close.

They gazed over the tall boy beside Istain. His fingers tapped against the flat of a sheathed claymore, a kind of greatsword she'd only heard about in songs and lays. The weapon was so long it stretched over both their laps and across the topmost board of a bookstack between them. Behind them was a goat seated like a faithful hound.

Anae spied on them for what felt like ten minutes. Istain gesticulated with one hand at their surroundings; the boy's head, puppet-like, followed the hand's every movement. They rolled off the beaten road, straight on toward the pens. Anae cursed under her breath, readjusted Ama's posture, pulled up her hood, and hurried back down to Reineshir's central lane.

She stalked around the warehouse and passed by the cramped crofts of the town's only neighborhood. The Ornhatter sisters, tending to the season's laundry, gave concise greetings to the Dammedottir before continuing with their work. Anae addressed them quick and moved on to the warehouse's far corner, sidling by a group of silenced workers. They waited for the girl to proceed before resuming their dialogues, undoubtedly rude in nature.

Peering around the warehouse, Anae found Istain and his young companion stopped before a bearded goatherd. Byraon was his name and, if she remembered correctly, he often purchased wool for his daughter Bayette, a spinner for the weavers.

Anae trained her eyes on the boy standing up on the cart bench, whose own awed eyes were unfixed, panning over the town's edge. He'd obviously never been within or near such a place in all his life. Anae tried to imagine what that could be like, how terrified or dazed he could be, especially once exposed to the admixture of stenches and the populace's homely gruff. She wondered further on how to approach this outsider, this local foreigner. Passing up such an opportunity was out of the question.

An idea came to her in a flash. Tightening her grip on Ama, she searched each of her cloak's inner pockets until she found a ball of daffodil yarn, roughly the size of her big toe. Without removing it, she pressed against the daubed corner of the warehouse and peeked around the stack of broken crates beside its back wall. She waited for the boy to notice her there.

He was ordinary, she decided. He wasn't physically attractive, not notably at least, but he held a certain gravitas uncommon in Reineshir. His astonishment of the town was so pure, so precious. This young man was untainted by the vices beyond Werplaus, the forsaken tip of Sarcovy Isle.

He probably knew no music, no songs—only the braying of sheep and the artless dialects of herder folk. And what of businesses and sacraments? Would he understand their functions, the means through which they were effectuated? What about those books beside him—had he ever tried to read them? Could he? Anae was herself sick to death of the leathery tomes left on her bedside table by Mester Alherde. It would be amusing to see this country lad take ahold of one, she thought.

Minutes passed before Anae snagged the boy's attention. She stood as a hooded figure, she imagined, a girl of fair age and perceptible hygiene, watching him beyond heaps of disused barrels. She prayed that he wouldn't be able to resist. They stared for a moment more. Then the girl disappeared from his view—a perfect bait.

As she did so, she tossed the yarn onto a little canyon of drying mud around the corner, praying that the boy noticed. The cat drooped over her forearm and glared at the ball intensely. They waited, crouched behind the abandoned containers. Then Anae leaned closer to the corner a second time and listened: the shifting of cautious footfalls. The girl and the cat continued waiting for a span no longer than ten beats.

Just as the light steps were upon them, just as they halted above the yarn, Anae released her small companion. And Ama spared no time. She viciously leapt for the ball.

To her surprise, they were met with a legitimate cry of distress, one which drew the attention of all the nearby workmen. Anae straightened up, concerned for an instant, and rounded the warehouse.

The boy stood sidelong, one hand held up in defense, the other clutching the center his tunic. His chest heaved and his eyes darted back and forth from the girl to the cat—who, meanwhile, was perched before the ball of yarn, watching the newcomer warily, her arched back sinking down.

Anae's concern vanished. She gave a heavy rasping laugh, the one her mother found unbecoming.

"What the—what—what is that thing?!" the boy exclaimed, pointing to Ama. The cat lost interest in him and proceeded to bat the yarn ball about. She immediately lost interest in that as well and stalked off.

"What are you talking about?" Anae said, her laughter receding as she pulled down her hood. "It's a damned cat. And a big one, at that." She paused. "Don't tell me you've never seen a cat before! Oh, what is the life of a Werplaus lad!? This must be the strangest day of your short little life."

The words were meant to be playful and embarrassing, but the young man instead furrowed his brow, relaxed his posture. Without response, he headed back to Istain and the goatherd. And all joviality flushed from Anae.

"Wait, wait!" she called after him. He stopped and looked over his shoulder. "I'm sorry. I really am, I'm sorry about that. Other than a few ridders and some traders, I don't often see visitors in Reineshir."

"That means good fortune in my experience," he muttered, then continued on. He truly didn't care, Anae now saw. She felt a small lump welling in her throat.

"I'm Anae!" she called, taking a step forward. She unconsciously folded her hands together—and shocked herself in doing so. She usually only put up this display of innocent grace when attending her parents or the ridders. When the young man turned to her again, she smiled. His poise softened. And the girl noticed his features again: his sharp ears poking out from under unkempt hair, his narrow eyes and head-to-toe thinness.

"You're...Are you an elev?" she asked.

"Halfelev," he answered. Anae approached. She was approximately a head shorter than him, she guessed. He watched her absently, occasionally glancing over to the wagon and the goat in its bed. "What are you doing?" he finally inquired.

"Looking at you," she replied without thought for etiquette. "Do you not want me to? I'm sorry, all I see are naemas like myself around here. I thought Damme Ellemine was the only elev on the island."

"Who?" he asked.

"She...Oh, I can't remember. She may only be from a story." Anae was gazing only at the boy's eyes. Discomfort twitched at its corners. "What's your name?"

"Fitzmorley. But I go by Morley. It's shorter and easier to say."

Anae cautiously wondered what to ask next. For once in her life, she was afraid of rejection. "Do you want to walk with me, Morley?"

He said nothing.

"I can show you around. Is this your first time in Reineshir? Why are— I mean, what brings you to..." She waved a hand by her mouth as if to waft away the befuddled speech. The faintest impression of a grin formed on the halfelev's face.

"Are you busy today?" she asked, feeling as though all charm had abandoned her.

"Istain and I—er, Istain's the man who brought me here, if you don't know him. We were going to sell things, see if we can make a silver piece maybe."

Anae tried to inspect their stock from afar, though the claymore was the only thing she cared to see. "Is the sword yours?" She caught herself and added, "I saw you two coming into town. You had a sword on your lap. And some books next to you." When Morley did not say anything—though he did appear to be contemplating—she spoke again. "You're not going to sell it, are you? Because, believe me, there isn't a single vendor in this entire county who can give you fair money for it. And believe me twice, all of them will try to convince you otherwise."

The lad scratched his head. "What should I do with it, then?" he said. "If I was to sell it?"

"My family can give you more than it's worth."

He made an unreadable face. "But you just said—"

"My family doesn't work on vendors' green, trust me." His features scrunched with incredulity. A weird belching noise came from the wagon. "What about the goat, what's he doing here?" she asked. Morley snapped his head to the horned beast and chuckled.

"Geat's his name. Minny's his wife, as we like to say, but she's back in Egainshir. Elmaen—he's in charge at our hamlet—says Geat's lost interest in her since they last had kids about eight years back. They were all sold off quick. So now he's here to see other males. Arrin—he's Egainshir's herder—says goats have more sex when they're reminded of competition, whatever that means."

Anae tried not to laugh at this odd boy, this fellow of the fields. "That's really interesting, Morley," she said. "Really interesting. So if it's your first time here, I can show you around. If you'd like. Can you let Istain take care of business? This *is* your first time here, right?" Morley nodded, then held up his finger.

"I think he wanted to show me how to barter properly. He's tried to show me back at Egainshir, but I didn't get it, so now—"

"Let me talk to him," she requested, smirking.

Without waiting for him to speak again, she grabbed the young man by the hand and marched over to the cart. Upon reaching Istain and his interlocutor, she stamped her foot twice and tugged Morley closer. Geat leaned his cordial head over the side of the cart. Istain, in attending the Bertriss girl, did a rapid doubletake, punctuated by a quick gasp.

"Ah, Damme Bertriss! How nice to see you!" He bowed his head then proceeded to gawk quizzically at Morley. Anae, still holding his hand tight, shot the boy a wink; he received it with further confusion. Istain searched the pair, then Byraon. The goatherd's expression hadn't changed and likely wouldn't. A significant silence passed over them, one that the halfelev clearly failed to interpret. Thus, ever impetuous, he banished it.

"This girl Anae wants to take me around town," he said. Blunt as a mallet, Anae thought. "And her family might want to buy Gale's sword," he added.

The trader gulped. "Why, yes. Certainly," Istain confirmed. "Go on, then. I'll tend to matters here."

Morley pulled his hand out from Anae's grip and went to the wagon, lifting himself up to the driver's bench with one foot on a wheel peg. He moved the books—of which there were two—into the cart's bed and tossed an empty sack over them. Then he reached for the sword.

As he placed a hand on its aged scabbard, Istain huddled close to him and mumbled a terse series of monotones, placing slow emphasis on a word or two. The Bertriss daughter couldn't hear any of it. She assumed the man was articulating to Fitzmorley the perceived nature of his situation: watch yourself around the gentry, she imagined him saying— they're a fickle lot and easy to offend. But as the lad clambered down and yoked the heavy sword across his shoulders, his demeanor was unchanged. He lumbered over to Anae and seemed to force a polite smile.

They headed off wordlessly, Anae leading by several paces. Once they turned the corner around the warehouse and its sordid boxes, she twisted her head back to him and asked, "What did he say to you?"

Without any regard for confidentiality, he answered, "That you're Anae Dammedottir Bertriss and your family owns Reineshir and that I must be careful not to offend you. And that I am, at this time, a representative of Egainshir. D'you know what he meant by that?" The girl chuckled again. She'd heard the word 'Egainshir' more times today than she had in her whole life.

"It doesn't mean anything, don't worry about it," she said back. "He was only joking, I'm sure."

They passed beside the storehouse. Most of the drinking men from earlier were now gone, though two remained—a roper and a dissembler.

As they too returned to their occupations, both stared at the couple, their gazes lingering on the weapon carried by the outsider. Anae reveled under their wide eyes, their patient and stolid prying.

She felt a strong desire for more—more of this particular breed of attention, that is. True enough, she was used to having everyone watch her as she passed by. But this was different. She now had an escort, a young man of the undomestic southlands, a boy in the midst of a small adventure. She felt as if she'd chosen a champion from beyond the Crouxwood rabble, a judicious guardian armed with book and blade like a subject of continental sculpture. His sword was certainly large enough to grant him this aura, if only since most Reineshir folk probably hadn't seen such a weapon in decades, if ever.

Morley was a subject most worthy of exhibition, in short.

But Anae liked the lad very much already. Genuinely. He bore no foul thoughts of her—or if he did, he was exceptionally good at disguising them. But no, they weren't there, she decided.

He was a sincere innocent, like Istain or Miccal, the ten-year-old son of the chief brewer. And the way in which the lad received her less than half an hour previous! He didn't know who the Bertrisses were, what their duties within the county entailed, why everyone had to be polite to them. And if he ever did understand these things, he still yet wouldn't become like all the others in Reineshir or beyond. It was too late for that. He could now only mature into a close friend or bold enemy. Either was welcome.

They stepped onto the main road and stopped. Two men on the atelier's crooked balcony hawked and spat simultaneously; the shrill voice of Gresha, the town tailor, berated an apprentice or patron around an unseen corner; a butcher loudly chopped meat. Morley beheld the grubby buildings around him, measuring their heights with his outstretched finger.

"What's…" he started, sniffing the air and lowering his hand. "What's that smell? It's horrible." Anae snuffed it up deeply—a challenge of endurance.

"Well, that warm smell of entrails is from the butchery," she explained. "And that rotten flesh smell mixed in with it is from the tannery. They both share the same space."

"It's horrible," he said again. The girl laughed in agreement.

"If you want a less awful smell, come with me." She patted his cheek and he blinked, touching where her hand had been. "Thirsty?" Morley nodded indifferently and they advanced up the street toward the manor gates.

Ignoring that house entirely, they ascended a flight of wood steps onto the raised deck of the brewery, just across from the block of houses. They slid inside its parlor, a wide room congested with anything but tables and chairs, though all were in use as such by the usual crowd of 'tasters,' all putting off their afternoon work.

As the pair took a table—a barrel topped by a small pallet—they pulled in the attention of every man present. Anae was used to this, as she and Amstudt Kochin were regulars of the unnamed alehouse. Of course, this time was different. This time, the patrons were transfixed by the sight of Morley. And the humorless incongruence of a boy carrying a man's sword.

Not long after they sat, Anae began whispering about the men around them. This was the only means, she found, of deflecting their scrutinies. Morley, of course, took nothing away from their secrets, though he seemed distraught by the fact that everyone he glanced at averted their eyes.

Moments later, Jhann, the masher and occasional assistant to the chief brewer, strolled over with two double-pint tankards. He grasped them both in one hand, as the other was lacking in fingers. The mugs were filled with the freshest beer in all the county—or so he boasted, meaning that it was the only fresh beer in all the county.

It was believable enough, anyway: Morley, who disclaimed he was not a heavy drinker and probably wouldn't manage to empty the vessel at hand, slurped down his share as if it were a mint-sweetened milk.

Anae, hoping to assuage his nerves entirely, later offered him the last sips of her own drink. She belched in his face as he finished them. At this, Morley laughed, the first disclosure of cheer she witnessed from him. With triumph in her heart and the soothing glow of insobriety under her skin, she led her new friend outside, urging him not to forget the sword. As was the way of things, she did not pay.

"What's life like where you come from?" Anae soon asked as they wandered by the inn and its adamant watcher, Maud. They walked with arms interlocked; and Morley, bearing the sword over one shoulder, tried awkwardly to retain some distance. His arm was stiff, his elbow outstretched like the handle of a ewer.

"Werplaus or Egainshir?" he replied.

"Either," Anae said, not knowing the difference. Morley seemed to dwell on the question.

"I guess they're one and the same, now that I think about it," he noted. Anae laughed.

"I've brought the question to Istain," she said, "and he once told me, 'Well, best come down and see for yourself 'cause it's not the sort of place one can describe with due respect.' I didn't understand what he meant, though I think I do now. Alherde—he's my teacher—told me there's nothing there but wind and grass and cold beaches. I tried to imagine Egainshir today. All I can see is a little spot of houses like the one we just passed, only smaller and cruder...*cruder.*" She paused. "More crude? Is 'cruder' a word?"

"I've seen it before," Morley asserted. "There's a passage—how does it go?" He mumbled to himself for a moment, then: "'Sir Chaisgott and his men then took up the clubs of their Piikish enemy and beat back the countering through cruder means.' That's from *Chevaliers of Bienvale.* Have you ever heard of it?"

Anae was speechless.

"It's an old collection of ridder tales I grew up with," he continued. "I used to read them every day until I found out most of the stories are untrue—though the men in them were real. There are stories of monsters, fornications, stolen loves, battles, all sorts of things. You might like it."

"I have read it, yes," Anae said quietly. She couldn't decide what to investigate first: Morley's alleged ability to read and recite, or the mysterious circumstances through which he possessed a copy of Mester Alherde's unfinished manuscript. Or which chevalier he favored the most. The choice was obvious.

"Which ridder do you like the most?" she asked.

"From the book? Sir Olivien." He cleared his throat.

"Because he died in a small battle? After surviving through dozens of more perilous adventures back on the continent?" She laughed. Morley didn't.

"Because I knew a man who knew him. Because I know he was real." He shook his head. "What about you, who's your favorite?"

"Sir Haubauld van Mirtl, but only before he became the fifth sword of Sir Cadmael. And after his courting of Wedhild. I hate that part where he talks to her through a wall for three years, though. Everything in between is so exciting." Morley hummed as though he disagreed.

"I think you mean Wenfred, not Wedhild," he said. "Wedhild was in Sir Lawren's tale, the one about the night-beasts. She was the woman whose watcher husband disappeared. Anyway, *I* always enjoyed the part about Haubauld and Wenfred, especially when I was young and didn't know what it meant. I'd read it over and over and over."

"I never would've expected a country boy to have a reading teacher," she said. "Who was your mester? My father sometimes jokes that there's fewer than a score of people south of the Crouxwood. Do they all know how to read the letters?"

"I don't know," Morley answered at a ponderous pace. "But I was raised by a ridder. I wouldn't exactly call him my 'mester,' but he used to read to me when I was very, very young. When I was older, he showed me how the alphabet works, how each letter is a sound. That was it, really. I suppose I taught myself how to read."

Anae was officially envious. Not of Morley's fosterage, not of his intelligence or the listless manner in which he presented it, but of his very *being*. Of his life and experiences. Truly, she realized of herself, to live with everything one could ever need was to live with a perpetual, irrational desire for more. More money, more acreage, more clothing, more lovers. It would never end, not even if she were queen of all the world. This was the curse of luxury, a bewitchment that prevented its subjects from speaking ill of lavish life.

She broke the silence with a hiccup.

They were strolling along the spot where they had first met, earlier in the day. Byraon and Istain were nowhere in sight.

"Is this the ridder's sword?" Anae asked, nodding to Morley's shoulder.

"Want to see it?" They stopped beside the fence of the grazing pen. "Istain and I looked at it earlier. It has some ugly brown spots near the end. You hold the scabbard and I'll pull the blade out. Ready?"

She did as she was instructed and the young man tugged the steel behemoth from out of its loose sheath. In trying to hold it upright, he lost his balance. Anae dropped the scabbard quick and leant her hands to the endeavor, holding the blade just above the cross-guard until the weapon was steadied.

"Careful! It might still be sharp there," Morley warned.

"It isn't," she murmured. "Well, it is a bit. But not enough to hurt me."

They beheld the naked claymore together: its finish was mediocre, Anae thought, compared to the swords her father's ridders carried. Though what it lacked in sheen and beauty, it surely made up for in size. And force, no doubt. She now tried to imagine the man who once wielded it, charging forth on his destrier, bellowing a terrible war cry.

Then her mind shifted to the thought of this same man, reading to little Fitzmorley, tucked away in bed.

"I'm going to put it back now," Morley said, carefully pulling it away. Once again they worked together, Morley sliding the sword into the sheath in Anae's hands. "If your family wants to buy it, they might need a new casing. I think this one was made for another sword, an even bigger one. Or it's just worn out."

Immediately after it was secured, the gurgled snort of a boar sounded out nearby. The girl paid it no mind. The halfelev, on the other hand, whirled about, holding the wrapped sword at a clumsy angle. The girl laughed, recalling Ama and the ball of yarn.

"I suppose you've never seen a pig before either," she said. Morley relaxed, taking in another deep breath. "Have you ever eaten ham or pork or bacon?"

"Dried pork," he answered, "though not much. We buy it here, actually. We don't have much meat in Werplaus. We don't have much of anything, really, just leagues of open land and a few animals. And the land's not good for farming because there's too much salt in the air."

His eyes drifted over the forlorn corpus of Reineshir, the mangy open-air market and its disinterested dependent vendors, the indelicate frames of the architecture, the way in which the pines around it all drooped, as if conscious of their eventual bane.

"Life there seems easier, I think," Morley said. "Happier, maybe?"

Anae understood him, though it stung her with self-pity. And doubtless that he was correct, she wished to prove him wrong. If only for the preservation of her dignity, her esteemed privileges. But how? By offering a taste of luxury, as she had done at the brewery not an hour past? He hadn't even noticed when she offered no coin for Jhann's service—did he then think payment was unrequired, that anyone could step in and slurp up a double-pint without charge?

In order for him to understand luxury, she thought, he would first have to be shown the intricacies of the 'Lord's System.' And what would be the purpose of that? He could live his whole life in the isolation of Werplaus. Why complicate it?

He was special—wiser than Alherde, more beautiful than Gerry the Woodcutter, more blessed than Chaplain Wyer, more precious than a

34

gemstone. She wished to possess him, to wield him as a glass optic through which the world was made more colorful. Would he stay if she asked? Could he be convinced that Reineshir had hidden finery?

Her father needed another stableboy, someone to shovel dung and tend to the destriers—creatures Morley had probably never seen in his life. Amstudt could use a kitchen urchin; Alherde might require an assistant. Alas, nothing seemed satisfactory. A life of servitude versus a life of total freedom in the south.

Istain was trotting over with a smile. His oxcart was left by the porch of the atelier. The goat was not present amidst its new supply.

"Have a nice walk?" he asked them both. Then, to Morley, "Geat'll be spendin' a night or two, gettin' to know the other rams, re-learnin' what it means to be a goat." He shot him a wink at this. "I'll be back to get him tomorrow if the weather's good, though I bet there'll be rain." Morley nodded and Anae caught him glancing at her. Istain stretched his arms and cracked his back through the stillness. "Ready to head home, then?" he said.

As if by instinct, Anae's hand shot to Morley's unburdened shoulder.

"He..." she started to Istain. Then, drawing her fingers away, she turned to the halfelev. "My family would be happy to—I mean, I'd like to invite you to the Bertriss manor tonight." Morley and Istain looked to each other with altered countenances—one dumbfounded and one hopeful. She explained further, "You've been very kind to me today. And I would like to repay you for keeping me company. You may spend the night as well, if you wish."

Morley searched Istain again. The older man's grin proved a fair hint.

"Sure," Morley finally said, hugging the sword to his chest. It was her second victory of the day, she thought, and likely her last. Another few hours with the young man seemed worthwhile.

"A day in Reineshir and you've gained the favor of its most beautiful lady," Istain said with a short bow before heading back to the wagon. "I'll be here tomorrow, lad. Sun or clouds. You two watch yourselves."

With that farewell, Anae again locked her arm around Morley's and treaded toward her hidden path around the estate.

She later couldn't decide between the greater difficulty: asking Morley to stay for the night or admitting to him that her family would never dream of hosting the likes of him. They would sooner burn their table to cinders before offering him one of its chairs. She knew this without having to ask;

it had been elucidated twice over the years, first with the Ornhatter sisters, then with Gerry.

Luckily, despite his momentary perplexity, Morley was happy enough with accompanying her to the stables—and compliant enough to accept the offer of sleeping there. He even claimed it was a fairer space than that of his house, though he was certainly just being polite.

Of course, there was shock and ensuing unease in him when introduced to its four tenants, the first horses he had ever seen. But as he soon insisted, he'd always wanted to behold such beasts. When Anae left to attend supper, duly within the hour, the young man appeared to be reciting certain cherished phrases to her mother's steed, his hand resting calmly between the beast's antler nubs.

"And Sir Aubin touched the face of Stridstein, his destrier," she heard him saying, "much as he would the face of his unforgotten Larenta."

Supper was long and uneventful at the Bertriss table. Alherde scolded Anae again for something—she didn't listen. Her mother absently discussed mid-Hetta tallage with her father: how many eggs were expected from the farmers and how many kegs of beer were needed from the brewers and so on. Lark, leeks, and pudding covered her dish. She ate half her serving, then left the hall without being excused. Afterwards, while making her way to the kitchen to get scraps for Morley, she was apprehended by her mester.

"Good Being beyond," Alherde called, "come here. Thought you could evade me even after supper? Well, if you won't be a damme of the courts, you'll at least be a bloody gardener. One lesson, at least one."

Carrying an herb box in his hand and *The Book of Roots* underarm, he sat the girl on a hallway bench, ignoring her exhausted pleas. He then forced her to read aloud the chapter they had left off on. After, he reached into the herb box and dumped a handful of gnarly dried petals between them on their bench.

"Now, what is this?" Alherde pointed to it, alternately black and pale with smidgens of fuchsia. Upon closer inspection, each of the shrunken leaves was covered over with a brownish powder.

"Chamomile," said Anae, speedily yet begrudgingly. "And ground akava."

"Fine," the mester allowed, dismissing the slight generality in his pupil's answer. She had neglected to include the precise type of chamomile. "And of what classes do they belong to, respectively?" Anae watched the pile at the center of the bench, wishing the answer would divine itself in the twisted petals.

"Herbs," she said, giving up. Alherde bit his lip and weaved his fingers together.

"No. Try again." His student didn't move a muscle.

"Xicitar," she murmured.

"No, absolutely not. Again."

"Acsifo."

At this, her mester grumbled a curse and buried his head in his hands. Anae spurned rhetoric, evaded dialectics, laughed at the classical arts, and now she was dispensing with pharma-craft. Alherde frowned at her as she continued staring down at the bench, her foot tapping.

"First—and as you only just read a moment ago—it's called acsifan, not 'acsifo.' Though, yes, akava belongs to that class. Second, chamomile and many other herbs belong to the class of uforian. The class of xicitar pertains to sugar and certain spices. Therefore, this particular blend is uforian-acsifan, which is meant to be steeped in hot water…for what purpose?" His features were still and waxen.

"For putting sick people to sleep."

"At a slower rate than…?" This time, the girl snorted discreetly and raised her head to meet Alherde's pale stubbled face.

"Slower than one of Mester Alherde's lectures."

Regardless of this little victory, she was immediately met with painful discipline as Alherde smacked her wrist with a measuring rod in two blurred movements. At the very least, he chose not to strike at the side of her neck this time.

Flustered, Alherde then gathered up all his belongings and stood from the bench. He marched off down the stony corridor, back toward the dining hall.

"You're an insufferable pupil, you know that?!" he shouted back at her.

"Tell it to my mother," she retorted at a moderate volume. "Or my father. Or anyone in the Bertriss staff. See how much they care."

Once Alherde was out of sight, Anae dashed to the pantry and buttery, fearful—perhaps irrationally—that Morley would not be there when she returned to the stables.

However, upon making her way back through the purple dusk, she found the young man stroking the nose of her father's bay destrier, still yet enamored by its size and gentility. He dismissed her apology, gratefully taking the bread, grapes, and lark she offered. He finished the meat in seconds. Finishing the bread and fruit, and admittedly resisting the courtesy of giving the horses a few of his grapes, Anae opened a cask of her parents' strongest wine, a bloody red from the Aubin traders.

The two of them then ascended the steps to the stable loft, a vault of broken bales lit faintly by the cerulean night. There, they shared the cask moderately, drinking from it with a long ladle as they rested on the ground. The sword was laid between them, hidden beneath a cascade of hay.

"I was afraid you'd be gone when I returned," she said after a long discussion on dinner habits in Egainshir.

"Where would I go?" he questioned. "Back to the hamlet? I'd get lost in the dark or eaten by wolves within an hour."

"Are there wolves in Werplaus, then?" She turned onto her side, facing him. She felt uncustomarily safe there in the loft, cozy even.

"I've only seen one," he said. "Lunferda said she saw one just yesterday. I think she was lying, though. She never sees anything while looking south." Anae smirked at this.

"I've never seen a wolf. Are they big?"

"Maybe. I think so. It was hard to tell." They quietened. The girl took another deep gulp from the ladle and passed it over to Morley. "Anyhow, I feel I've spent the whole day talking about my own life," he said before taking a sip.

"And an interesting life it is," she interjected.

"Tell me about yours. All I know is—" He hiccupped. "All I know is that you're the daughter of the man who owns the county."

"The Earl, yes. Though, he doesn't quite own the land. It's more like he bought the title and now he's charged with *watching over* the land. But even so, my mother—she's called the 'Damme'—she does most of the work nowadays. All for the sake of Aetheling Roberrus. He's the man who truly owns the land."

"I know of him," Morley confirmed. "I've seen his name in *Chevaliers of Bienvale*, nearer the end. In the part about Sarcovy. Roberrus was the one who brought all the best chevaliers here."

"My book doesn't mention Sarcovy," she said, thinking of the lean text on her bedroom table. "Mine ends with 'The Love of Sir Aubin and Larenta.'"

"But their story ended on Sarcovy. Many of them did."

"True." At this, Anae thought over the details she'd read so many times over. She could remember no references to Sarcovy—no place-names whatsoever, in fact. It only mentioned a conquest that set out across the southern sea, that carried all Bienvale's heroes to their graves. She'd believed it a poeticism.

"Were you born here?" Morley asked.

"No. I came from Triume, the continent. Most of my life was lived in a town called Oxhead."

"Did you like it there?"

"Yes. It was much nicer than this place. Brighter. Filled with all sorts of people who'd come and go like the day's sun. I like people—nice people, that is. The people around here aren't so nice—besides you and Istain and a few of the younger folk, they're not so nice. And I feel like they've made my family nastier, just by living around us."

"Why'd you leave the continent?" asked Morley, offering her the filled ladle. Anae gulped the wine down quick and handed it back.

"My father only became an earl here," she continued, wiping her lips, "because Rien Debois—he was the last earl—died a few years ago without a successor, so Roberrus needed his position filled. Normally, Roberrus would just install one of his kapitains, as he did for the other counties. But I think he needed money to pay war debts, so he auctioned the title instead. My mother pushed my father to it, my father was highest bidder, and thus we moved here." She chuckled quietly then.

"My family is of merchant stock, which I don't think pleases Roberrus much—though he knows of our benefits. He ignores us as best he can. My mother, for one, has been trying to plead for him to change this land's name to 'Bertriss County,' instead of 'Debois.' And Roberrus repeatedly inconveniences her by sailing off to war all of a sudden. That's his reply to every request my mother's made. Except one."

"Tell me," Morley insisted, drinking more.

"My parents are trying to marry me off to Roberrus' son. Felix, he's called. They won't say it, but I think they want me to become the Damme of Sarcovy and raise sons who will inherit the family legacy or something."

"What's that?"

"Legacy? It's something that remains after you die. Like the stories written for Sir Olivien or a statue of a dead king."

"Or a sword," said Morley gladly.

"Maybe," Anae conceded. "I liked the idea at first, the idea of leaving a mark here forever. But then I think, why? I think of my grand tomb or a church built in my name or a monument in my likeness. They wouldn't please me for all time if I was alive to see them. If someone sculpted my face and figure, I would desire another that corrects the flaws of the first, which I would spot even if they weren't there. My sons would inherit what? The Crouxwood, the swamplands, the Lightrun River and Larenta's Creek? What pleasure would I gain in surveying them from the heavens— where my soul has already inherited a knowledge of all things?" At this, she shook her dizzied head.

"I don't want to marry anyone, especially not Felix," she said. "It isn't my decision to make, so I don't wish it made at all. I've never met Felix but I think he's probably cruel. All men like that are cruel."

"Men like what?" Morley asked, offering another ladleful. Anae didn't accept it, so the halfelev slurped it up himself.

"You know. Aethelings. Princes. Sometimes kings. Like in all those stories we know—like Sir Haubauld and the Baron of Lumnir. If aethelings and princes don't get what they want, they hurt other people. And they do it with impurity—ehm, *impunity*."

"Impurity sounds right to me." Morley spoke, pushing aside the cask.

"You know more words than most of the townsfolk here, Morley," Anae said, again reclining to face him. His features were dimmed under the sparse coppery moonlight beaming in from the holes in the ceiling. He looked older in this shade, nobler, like a sculpture.

"Maybe. But I don't know what they all mean exactly." The girl giggled at this.

"Do you know…Do you know what 'virgater' means?" There was a rustling sound as if he were shaking his head against the straw. "Do you know what 'hallmote' means?"

"Halibut?"

"No, 'hallmote,'" she repeated.

"No."

"Do you know what 'benefice' means?" Against the dimness of the loft's open window, she could see the silhouette of his finger, pointed upward.

"It's a piece of land given to a ridder for his service to an aetheling." She playfully swiped at his finger. In taking ahold of his hand, her fingers laced with his and rested between his knuckles.

"You grew up on one, didn't you? With that ridder. What was his name?"

"Gale. He built our house under a hill—it was very nice. Have I mentioned that?"

"You haven't. Was…" She wondered if the question in her mind would sound too silly. "Was he your father?"

"No. He wasn't. Though I wish he was." The lad turned over onto his side, facing her—as she heard through the dark. "I admired him. And his stories. He fought for this land alongside many of our favorite chevaliers, back when they all first set foot on these shores."

"Who was your father?" she asked.

"I don't know," he said simply.

"You never asked Sir Gale? Or did he not know either?"

"I didn't really know what a father was until I moved to Egainshir. I just assumed that—I don't know—that people came out of the ground or something. Like celery." Anae's laughter seeped through her nose in clipped snorts. She slid her free hand over her mouth. "You can laugh all you want. It is funny." He chuckled quietly along with her.

"That's not what happens, Morley."

Without thinking, she wriggled closer and kissed him. When his lips did not part, she lifted her head and looked at him: he stared back, shocked or terrified, mouth now agape. She tried again, nudging his jaw shut with a knuckle. He did better, though the movement of his lips was poorly timed. She lifted her head again, tried not to giggle again. It was clear from the start: this was his first time.

Regardless and with some guidance, he fulfilled the role adequately. They were both fully undressed after a foggy interval—skin clammy, patched with hay, sticky from spilled wine. The sword clattered beneath them. The destriers fussed below. And Anae found herself thinking about candles and rainstorms.

She stayed with him afterwards for an unknown duration, holding him, watching him, dozing in his arms. They had no energy left for words.

When she knew he had drifted to sleep, Anae gathered up her gown in a bundle and whisked across the manor's front toft, through a back door, up the nearest stairwell, into her chamber, and under her blankets.

She thought about Morley—not with affection or admirability, but with a weighty concern. She wondered if she had erred.

41

Before fading to sleep, she attempted to plan out the impending morning hours: get him out of the stables, take him to the pens, get back in the house in time for her breakfast. Until then, all she could do was pray that nobody needed anything from the stable loft before she woke.

In the morning, Anae found Morley waiting for her there, trying to find his reflection in the flat of the blade. He was a man now, he probably thought, so his features had to be magically matured. All Anae could see was a sweet boy, oblivious to the possibility of getting caught by the stableman.

She imparted some spirited ridicule as she rushed him into town. There, she tried her best to ignore the lethargic, yet watchful populace as they gathered their work tools or went to fetch a sausage or two from the butchery. When the two of them arrived at the animal pen's barred fence, Anae embraced him fondly. And hastily.

"I'd like to wait for Istain with you," she breathed, "but I need to meet Mester Alherde back at the manse. Lessons and all that. Mentoring."

"I understand," Morley spoke, well rested. "If I come back next time we need to re-supply, will I see you?" Anae simpered at him.

"Of course. You're a very nice boy, Fitzmorley." She glanced at the ground. "Meet right here?"

"Yes."

"Good." She started back for her house, slowly. "How long until you return?"

"I don't know. Next week—no, three weeks. I don't know."

The girl bobbed her head. "I'll look every day. Or try to." They stared at each other. "We'll meet. One way or another."

She dashed back over to him and pecked both his cheeks, then headed off. At a distance, she heard an exclamation from him: his goat Geat had dashed over to meet him, deftly scaling the fence. Morley hugged the odd little creature close, gripping his horns.

Yes, she thought. We'll meet. Once or twice more.

A season passed.

*   *   *

The four cogs came into view during the hour of Vosses. Felix watched from the highest turret of his home, squinting against the ocean's sharp effulgence, trying to discern the flagship's topmost banner.

42

Its mainsail, which was being furled by invisible crewmen, plainly carried his family's mark—two violet bolts crossing one another over a neutral blue field—though he surely didn't need *this* indication to know it was his father's ship, returned from an ill-advised incursion unto the Talioran coast. There was a streamer at the tip of the mast—he could see it now—like a silk-thin tendril wrapping and unwrapping itself around its pike.

Was it white or black? Felix couldn't tell. Or, he thought, perhaps he just didn't want to. He stared on. Then, when his denial crossed beyond the border into impracticality, he abandoned the window.

He stepped lightly down the spiraling slabs so as not to be heard by his officials, waiting below in the astronomer's scriptorium. The stairwell was lit only by intermediate arrow loops, each shedding a flat stave of light. Felix paused at each one, looked out, kept going. What he saw through these vertical slits were the ever-accumulating portions of Sarcovy's demesne: there was the sea, then the harbor, then the steaming burg of Wallenport, then the Crouxwood's treeline, then the highlands beyond the roof of their motte-based keep, then the north coast's mounting seaside crags. After that, it was the ocean again. And still yet at the bottom of the stairs, the household staff waiting in the cramped studio of the sciences.

Felix—dark-haired, primly bearded, tall-eared, sharp-eyed—searched his servants. As he did so, his mother, Ellemine, shifted into the room and stepped to the throng's foreground. She wore the same expectant face she always wore, though with a small frown ridged between her eyes.

Felix joined his hands behind his hip. "Black," he stated of the ship's streamer.

A morbid hum filled the room. As if by routine, the marshal removed himself from the chamber to prepare the horses. Ellemine's downcast eyes did not glisten but, as her son recalled, why would they? Nobody wept, in fact, and Felix expected this much. He had seen and heard so many ancient dramas and songs outside St. Maguir's, and knew well that catharsis only occurred before the denouement of tragedies. But the death of his father was not a tragedy.

Roberrus Sivliére, Aetheling of Sarcovy Isle, was not a moderate or satisfied man, nor was he of pleasant spirit. Granted, he wasn't boastful either, and he never did anything with cruel intent. Roberrus was a man of enterprise. He was naturally determined though uninspiring, Felix thought, a subject incapable of being rendered into memorable art: if there were to be a monument of him, it would most appropriately be an enormous stark block placed atop his grave. If there were to be a song of his deeds, it would be composed without a melody—a static monotonous rhythm with an efficient meter, like that of the rowers' drum.

His mythos would be a chain of victories—his recent death the climax, the peripeteia, and the only instance of pathos, all meshed into one scene. The end, a pitiless exhibition of characters yet unseen—besides Felix himself, Esteran the Edma, Ellemine and possibly her bastard, Willian—could not possibly evoke tears.

Thus, Felix imagined the herald of the overture: "Settle and hear of Roberrus Sivliére, of the Isle of Sarcovy so fruitlessly sundered, of the Piikish corsairs and their coarse seaward crafts, of the barons in Bienvale he battered and bolstered, of the treacherous Taliorans who so tattered his pennant…" Even that ridiculous set of verses would be too colorful for the likes of him.

Felix Sivliére contemplated all this during the silent procession down from the scriptorium, through his house's upper gallery, down into the court, and out the front gate.

Upon setting foot outside, a briny wind surmounted the high motte. It whipped the hem of his mother's dress and knocked away several guards' caps. The marshal and his apprentice brought around four horses. Still, nobody said a word.

Knowing their duties, Felix, Cato Clerici, War-mester Herman, and Iacob—the new edma, as was implicit—climbed onto their desired steeds. They set off down the long graveled steps toward the heart of Wallenport, now nearly half the size of a proper city.

The landing led onto a wide street of stone and grout, currently unglutted by the citizenry. The buildings across from the palisade, all squat and prim, were neatly dwarfed by the ridge-roofed insulae houses circling the town's central plaza, the nave of which bore St. Maguir's Church.

Iacob the Edma was the first to canter up beside his new lord. The young man was dressed almost identically to Felix, as was the custom: a dark wool-padded gambeson, breeches, and a riding cloak—the difference in their attire being that one cloak, Felix's, was much filthier than the other's.

"Well," Felix said to his mate, "it happened."

44

"Exactly as you predicted, at that," Iacob replied. "It's midday, streets are empty. Rainclouds are on their way. It's the end of Sarcovy's first era, my friend."

"I wouldn't say that," said Felix. He turned his head to see Cato, swathed in the fresh habit of a prioress, and Herman, garbed in heavy wool. Both watched him as if waiting for a command.

"How do you think he died?" the edma asked. Felix had already prepared a conception, partly from the details of his recent dreams.

"Sustained wounds. Passed away in his cabin, reticently. I hope it was in his sleep. Otherwise, his last breaths were sucked-in, frustrated. Ah, and the wound was caused by an arrow. What do you think?"

Iacob sagged. "I thought it'd be something more heroic," he said.

"What? Skewered by a lance? Thrown from his horse, lifted over the heads of his fondest ridders? Carried away by a harpy? No, maybe there was a river nearby and he floated along with its current. Like Sir Olivien and the other one." The edma said nothing to this.

"I'm sorry, Iac," Felix proceeded. "Didn't mean to make things grim— or grimmer. Here, a first task for you as my edma: change the subject for me."

"With pleasure," he said. "What's next for us Sarcovians?"

This time, Felix had to muster a response from scratch. "I suppose we'll have to deal with the Taliorans one of these days, if only for the dignity of our countrymen," he proposed. "We could try to raid one of their smaller ports again. Or harass their westward sea-traders—better yet, hire the Piiks to do it."

As he spoke, Felix caught the eye of a grizzled elder. He was sitting on a stoop under a faded signpost and nursing an elaborate flagon. He was one of only eleven commoners in sight, the rest being further up the road.

"What do you think of that?" Felix asked his companion. He could hear Herman's ride clopping up to the edma's side; Cato's followed suite on Felix's own flank.

"Call me bold," Iacob started, "but Roberrus had some capable colleagues back in Bienvale. Think of the favors they might fulfill, knowing you're his son. We could try and gather together an army on the continent, invade Taliorano by land. Think about it—that's how Roberrus took Sarcovy. He brought together his friends and other aethelings, promised them land, benefits, glory, all that. And he was only a few years older than you are now."

"Do you know how big Taliorano is, edma?" came Herman's voice as they treaded around a corner. They were headed straight for the plaza and its church, a windowless block of grey brick and mortar with three apses on its harbor-facing side; a rigid square bell tower stretched over the front door and narthex. People milled about the courtyard, though not too many.

"No. Do you?" the edma challenged.

"I know well enough that it is a hundred times bigger than Sarcovy. At least. If you'd listened to or attended his councils, you'd know Roberrus never wished to take Talioran land. He only meant to plunder a few of its lesser ports—Criccaci, Daargate, and Saduan namely."

"Ah yes, and why did he wish to do so?" Iacob asked rhetorically. "To raise funds, to settle our debts to the king—debts which are now chiefly *our* concern. Taliorano is under so much strife these days with the infighting and the invasion from the north and such. Taking one port would go unnoticed, I'm sure."

"We can plead for more time," Cato Clerici's smoother voice came in. Fleetingly, she rested a hand on Felix's shoulder as they trod across the open plaza. "The king will understand the difficulty at hand. He inherited his own father's debts, if you recall. If I may make one proposition: we should ask for one year, levy twice as much money as he demands, then repay him with additional recompense."

"That's the crux here, cleric," Iacob resumed. "As far as I see it. I suppose you're against the idea of levying those sums through warfare— that is, the quick and easy way."

"Quick and easy, eh?" Herman came in. "When was the last time you went into battle, edma?"

"Undramon's Isle, three years back," the edma said confidently. "Felix was there as well. It took a season and a half, there and back. And the prisoners we brought back with us were two plummes each in the western market. What?" Herman had been soundlessly snickering all the while.

"As mester of war," he began, "I can assure you that slaughtering a load of cudgel-wielding goat herders is quite different from fighting continental troops, no matter the country. I can also assure you that this particular excursion you so boldly joined was not free of charge. Roberrus had most of the ships loaned to him from the coastal earls and, as you must know, two smashed into the sea stacks and one was set aflame by the Piiks. In the end, Roberrus had to pay for the three ships in full with what he earned from selling the prisoners. Do you know how much was left over?"

Iacob glared at the war-mester then looked to Felix, hoping he would know the answer.

"Twelve nickel plummes," said Herman, "hardly the value of one argen. A good brewer makes more than that in a week. Now, since you've obviously been paying attention to the curator's addresses over the recent years, can you tell me what amount we owe the king and why?"

Again, Iacob the Edma made no response. Felix's face reddened. The purpose of the edma's station was merely to provide an aetheling with someone who could be more of a friend than an advisor; it was strictly a Bienvalian tradition and had been for centuries, they'd been told. The edma was never meant to be a voice of reason or a fine guide, but a corporeal reflection of their governor.

So, during those incidents in which Felix had no desire to speak or sound foolish, as was the case at the moment, Iacob was purposed with speaking for him, for they both were perpetually of the same opinion. However, this tended to mean that whenever an answer was unknown, it was unknown to the both of them.

"That's what I thought," Herman said eventually. "King Hugon is owed three aureons, seven argens, and twelve plummes in total. Now, Roberrus was not an idiot for allowing this debt to rise. He was a strong leader and everyone knew it. Strong leaders do well by staying indebted to their superiors, as kings don't often turn a blind eye to borrowers. If a debtor is needed to break a rebellion or meet a foreign legion at the borders or go on an expeditionary march, they're duly called upon.

"In Bienvale, service means war and war means plunder. And plunder is easy to purloin in the field. Some arrears are repaid, some honor is restored, some money is pursed and kept out of sight. Thus, distinguished men benefit from debt. And with all due respect, Aetheling Felix…"

The young man avoided his advisor's heavy gaze. Herman said no more.

They were passing onto the strand of the harbor. Its jetty was of the same material as the church, but the bricks were much larger and copiously speckled with sessile barnacle beaks; the wooden piers beside it spewed out from the mouths of fisheries and boatwrights. It was largely quiescent at this time of day, when the fishermen were still out to sea and the grocers were counting their earnings from the early morning.

The riding tetrad halted before the jetty. Roberrus' flagship was half a league out, too big to moor by Wallenport's adolescent quayside. The other two ships were dropping their anchors further out, each giving the others an appropriate berth.

"Well then, now that we have the preliminaries out of the way," Felix said, watching the distant sailors prepare a dinghy, "I'd like to hear more proposals. Cato Clerici says we should appeal to the king, acquire a year, and repay him honestly. Without shedding anyone's blood."

"Highly implausible at this point," Herman grumbled, though not unkindly. Cato did not react either way.

"Iacob says we should appeal to my father's closest allies in Bienvale— the barons, burghers, and earls who've fought beside him in the past— then invade Taliorano by land."

There was a brief stillness. Iacob smirked through it. Then Cato cleared her throat.

"To add to the war-mester's earlier statement," she said, "have you heard the phrase, 'Fine fathers pave the road for miscreant sons,' Aetheling Felix?"

Felix and his edma eyed each other questioningly. Herman bobbed his head.

"It is an oft-honored maxim throughout Bienvale," she continued. "I employ it here not because I think you a miscreant but because I think Roberrus was known to many as a great ruler. A fine father. Imagine what the aethelings of Bienvale, your father's friends, would think when Roberrus' young son appeared before a hallmote of some southern hertog—and thus demanded a coalition and a foray into the unpredictable Taliorano countryside. And all for the sake of his debts to the king, which is undoubtedly how they would perceive such demands. I'm sure they would think you a miscreant."

Felix, though he retained composure, felt as if his authority had been sapped by an eminent ghost. He was immediately disgusted by his naivety, by the silly notion he had absently carried down from the keep's turret like wooly lint in a cloak pocket: that nobody would notice the difference between Aetheling Roberrus and Aetheling Felix, the father and the son.

All of a sudden, the young man had no desire to rule. He distantly wondered over alternatives, ways in which he could either abandon the role or pass it along to someone more willing or self-reliant. But there were very few feasible methods of escape. And in terms of a new ruler, nobody besides his mother came into mind.

"A good addition, cleric," Herman soon followed, "but I do know these allies well. Almost as well as Roberrus knew them. Convincing a few earls to lend us arms is not wholly futile, though it'll take time. And relentless determination. Before you can gain faith from aethelings abroad, you must first gain faith from your subjects. From the barrens to the barracks."

As if in rehearsal, Cato produced a vellum from the insides of her robe and handed it over. The young aetheling unrolled and looked it over: it was a small map of the island, or so he figured. Iacob leaned over as far as he could to inspect the cloth.

"I took it from the scriptorium upon hearing your announcement of the black flag," said Cato. She then began to speak as if every word were made of marble: "This is now your demesne. You have a hertog, a castellan, two earls, and ninety-eight and a hundred ridders. And by the account of our last survey, just over three thousand landed tenants throughout the island, the ridders included. So…what do you believe is the best course of action right now?"

Felix thought back to his lessons with Chamberlain Raul. The answer was an easy one.

"Tour the demesne with my best men in tow. Check up on my earls, their manors. My people." Cato gestured to the map in his hands, as if requesting him to specify his exact route.

"First ride to Chaisgott's hill," Felix went on, "and gift the castellan with…something. A new sword or coat. From there we ride to The Stead, then Hoerlog. Then we move around the high hills to Westley, give respects to Michel Laisroch, and take a boat across the channel to Aubin. I suppose that's where I am to be officially initiated as aetheling, yes?" Herman and Cato nodded.

"Right. After seeing Hertog Pourtmann, we sail back to the mainland, go to Reineshir to visit the Bertrisses, then finally pass over Olivien's Ford and come back here. It can all be done in half a season. Less if the weather is kind and the horses are fast." Nobody said a word in reply.

"Did I miss anything? Iacob?"

The edma swayed his head in a reluctant fashion. "There is a matter you left out, my friend. One which I *know* you have no desire to hear." Felix knit his brow. "The Bertriss daughter. Anae. I know you'll want more time to…you know." He mumbled the latter words so as not to displease the cleric. "But the Bertrisses have been requesting this marriage for a long time now. Considering their wealth back in Oxhead, we might do well in humoring them."

"That is key here, as well," Herman came in. "If we are to gain the trust of the continentals, we need to show them a semblance of ability. That is to say, men of your position do best in purchasing their proficiencies and taking great risks—Stewardess Allesande's method. We need an army, though not an army of peasants or hirelings."

"Ridders," Felix agreed. "Chevaliers. Veterans. That's what my father had in bulk when he took this island. A retinue of able officers, like the ones in your stories, Herman. Chaisgott, Olivien, Rien, Rolle, and all the others. My father fostered them all, united them. That's how the earls of the southern coast knew he was capable."

His father's dinghy was jouncing closer and closer to the lowest pier. Three figures were seated on its thwarts: two of them rowed as one tried to stand with his palm against the tall bow. Felix could tell without scrutiny that it was Esteran, the previous edma. Between them all, stretched out across the burden boards, was the shape of a man wrapped in wet white cloth. Silence crept over the mounted group once again.

Eventually, Cato Clerici turned her ride around and, before departing, leaned over to Felix.

"I'll have my staff prepare a catafalque for him in the church. When do you wish to see him buried?"

"How soon can a grave be prepared?" he asked.

"If it pleases you, he can be buried by this evening. Wherever is most appropriate. The decision is all yours." This was more than satisfactory.

"This evening before dark," the aetheling demanded. "The promontory, if that is possible. Send a man to the quarry as soon as you can. I want the largest block of stone on this island to be placed over his mound. The stonecutters may have as much time as they need to prepare it—No, I take that back. I want to see it there by the time I return from my tour."

"Inscription?"

Felix took a moment to imagine the most evocative words: HERE RESTS AETHELING ROBERRUS VAN SARCOVY…AETHELING ROBERRUS OF THE ISLES, HERO AMIDST THE BIENS…

"No inscription," Felix said at last. "Just solid rock. He would've preferred that."

For two and a half hours, Roberrus' body was displayed for the public atop a perfectly sized catafalque at the center of St. Maguir's chancel. The full populace, as Iacob reckoned, seeped timidly from their homes and businesses to behold him, the greyed progenitor of their home. Neither Felix nor Ellemine entered to see the man. Instead, they waited without, anticipating the hour of Spaken when the body was to be removed, carried up to the north cliff via its undulating trail and lowered down into a speedily prepared grave—a trifle shallow, no doubt.

That time came and went without issue. Only the Sivliére family—now only Ellemine and Felix—their household staff, and the town clergy made the ascent. Many respectful families hung their heads along the roadsides as the procession moved on, guided by prayers of passage.

Felix and Ellemine followed behind the pall, their arms interlocked, their retinue tailing. Just before they moved beyond the palisade gates, Felix spotted two familiar women, standing at a surprising proximity. One was a younger girl, the blonde-haired and widely envied Enriet; the other was much older, an infertile beauty by the name of Ranneka. The new aetheling eyed them both and subtly moved his lips: "Later," he spelled out. Both understood without noticing the other.

Thus, soon after the funeral, Felix fled in secret to a house near an end of Wallenport's largest fishery, the residence of Kabb Browncobbler. He entered without flourish and urged Kabb to leave for a time, then slid into the room of his daughter, Enriet.

Not long after—and with the request of a later liaison—Felix departed and made his way to the insulae, the craft-workers' apartments. Ranneka, who lived above a prominent weaver workshop, had left her door unlocked. She was older than Felix by at least twenty years. He admired her attitude, her rich condescendence. And her fair seniority. He stayed with her for much longer, left late into the night.

For days after, Felix's staff planned his trip around Sarcovy, deciding upon which gifts to grant, who would receive them, and whether or not such was within their dwindling budget. At the end of the week, messengers were sent out to herald his imminent arrivals.

Only hours after this, the aetheling, his edma, most of his advisors, and a handful of house-ridders rode out for Chaisgott Castle, a shell keep built on the foothills at the northern edge of the Crouxwood. Its castellan,

Bertram, son of the keep's eponymous builder, was promised a team of masons; he'd requested them after the Skonhet season, when the heavy storms flooded the central courtyard. From there they moved to The Stead, a commune for aspirant ridders at the Crouxwood's western end.

They then made their way to Hoerlog, a watchtower over the island's northwesternmost cliffs, where Felix unamusedly noted the absence of his brother. They left promptly without imparting a gift of any kind.

Moving south and keeping the Crouxwood at their sides, they reached the town of Westley, seat of Laisroch County. Its earl and damme, Michel and Mennia, both pleased or feigning pleasure over the expectations of his patronage, were given an inexpensive collective of brooches and gilded horse collars.

Felix was also introduced to the earl's stewardess, Allesande, a woman who exulted the competence of her Westleyan ridders. She was justified. He deigned this upon viewing a brief pageant of her frog-helm warriors. They could serve as excellent vanguard, he knew.

From there the cavalcade descended to the lowlands, met the ferrymen of Rolle's Channel, and took a longboat to Aubin. Hertog Pourtmann, the legal overseer of the island's rare assemblies, officiated Felix's status as Aetheling of Sarcovy within the day. The hertog then hosted a large feast—as large as his coffers could concede, Felix convinced himself— within a cloister of his manor.

Early the next morning, the young aetheling's party set out for their next destination: Reineshir.

When they trailed up the southern road and stopped before the manse's gates, the townsfolk either hid out of sight or watched from their respective distances. Aetheling Felix paid no mind to them. He was irritable, already fed up with riding through the day and sleeping with a stone or root under the matting of his tent. The campaign to Undramon's Isle wasn't even this bad, he thought, as he'd had his own cabin and a soft feathery bed to cradle asleep his anxious mind. Meanwhile, all his previous ventures around Sarcovy throughout the long years had been mere day-long hunting excursions, a hobby he long since abandoned for other more pubescent indulgences.

Tired, the aetheling and his men trudged onto the turf of the Bertriss estate, where they were received by the manorial staff: Earl Lammert and Damme Fruela Bertriss, and their daughter Anae.

The girl was very much a youthful recreation of her mother, whom Felix discontentedly found far more beauteous. And yet, Anae was also lovely. Her body seemed shapely enough under her gown; her face was fair and bore a disinterested expression—this was what set her apart from her mother, actually, as he soon realized.

Earl Lammert was elated to the point of tears. His daughter, his only child, was to be the aetheling's woman, the Damme of Sarcovy. The happiness made him uncomely.

Anae, on the other hand, looked upon her future spouse with a realistic, sullen indifference. She was certainly the type who spoke her mind freely and expected a clout of some sort. But Felix wasn't that kind of man, he often reminded himself. If she attempted to irk him in any way, she would be met with a counter-argument, a commendation, a laugh maybe.

The young man approached. The girl tilted her head, inspecting his ears and eyes from where she stood. Damme Fruela simmered behind her, prepared to reprimand the girl for her aloofness. She forgot to curtsy, Felix noted, and he himself forgot to bow and take her hand. They would get along exceedingly well by the following day, he thought.

"Anae Dammedottir Bertriss," he said, ignoring the heralds as they blasted their ceremonial announcements behind him.

She held out her hand for him to kiss. He played dumb for half a moment, then let out a careless "Oh," grasped her fingers, and kissed the middlemost valley of her knuckles. His eyes roved up her body, over her plain bodice, her flat breasts, the new Yeltiin Voss pendant at her neck—all the way up to her face. A corner of her mouth twitched as she slowly blinked. Her mother stepped forward.

"Aetheling Felix, this a crucial occasion for both our families," said the damme. "I need not prod that sentiment further." The young man vaguely rolled his eyes, hoping Anae would notice. She did. "But…well, perhaps we can speak somewhere private."

Fruela was tall, her skin pale as cream. Her husband had a similar hue: they didn't travel much. Anae, however, was moderately tanned, as if she spent much of her time out in the clearing of the town proper.

"Speak about what exactly?" Felix asked carelessly. He could tell the damme was writhing internally. "If anything must be said, it can be said before my retinue." Fruela took time, as Felix assumed, to conjure up a new response. As she did so, the young aetheling leaned close to Anae.

"Do you have a preference for a main course?" he asked. "At our wedding feast, I mean." The girl raised her shoulders diffidently.

"Anything but leeks," she murmured, her voice flat and appealing. "And chicken. Anything else is fine."

"Too bad. That's all we have in Wallenport," he joked. He withheld a smile and the girl withheld a laugh.

"The marriage need not take place immediately," said the Damme. "We're willing to acquiesce your, ehm, convenience. My daughter may not be prepared to fulfill the role and, I suppose, as the new overseer of this land, you have much work to do. A marriage is not a trivial event, Aetheling Felix, and I fear that it might seem rushed if she were to go away with you this evening."

"Who said anything about the evening?" Felix said, searching the men behind him. "We plan to leave as soon as possible—within the hour, if that's permissible. And we would be honored if you and your earl came along, as I wish to be wedded within the next three days. Your presence within Wallenport will be welcomed."

Earl Lammert's and Damme Fruela's harried looks were all Felix needed to see.

Now, truly, he was Aetheling of Sarcovy.

Anae and her parents disappeared back into the manor and, when they reemerged, they were dressed in riding clothes. As their stableman headed off to fetch their horses, Aetheling Felix took his fiancée by the hand and led her tenderly through the estate gates, much to the confusion of the damme. He mounted her atop his own ride, placing a generous pillion in front of his saddle.

He climbed up after her, ready to take to the roads before anyone else had set foot within their own stirrups. Without warning, he gripped one of his horse's nubbed antlers and spurned the beast forward up the north road. He was satisfied by his performance for Anae, happy to finally be away from the useless pomposity.

"Now," he said to her, wrapping an arm around her waist, "we have the better part of an hour to properly get to know each other. If that is your desire."

"It is, Aetheling Felix," she said, her voice still flat and awkward.

"No need for titles," he requested. "Titles are for epitaphs."

As he rode past what appeared to be an innhouse, a thin youth crept out from its side and stood in plain view, his face largely hidden behind a mop of brown hair. He watched them pass anxiously. Felix nodded and grinned kindly at him.

Chapter III – The Misadventure

Again Morley stumbled into the dry ditch at the barley-side of the road. After gathering himself up and regaining his sword, he moved closer to the wheat-side, grumbling.

He unsheathed Gale's claymore and swung it at the wheat grass, cutting it, beating it down, occasionally stomping on the bronzed heads of the overripe grain. He then put away the blade and continued on toward the distant trees; soon enough, he removed it again and continued thwacking the stalks. All the while, he shouted every curse he knew.

His voice echoed over the swaggering fields; a crow answered somewhere, then beat its wings. Morley stepped back to the middle of the road. He listened for a time, staring down each direction of the trail in turn. Nothing. He continued on.

"Ugly bastard. Stupid ugly slime-slurpin' git bastards," he muttered, quieter now.

Not far from the field's end, Morley dropped his trousers down to his ankles and urinated on the barley. "Drink this'n the next batch, Reineshir. Cursed buncha—*hic*..." He moved on momentarily.

*   *   *

Morley's excursions to Reineshir sapped away all other thoughts of work or relaxation. Whenever Istain mentioned a resupply trip, all that occupied the lad's mind was the image of Anae, spiritless and silent under the eye of Mester Alherde. Her own thoughts were surely bent on him, as she insisted during their moonlit walks around the estate's wooded croft. She had never lied to him, not once.

"You're not still set to marry the aetheling, are you?" he questioned once as they settled under a bald red oak and splayed a blanket over their legs. It had been two seasons since they first met, since she first offhandedly mentioned the arrangement. He wanted nothing else but to hear the words, "No, he has been promised to another and I am free to marry whomever I so wish." But he was met first with silence, then a sigh as gentle as a minnow kissing the undersurface of a pond.

"He isn't the aetheling, not yet. Roberrus is. And he hasn't had words with my parents about it. He's busy, the messengers say. Always busy somewhere off the island. The damme tends to the business of Wallenport, from what I've heard. Felix, meanwhile...I suppose if he wanted to take my hand in matrimony, he would be free to do so. But he's made no motions, sent no proposals. I've never met him, not even when I first arrived in Wallenport from the continent. I'll bet he's perfectly content with the women there—he could get any of them at any time, you know. There are many pretty girls walking those streets, if I remember right." This was satisfying for a moment.

"So you don't want to elope with him? Or climb into his bed?" Her face was not entirely clear in the night's gloom, though he was certain she bore a revolted cringe.

"No. Reineshir is a vile pit on the fringe of the known world, but I think I'd rather be here than in Wallenport, caged up in their keep. And in becoming Damme of Sarcovy, I'd have less freedom to go where I want." An owl leapt from a high branch, swooping down to catch a dormouse. Morley gripped Anae's hand. "But I say again, country boy. It won't be my decision when the time comes. And the time will come, probably soon."

"What if he's promised to another? Someone back on Triume?"

"I doubt it." The reply came with such speed that Morley gulped. "My parents have more money than the Sivliéres—or so they sometimes say. Not as much influence but definitely more money. And I hear they're in debt to the king. The only other option would be for Felix to marry the Princess of Bienvale, but that's not likely. She's engaged to a prince somewhere else, much further north. But anyway, even if Felix were given to someone else or chose to marry another on his own accord, I think my mother would sell the manse and move us back to Oxhead. I think she and my father might do that anyway once I'm married off—she always says she will. Since there's better business to be found there. She just wants a marital tie to an...aetheling so she can stand...stand out...among the other merchants."

Morley had stopped listening. In fact, he had begun to glide his lips up and down the length of Anae's neck, kissing her. There were no more words after that.

The pair had become uncareful with their promiscuity. Several times already, she'd sneaked him into her bedchambers and barred the door. Once, they had fallen asleep and the boy had to be expelled out the window in the early morning—like in the tales of Sirs Cadmael, Rolf, and

Tretain, they laughed. And yet, despite the ebbing secrecy, not one member of the household suspected anything.

Such was not the case, however, with good Istain the Trader, who knew immediately that Morley and the Bertriss girl were up to something devious. It showed through the young man's silly smirk on the very first morning after.

"I don't wish to hear out the finer details, boy," Istain said during their ride through flat Werplaus, "but I'm obliged to ask what you got yourselves up to last night. I guess you tried to sell off the sword?"

Geat tried to climb out of the wagon bed and onto the driving bench, but the lad pushed him back. "I unsheathed it a few times," he said. Istain hummed dubiously. "But she never got around to asking her father about an offer. It's fine, though. I'll just bring it back next time." The two stayed silent for a spell.

"You need to be careful around people like that," he cautioned. Geat brayed, as if he were asking why. Istain chuckled. "See, the Bertrisses have ridders in their service and…Well, lemme put it this way. It's common—very, very common for women and men of the gentry-kind to preserve their, eh—their, eh, purity, say. Till they're bonded in marriage. See what I'm sayin'? So, if Earl or Damme Bertriss ever found out that some kid from the south county was soiling his daughter's purity then, like I said, he's got ridders employed. And the act I'm implyin' is illegal, anyway."

"I see what you're saying," said Morley. "But it was *her* move, mate, not mine. And Arrin and Ceridwen aren't married. And I'm sure Anae's been with other boys before me. Unspecial boys. I'll bet none of them have been caught before."

This wasn't enough for Istain, of course. Either way, he allowed the young man to join him every time he rode off to Reineshir. He even stayed the night himself several times, when he was free of the burden of picking up Tommas and his supply of wood. Though afterwards, at the start of the Hosten season, Morley was forced to make the morning journey to Egainshir on foot, as the trader couldn't be bothered with repeatedly riding out a second time in as many days.

There were mornings of relentless rain and cruel winds, sweltering heat and horrid cold. Yet none of these were half as bad as the day of Anae's departure with Aetheling Felix. Thirty-some weeks after Morley had met her.

Though he'd just arrived in town with Istain, he abandoned the place forthwith, paced his way across the breezeless fields, treaded weakly onto the hamlet's green. He entered Amarta's house as she was guiding her young son, since named Galey, through the basic principles of walking. She saw the halfelev's crinkled face and, like a true mother, knew what was wrong without question. Morley rushed into her arms and sobbed against her chest. She held him there as Galey wandered the small house on his own.

In the early evening, Yeva came by after returning from the west shore with Serryl. She found him sitting on the corner bed, a blanket over his shoulders and Ceridwen beside him. Amarta had warmed a small loaf of wheat bread for him. Ceridwen explained the circumstances to the best of her understanding.

"I told you she wasn't worth the trips to Reineshir," she scoffed. "It's a sick-ridden heap and always will be. Wallenport is worse in certain ways, though—I hope she realizes that quick, right? Then she'll see what she's given up, who she's given up." Morley did not speak, nor did he cast an eye over his friend. He continued watching his covered knees, rubbing his fingers, sniffing. "If I had the means, Morley, I'd stride right up to the aetheling's castle and bang on the door. And once she answered, I'd pull her out by the hair and, and—"

"Yeva," Amarta hushed near the mouth of her kiln. Ceridwen, too, trained an admonishing stare over the young woman. After the quiet, the conversation shifted quaintly onto little Galey's progress with walking. The whole while, he'd been maundering around the house all on his own.

Morley did not eat or speak, not even once darkness fell over the hamlet. At this time, Yeva pulled him up and led him back to Gertruda and Lunferda's, where she shared her sleeping mat with him—largely so that he didn't have to stay with Arrin and Ceridwen, the young lovers, that night.

Through the days that followed, he distanced himself from the others and spent most of his time working. When he wasn't preoccupied with those varying duties, he sat with Geat and Minny. After a week and half— which in his distressed mind felt like a year and a half—the others began to approach and give council. Morley said nothing to most of them. The rest, meanwhile, he was inclined to revile.

"Y'know, I was sweet with a boy when I lived back in Bienvale," Lunferda said to him once during her watching hours. "Hyart was his name. I was about your age, too. Small village place, he loved me and I loved him—that sort, see. Neither of us had other lovers. I sense that was the case with you and the girl, eh? Her case is a tough one, see, since she's more bounden to show her faith for the king's system. In a way, everyone's watchin' her and she knows it.

"Anyhow, I left Hyart when my father passed and his property was bought up by some northerner. Gertruda and I had to leave, head off to the cheapest place within good distance. Here. Hyart said he wished to join us and I would've let him. But his own father had other plans for him. The choice was an easy one to decide and a tough one to make, if there's any sense to that. I stuck with my sister. Maybe there's some similarities in our stories, eh?" As she walked off, Geat groaned.

A day later, Arrin climbed the goats' fence and sat above Morley.

"Mate, I don't know if you've proper noticed it…but Yeva's been acting odd around you of late. Haven't you noticed?" Morley shook his head once, continued glaring southward. "I mean, she slept beside you last week, didn't she? Did she, y'know…?" The young lad did not reply. "Not something to ask, yeah—but wait. All I'm trying to mention to you is, well, y'know? I think if you wanted to, you could get cozy with her now. Y'know, like how you wanted it all those years back? Remember?

"Never you mind the likes of Anae Bertriss, the girl's nothing but trouble. And besides, you met her how long ago—last season? Yeva you've known for years and years. And I reckon she was jealous of that Bertriss girl, but not 'cause she's rich. But watch it, should you take my advice. Yeva's trouble of a different kind. Get what I'm givin' you?" Again, Morley shook his head.

Arrin sat with him for a moment, added, "I tried," then hopped off the bars to count the grazing sheep again.

Elmaen, Reffen, and Semhren came to him once before heading off on a half-day stroll.

"Still grieving the loss of your young damme?" Semhren spoke up. "Ahh, you're better off now, my boy. Never a good idea to get tangled with the courtly folk when you're not of their rank. Though, I will say," he added a laugh, "it is much easier to get away with lewder deeds when you're invisible to those of the higher birth."

"Take it from him," Reffen added with elderly impetuousness.

"Might as well," the ex-scholar continued. "But Morley here was never apprehended for his crimes. He's an admirable one, yeah? A cunning artist."

60

"You're free to come along with us, Morley," Elmaen offered. "Though we'll be out long, I'm sure." With that, he stepped slowly around the pen. Reffen moved away as well, but Semhren came closer to the fence and the seated halfelev.

"Some bonds blossom through fortuitous coincidence, lad," he said, quieter. "You need only trace its origin, the occasion upon which you met. That alone can tell you so much about the flesh of your relationship. I sense she was the one to pursue and you were the hare who gave chase, perhaps without intention. Ahh...I suppose you had no idea who she was at the time. Still, that had to be a rude awakening. Anae Dammedottir Bertriss. I wonder if my old pupils have met her yet. Well, if they do—or *when* they do, I imagine they'll—"

"Will you shut up?" Morley said, softly and sharply. "You're an ugly old man and you'll die alone. So go away. Go on your walk. Join with the other ugly old men and go away."

Morley did not face the ex-scholar as he growled the words. After some quiet reflection, Semhren abandoned the effort, treading lightly away over the grass. Morley soon regretted his spiteful incantation.

After another week, once he had begun to focus on other matters—watching the sheep for Arrin, combing wool, cooking with Amarta or Reffen—his active thoughts shifted from Anae to Aetheling Felix, how he probably treated his new wife, how she probably reacted to his abuses. It gave him stomach pains.

He imagined the Sivliére castle as dismal and twisted, quite similar to his early conceptions of the Crouxwood. But as he later noted, the Crouxwood was only bleak wherever people had settled. Like Reineshir. If Wallenport was over three times the size of Reineshir, as Anae attested, how could it be any better?

Reineshir. He wanted to burn that faithless clearing-town to the ground whenever he returned—which would have to be soon, as he'd left his sword hidden in the stable loft during the penultimate visit.

On the day before Istain's next resupplying trip, Morley and Serryl took a boat out to sea, out where her game tended to put up the hardest fights. It was predominantly a silent excursion. The woman combatted three lesser pikes within two hours; her companion received few bites and put little effort into securing them. Later on, as she rowed them back to shore, Serryl gaped piercingly at Morley's face, averted under her unbroken scrutiny.

"Yer goin' to Reineshir tomorrow?"

It came out as a statement, but the young man could also tell she was making sure not to wait on him the following morning. Morley glanced at her and nodded. The silence under the swishing and plopping of the oars returned for a short time. Then: "Will ye be comin' back?"

Morley knew this woman was, like everyone else, well aware of his recent woes. He eyed her suspiciously.

"Why wouldn't I?" he replied. Serryl's question was either absentminded or, as he began to suspect, formed of a sapient insight. He added, "There's no point in staying."

"No, course not. I don't expect ye to stay there fer more than twenty minutes. But will ye be coming back *here*?" Morley said nothing, preferring not to lie. He frowned, wholly unsure of what Serryl suspected.

"When ye first came to us," she continued, "ye told Elmaen all that happened at the hill-house. Gale wanted ye to run on to us, to find safety. But ye didn't, did ye? Ye stayed till it was over. Ye watched the ridders fight and waited till the end. Mayhaps ye had faith in Gale and knew he'd win. Mayhaps ye intended to kill the other if he didn't. But what happened happened and can't be changed now. What I wanna know is…well, what would ye do if ye could go back and do it again?"

Morley said nothing.

"I won't dare ye to prove me wrong," Serryl said. "But I think ye've got some knots to tie. I think ye'll step into that town tomorrow and ye'll find yer sword, wherever it is, and ye'll remember everything—hells, ye'll have time enough to think on it. And ye'll pump some air into that fire yer tendin'. I need not say anythin' more, yeah?" She turned to check their distance to the beach. Morley continued eyeing her as she swung back.

"Well, except this," she said. "I've two brothers in Olford—I've told ye about 'em before. Sethan's about yer age and Sieger's about mine." She chewed at her lip, hesitating. "If ye wanna get to Wallenport, one of 'em can take ye. But listen here, Morley…Don't do anything which'd get ye in chains. If ye wanna see that girl and settle everythin' up, then do it and be on yer way. I know ye too well. And I know ye can be unpredictable. Reineshir gave ye a taste of somethin' ye can no longer live without. I know well enough what that's like."

The boat soon dug into the sea bank and the pair hopped out to carry it. Still yet, the lad watched the fisherwoman, waited for her to expound more.

"Do what ye will with what I've told ye," she added, "but like I said, stay outta trouble. Or in messin' that up, avoid it whenever it comes yer way." For the first time in several weeks, Morley smirked. "And fer Being's sake, get back here as soon as ye can."

Evidently, Serryl was much more sagacious than anyone else at the hamlet. It seemed she was able to join together her empathies and her surprisingly keen hindsights, a rare social logic that Semhren himself could never master.

Because of those few occasions where Morley gave in to or raised high his passions—the day of Gale's death, the many journeys to and from Reineshir, the endless praises he shed over Anae in her absence—Serryl knew everything. It were as if she saw herself in him and proceeded to consume his body and mind, to make the decision he'd already made three times during the preceding weeks. And from her astute expectation—or wild assumption—she thought it vigilant to give out a scrap of information, not words of self-perceived wisdom.

For this, he promised to thank her once the task was done.

The next morning, Morley helped Istain load up the cart and yoke it to Nudd, then went about the hamlet circle to deliver tenuous goodbyes to Amarta, Yeva, Elmaen, Geat and Minny, and others. None of them seemed to suspect his intentions, though Yeva stepped outside to watch the pair roll off. She wore a mask of blatant mistrust, distantly distinct.

Istain, meanwhile, if he did have a hunch, gave off an air of singular fondness that day. "I appreciate all the help you've handed me in these trips," he said at one point. "I know they may've ended up bein' more trouble than they were worth. Mayhaps you see it differently. Here." Istain held out two nickel pieces—or 'plummes' as he called them. "Buy somethin' nice for yourself in town today. Remember, it's worth ten coppers, so don't let any of those townsmen cheat you. Should be worth two barrels of beer, that. Usually. But don't waste it all on drink, hear?" The young man took the coin, slipped it into his shirt pocket, and thanked his old friend.

Later, when they entered Reineshir, Morley gave the trader a subtle farewell and sped off to the manorial stables. He passed Jhann and Gerry on the way there, but avoided them as best he could, knowing well how much they disliked him. Closer, he waved to the Ornhatter sisters, who each withheld their greetings, no doubt confounded by the sight of him.

He soon arrived at the manse's open gates: the stables' side doors were gaping wide. He breathed deep. Then he moved.

Rush in there, up the steps, second mound on the left—second old mound. Run across, don't stop to look, run on, keep going. Up the stairs. Hear that? Stableman. Don't stop—keep going, dig through the slime at the bottom, grey fuzz. Good.

The claymore was still there, still resting under a haystack. He took it up, remembering its weight, listening for the stableman below.

Check the blade later. Man under the floors—now by the door, by the forks. Leave, quick, quick. He'll see—leave.

As he descended from the loft, the stableman spotted him and shouted, "Aye! Boy!" Morley stole no glances of his interceptor, down past the emptied pens. Instead, he flew back out through the side doors, ignoring the yells of "Stop! Get over here, rat! Stop!"

Don't look back, don't look back—hear him? Take out the sword if he dares follow—he's following now. Won't really hurt him, no, he doesn't know that. See over there? Brewery door? No one there, no one looking. Quick, take some for the road. Who cares—it's Reineshir, it's filth, hate it here. Take it.

The halfelev made a sound like a humorless laugh as he dashed up the northward road. The stableman had pursued to the edge of the estate, to the gate across from the brewery; and from there, he watched as the young man, armed with a greatsword in one hand, wrapped his opposite arm around a five-gallon cask at the edge of an untended wagon, then raced off into the deepening Crouxwood.

Go, go, go, go, go, go, go.

Two others yelled from unseen spaces behind him but nobody followed, at least not further than Maud's inn. Reineshir was out of sight within ten minutes.

From then on, Morley strode slowly and timidly over the leaf-ridden road, through a tunnel of overripe foliage, beyond all familiar life. And gradually, his fear of the forest's menace returned to him for a time.

*   *   *

Hardly an hour later, he saw a man in a black and white robe coming down the trail ahead. Without pause, the lad shifted into the overgrowth and waited, frozen under the young trees. The man up the road began to sing, though the words were either muddled under the breeze and birdsongs or the words were of an unknown language; its rhythm, too, was difficult to follow.

Once his footfalls were clear as the sun, the man interrupted his verse, calling out, "Hello there, wherever you are! Lovely day for a walk, don't you think?" He then continued his song without slowing. Before long, he was gone. Morley, dissatisfied by his cowardice yet relieved by the short rest, gathered up his things and moved on.

By the early evening, he reached a church-house, much larger and better kept than the one in Reineshir. According to the carved board atop its main entrance, it was dedicated to St. Berthe, the matron of sibling love. And it was apparently unoccupied, much to his misgiving. The main prayer hall was chilled and unlit, the adjoined house bore no active host—even the odd plot of weaved domes and swarming bees some distance across the road was untended. For all he knew, this place was long abandoned.

Thus, he left the cask and sword nearby, approached the wattled storage shed behind the church—a construction much like Istain's though far bigger—and as best he could, utilized Arrin's method of prying open the laced surface to seek out the door's lock. After less than a minute of toying with an already impaired section of the wall, he reached inside and instantly found a cord holding the door shut. He removed it quick, raided the kempt space for its cheese and bread, all neatly wrapped within a basket, then fled up the lane for another half-hour, his arms full. It eventually occurred to him that the place likely wasn't abandoned. And that he was now twice a thief.

Once night fell, he stumbled upon a bed of ferns off-trail and, using the cask as a headrest, he blinked into a severely discomforting sleep.

Then he was back in Reineshir, which had since subsumed all of Werplaus and the circle of Egainshir. He was again trying to steal his cask from outside of the brewery, now guarded by ridders and other men on horseback. He spied on them from the manor's toft. The sky was bloody purple. "Someone's watching out for us," came a startling voice behind him. When he swerved to face its origin, he saw that the manor was now gone, replaced by a wild bosk of reddish ivy and tree stems. Naked people with tufts of animal fur seeped from between the squat trunks.

Morley woke before dawn and resumed his journey.

At noon's rising on the new day, as he struggled up a slight incline, he finally recognized the sheer weight of his luggage. And the unnecessity of its bulk: the cask of beer. Worse, he was forced to carry the small barrel under one arm while balancing his two loaves and block of cheese on top of it. He stopped intermittently to slacken the effort, abandoning the road for the heavier shade of the woodland, under which he uncorked the barrel and soaked hard chunks of bread in the ale.

More than once, he noticed small huts hidden under veils of thick-needled pine branches, all of which were only dozens of strides from the main trail. Consistently at first sight of these ominous abodes—perhaps seven in all—he crossed back over to the opposite road-bank, where he held a better sense of ease.

Meanwhile, throughout the day, he combatted the temptation to leave the beer behind on the wayside, where its original owner could potentially find and reclaim it during his potential respective trek to Wallenport. However, every time he paused to set it down, he couldn't help but open it back up and drink, spilling the brew all over his jaw, neck, and tunic as he lightly upended it.

A better plan consumed him that night as he laid down to rest.

He dreamed he was climbing trees as Tommas ineffectually chopped at the moaning chunks below. After a time, the lumberman gave in and left, forgetting about young Fitzmorley up in the highest boughs, despite the lad's cries. He tried to climb down, crying, fearful of the height and the awaiting world below. Then he knew he forgot something, high up in the palm of the pine. He ascended, cautiously as ever, toward the swirling mouth in the skies. He missed a narrow limb and fell upward, screaming into heaven's abyss.

Morley woke and swatted a spider from his cheek, plucked the snails off his trousers.

Believing he could reach Olford by the new day's dusk, the lad stuffed his gullet with the cheese and remaining bread just after sunrise. For a time afterward, he forced down the rest of the ale, determined to be rid of its heavy casement. Largely, he succeeded in this feat. Without granting much thought to the outcome.

With wobbling knees and a brash temper, he threw the cask at a sturdy oak, spat at it with a curse, then left it behind. His balance came and went with the blustery Hosten winds. Thus, the day's journey passed over him at a woefully unreliable pace as he trudged through a cropland of wheat and barley, grumbling to himself like one of Reineshir's nocturnal citizens.

"Doubtin' me? I'll shoulder ye some doubt—ye cheeky, thin-eyed...I'll clout ye right good on yer...*mmhmmh*," he slurred with a punctuating belch and a swing of his fist.

It was typical for his unexpressed affections to surface after such binges: the time in Arrin's shed when he discovered his naïve love for Yeva, the first evening spent in the stable loft, the night beside Anae when he wept with love. But now he had no one, no subject of youthful worship. Only the thought of Aetheling Felix, inflamed by his perversions and depravity, tainting his new wife's beauty.

The lad had decided, in the haze of his afternoon stupor, that his was not a quest to retake what surely, rightfully belonged to him—the admiration of Anae—but a pursuit of vengeance. He believed that, if he could seek out the opportunity to do so, he would harm Felix. Laugh over his damaged body. Cut it up into little pieces.

Fatigue conquered the halfelev just past the edge of the fields. He sat by a tree for a moment and, when the earth began to tilt this way and that, he prostrated himself and retched over a spread of damp leaves.

He got up and continued walking, shutting his eyes as he advanced north—or east, or west, or whatever direction it was. He could no longer tell. He soon vomited a second time at the wayside, then chose to rest for a little while. He fell slowly into a sour-tongued slumber.

Waking to a black weald, an irate stomach, and a sore head, the young man swore off beer. He then slumped down on his side and went back to sleep.

His dreams came to him in disparate flashes, like voices in a crowd all bellowing one after another, each more prominent than the last: a castle, a piling of stone boxes with walls of black steel atop a sea stack, its highest point cradling a woman, a beacon like a bright moon. He stood beneath it with all his friends. Then he was alone.

The drilling gallop of a horse pattered by, somewhere. "I'll give a hand or two if they're needed," said a new voice. "Can't promise much." The lad chose not to face the source of the words.

*   *   *

In the morning, Morley did what he could to shake off the numerous aches, then spent some time harvesting moist clumps of moss, squeezing fresh water from their soft emerald furs. He later yoked the sword across his shoulders and stomped up the road.

Fortunately—and somewhat perplexingly—Olford was a mere kalcubit away. He assumed it was Olford, at least. There were four buildings in sight, each situated near the turfed corners where the trail met a tinkling creek, a highway of water flowing over a shallow stone bed. The infamous Lightrun River.

The stone bed joining the ends of the road matched Gale's description of a ford, from what he could recall, though it was a bit wider than expected. Its area exceeded that of each house, he reckoned, yet the water would likely only submerge his feet along the ford proper.

A second roadway split from the main trail just before the building on the western edge, the one closest to him. This structure was the largest of all the others with a base of mortared cobbles, a daubed second floor, and a shingled roof not much higher up than the loft of the Bertriss stables.

A niched door on its furthest end opened and a woman treaded out, dragging a wood-bearing thong behind her. As her head was low and wrapped up in a cowl, she didn't seem to notice Morley stepping toward the intersection. She instead wandered out of sight, staying close to the westerly path.

Across from her barnlike residence, there was another, less attractive house: a squat domicile with a porch of weathered grimy ashlars, each crumbling along their shared ledge. The whole of the place was approximately half the size of Egainshir's cow pens, perhaps smaller. Most of the space, anyway, was comprised of the front porch.

And upon this decrepit platform was a young man, a naema, settled atop a stool.

He was only a few years older, Morley estimated, as the skin around his eyes was in the earliest stages of wrinkling and his short beard was untended. A mud-stained and superfluously large cloak was wrapped around common garb. A hood hung against the back of his head, just over the ears. He wore no shoes and, according to his blotched and begrimed feet, he had none in his possession. Presently, he was tending to a longbow much like the one that used to hang untouched in Gale's house. This limb, on the other hand, was actively admired, polished with excessive care, curved at the ends with yet unseen craftsmanship. The man had it resting across his knees as he ran a drab cloth along the wood.

His head shot up once Morley was close enough, then went straight back to the bow. He began to hum a song then, a tune the halfelev swore he once heard coming from Maud, the innkeeper of Reineshir. The archer was ignoring him—despite the claymore held behind his head, across his shoulders. Morley remembered Serryl's tip and, tiredly, he approached the base of the stone deck.

"This Olford?" he asked, it being the first question to come to him. The seated archer lifted his head slowly as if feigning lethargy. Or perplexity, as an eyebrow was raised. Then, he twitched the side of his nose, sniffing.

"Nah," he finally said, his voice vibrant with youth. "Wallenport. I'm, eh, Aetheling Felix. Pleased to meet ye." He returned to the bow at hand.

"Right, right," Morley proceeded, unamused and unfaltering. "Where's Anae Bertriss, then? Also, I'm here to kill you. Any final words?" The archer let slip a smile. Erasing it, he looked back up.

"I've more regrets than a slug at the seaside. Allow me to list them off, then ye may have yer foul way with me." Surprisingly, he put aside his bow and leaned forward. "Anyhow, what d'ye really want? And what's yer name, if ye don't mind givin' it?"

The halfelev brought down the scabbarded blade from behind his head, rested its tip between his feet. "Morley. Short for Fitzmorley," he said after clearing his throat. "I'm on my way to Wallenport. And if this truly is Olford, I'm searching for someone named Sethan. Or Sieger."

The archer swayed his head pensively, his eyes jumping to each visible house. They settled on Morley below.

"Wallenport's a few days' hike down the road there. Ye take a right at the big round castle, then stick to the center road. It'll be in yer range within two nights if yer pace is good." He scratched at a nostril. "Sieger's my name, by the bye. If ye need vittles or a bed..." he pointed first to a shack of sticks and daub across the river, the ugliest house of them all, then shifted his hand to the tall building close by. "Good morning," he dismissed, abruptly picking the bow back up.

"Sieger, you say?"

He glanced up. "Ye heard."

Morley lifted the sword back up onto a shoulder. "So your brother is Sethan?"

The man shrugged, rubbing a spot on his bow with a thumb. "Haven't seen him in a while," he said.

"Well…you also have a sister, right? Serryl?"

His head came up with the same sluggishness he employed earlier. Now, though, his expression was doubly stupefied. "I do, yea." Once again, he put the bow back down beside the legs of his chair. He leaned forward. "Ye know her, do ye? Haven't seen her since I was a tiny-man—where's she now?"

Morley was now acutely reminded of a long-forgotten fact: Serryl and Tommas, two forbidden lovers, had fled from Olford when they were younger. They hadn't left calmly and with a communal send-off; they had fled into the night without any idea of where they might settle. Morley was overtaken by a strange speculative wariness as he absorbed the archer's stare.

"Why?" he tried.

"Why?" the man emphatically echoed.

"Why do you want to know?"

"Are ye really askin' me why I wanna know where my sister is, Fitzmorley? After not seein' her fer years and years?"

The point was fair. The lad mutedly apologized to the fisherwoman, hoping his words would cause no complication.

"Egainshir, down in Werplaus."

The archer mouthed the words, rolling his eyes in calculation. "Never heard of it. She doing all right there, then? She still with Tommas?"

Again, Morley confided, now sharing everything he knew.

"Robi, eh? That was our uncle's name, that's nice," said Sieger. "Yeah, mum wanted Serryl to leave fer Wallenport to find herself a sailor or a mason. But she just wanted to stay here with Tommas—whose own father wanted him to take off fer Westley to get a few acres. They left, eh, almost ten years back, I think. She won't mind a visit from me one o' these days, I'll bet. I'll have to go durin' the Frysa, when she's not all that busy with the fishin', as ye say. Yeah, that'd be good—bring her a few bunches o' grapes, some o' Marion's porridge…"

He sat weightily for a moment, plucking the hairs of his chin, smiling as if lost memories had been found—rather, returned to him. Morley stood in a similar state, thinking over the information he'd just given out. If anyone came to disrupt the married couple's life, he concluded, they would first have to surpass Gertruda and Lunferda, the able guardians of the hamlet. That couldn't be an easy feat.

"Well," the seated man continued, chewing his lip. "Eh. Didn't expect my day to unfold like this but, eh…Listen, this is right stingin' embarassin', but I'm not really Sieger, see. Sorta just, eh, pretendin' to be him. It's one o' those days, if ye happen to know what I mean. I'm his brother, Sethan—call me Seth. I'm, eh, well…sometimes there's, ehm…*feh*."

He made a dismissive sound, then grasped his bow and stood. Morley clung to every one of his broken utterances.

"I feel virtuous enough to let ye in on a good bit of input, Fitzmorley. Stay off the roads, take off yer shoes, walk down the river here till ye get to the coast, follow it north—there's Wallenport, big and stinky. Now, here's your problem: Sylvan's a dangerous tract—that's the wetland before the coast, between the Lightrun and Larenta right over there." He attempted to gesture to an area around the side of his house.

"And I don't recommend ye goin' down that way without me, my bow, and a sling of arrows. Now, here's your bigger problem: I won't be goin' down that way fer nothin'. Yer options are three coppers," at this, he stuck out a thumb. "Or cook my supper and breakfast on the way there, to my liking. Or…" He stuck out a forefinger in addition to the thumb. His pupils swiveled around again. "Or steal me a jar of somniferum seeds from Old Sylvain's shelf, whenever and if ever we get ourselves there. Trust me, ye don't wanna make an exchange on his terms."

Morley was now quite clueless as he peered at Seth, resting his jaw against the bow's notch, his three fingers sticking out. "Pray tell," he said directly, "why should I nix the dry trail?"

Seth gave a small grin. "If yer the same Morley as descripted to me— tall lad, shaggy hair, halfelev, big bloody sword o'er his back—then ye've got Ridder Einaar after ye. And I'd predict that he's on his way back south by now."

Morley's heart sank with dread, his oldest enemy. He was now a witnessed thief, an identified criminal. Most Reineshir folk knew him as Anae's 'bodyguard,' had seen him strolling around with their town's noble daughter. Someone likely notified Istain not long after he ran off with the sword and cask. The whole south of Sarcovy could now recognize him— the beer thief, the boy with the big sword, the only halfelev within a hundred kalcubits or more.

"Shoulda saved some o' that ale fer me, friend," said Seth. "Woulda been decent payment over three coppers."

"So," Morley retorted, annoyed, "you were prepared to send me off down the road, despite knowing there's a ridder tracking me?" Seth raised a hand, as if he were tossing dust over his head. "Then you share with me a false name? Then you correct that name and demand to service me for a fee of my choice?" The archer swayed his head around guiltlessly. Morley gathered up the sword. "I'm thinking I'd be better off following the road through the overgrowth. Or hiding away at the first sound of thumping hooves. But I appreciate your offer, however unreasonable." With that, the lad gave a nod and made for the ford.

"Fine, fine, fine, fine!" came Seth's voice behind him. "One copper instead o' three—no, forget the coppers, I'll throw that option out—no, better yet, one copper and I'll get ye somethin' to put in yer stomach afore we leave." Morley turned back around at this. "Ye look real hungry, is all."

He was right. The bread and cheese from the previous morning was his last meal. The lad sighed, realizing he was beginning to like this harmlessly inept bastard.

"I only have a nickel piece," he lied. In truth, of course, he had two. All the same, Seth's face contorted, his lips shrinking into a pucker, one eye narrowing as the other stretched open.

"A'right," he said. "New offer. One nickel piece, I break yer fast this morning, I go check my traps and take whatever I've catched, we head down the river, ye cook what I hunt, we stay at Sylvain's place, I leave ye at the beach after it all. Deal?"

"I don't know how to prepare rabbits or venison," Morely replied. "If those're the creatures you're expecting to hunt. I sense it'd be easier for you to just buy, I dunno…bread, cheese, vegetables, beer?" At this, Seth sagged. "And I'm also not sure why I need you to come along with me in the first place! I don't need your protection, I've got this." He struggled to hold up the sword with one hand.

"Swords won't do a sliver against vodniks," Seth said. "Ye trust me on that."

"Against what?" Morley asked.

Seth smirked and nodded. "Right, exactly. Ye'd be bloody dead if I let ye go down that way on yer own."

"Why don't we just take the road north and, like I said, jump off the path if we see anyone coming up or down it?"

Now the archer shook his head. "Ye've never been further up than Reineshir, have ye, Fitzmorley?" The lad made no motion, waited for Seth to continue to his point. "Right. No matter what ye do in goin' north, yer still gonna go by Chaisgott, which is itself between Wallenport and The Stead. Ridders and asp'rants are all over the sodden place. And lest ye have a cart and a record of yer goods, any one o' those bastards'll come down on ye—oh, mark my bloody words, none of them'd pass up the chance to grab a greatsword off a scrawny fella like yerself. And better yet, if ye so desire to tramp through the wilderland and stay off those roads, ye'd likely get caught in a trap or spotted by the wilderfolk and hunted through the night or—"

"You've made your point," Morley wheezed. He brought his claymore back down and rubbed his face with his free hand.

"How's about a bit o' frumenty?"

The halfelev's head shot back up. "You have that here in this…place?" He caught himself before saying 'heap.' The lad had only tasted frumenty twice or thrice when visiting Anae. It was one of the easier foodstuffs to smuggle out, as she could simply claim it was a treat for the horses.

"Well, it's what we call it round here," Seth noted. "Come on back."

Rather than retreating into his house, Seth put an arm through his bow, hopped down from the porch, and led his new associate around to the back of his house. There was a patio of buried boulders covered over with three-legged stools, a maimed ladder, broken pottery, a rudimentary quintain dummy, and other timeworn miscellanea. The archer soon disappeared back to the front, recommending that Morley sit against a wall if he were to use one of the stools. The young man did so and rested his sword down, leaning on the stead's pale walls.

When Seth returned, he carried a leathern sack of arrows and a clean clay bowl, inside of which was a cold mush as yellow as a herder's teeth. He dropped the arrows and held out his free palm, slapping his fingers against it. Morley moaned and reached into his tunic flap, then proffered one nickel, surely warmer than the porridge he was given. Seth smiled and vanished again around to the front of his house. When he was again in view, he was crossing the ford with another sack in his hand and a smoking pipe hanging out his mouth. He lifted the full hem of his cloak as he crossed.

As the halfelev dug out the frumenty with two fingers—the 'frumenty' being a mound of mashed carrots sitting in a puddle of water—he ambled his seat to the riverside corner of the archer's house and observed him.

Seth had entered the shack immediately across the Lightrun, the crumbling wattle-daub hovel, the nearest side of which appeared to be drooping toward the shaded bank. When the archer emerged from it, his one sack was bundled underarm: he'd supposedly taken Morley's advice of purchasing food instead of going through the headache of scavenging downriver.

From there Seth trotted across the road to a house quite similar to his own—a moderate rectangular dwelling bereft of a stone porch. There was a circle of rocks laid out near the front door and, on the heaviest block, there sat a camouflaged youth, dressed up in grey and brown linens. The way he sat and the manner in which he dodged a playful swipe from the archer reminded Morley of Robi.

Morley leaned further from the corner and continued watching Seth: he bypassed the second house and went upstream to a previously unnoticed structure. Peculiarly, this one had a giant wheel attached to its side which turned languidly within a manmade trench dug into the riverbed. Its watery current passed between the mud shore and a wall of stacked stones rising from the shallow depths.

He saw Seth knock on a door beside the foremost fence of a side-croft, its recesses fading into the wilderness. Nobody answered, so he knocked again. After a third attempt, he blew a cloud of smoke, threw up his free hand and hopped over the fence. Moments passed.

When he reappeared, a plump drinking skin was strapped across his torso over the bowstring. He turned as he walked, taking in every detail of his surroundings; then he hesitated before the ford crossing, his head shooting from one end of the road to the other. Upon completing this surveillance, he marched back over to the halfelev, lifting and lowering his feet into the water without making the slightest splash, now dragging the oversized cloak through the stream. All the while, a bearded elder had appeared, ambling down the northward road. He watched Seth intently as he walked, receding into the hideous shack.

"Ready?" Seth asked upon his return, checking over his shoulder again. He removed his pipe and stuck it into the threadbare head of his quintain. "How's the porridge?" Morley glanced at the empty bowl. It'd been sufficient sustenance. But would've been better if Seth had not earlier referred to it as frumenty.

"Fine. We're to leave right now, are we?"

"That's right," he answered without pause, exchanging the bowl for the supply bundle. He strode to an eaten plank nailed into his house's wall. Morley hadn't noticed before but the bar was covering over a hole in the bleached facade. Seth knocked a fist against the softwood.

"Mum!" he called. "Mum, ye awake in there? Mum?!" There was a sound of muffled movement from within. "Mum! We're goin' to Westley to see Sieger, Mum! We'll be back soon enough! Call Tomak if ye need anythin', Mum! Ye hear me?!"

A weak moan seeped from the room. Seth put the bowl down into a ruined box, checked to see if he had all his gear, gestured eastward with his head, then moved off.

Morley followed after a deep breath. "Did your mum know what you meant by 'we'?" he questioned after the first few steps.

"Me and someone else, o' course," Seth said. "What, ye think I'd lie to my mother?"

Morley, confounded, gave no response for a moment. "Who's Tomak?"

"That little string bean sittin' across the ford there," he said, pointing without looking. Morley glanced back, but the child mentioned was nowhere in sight. "Marion's been watchin' after him since his father went to Westley and didn't return—that was 'bout a year ago. We don't miss the sod. But we all miss Tommas, the eldest son o' that family." Morley peered back again instinctually, as though to match the vanished boy's distant features with those of Tommas'. But the child was still nowhere in sight.

Not so far downstream from the ford's shallows, the deepening river split into two branches. Keeping to their current bank, the duo marched along the Lightrun-side, a much deeper and wider current. The trickle of Larenta's Creek remained audible just past a dividing spinney of nephrite firs, their heavy, glossy needles like glass in the sun. It would soon begin to flow northeast, Morley knew, away from its parent stream. Gale often spoke of these waters. He'd fought over them, he said.

Before Olford was entirely out of sight, Seth handed over the drinking skin and trooped into a thicket. Morley waited by the bank, impetuous. After several minutes the archer returned with a mangled rabbit's foot at hand.

"Waited too long," he said. "Foxes must've nabbed him in the trap. Here." He tossed the crusty blood-matted appendage to Morley, who dodged it apprehensively. "It's fer luck, they say—no need to cringe!"

"I don't care what it's for, I'm not carrying it. I've got no other pockets. Unless you wanna wrap it up with the bread or meat or whatever it is you've got here." He raised the bundle in his arms.

Seth picked up the elongated foot and blew on it twice. With that ritual complete, he stuck it inside a neatly sewn flap against his breast, right within the confines of his shoddy cloak.

"More fer me, then," he said. "Oh, watch out fer snakes. They stick to the shallows."

They continued on for the better part of the day. Time after time, Morley recalled the words in *Chevaliers of Bienvale*, the timely passages on Olivien's and Aubin's death. How they floated with these very rapids, how their blood so purified the tempestuous ocean.

"And with a stubborn shame, they gave in to their old fates; how Aubin wept for his weeping love, confined to her cave in the hills; how Olivien beat at his battered chest, closed his hands over black wounds. A cry of rage and a cry of longing, how these so filled that air over the Piiks' dire bridge."

*   *   *

One early morning during the Hosten of Fitzmorley's first year in Egainshir, Tommas woke him. "Ready to see something new?" he asked as the lad crept out from the new wicker shack they'd built. Plump Istain was waiting on the driver's bench of his cart, loaded now with goods for Reineshir. "Need another set of hands today," Tommas said as he helped Fitzmorley into the cart bed. "About time you met the Crouxwood anyway." They left in that moment.

At first the boy was timid of the looming forest: from a distance all the trees looked alive and uninviting, bobbing in the wind as if on a stationary march. Closer, they were defunct. Careless, even. One could rest under their shade and wake unharmed.

The woodland, contrary to everything he'd been told as a small boy, was a place of peace. No ghouls, no geisters. Perhaps the Crouxwood was different during Gale's days as a ridder.

Moments after they reached the tree line, Tommas and Fitzmorley hopped down from the wagon, letting Istain carry on to Reineshir. While Tommas set about sharpening his handsaw and replacing an axe head, he ordered his young companion to seek out popped pinecones, dry sticks, and abandoned bird nests. Naturally, the last of these were settled up in the higher boughs.

"Climb?" Fitzmorley questioned before they started. "All the way up there?" They stood before a nephrite fir, as Tommas called it, no taller than the ones behind or next to it yet still the tallest thing Fitzmorley had ever seen—at least five times the height of Gale's hill-house. The brawny man beside him shot a perplexed eye.

"Yeah?" he rumbled. "What of it?"

"Well…" The two were in equal confusion. "It's very high, isn't it?" Tommas gazed back up.

"Yeah. Again, what of it? Yer a kid, all kids climb trees. My baby brother knew how to climb afore he could walk." This, the lad knew, had to be untrue. "And yer part-elev. Elevs are born to climb trees."

Fitzmorley didn't know what he meant by the comment but, in an odd way, he still didn't believe him. He also wasn't sure why he used the term 'kid.' He wasn't a goat.

"I've never been north of Werplaus," he said. "I've never even seen a tree before."

At this, Tommas broke out into an unreserved laughter which, as Fitzmorley estimated, could probably be heard at every corner of the island. At least the man's confusion was dissipated; Fitzmorley's was thoroughly bolstered.

"Fine, fine," the lumberman continued. "Then just go as high as ye want. Don't take any with eggs in them, else a hawk may swoop down at ye. If ye find any with empty shells, ye can take those. Eh," He sized up the tree again. "Ye'll do fine. Anyone can climb, we're born with the skill. Ye'll figure it out."

And he did with great success. By the evening, when Istain returned from Reineshir, Fitzmorley had two bags' worth of kindling material, all neatly arranged by type. Tommas in the meantime had felled another tree all on his own, hours before. He was now working his way down from the tip to the base, chopping off portable chunks and throwing them into a pile.

Fitzmorley bundled up his sticks and, for a short time, assisted the other two men in loading up the rest of the cart's space. Istain had successfully traded all of the Egainshir supplies, acquiring fresh and dry meats, plenty of grain mash, extra vegetables, three small barrels of beer, ingredients for Reffen, and some other supplies both necessary and unnecessary. They headed back home.

*　　　*　　　*

Not long before the sun began its northward descent, hours into their journey, Seth and Morley were so deep into the Crouxwood that an uneasiness again crept over the halfelev. Traveling this wet road wasn't incredibly different from the beaten path between Reineshir and Olford. But this place had an eeriness to it.

It wasn't much darker under the leaves' modest awning. And the sonorities of the birds and elusive fauna weren't much heavier than they were around St. Berthe's church-house. But this land truly did have a wafting air to it, unpolluted by the breath of aethelings, untouched and unseen for countless centuries—at least, by anyone aside from Seth the Archer, who expressed a masterful acumen of the territory.

He knew precisely when the river thinned, when it deepened, when it turned to gentle rapids, when the rocks became sharp as arrowheads. Dually to Morley's comfort and disappointment, there were no conversations between them, only brief indications of distance and the occasional consultation: "stay to the south bank for this next bit" or "watch out for the big green bugs, they'll fly into your face." Otherwise, he would ask for an occasional strip of dry meat from the bundle in Morley's arms.

Thus, they sloshed in silence for most of the first day, until the sun's aura could no longer cut through to them. By dusk, after the lad began to stumble copiously over unseen stones, Seth decided the time was right to rest.

"We're not far from Sylvan, but we're far enough to sleep in peace," he stated as they set down their equipment over the inland sedge, their eventual bedding. Seth collapsed in a comfortable space between a pair of trees and wrapped himself in his gigantic cloak, still soaked around his newly washed feet.

"Very good progress today. We'll make it to Sylvain's house by this time tomorrow, mayhaps a trifle later, mayhaps a trifle sooner. I'll wake ye when it's time." With that, he hid his face under his hood.

Morley, not yet cozy enough to sleep and not fully credulous of Serryl's sibling, cleared his throat. "I'd say now's as good a time as any for you to explain a few things," he propounded.

The archer poked up the hood's cloth from over his eyes. "Right back at ye, Fitzmorley."

"Why did you lie about your name this morning?" Morley asked, rubbing a nostril.

The archer took his time. "'Cause," he said. "I'm a convict. A scofflaw. The most wanted man on the whole damned island o' Sarcovy."

He mumbled the words without pride or disgrace. To him, the statement seemed to resemble casual fact. A claim like this would've normally struck Morley with awe or even fear seasons before. But after knowing Seth for less than a single day, the lad was more than skeptical.

However, as Morley quickly considered, he was now fundamentally a criminal himself: he'd stolen and consumed a cask of ale, the merchandise of Reineshir's brewers, and now finally had the minor charge of trespassing in the Bertriss stables. They'd even sent a ridder after him. On top of all that, he felt no remorse for the actions. And besides the beer, he had also lain with a noble girl out of wedlock—several times, at that. All of a sudden the status of "most wanted man on the whole damned island o' Sarcovy" was a trifle more believable.

"Really?" Morley said after a long pause. "Why's that?"

Seth shrugged under his cape. "Ridders don't like me much and I don't care fer them at all. And we keep comin' by each other." He let the odd confession hover before them for a time.

"I'm listening."

"Oh, well that's bloody good, innit?" he barked, straightening himself up against the tree at his back. "What d'ye want me to do, list off every crime I've gotten away with? We'll only get two hours' rest if I go like that, y'know—one hour's rest if I cover the ones I *didn't* get away with."

"Fair enough," Morley muttered, his disbelief restored. "Then just tell me about the memorable ones, quick as you can. And I'll tell you about my own crimes." He crossed his sleeved arms and glared patiently at the archer across from him.

"Fine. Let's see. When I made my first bow—this one over here's my fourth—but when I made the first one, I was about, eh, sixteen years of age. And my good brother Sieger saw a ridder comin' down the road to the ford and he dared me to climb up Nanci—that was our favorite tree, the big elm next to our house—and from its tippy-top branch, I was to string up an arrow and shoot it over the man's head. Give him a little scare, y'know, all for a lick o' fun. So I made the climb, the ridder came round, I nocked and gave a weak loose, and—*ting*! Got him right on the ridin' helm. Man fell off his horse, Marion came out and screamed, horse charged off. A good thing he didn't have stirrups, I'd say. And a good thing I didn't aim, else I'd have stuck him through the head. Well, anyway, he ran off and we ran off, laughin'. Came back the next day and all was well."

Morley chuckled through his nose. Then he added, "That was your first crime, then?" Seth nodded once.

"Employered arms 'gainst a sergeant o' Sarcovy, as they say."

"It's a good one. And you say you've been caught before?"

"Sure, plenty," Seth said. "They once even got me as far as Chaisgott afore I gouged at a bastard's eye, the fella who had me by the scruff o' the neck."

Morley's good spirit, so short-lived, vanished. A hush came over them for a time. "Have you..." he tried, making laggard cutting and stabbing motions with one hand. "Have you ever killed someone?"

"Oh yeah, four times," Seth replied, yawning. "Twice in defense, twice for wellbein', see."

Morley thought then of Semhren back in Egainshir, as he often alleged his courting of the Princess of Bienvale when he served as Wallenport's scholar and record-keeper. Though nobody ever humored him or accepted his personal account, he maintained the truth for himself. Why? Probably because it was the truth he preferred, the truth nobody could or would want to disprove. There was always a purpose behind lying, Morley thought. But admitting an act of murder?

The lad tried then to understand Seth's perception of the world, of the people he knew in passing, his attitudes and uniform emotions. Though he'd 'acknowledged' his mortal crimes with such ease, there was something in his voice. It was the same gentle tonality he'd used when introducing himself as Sieger. It was the sound of a lie or, as the halfelev alternately guessed, of masked sensitivity. Sethan was skilled enough to hide himself within his words; Morley, when listening to Anae speak of her future away from home, could only hide himself in silence. And carnality.

"What does it mean to kill for your wellbeing?" Morley asked after another muted lapse.

"Well, wasn't just fer my *own* wellbein', see," the archer said. "'Twas fer me and the whole rest of Olford. Not sure if ye noticed durin' yer short visit, but my home's not the most well-off plot on Sarcovy. Our tradesman's a tactless drunk and our only livelihood's the inn across my house. Oh, and the miller's wine—which reminds me, hand that over."

Morley absently had been carrying the skin through the entire day. He handed it over to Seth. The archer unplugged it and took a long draught before continuing, passing the bag back to his companion. "If someone in Reineshir or Westley wants a cup o' wine, they have three choices only: take a boat over to Aubin, where they get it shipped from Taliorano; ride all the way to Wallenport, where they get it shipped from Bienvale; or come to Olford where the grapes are grown, squashed, turned to wine, and priced beyond good sense." Morley had taken small sip.

"It's very sweet. I like it."

"Where was I?" Seth asked.

"Eh, killing for wellbeing."

"Yea. There were two times—both durin' the past two to three years, I'd say—two times when we could only pay fer bread and a slurp o' beer. Not just me and mum, but the whole place. As I said, it's 'cause our tradesman, Haarka, makes crud deals without tellin' the rest of us—makes 'em with the shippers who pass through on their horses and oxcarts. He just buys what he wants, not what his neighbors might need, see. But he's the tradesman, he's the one with all the goods—and property's property till death deploys it off."

"Why not just...kill *him*?" The words surprised Morley as he spoke them. "If you can kill."

"Why not just kill him," Seth echoed, relaxed. "Ye say that as if it's so easy, mate. Ridders are no hassle to me—they might as well be scarecrows or practice-shootin' dummies. In essentials, a ridder's job is to not die, y'know. And not all ridders do their job real well. Nah...I've known Haarka since I was a tinyman. He's always been a bastard, always been despised, don't get me wrong there. But that's just the thing, innit? I know him as that rat bastard—I despise him like the rest o' the Olfordians. Kill him, ye say? Nah, that's too heavy.

"Maybe, yeah, doing that'd be the best thing fer everyone else in Olford. Not fer me. I'd have to live with that thought fer the rest o' my days, y'know. I've seen so much of him, heard lots of his words—I've seen him happy, I've seen him raged. I dunno how to say it. Killin' him would be like burnin' up a wheat field that's been growin' fer twenty-five years or somethin'. But the field is Haarka, or my memory of him. Every time I'd pass by it, I'd see all the ash or the little sprouts. And I'd have to remember the time I set it aflame every day, right?" He quietened and pinched at his short beard. "Anyway. Ye can't kill someone ye know well."

"I'll keep that in mind," Morley said, though he'd been struggling to keep his eyes open for several minutes. He yawned and said, "So, who were the men you killed, then?"

As if by contagion, Seth yawned himself. "First man I did in..." he grunted, repositioning himself against the trunk's lower roots. "Well, I'll say this fer a start: they were all ridders. Northern ridders from Chaisgott, Wallenport, The Stead—not any o' the landed men from Westley or the other place—Reineshir. So, first man I did in, I was coming back from there after buyin' a new whittle knife. The ridder was coming down the road, figured he could take a look at my bow—took one grab at me and I stuck the new knife under his arm. He didn't know what to do about it and I didn't know what to do about it, so I ran off. Heard later he was dead on the road.

"Second time was durin' a northward hunt. Again, ridder was coming down the way—this one was on a horse with real big nubs on its head—and somethin' in his head told him to start chargin', runnin' past me and runnin' back, over and over. He was swipin', laughin'—it was all a bit o' fun fer him. Ridders must often get bored round here, I reckon.

"So, I had my bow over a shoulder as usual, and a full sack of arrows. Didn't *really* mean to hit the bastard but, when he saw me nockin', he made some real swipes on his comeback. Missed the first time, I did. My second point went into his coat—not sure if it cut his flesh, but the force or shock was enough to push him off the back o' his courser. Didn't get up. Went over to check on the bastard and he was dead. Broken neck or battered brain, I dunno what it was that did him. But I just went home.

"And like I said, the other two times were fer the well-doin' of Olford. And in a sense, they're the ones I feel worst about. Both times, I just went up near Chaisgott, climbed a tree, waited fer a rider to come round. Not much more to say about it. Just loosed, made it, checked the bodies fer cash. First man had a pouch o' nickels and coppers, second had just coppers...Damn. And I was caught right after that one, right as I was cuttin' away his purse. There were two others laggin' behind him and they didn't waste a breath when they saw me over the dead sod. I suppose he was a friend of theirs.

"Got smacked with a sword flat right here," he reached into his hood and touched the back of his head. "Bit humiliatin'. It only stung fer a short while after, though. But they didn't know that, o' course, and I got away with playin' off a skull-cracked dullard. All confused and the like. Did it till they dismounted near Chaisgott, then swapped an arrow from the sack they took and jabbed it into the closer man's eye. Ran off—other man mounted, but I was well off the road by then. Had to make a new bow after that, too."

To his own surprise, Morley was now fully awake, captivated by the archer's small stories. The tales shared with him by the populace of Egainshir over the years had typically been insipid anecdotes about life beyond the south county, long and dully formed accounts with an excess of unneeded detail; Anae's stories were hardly any better, often filled with fragments of intended humor that far surpassed the lad until she explained them.

Sethan. What he shared was comparable to the half-true yarns shared by Arrin or the empty short-lived myths of Serryl's making. Though, there remained the factor of Seth's style: it had a trace of the familiar—the dialect he and his older sister possessed—and a fine homeliness to it, a backwater intrigue. Even though he'd lied earlier in the day, the archer's stories, with their natural pace and scattered, just-remembered minutiae, were the realest Morley had ever heard.

"What about yer own crimes, mate?" the archer spoke up. "Stole a cask 'cause ye were thirsty? Hope that's not the worst of it." He snickered.

"Nah," the lad mumbled, caressing the sword blade beside him. "I trespassed on the property of the Bertrisses. Several times. To make love to Anae, the Dammedottir." He paused, as Seth tended to do after presenting a plot; likewise, the archer hung on, waiting for more. "We kept meeting for a year or so, up in the loft of the family stables, but…I dunno if they passed through Olford on the way back to Wallenport, but Aetheling Felix took her not too long ago."

"Yeah," said Seth. "They stayed fer a night at the innhouse, I think. I left right quick, first sign o' horses."

"He took her as if she's a sheaf of wheat or something. I dunno—he came to Reineshir, called her out of the manor, put her on his horse, and off they went. Nearly barreled over me on the ride out, too. So now, well, I'm going to go get her. I suppose. That's why I'm heading to Wallenport."

A pause.

"But why did ye take the beer afore leavin'?" Seth asked. The halfelev shook his head. Obviously and rather appropriately, Seth didn't believe him. "Correct!" the archer added. "No reason not to! Ah…" Seth sunk down until he was lying flat on the ground. "Best we get some sleep, eh?" he proposed. "Lest ye have somethin' else ye've been meaning to ask or say or somethin'."

In fact, Morley did have a final query, a question he'd neglected to bring up through the day. "Where exactly are we going tomorrow?"

"Sylvain's place," he answered. "We're already within the boundaries of his land, which isn't really *his* land by law, see, he's just the only man foolish enough to set up his house here. It'll be dark by the time we get there, I'm sure. And, uh, the water's gonna get murkier. And there are vodniks in it, so we need to keep our eyes peeled fer them."

"I'm not sure what a vodnik is or what it looks like. As I said before." He imagined a serpent, grey and scaleless and thrice the size of the stringy water snakes they'd spotted through the day.

"Ye don't need to, Fitzmorley. Ye'll know one when ye see one."

*   *   *

By late afternoon on the next day, the forest was no longer a range of tall trees with a comely awning of pines and mid-year leaves—nor was there the sweet coolness and chime of the rushing Lightrun, its course now shattered into ripples over the buried stones. Without warning, the banks faded away and the water turned to a deep weedy green, the bottom of which was imperceptible to sight. The high trunks, now crooked weakling stems, rose from the foul murk like drowned crop sprouts. Spread between them were small incomplete fingers of wood and spidery bushes with knife-sharp fronds. The birdsongs had receded as well, giving way to the monotone of toads and insects, the plopping of their unnoticed retreats, the succeeding splash of fishes on the hunt.

And yet, though the whole of this land was out of the ordinary, not one of its parts could truly be called eccentric. Within an hour of entering the depths of the swamp, Morley believed he had adjusted to its dreariness. If the day had been brighter, bereft of the blackened storm clouds overhead, the area would be almost pleasant. Indeed, before dark, he also came to the conclusion that the 'vodnik' was nothing more than an oversized sea bass, like the one which twice swam between his legs, almost tripping him over into the filmy pool.

Then dusk fell, pale and blue. And a dim hut came into view, raised on an impossibly tall platform, its sides squashed between two trees.

When the dwelling was a mere fifty-some paces away from them, Seth raised his hand haltingly. He pointed north, away from their destination.

"What?" Morley whispered, examining the slender lines of bark against the grey. There was no movement, though he was repeatedly tricked by the mangled roots, their heads smoothly breaking the water's surface. "I see nothing."

"Quiet!" Seth hushed, removing the rabbit foot from inside his cloak. He raised it slowly over his head, stretched his arm back, then chucked the limb as far as they could see. Seconds later, there was a scraping noise then a soft plop, like a branchlet falling into the shallows.

They waited. The void made no reply over the gurgling of its denizens.

"Listen very carefully to me, Fitzmorley," he murmured articulately. "Don't move yer legs when ye do so. But take a peek at the hut up there."

The lad did so: it seemed completely built of shingles, like the oblong layers of the Olford innhouse, and its cramped porch was comparable to a balcony, accessed only by a swaying ladder of interwoven brambles. It was the house of Sylvain, he assumed, the only known resident of Sylvan.

"See the ladder?"

"I do," Morley said more quietly. "We have to climb that thing? Will it hold the both of us?"

"No," Sethan grumbled bluntly. "Always breaks whenever I climb, always fixed whenever I come back. Well, not *always*. Most times. Now listen. I'm gonna climb first and try not to break it this time." He paused, as if waiting for his companion to make a comment. "Then, when I'm up at the top, ye need to follow me up as careful as ye can. Get it?"

"Yeah," the lad replied, still whispering. "Why aren't we going right now, then?"

The archer emphatically breathed the swamp's fumes. "Because they're watchin' us. Ye can't see 'em, but they're watchin' us. Underwater. We make one move and…I dunno how many there are, but they'll be after us. All of 'em. We both climb, we both fall. But ye have a sword. If they get close to ye…Nah, I take it back. We'll just run there together. I'll climb as quick as I can, call ye when yer safe to follow up. Right?"

Morley had paled. Though he had earlier dismissed these creatures as misconstrued fish, Seth's suggestions welled fear in his throat.

"Ready?" came the word as he strapped the bow back around his torso and gathered up all the valuables hanging off him. Morley gripped the hilt of his sheathed sword in both hands.

The archer, instead of making another audible indication, leapt forward through the murk, disseminating the macabre peace with his hurdles.

Morley pursued with a mimicked bearing—and was almost provoked to stop when, nearby, the scummy water twice exploded upward, once behind them and once before them, further past their destination. Sethan was at the ladder within seconds, calling out, "One foot and one hand to each rung!"

The instruction bore no meaning to the halfelev at that moment, for he'd just laid his air-stung eyes on the strangest creature he had seen since the horses of Anae's family stable.

Its head could've been likened to that of a toad's, with two bulbous eyes and a wide mouth, though it had two web-like dewlaps on either side of its moss-colored neck. From its bulbous throat downwards, its flesh was covered over with a blood red chitin, itself glazed with an algal coat. Its arms were stout and short, barely jointed, affixed at their ends with four malformed, clawed phalanges.

Morley was only able to make a sufficient examination of the thing as he stood gasping at the base of the ladder. The vodnik, meanwhile, waded toward him, parting the vivid froth with its curved claws, the orbs of its eyes unfocused and outward. Morley glanced to the other beast behind him: it was the same breed of monster, though much more horrid, with one eye missing and brownish fungal growths forming through the fissures of its chitinous armor. This one swam faster, its arms flailing about.

"Come up, come up!" came Seth's call from the platform above. Morley gripped the highest rung he could reach with his one free hand—his other still holding the claymore scabbard at its strong-point—and set both feet upon the lowest, which immediately split down the middle.

Dangling with his feet under the water's surface, nearly within the first creature's reach, he forced away the morbid temptation to fall and try a second time and, instead, lifted himself with what little strength he still had and wrapped a leg around the vine-rail.

The vodniks were just below him. An imperious stench wafted up from them, like the feculent air of the swamplands made manifold. Morley was again drawn into the danger of the moment, felt the urge to kick or jab at the piteous vile beasts, both groping helplessly at the base of the ladder.

Halfway up, he again forgot about the archer's advice concerning the rungs and, in placing two hasty feet against one, the brambles snapped beneath him. In this instance, he lost the balance of the heavy sword in his hand.

While hanging, searching for a foothold below, he held the sheath so that the blade's pommel was directed downward. Within a second, he noticed the sword sliding out from its casement.

And Morley lost himself—the archer, the ladder, the vodniks, the swamp. He had forgotten about all of them.

Quite deftly, and with a yet unutilized might and acuteness of hand, he swung the half-clothed weapon upward. At the limit of his reach, only an ell's length of steel was yet stuck inside the solid scabbard as the rest leaned for its escape.

In lowering his arm again, the sword fell away. He released the empty sheath—snatched at the midair blade, caught it along the end of the fuller's groove.

Its edges dug into his hand. There was no pain.

He senselessly scaled the remainder of the ladder.

Upon clutching Seth's outreaching hand, letting him labor through the rest of the escape, he gave in. Still, no pain. And there was no sound except the muted hissing of the vodniks. And that too faded away with all vision and feeling. And yet, even in his sudden slumber, the stink lingered in his nose and against his tongue.

Less than two minutes had passed since they made the run for the brambles. Within that time, the halfelev unwittingly passed beyond the sphere of simplicity.

*   *   *

When he woke, the smell was less oppressive yet still present around him. He was indoors, resting over a spread of rushes or straw, curled up under Seth's cloak. Opening an eye, he saw he was at the corner of a room. His hand was wrapped in cloth, coarse and tattered, and stung whenever he made a fist. The wall plank nearest his head had a gaping pore revealing the world outside: night had fallen, though the flicker of torchlight shivered against the water and the bobbing, swimming heads of the now ample amphibians. The horrid vodniks.

As if deranged, Morley smiled at the beasts. Gale once spoke of them when recounting the tales of the conquest, though he hadn't referred to them as 'vodniks.' Just 'poison-blooded swamp dwellers.' He almost laughed, dispelling all the terror of the recent chase, which itself felt like the memory of a dream.

Then, as if in resumption, a speaker sounded out at the other end of the room: "So, what *is* the difference?" It was Seth, his tone haggard.

"The difference is both his parents en't elevs," came a response, a voice that creaked with age. "One's a naema—probly the father if his mother's blood en't so strong. I've only known one o' their kind in all my years. They say elevs can breathe the vodnik breath. But, eh, this one can't, ye see."

"I thought ye said he'd be fine," said Seth.

"He will be by the morn-time. Ye can be on yer way then, when the toads're all asleep. Still don't get why ye want to go up that way—ye haven't said. Wallen's port is a nest of bloated gannets and ye know it well."

"Better than a bank o' rottin' lampreys," the archer spoke again. "That stuff almost done?" A pause followed. "It's frothing over, old man—it should only bubble. Hard enough to get here as it is, I won't have ye bugger this up again! Just look!" He made the statements with a raised voice, as if the elder had answered his inquiry with an upbraiding scowl. A second quiet proceeded.

"I live where I live and have all the right to it. I'd say the fault's in yer own hands—ye coulda had 'im climb first."

"Not a better choice. He'd have split the rungs and I wouldn't be able to follow. But that's all past now. We made it, he'll be fine, we'll be gone afore ye wake tomorrow. If ye sleep at all, that is."

"Hurryin' all about. Hurryin', hurryin'. No use in hurryin' less yer late fer somethin'." The elder hacked.

"Easy enough fer Sylvain the Hermit. Sylvain o' Sylvan. Reckon ye haven't left this hole in twenty years," said Seth.

The other grunted without mirth or annoyance. "Longer now, boy."

"Got any vittles to spare? All we've had is old cheese and old bread." There was a grating sound, like a bowl being pushed across a tabletop.

"Never mind. There're giant crabs on the east coast, we'll just get a few o' those. And I've heard that dune pheasants strut the sands further north. Won't expect a thing. Right, that's done. Hand it over, old fool."

There was a second growl of crockery across a wood surface. Morley took the opportunity to shift onto his back. Amused by their discussion, he did so furtively.

The room was surprisingly small, incongruent to the house's outer aspect, though there was a moth-eaten curtain over a doorway opposite his peephole. Even more shocking, the space was stuffed with more vessels, chattels, and rubbish than the houses of Semhren and Reffen combined. The lad wondered how it was possible for him to stretch the full length of his body across the floor; then he saw he was situated under a three-legged table.

Ahead, Sethan and Sylvain were perched on stools before a workbench of sorts. A black spike burned like a candle between them. Both of them were shadowy and blurred through his exhausted eyes, but several details were clear enough: Sethan was dipping and raising a perforated ladle into a pot with one hand and shaking an opaque bottle with the other. And the elder had an impossibly long beard, white as wool, that hung down beneath his boney, bent knees.

"What's yer purpose in Lordtown, eh?" Sylvain muttered. "T'ain't wise fer a part-elev to walk those streets. Caution the lad. Tell 'im to watch fer the damme. Better yet, steal 'im a hat fer measures, *keh heh*."

"I dunno what yer talkin' about, ye loon," said Seth. "He'll be fine."

"And what of yerself? Yer face en't so guiltless neither, as ye say. Have ye told yer friend what ye've done, *heh heh*. Eh? What'd he think—"

"I've told him everythin'," Seth said. "He has his own crimes. Better ones than mine, even."

"Two snakes slitherin' unto a hawk's nest," the elder said. "And the hawk's hunkered down." Sylvain then gave a shrill wheeze, something between a laugh and a cough. "Think the boy'll want ye around longer?"

Sethan made an ambivalent motion with his head as he scraped something from the base of the ladle into the thin-necked ceramic bottle at hand. "I dunno. I'm hopeful. Won't be misleadin' him or anythin' low like that. I'll just keep goin' with him till he makes it plain I en't wanted. Or till I'm fed up. We'll see."

"And what if the lad's caught while breakin' into the castle there?" asked Sylvain. "What'll ye do then?"

"Depends," said Sethan. "Depends on my chances of freein' him without gettin' locked away myself. I've been thinkin' about all that, too—I've got my predictions. Lad has too much stupidity or passion. And that's why I like him so much, I think. Ye didn't see him catch the sword when he was climbin' up, it was bloody wild. I thought that'd be the end of him, but…Anyway, like I said." He took a stub from an overhead shelf and plugged up the bottle. "I'm bored. Very, very bored—damn bored. Ever since Sieger left fer Westley and the stupid ridder-hood, I'm…I dunno. Bored. Got nothin' to do but watch over mum and help round Olford.

Morley hadn't realized it until this moment but, over the course of two days, he had forgotten Sethan's original intent: lead him through the swamplands until they reached its end, then separate and move on with their lives. It seemed now the archer was going to go a bit further.

A noble killer—or a skilled liar—and a beer thief against the Aetheling of Sarcovy. Infiltrating the stone keep of Wallenport, rescuing Damme Anae from its dark recesses. He was reminded of the Idyll of Sir Tornau and Black Coney, a comparable romance of stolen love, curious friends, adventure.

Theirs would be a different tale, of course. Theirs wouldn't end with the deaths of all involved.

Come the new day, Morley would not dismiss the archer, he decided.

"Right. What do I owe ye?" Seth asked the elder with a sigh. Sylvain held up a miniature saucer, no wider than one of the skipping stones on the northwest shore of Werplaus.

"A bit o' blood," he said with disturbing geniality. "And the old cheese and bread. And I'll want back one of the halfelev's bandages."

"Course ye will. Sick bastard."

The old man wheezed a second time.

*   *   *

Morley could not remember the first time he'd been called a 'halfelev.' Nor could he remember the first time he realized it distinguished him from a 'naema.' From everybody else.

Reffen the Apothecarist had once tried to explain the term. In his words: "There are four different types of rational animal, boy." Here he paused and gawked for a long unfocused moment. It were as if he had fallen asleep, though his eyes were open and glassy. It passed.

"There are six different types of rational animal, boy. You are of the fifth kind, the halfelevs. The rest of us are of the first kind, the naemas. You've got the naemal features—the wide eyes, the drab hair, modest nose." He prodded each indicatively with a whittled rod. "But the ears are too long. And the general physique is too, eh...thin. Those are both elevi features, see. So you've got some elev in you." He poked at the lad's heart.

"Stop that," the boy said. The elder compliantly sat down at his table with a childish smile.

"The other kinds of people are..." He stopped again and stretched his arms, cracking them, almost inverting their joints. "Naemas, eh. Everyone in Egainshir is a naema aside from you. Then there are elevs, who live back on the continent, far away in a place of dark—"

"Do you get a halfelev when a naema and an elev have sex?" Fitzmorley asked impulsively. Reffen's face froze up like a cracked clay mold.

Fitzmorley knew what coitus was by that point, the age of seventeen. To a certain degree, at least. He had helped Elmaen lead one of the cows into Nudd the Varken-Ox's pen not three weeks prior.

"Eh," the elder said, reaching for the mint leaves on the table's nearest corner. "Yes, that's right." Fitzmorley wasn't finished, though.

"Does it matter who is the female and who is the male?" he asked. Reffen raised an eyebrow, taking up an opaque jar of liquid. "I mean, does the mother have to be an elev or does the father? Or does it not matter at all?" The apothecarist continued with his ponderous grimaces.

"I, eh...can't say for sure," he soon admitted. "Now, what's it you wanted? Chamomile, was it? I'm sure I've got some on the, eh—could you pinch for me a bit of ire salt? It's right over on the—oh, you found it."

Fitzmorley picked up and handed him the round saltbox without having to take a step. Reffen's house was small and musty, characteristic of its occupant. For Fitzmorley, its girth was three strides in any direction. Despite this size there were three tables, all covered over with a mess of powders, leaves, and finished solutions, and nearly ten overhead shelves which were themselves packed to the edges with clay jars and notes, paper scraps and vellums.

"You sure this is the ire salt?" Reffen mumbled. He was about to add it to a mush-filled mortar when something inside the saltbox seemed to catch his eye, perhaps the hue of the grains. The house's one window was curtained behind him and, as Fitzmorley presumed, he failed to consider

91

the effect of the room's current lighting: the miniature brazier at his side. Even so, Fitzmorley opened the palm-sized box and extracted a flake, then pressed it against his tongue. After two beats, he confirmed it as ire salt and sputtered away the flavor.

"I was probably trying to move things around recently." Reffen sighed and rubbed his scruffy beard. "I've taught you well, boy. Ech, I'll take your word for it. What were we, eh, chattering about before?"

"How a halfelev is bred," he stated, returning to Reffen's dim workspace.

"Ah, eh. You're right." He gaped down at the ingredients before him and, once again, his mind turned off. After a full minute, he raised his head. A punctual crack sounded out. "Maybe go to Semhren with the query, he'll know. Eh, or read up that holy-man's tome you left in Gale's house. Maybe the answer's in there somewhere, *heh*."

Fitzmorley was silent for a moment. Whenever he told the others at the hamlet that he was taking a day-trip to Gale's, he never mentioned that he remained outside, many strides from the benefice. The place frightened him now: the empty goat pen and deceased garden, the bump of earth that hid the horizon.

His face sagged. "It isn't," he said. "I know. I'd read the whole thing twice with Gale. It's just so, eh…I'm not sure of the word. Boring? Reading isn't supposed to be boring. It's supposed to make your mind wander and, you know, think up images for the words. That book just makes me wanna go to sleep."

Again, Reffen was casting a curious eye over the youth. "Why not read the old, eh, the old chevalier book, then?" he tried.

"I'm sick of it, I suppose," the lad said. In truth, he had hated the book for a long time now—before even Gale's death—as it only reminded him of the man's made-up stories; and of how, as 'fabliaux,' they deliberately painted over the greyness of Reality with a much brighter, more amusing color.

Despite this, however, he remained steadfast in his smaller beliefs. Gale's strange creatures and magiks were out there. Somewhere.

*   *   *

Wallenport came into view on Morley's and Sethan's fourth morning up the western beach. Few hours later, it dominated the seascape before them: a sheer wall of shaved lumber, its pegs shrugging aside the sands and the withdrawing woodlands. The land all along its northern boundaries was a lush stony slope rising away from the city proper; and at the edge of its foremost peak was a thumb of rock, its contours unnaturally sharp against the sun's subdued light. Closer to their end of the ocean, stretching over the city like an eagle beside its aerie, a magnificent house sat upon a tiered hill, an assembled elevation of sod piled against the pinnacle of a marooned sea stack. That, Morley reasoned, had to be the aetheling's castle.

They took their time on the half-forested lowlands before the west-side gate, shuffling their blistered toes through the grass and watching timidly the occasional exit and entry of the workmen. Soon enough, they surpassed the gate themselves and settled in the first inn they could find, right near the base of the castle's hill—or 'mutte,' as Seth referred to it.

The archer ordered two double-pints with part of the nickel Morley had given him back in Olford, well over a week prior. After that, they inhabited a table in a private room, away from the laughter and repetitive dialogues of the craftsmen in their main lounge.

A grizzled man fulfilled their drink request, carried the overflowing tankards to their seclusion, and set down the cups with marked scrutiny. The pair, after presenting equitable glares, became readily aware of their odd raiment and odder gear: Seth had on his oversized cloak with the hood drawn up to the peak of his skull and, beside him, there rested his bow, a full pouch of arrows, and a deflated drinking skin. Morley, meanwhile, who had placed his greatsword at the center of the table and whose filthy clothes suggested he hailed from Reineshir, couldn't help but smirk at the foamy ale.

"I take it you lads are here to attend the banquet?" the man said after a time. Thinking he meant the small gathering in the adjacent room, Morley spoke up.

"No, no, we're just stopping in for a quick drink. We're…" He took a slow gulp of beer in order to come up with a fair evasion. "We're taking a ship to the continent. We've been on the road for a long while now." Seth nodded beside him. "Two weeks now, I think."

The server chewed his lip. "Whose ship are you taking?"

Morley had recommended his drinking, so Seth came in: "Haven't yet decided, see. Haven't even stepped as far as St. Mag's—we came in through the gate only moments ago." He pulled his ale over and imbibed its peachy head, averting his attention to the bare wall as he did so.

"I get you," the man mumbled, crossing his arms. "Well, it'll cost more than a nickel piece to get you a half-decent cabin—if there *are* any docked ships with cabins, that is. Otherwise, you'll have to take a trade ship. And everyone knows trader captains charge unreasonably, unless you're willing to pay through service." He was now staring over Gale's sword. Morley was possessed by urge to pull it away, conceal it under the table.

"Haven't seen an arm like that for decades now," the man added, "not since the first arrival. Where'd you get it?" Morley had a mouthful of ale and almost choked in forcing it down. "If you stole it, that's your own problem. I won't ring the bell."

"No, no," Morley said, wiping his mouth. "I inherited it. I suppose."

The stranger leaned over it, scratched his stubbled chin. "When's the last time you oiled it?" He squeezed its tip with his fingers. "Still sharp there, at least. It has its uses. No scabbard?"

Morley shook his head and pulled the weapon slightly closer, though not out of the server's reach. He wasn't sure what the man meant by 'oiling,' but guessed it had something to do with the russet specks at the edge of the cross guard and along the fuller. There were also cloudy blotches further along the blade, contrasted by smaller chromatic tracts.

"No scabbard," the lad replied. "Lost it in Sylvan. Carried off by vodniks." The last of his words were cut off as he again lifted the tankard to his mouth.

"Sylvan? Where's that?" the man asked.

Seth scoffed into his cup and spilled some beer onto his lap. "It's 'tween the Lightrun and Larenta," he condescended, pounding the tankard down on the table. "If ye even know where those are."

The man moved his tongue around inside his mouth and narrowed his eyes at the archer. "Didn't know it was called Sylvan now, is all." He took a step back. "Well, if you need someone to fix that blade up for you, my brother works at a smith. North end of the square, ask about for Smid or Bedweir. Fairest price you can find in Wallenport—fairer price if you tell them I sent you over." He took another few paces back toward the main room. Morley and Seth dually relaxed as they sensed his departure.

However, with a hand against the doorframe, the server added, "Even if you're not here for the feast, might as well head up to the keep with that monster underarm. I doubt any of the others carry such a fierce blade. Can't imagine a finer key to the banquet, myself." The man sidled away.

So it was Felix who was hosting a banquet, Morley thought. For what purpose? Why assume *they* would be in attendance?

"Wait, wait!" he called, suddenly piqued. The man didn't reappear.

"Keeper!" Seth shouted for him. The server, still standing close by, leaned his head back through the egress. Morley beckoned him back to their sequestered table with a wave.

"Pray tell," he said in imitation of Sir Olivien, "what is this banquet you keep mentioning?" The man almost laughed.

"Aetheling Felix's feasts. What, you really haven't heard of them?" He spoke with a mocking loftiness in his tone as he peered over at Seth, who received the jest fairly. The server continued, "Yeah, Felix gave a sort of call to arms about three weeks back—wants to send more aspirants to The Stead or wherever. So, he's been hosting banquets every night for the past, eh, three days, four days? I know tonight's the last one, though, since the recruits are all marching out tomorrow morning. Anyway, it's all a bit irregular." He placed a hand on one of the two free chairs across from the pair.

"Why's that?" Morley ventured, nodding to the free seat.

The man settled down. "Well, back in my day, back in Bienvale, ridderstaat—as it's properly called—was both bought and earned. There were no *aspirants*—besides the squires, of course—and there weren't any allotted training grounds like The Stead. This was a ridder: a man, either of the nobility or of a wealthy upbringing, who had his own horse, his own set of armor, his own weapons, and his own experience—which is to say they were expected to tour through Bienvale and Taliorano all on their own for a certain span of time.

"But Roberrus, being the aetheling of a little speck of earth away from all that open land in Triume, had to change things a slight. If you wanted to become a ridder, you had to 'aspire' and go live for a time at The Stead out west. Then you had to be squired into the service of a proper disciplined ridder for a while, then you had to be assigned to an earl as a journeyman. After all that, you finally become a ridder and get to sail off to the Piik Isles for war, where you can die memorably.

"Felix, however, is making things…well, worse if you ask me. Don't mistake me, Roberrus' system worked fine for everyone involved, despite what a typical Bien—a continental, see—will tell you. But from what I hear, Felix's system is all wrong. Unless I've been fed the wrong words, our new aetheling wants to gather up hundreds of aspirants, send them to The Stead for a few seasons, then simply dub them ridders and send them off to war. He has the right, regardless of how illegitimate it all looks.

"He doesn't get it, the way I see things. They all still have to buy up their own gear and their own horses—resources we don't amply have on this island and can't afford to import in bulk. Worse, Felix has been to war himself before. And though he's more than a mite proud of that, everyone knows he saw no battles up close. I'll bet he doesn't have an idea what they're really like. I'll bet he knows them only from romances and tall stories.

"Yeah. Only a matter of time before Sarcovy plummets. We've no wealth, no respect from the continentals, and soon we'll have no real ridders. Just a load of shivering boys and old dust-throats. All-Being, how I miss Triume. A ridder of honest recognition could crop the favor of a lesser lord and declare his vassalage, lesser lord could crop the favor of an aetheling, aetheling the favor of the king. If the ridder chose his lord well, he could grow to be right popular."

"Like Sir Olivien," Morley interrupted, looking to Seth: the archer was fumbling through his quiver-bag, disinterested. The man across from them folded together his arms again.

"He was praised in a few coastal towns, yeah. And that does bring up another point. Nothing acclaims a ridder faster than a song-worthy death."

At this, Seth gave a single cynical laugh. "Hardly worth the effort, nah?" he said, pulling out the bottle he acquired from Sylvain's house. "Oh yeah, yeah, love to be a ridder." He deepened his voice. "'Remember that ole Sir Whosit? The one who stood up fer the weak and died drunk in the alley?' Nah. 'Remember Sir Asshead, the rich bastard who cut up other rich bastards and died under the sword of a nastier rich bastard?' Yeah, great song, great song." He sputtered derisively and shook the dark vessel in his hand, letting his hood fall away from his head. Morley wondered briefly what Gale's song would sound like.

"That's the way of things, sure," the server agreed without contempt. "When the news came to us here that Olivien and Aubin died at the ford of the Lightrun, oh...I'll never forget those lamentations. I watched grown men—bearded, full-bodied men-at-arms—weep and bawl like infants."

Morley choked on his beer. "You fought in The Acquisition?" he said, clearing his throat and coughing softly.

96

"Sure, though I never made it to any of the front lines. And I wasn't a ridder, just a levy. With a spear, a wood board, and a wool coat. Find me a song about a hero peasant and I'll let you stay an eve for free."

"Did you know a ridder named Gale?" the lad asked distractedly. The man shook his head. Seth caught his companion's eye and shrugged.

Over the past week as they traipsed over sand and stone and feasted on half-cooked crabmeat, they had divulged every conceivable particularity of their past lives, every monumental or insubstantial reminiscence, every minor and major character—Serryl being of greatest interest. Indeed, Seth could now claim to know more about his new friend than anyone else on all of Sarcovy Isle. Including Anae.

"Well, as I was mentioning," the man came in, cutting through the conspicuous silence. "Aetheling Felix wants an army and he wants it by the year's end. For what reason, I can't say for certain—something about invading Taliorano, some tell me. And he thinks he'll muster men quicker if he promises a ridderstaat to anyone who volunteers. It's not a *true* ridderstaat, as I said, but I don't think the aspirants will know the difference. Or even care too much. They'll get a sword and maybe a horse if they commit themselves. And that's good enough for the sons of sailors and tailors. It'll be grim sight whenever they sail off to war." He reached for the claymore between them, then stopped. "May I?"

Morley nodded his permission and the man pulled the blade closer. He scratched at the reddish dots, held the blade up horizontally, checked its girth with one eye. He then stood up, gripped the hilt with both hands, pretended to wind up a swing, then a chop, then a thrust. Morley rested his chin against his knuckles and watched, fascinated. Seth had uncorked his phial and was sniffing its hidden contents with some repulsion.

"So," Morley said finally, "if I was to go up the hill this eve with my sword...and if I offered my services to Felix..."

"You've already got a weapon," the man emphasized, placing down the claymore and pushing it back to its owner. "Only problem is you look like an urchin up from Reineshir—no offense to you. You'd be wise in buying a new tunic at the very least. Or better yet, snatching one up from the laundress on the south end." At this, he winked. "You lads take care of yourselves. Need another ale?" He pointed at Seth, whose cup was turned upside-down.

"Please," he requested, pushing it across the table's smooth surface. The man took it and left them. Seconds later, Seth spoke up again: "Looks like the ole sayin' isn't all that true." Morley took up his tankard as he leaned over to his mate. "'A barman's above all a purser of rumor.' Eh? This one didn't care about *our* rumors so much as his own. Shame. I'd prepared a few." He carefully placed down his phial at the edge of the table.

"What is that?" Morley asked finally.

"Somethin' I got from ole Sylvain," he said, tapping its tip.

"But what is it?" The archer uncorked and handed it over for Morley to sniff: it smelled like burning fumes mixed with the swampland's stench. He recoiled. "Fine, but what is it?"

"Medicine."

"Medicine for what?" At this, Seth shook his head.

"Better dreams, I guess."

The halfelev grunted, finished his drink, and ran his wounded hand through his knotty grease-laden hair. His thumb brushed by the point of his ear and the parallel cuts stung mildly. He remembered the night in the mire, among other peculiarities.

"What did Sylvain mean when he said it's dangerous for a halfelev to be around here?" he asked. Seth drummed his fingers on the table.

"Who knows? I don't rightly fathom half his babblings. Ye were awake fer that, then?"

"Partly. Didn't catch most of it and might've faded to sleep a few times, but I remember him saying something about part-elevs and…Maybe I dreamed it. I don't know." They sat in silence.

"Why d'ye ask?" the archer pressed, leaning back into his chair with a tired stretch of his arms.

"Because I'm going up to the keep," he said. "Immediately. Right now, in fact." He got up, but didn't move further. "I'll need to borrow yer cloak, Seth. Think I should have another double-pint afore I go? Or would that get me too drunk?"

The archer had raised an eyebrow and was on the verge of smiling. "Considerin' ye just said 'yer' instead of 'your' and 'afore' instead of 'before,' I'd say yer well filled. Looks like I'm rubbin' off on ye." He chuckled and scooted his chair back, then stood as he unclasped the square brooch holding together his cloak. "They'll probly pour ye a cup or two at the banquet anyway. Try and sneak out a hunk o' pheasant or a couple fish, yea? I'd rather hold onto yer remainin' coppers fer a while." He handed over the bundled cape and hood. "Just mind the tear there in the inner right side—yer right."

Morley tried on the vestment, latching the pin slightly lower than where Seth tended to stick it. It fit the tall halfelev better than its owner, its hem drooping just above his heels.

"Very good," the archer approved, hunkering back down. "Right. Fill me in."

"Fill you in?"

"Tell me yer plan. Or whatever ye hope to achieve or when I can expect to see ye again." Morley picked up the greatsword and held it point-down against the cement floor. He prodded his lips pensively and squinted. Seth snorted. "Is this how ye stole the cask and decided on comin' here? Ye just...got up one day and left home?"

"I thought through that one a bit more. But the beer was a spur of the moment." He pressed the sword's flat pommel to his cheek. "In my own defense, I didn't know what to expect of Wallenport in the first place. I expected I'd draw up a plan once here. Like Coney and Sir Tornau when they got to Irongate."

"Isn't too late to think it through, mate," Seth suggested.

"I disagree. You heard the man, right? I have a chance—*we* have a chance of getting into the keep tonight unharassed."

Seth shook his head at once. "I'm not goin' with ye if yer goin' tonight. If there's a gathering of asp'rants, there'll be real ridders aplenty. I'd rather sneak about than show my face round them."

"Then sneak about tonight while I'm at the banquet!" Morley pressed as quietly as he could.

The archer groaned. Incrementally, its pitch mounted until he gave a curt punctuating shout. They were hushed for a moment; the keeper came in and delivered Seth's refilled cup. The man cast an eye over Morley as he strode back out of the room.

"That'll do too," the man affirmed, indicating the cloak. Then he was gone.

"So you're now unwilling to help me?" The lad couldn't help but feel an ache of selfishness as the question left him. He had, after all, dragged Seth from his home for no more than a nickel piece—which he had just now invested in their drinks. And bored or not, the archer had made the choice to accompany him much further than they originally agreed and, during that trek, afforded the endeavor of preparing their daily suppers. He had never promised to lend his hand in infiltrating Felix's castle or rescuing Anae.

Indeed, after no more than two weeks, Morley had come to rely too much on his new friend—who at present was tilting the phial from Sylvain over his tankard, dribbling out a greyish silt and agitating the ale. When the bottle was upended and empty, Seth pulled his beverage closer and looked back up at his companion. He had not answered Morley's previous question, probably because he knew its provision would be superfluous.

"You'll be here, then?" Morley checked.

Seth peered down into his cup. "There's some likelihood o' that," he said.

"Where else would you be if not here?"

The archer upraised his hands unknowingly. "The fishery, the church, a ditch somewhere, bottom o' the ocean—I can't say. Here's an idea. Ye rescue yer love, ye hide on the beach fer the night and catch up a bit." He cleared his throat and rubbed his nose. "Then ye meet me back here in the mornin', we leave down the east bank again. Yeah?"

Morley gave a dense sigh. Anae wouldn't be very pleased about traversing Sylvan's waters. Nor would she be partial to the days of hiking down the shell-covered beach or up the ophidian waters of the Lightrun.

"Seems risky but it's fine by me. Anae will know what to do, I'm sure," he resolved. "Take care of yerself, Sethan."

"*You* as well, Morley," he grinned. "Steal me some food. And mind the cloak."

The lad left.

* * *

It took over two years for Fitzmorley to gather the confidence to ask Elmaen van Egainshir about the *truth* of Sarcovy's conquest. Whenever the halfelev hazarded to express knowledge of the event to the elders of the hamlet—knowledge he'd gathered from Gale, who had been in the thick of it—Elmaen waived the validity of his claims. The crabs along the coast weren't really thrice the height of a foot soldier; the reports of jotuns wandering the high northern cliffs were all comedic hearsay. From these and others, a dismal and easily fed fear of disappointment had enrooted itself in Fitzmorley.

The old campaign aside, however, Elmaen was an intriguing figure. The plot of Egainshir, a full hide of acreage, all belonged to him; that was double the amount Gale had been granted for his own service as a ridder.

Elmaen's wife Gaeshena, a woman of the continent who gave up her riches and followed her love across the sea, was the first of her husband's landed 'tenants'—as he called them. Fitzmorley had never met the woman before but had seen her twice when he was young, leaning out the door of her house and calling to her husband. And as a youth, he often reflected on how strange it was for a man to live with a woman.

During his third Frysa within the hamlet, Fitzmorley brought his questions to Elmaen. The lad had just leashed up Minny and Geat, intending to take them on a stroll over the hoarfrost, when he spotted the elder nearby. The man had also decided to go for a walk on that cold day, wrapping himself up in apparently every garment he possessed. The same went for Fitzmorley, which only meant his tunic and trousers, though he additionally wore a rough woolen sweater given to him by Amarta. It would've fit Gale perfectly, he'd thought, as its hem went as far down as his knees.

"Did you know Gale during the war?" Fitzmorley inquired as soon as Egainshir was out of sight. He tugged at Minny's leash whenever she was distracted by a patch of frozen weeds, which was proving to be moderately often.

"What war?" the elder replied. Fitzmorley said nothing, thinking it a jest. Elmaen eventually proceeded with, "Roberrus' campaign, you mean?" His companion nodded. "Ah well that was no war, see. Just a—what's the damn word?"

"A conquest?" That was how the *Chevaliers* book referred to it. And the word choice would make Gale scoff.

"I wouldn't even call it that, boy. It was more like a push to acquire land…" He scratched at his coifed head. "A land acquisition? I thought there was a better word for it, but I s'pose that's as good a description as any. The Acquisition."

The elder pulled out a small pouch of ennichfir, a sweet chewing leaf, and slipped a pinch under his tongue. He held out the bag to Fitzmorley, who took a bit for himself.

"Yeah," he continued, his voice distorted faintly by the herb. "Some still say Roberrus did it all for his big brother, Willian. Man was dying of some ill—can't place the name now. In any case, that was partly how

Roberrus got to convince the earls Rolle and Rien to come along. They were fine friends of Willian's and thought it'd be good to please their king with more land—rotten bastard that he is. But when Sir Olivien committed to the march—Sanct's Bones. Every man in the region conscripted themselves to Roberrus, myself included.

"Hetta was ending and we all turned an ear from the risks. And off we went. Wasn't a whole lot of fighting when we arrived. The Piiks had never seen horses before, y'know. Imagine seeing one for the first time in your whole life and it's barreling after you, head swinging all around, rearing, neighing." Fitzmorley didn't bother admitting he had never seen a horse either.

"Set up camp on the coast," Elmaen went on. "That's where Wallenport is today—imagine that. Day one, the city is well in order. Anyhow, Rolle—good friend, I named our fishing channel after him— Rolle was too sick from the sailing by the second day, so his best man was put up in front of the foremost march. Chaisgott was his name, a man out of Garm. To all our surprise, he met the worst of it on the route to the highlands out west. Had to come back when the snows began to get heavy. Yeah, a tough Frysa it was. Toughest one I've ever seen, but I've got life enough left. Me and the coastal folk kept on chipping at the rocks out where the quarry is now, sleeping in the caves we found. That kept us warm enough. And the ships were going back and forth to Triume, so we all ate well. Could've been worse.

"When Skonhet and the new year rolled in and the marches picked up again, the armies went off in all different directions. I went south down the beach—Gale went my way too, but I didn't know him till we became neighbors. He, 'midst very few others, was given a cozy piece of land on this side o' Sarcovy. Must've done something important, I figure. I was given my piece because I was first overseer of the quarry. But Gale never told me a lick about his role during it all. He ever tell you anything?"

"Not a word," Fitzmorley heard himself say. "Well, that's not true. There were many words but I'm not sure which were true. It's like what you said before. Most of what he told me was all imagined. Wicchas, jotuns, water goblins, giant crabs. I've never seen any of those things."

"Neither have I," Elmaen mumbled. "But we're only two people, you and I. Just because we've never seen those things doesn't mean they're not out there, eh? Yeah? Could be that they're all living flukes. Serryl has all those stories of sea creatures, yeah? And she said she's seen a few a while back. Reffen, too—he's familiar with all sorts of odd beasts. And Yeva claims she used to live on satyr ground back before she came here."

Fitzmorley's ear perked up at this new word: Satyr. It sounded like a type of snake or mire-dwelling reptile. Regardless of what the sound signified, it had been a tremendously long time since the lad heard any new words.

"What is that?" he asked.

"Oh, I'm not sure," Elmaen answered. "I do know it eats flesh, though. Or bone marrow."

"Where did she come from?"

"Who? Yeva? She may've been born on one of the Piik Islands, brought back by a remorsed sailor under Roberrus or something. Might as well ask her yourself, yeah?"

Fitzmorley's thoughts swam and he realized he couldn't stop there. "Where did the others come from? Lunferda and Gertruda and Arrin and all the rest? And what else did you do during the rest of The Acquisition? Did you ever meet Roberrus in person?"

He managed to spit out a half dozen more queries before Elmaen silenced him, prodding his chest with the knuckles of his bony hand. They halted for a moment and the old man expelled the ennichfir from his mouth, smacking his lips. Minny instantly pranced over and ate the soggy lump; Geat watched her with the categorical blankness that only he could convey.

They continued on southward, the wind behind them. And the old man shared everything.

*   *   *

Upon reaching the top of the artificial hill, Morley—the claymore held confidently over his shoulder, the cape wrapped tight around his tunic—beheld its colossal house, surrounded on all sides by cloaked and armed men. Each was more or less attentive to the new arrival.

The sun was beginning to sink into its northern bed, setting aflame the horizon and the apparitions of distant islets. More fascinated by the southward vista though, the halfelev wandered away from the group of men conversing by the wide ironwood entrance nearby. He stood over the unnatural elevation of turf and rock, wondering if he could survive a fall from that vertiginous height.

Lifting his head away from this decline, he rested a foot on the uneven rampart of ledgestones and stared over the borough below, pulling up the cloak's hood. For a time, he was captivated by this vantage: the peace, the drifting steam of labor, its unheard wind-lost din. Ships floated beyond the harbor; Morley had never imagined that sea vessels could be so large. How were they not sinking? Why were they moving so slowly or not at all? They couldn't be fishing, for that was a task restricted to smaller boats, wasn't it?

"Boy!" came a shout. Morley whirled around: a man wearing a padded dress-like garment was standing close by. Another, armed with what appeared to be a giant unfletched arrow, was waiting further off. "Good Being above, I called to you twice. I asked what's—" A gust carried off the rest of his words. Morley stepped forward, silent and almost terrified.

"Say again?" he requested. Once near enough to the sentinels, he halted and stuck the blade into the ground beside his foot. He presented a fortitudinous frown as he did so. The closer man peered away at the other. Turning back, his face was curled in amusement.

"Where'd you get the sword?" he asked, apparently discarding his previous question.

"From my father," Morley fibbed. "Sir Gale van Werplaus."

The man holding the metal-tipped pole approached. "I'll bet it's a fake," he said snobbishly. "Look at it—doesn't even shine. Wood painted white, rubbed with ash or something." At this, Morley lifted his wounded tremoring hand to his head, showing the deep cuts on his palm.

"I'll take that bet," he said calmly. He then held the sword out vertically, its tip pointing up. "Wanna test the edge?" The first man set his arms akimbo with another satisfied smirk; the second eyed the back of his cohort's head, as if attempting to see through it. The muscles of Morley's forearm quickly began to shiver under the weight, so he set the blade's point back down between his toes. He had their attention.

"I heard Aetheling Felix needs ridders," he said.

The armed man blinked and walked off. "He does," the other spoke. "He's fattening up the rest inside. What's your name?"

The lad jostled through an internal debate. "Fitzmorley," he decided. "Fitzmorley van Reineshir."

The sentinel chuckled and seemed to roll his eyes. "Bit of a mouthful, that. I'll settle with 'Fitz.' Wait here." With that, he strolled back to the castle doors.

Morley returned to the ledge over Wallenport and huffed, shocked by his success. The cloak, he guessed, was hiding his unimpressive frame excellently. He hoped now that nobody would demand him to remove it before entering the keep.

He then thought about the aspirants already inside. How bulky would they be compared to him? Or were the doormen just letting in anyone who ascended the hill? Not likely. If such were the case, every man in Wallenport would knock at the castle doors, promise to join the ridderstaat, eat their fill of the aetheling's stock, then scurry back into their houses, hoping they'd never be seen again by the higher powers. Morley, of course, had no intention of becoming a ridder, but could evidently pretend to be one, at least for one evening. He'd be gone by the morning anyway, with Anae at his side. Damme Anae. The Aetheling's wife...But wouldn't he—

"Fitz!" came the familiar voice. The sentinel, waiting several strides away by the front door, beckoned the lad to him. There were now two richly clad gentlemen watching him from the castle's cracked-open entry. As he paced over to meet them, all the other idling guardsmen ceased their conversations and stared. Morley ignored them with fabricated pretension, focused instead on the blond-haired and mustached man in wool, then the robed and bald-headed youth beside him. The latter held a pair of wood frames, loosely bound like a manuscript, and a stylus that was slightly larger than the one Semhren used.

"Fine blade," said the older attendant. "Can't even *steal* a weapon like that nowadays. At least, not around here. And even if you did, I'll guess its last owner had no more use for it..." He trailed off, as if lost in his recognition of the sword. "Your name?" he soon asked.

"Fitz." The robed fellow carved something into his book. Morley now presumed it was a set of wax tablets.

"Fitz from...?"

"Reineshir." The young scribe made another careful etching. The man with the drooping mustache raised his brow in surprise.

"That's a first," he mumbled. "Can you mount and ride a horse?" Morley shook his head. "Have you money enough to rent or purchase a horse?"

"No."

"Are you skilled in the use of that weapon?" The response to this was difficult to decide. Yes or no? Would he be asked to demonstrate if he confirmed such?

"Skilled enough." He had, after all, watched Gale fight. Shortly before his death. And the memory was ever vivid—how hard could it be to mimic what he recalled? The interlocutor stepped back closer to the door.

"You'll do, then," he judged, pushing his hand against the umber planks. "My name is Herman, by the way. I serve Aetheling Felix as warmester. This one here is Fien, he's the court scholar's apprentice." The bald student said nothing and continued to write, turning as he did so. "Come in and take a seat at one of the benches." As he spoke the words, Morley passed into the threshold of Castle Sivliére, the true domain of his chosen rival.

Awe. Beyond the tall doors was the most tremendous room he had ever seen, currently resounding with countless percussions. All the floors and walls were of masonry, all capped off with a timbered convex ceiling. The hall's width was twenty strides at least, perhaps fifty from front to stern. Five open and unreachable windows yawned the evening's light along each lengthwise wall, the lower portions of which were draped with embroidered curtains depicting flowers, people, beasts, and an indiscernible narrative flowing through them all.

Two excessively long trestle tables, much like the one Anae described as being in the Bertriss manor, were situated before him. Their benches were packed almost to their brims with naemal men and youths, their clothes diverse and drab. A modest gap divided the tables, a passage for scullions to deliver and receive the variously-shaped kitchenware.

Somewhere over the incessant intoning of a hundred voices, music was being played—much to Morley's puzzlement. On those rare evenings in Reineshir when he and Anae entered the brewery to listen to Jhann and his fellow performers, the upper parlor was stuffed to the walls with townsfolk. And yet all of them quietened when the musicians made their noises, cheered when the song was finished. Here, what was their purpose?

Nobody paid any mind to the thud of the unseen tabor or the rebec's haunting gull-like whine, squawking through the laughter and the clacking of bowls. Most shameful of all, the halfelev could discern his favorite sound through the noise: the spirited coo of the short cornett, an instrument favored by the goatherd's daughter in Reineshir. Whenever he heard the flute's song, gliding listlessly over the drum's softened patter and the slowed buzz of the strings, something inside him shrank: often it called forth his memories of childhood, of walking the breezy flats or watching the north sky burn into night. Now, here amidst the feast's raucous madness, it might as well have been a ghost.

The music emanated from the furthest end, where a third table—to which Herman was steadily advancing—was placed: two figures sat behind it in highbacked chairs, facing all the others. Felix and Anae, as Morley guessed.

Unheeded, he settled onto one of the benches and occupied its end, concealing the claymore under his thighs. Beside him was a middle-aged man with an unfortunately fat neck, stuffing his cheeks with half a baguette. Not many helpings of food were within Morley's close reach, as the servants had not yet noticed his arrival or passed by him. Closer to the tables' gap, though, there was a steaming crock which nobody had yet touched. He stretched to it without deliberation and pulled it over. This snatched the attention of the eater at his side, who dipped his last piece of bread into the basil-green stew. He then drawled a few words to the lad, his mouth full and words unclear: "Wahnah dees?"

"Eh?" Morley muttered with a similar lack of clarity. The man offered him a generous loaf of seed bread. The lad took it and thanked him.

A quarter of an hour passed. After having his fill of spinach and beef stew, soaked bread, fish with lemon, and mashed beets, he grabbed several fistfuls of pecans—storing a fair amount inside the hood for Seth—then ate two small potatoes and an apple.

Minutes later, he felt ready to vomit.

He needed an escape, somewhere to purge. His first thought was to do it under the table. Not subtle enough, he resolved, perhaps incorrectly. Earlier, when entering the court with Herman and the apprentice called Fien, he did not take the opportunity to find other passages leading out of the great hall. From his current position, he could descry little more than the exit and the feast around him, its bantering aspirants and the now sickeningly ample fare. And yet, Fien seemed to have vanished immediately…

He twisted his head around: a dark opening hid against the closest corner of the room. Before he could bolt for it, a hand rested on his shoulder.

"Aetheling Felix would like to meet you," said the war-mester. "And see that sword of yours."

Morley gulped. "After y——" A lurch in his throat. "After you."

Herman turned away at precisely the right second. Morley yanked over the pot he had so rapidly emptied, placed it down on the vacant side of the bench, and stealthily did what he needed to do. Clammy and pale of face, he set the refilled crock away from the rest of the victuals and abandoned his seat with all haste, taking up the greatsword.

As he passed behind the line of feasters, he caught multiple sets of eyes, largely from the men at the opposite table. He almost felt the chamber quieten. Ahead, Herman waited with his hands behind his back; there were two doors behind him, both barred with black ingots. Not many paces to his side, meanwhile, Aetheling Felix waited, beaming up at Morley and the sword resting on his shoulder.

Morley froze: Aetheling Felix was a halfelev.

Averting his eyes, he found Anae sitting next to him, distracted and seemingly disgusted by someone further down the hall. She was beautiful as ever. Even with her restrained displeasure.

When walking the streets of Reineshir, she would exude an aura of calm satisfaction; when intimate, she would dispose of all sophistication, give in to the weight of her impulses. Now, here at the aspirants' feast, her hair was braided up with a striking artistry and her blue gown was of a material which the lad couldn't hope to determine. But of course, Morley saw them as nothing more than spurious layers piled over her true psyche: the naema girl who allowed herself to fall in love with a halfelev boy from Werplaus, the girl who once wished for little else aside from the day of their next meeting. Strangely, he hoped that she wouldn't see him, that he could surprise her in private—somewhere, anywhere else within Felix's vast house.

Morley stood at a comfortable proximity between Felix and Herman, trying as best he could to block Anae's view of him. At the end of the bench, another young man of similar age was situated: inversed, he reclined against the table's edge, his elbows over its surface. He and Felix shared the same trimmed beard and the same bluish garb—a thick wool sweater interweaved down the middle with helix patterns.

"No need to be nervous, friend," said the aetheling, probably in reference to Morley's post-vomit pallor. "You know, you're the first one out of all these men—not just today, but yesterday and the day before—to bring their own weapon into my hall."

Felix's nearby attire-twin snickered. "That's not true," he proclaimed, leaning forward onto his knees. "Remember the composter's son and his *pike?*" Then, to Morley, "Decapitated shovel with its edge shaved down to a point. Said it belonged to his grandfather." There was some movement behind the lad: Herman was making his way back to the hall's entrance.

"Ah, and there was the farmer son who brought along a scythe," Felix recalled. "That was good. He came from the dairy near Chaisgott, right Iacob?"

The other sniggered again. "Nah, had to be Westley. Why would a dairy farmer need a scythe?" Instead of chiding the retainer, Felix prodded the side of his temple.

"Even a dairy needs a furlough. Imagine all the fodder he has to reap for his cows. Or goats or whatever he has there. A lord must know his land, Iac. The scythe-wielder was from the dairy, I'm sure of it." With that settlement made, he readdressed Morley. "Where did you come from, eh…Fitz, is it?" The lad nodded, hoping that, by presenting himself as an untalkative commoner, he could be allowed to return to his seat. He glanced at Anae, who was now carefully tearing at a strip of roast pheasant. "What part of this land do you call home?" the aetheling asked again. The lad debated, carefully scratching under his mop of hair.

If he were to say Egainshir or Reineshir, the two places he was most familiar with, there was the risk of drawing Anae's awareness—which, still yet, he preferred not to do. He could say Westley or Aubin, though he knew virtually nothing about the places. Then there was the option of Olford, a village even smaller than Egainshir. Before he could arouse uncertainty in the aetheling and his attendants, he resolved to the most general satisfying answer he could come up with.

"I call all of this land my home, Aetheling Felix," he said listlessly. "I've settled nowhere." Felix and the young man named Iacob exchanged looks of affectation.

"This one's full of surprises," said Iacob. "Few words and a big sword. A rogue of the road. I like him already."

"So do I," Felix confirmed. "I sense a thousand stories will come of you, my friend." He adjusted himself in his chair.

Anae twisted her head in his direction. The lad stiffened, thinking she would now apprehend him; but she merely glimpsed right through him, then resumed her lethargic meal, her face still sagging with discomfort. Felix leaned over and whispered to her. Morley, dreading an inopportune introduction, tilted away. Seconds later, the aetheling angled back to his favorite new recruit.

"You may return to your seat now, Fitz. Enjoy the rest of the feast. I very much hope we will meet again soon."

After giving a short bow and receiving appreciative tilts of the head from both Felix and Iacob, Morley made his way back down the hall, puffing out an uneasy breath once far enough away from the pair. He was overtaken by an inordinately strange feeling then as he reflected on the manner of that exchange.

He hated Aetheling Felix, that rat who stole away his love, that arrogant power-drunk halfelev…And he found himself forcing aside a regret of this hatred. Upon their first and hopefully only meeting, he was cordial beyond all expectations. Indeed, he was almost excessively friendly, more so than anyone he'd ever met outside of Egainshir. Even his right-hand man was likeable.

So, why did Anae seem so upset? Was Felix's courtesy a public façade, a means of assembling the love of his lower subjects? Believable enough. What did he whisper to her when he bent to her side? She made no reaction—perhaps he was ragging her for bearing such a foul mood in front of the throng. Why else would he have to convey the words so privately? To scold her aloud would break character, resurrect his domineering ethos—that he no doubt hid away. Yes, Morley thought. Felix really was a rat bastard. He had to be.

But why the hell was he also a halfelev?

Not far from his previous seat, Morley passed by War-mester Herman, hands still behind his back as he returned to the aetheling; he gave a cheered nod before passing the lad's periphery. Seconds later, the lad saw that a new aspirant had taken his place at the end of the bench, a plainly dressed elder with sun-darkened skin. He was preparing to tug over the wretched crock.

The opening at the dark corner was still untended. It was now or never.

Readjusting the claymore underarm and lowering himself to a near crouch, he scurried forth into the passageway.

A dark narrow stairwell hugged the outer side of the courtroom's wall: Morley stumbled his way up its black steps. At the top, a long and equally cramped corridor extended marginally further than the length of the great hall, its cobbled flooring lit by a series of iron-barred skylights, each above a rusted drain plate: Morley sprinted to the light at the other side, fearing that someone's menacing shadow might emerge at any second against the stones ahead.

Upon reaching the tunnel's end, he peered around the corner. At the center of the closest wall, a gaping window overlooked the court and the feast below. At the wall's ends, two doors presumably led down to the massive space. The one within his reach, as reason insisted, had to descend to one of the doors he'd seen behind Herman earlier.

The wall opposite was lined with identical posterns—much like the portal Anae used to sneak him through—each set into an alcove. Above this same side, evening light was cast down through broad lunettes in the stonework, all fitted with adjustable shutters.

Morley's first thought was to open each door under the lunettes and inspect the chambers behind them—the fastest means of getting caught, he quickly surmised.

However, before he abandoned the notion, the soft treading of footfalls came from one of the two archways at the other end of the hall. He slipped into the nearest alcove, wondering if it were a better hiding place than his previous spot.

He leaned minutely out of his niche: an exasperated scullion maid lumbered up through one of the arches ahead. When she reached the landing, she removed her grubby apron, then issued the heaviest sigh the lad had ever heard. Not a moment later, she'd proceeded through one of the doors, slamming it behind her. A hush followed.

He soon slid out from his seclusion. And immediately after stepping into the open corridor, another sound—a firm voice that surpassed the noise of the banquet—echoed from the same arch the woman had come through.

He froze, again debating where to conceal himself, then scampered into the second alcove and hugged the greatsword to his chest. The speaker loomed further into earshot.

"…already told him that, too many times. Two gatherings were one too many, but three is an excess he'll regret before the end of the season." The voice was both gruff and nasally, and Morley couldn't yet tell if it belonged to a man or a woman. "But he's determined that it will work. He has far too much confidence, that boy." The speaker hacked and coughed extravagantly.

"You certainly have little faith in him," came a woman's voice, "given that you still refer to him as a *boy* behind his back."

The conversers were now in the long room, moving at a steady humdrum pace. This worried the lad: if they were walking so slowly, they might detect him. He pressed himself deeper into the nook, furling the cloak around his front. The man continued speaking.

"He *is* a boy, cleric. Though he legally came of age years ago, he's still a boy. I thought Roberrus' death would set him right, but he hasn't changed enough. I try to speak with him about his expenses, you try to speak with him about his people—he won't have it. He knows it all well enough, he says. So, he'll have to learn the hard way."

"But is it not our job to protect him from the hard way, Arnaul?"

"It is. And we can try all we want, but we've already walked and split the gangplank, so to speak. Some will starve come Frysa, mark my words."

"Maybe," said the woman. "But the aspirants have been served at the aetheling's table. They know it's a luxury, they know it's costly. But Herman says we have over five hundred recruits. That's five hundred fewer mouths to satiate, at least in the city."

"I have doubts those five hundred men know what they've agreed to. They'll take their bread and corn without complaint at first, but most have been fattened by the bounties that only Wallenport provides. Just watch. Fifty days into Frysa's cold, there'll be trouble."

They were now in sight, idling their way to the other end of the corridor. Morley could only see their vestments and the backs of their heads, but tried not to look for too long, shrinking against the cold surface behind him. They both wore gowns tied at the waist: the woman's was black with a mantle over the shoulders, and the man's was green and grey.

"I'm surprised you're defending his immoralities as much as you are," said the one called Arnaul.

"Just trying to keep faith, curator."

The man gave a churlish laugh. "Given the circumstances, that's another way of saying you've lost faith, priestess."

"In some things, I have," she said sadly. They stayed silent for a short time, then a knock sounded at the door in the adjacent alcove.

"I suppose you've heard about Hoerlog, then." The woman did not answer. "No? Then we have much more to discuss. Perhaps tomorrow after mass, once the aspirants head out for The Stead." Another knock at the door, then "Raul!" He kept knocking, calling, "Better not be sleeping in there again!"

"Just open the door," said the so-called priestess. "He might not be in there." The latch clattered up and down. "Let me." There was one solid chink, then, simultaneously, a grunt and a very loud bang, like an ashlar chunk being tossed over metal and hardwood. This was followed by gentle footfalls. A second, less violent clamor returned the hallway to its relative peace.

Morley, relieved by his newfound competence, poked his head out of the niche: nobody was there. He propped himself back against the wall of his hiding spot, exasperated.

The door beside him opened inward.

The lad didn't react. A tall and impossibly gorgeous woman stood there, blinking at him. Her eyes were bright and slim, much like his own. Really, the whole of her head was slim, topped by threads of silver hair which couldn't possibly be real. She was tall as well, towering a full head higher than the awkward boy before her. She was unsurprised, though her face changed into something that, at first, made Morley gulp down his nausea.

She seemed…affected. She tilted her head this way and that, inspecting the frozen halfelev. Lifting her hand, she skimmed her fingers against one of the lad's cheeks. Then she brushed back the filthy hair from the side of his head.

"Hm," she said. "You're my son."

*   *   *

Damme Ellemine handed Morley a small cup of chamomile, poured seconds earlier from her painted earthenware kettle. One lithe helix of steam slithered from it.

Reasonably, he was unconvinced that she was his real mother—really, he wasn't sure if he even wanted her as his mother. She told him that, as of the recent Hetta season, he was nineteen years old. He had suspected he was far older than that.

Much to his displeasure, a fair deal more confirmation was set before him: for example, an entire account of his conception and birth was laid, ending abruptly at his delivery unto Sir Gale's doorstep. Ellemine, senior of the Sivliéres, one of the highest authorities of Sarcovy…thus far the only person beyond Werplaus to bring up Gale's name before Morley himself could mention it.

All of this was conveyed within ten minutes of their chance meeting. Morley, slouched at the edge of her baldachined bed, the sword under his feet, shook his head with a frown.

This woman meant well, but the way in which she conducted herself irritated him. She found him hiding outside her door, noticed he was her son through some dynamic instinct, then spared no excitement in making the announcement to him. True enough, he didn't expect to ever find his mother; but weren't mothers supposed to embrace their sons the way Amarta and Serryl embraced theirs? It were as if he didn't matter to her at all. But maybe that was fair. She meant nothing to him prior to their engagement in the upper hall. Perhaps he was just being selfish.

"Did you know that Sir Gale first came from the town of Garm?" she asked, her voice clean and lustrous. "And that he had a father named Morl, from whom you surely acquired your name?"

Morley shook his head again. "Nothing you've said was known to me," he said. "Besides that I was delivered to Gale when I was an infant." He reflected for the fourth time in that quarter-hour. "So, Felix is my brother, then?"

"That is right," she replied. "Though, I suppose 'half-brother' might be more accurate a term around the Biens, since the two of you do not share the same fath—"

"I know, I know, you said that already!" he snapped. Moaning, he lowered his perspiring brow onto his open palm, then he set the emptied cup on the floor to disrupt the moment's silence. Restless, he peered across at her, still in disbelief.

"The Earl of Laisroch County is my father," he added. "And his name is Michel?" Ellemine nodded. Another set of details she'd blandly shared within their first moments together. "And the two of you birthed me out of some loveless relation? While Roberrus was off to war and Felix was only a baby?" Again, Ellemine nodded. "And you both had to dispose of me once I was born because my being in the castle would be seen as scamerous?"

"Scandalous," she corrected. The young man sighed.

"Fine. But why?" The woman tilted her head. "If you knew I couldn't be kept around, if you knew what would happen if I was birthed, why would you still do it? Why would you still…?" He shook his flushed head.

"Unspoken portents," she said. The lad waited for her to say more. Time passed.

114

"Go on," he soon requested.

The woman straightened in her slender chair. "About four hundred years ago, I learned how to read all the heavenly asterisms—the sentences of the All-Being, as the clergymen refer to them, the patterns in the stars. They have many utilities, all at once. Sailors use them to map their course through the night, farmers watch them to tell the precise time of year. And astrologists—many of whom claim to serve me—irrationally conduct their experiments under the stars' pale light. All of these uses are secondary. Or mistaken." She paused as if to give Morley a chance to speak. He was, however, still latched to the notion of her profuse age.

"You see, the clergy believes that when an individual star in the celestial ring shines out the brightest, it is an indication of circumstances to come. This is a fallacy. In truth, only one of the eleven binding-stars tells of the future. It is called Blanc, the year's final sun, the adjoining body between Haem and Synesti. Of all the many others, Blanc is the one I have best learned to—"

"I don't know what you're talking," Morley heaved. Ellemine smiled.

"Of course not. I will not confuse you further. Just know that, through this final sun, I can receive unspoken portents. It requires immense ability and decades of painful practice, but it can be done. By an elev, at least. Naemas are too weak-willed to succeed in a reading such as this."

"But what does any of this have to do with my damned birth?" he snapped again.

The woman's face darkened. "I saw myself in the act of conceiving you," she said bluntly. "And Michel Laisroch was my partner. So, as Roberrus was absent as usual, I sent a messenger to Westley, urging its earl to come here. He did so without question. We feasted, he passed rude flirtations, and the deed was soon done. I had him removed in the morning. That was that. You were born later that year and the cleric and chamberlain dissuaded me from keeping you, as expected."

The lad's mouth hung open.

"You just…had a dream of conceiving me. And you went through with it because…" He let the words float about.

"They were not dreams," she corrected. "A dream is nothing more than a boundless meandering of the soul. A portent is a containment of Reality yet untouched."

"But why follow it? Why obey it, why let it happen? If you *didn't* conceive me or birth me, what difference would it make?"

At this, Ellemine shrugged with her eyes. "That remains to be discovered, I suppose." The young halfelev groaned and lowered his head into his hands again. "I have lived for nearly five hundred years. Some wishes, over those long centuries, have not even passed over me yet. When the truths are ignored, I face hardship. When they are honored, I find solace and sometimes joy—no matter how foul an entailing deed."

"Fine," he said, raising his head again, still lost in her arcane babblings. "Did the potents—"

"*Portents,*" she corrected.

"Did they tell you to take me to Gale?"

"No, they did not," she said.

Morley felt the color leave his face. An exasperated fury writhed in his stomach. "Why did you take me to Gale, then?" he murmured.

"I owed him a favor of my gratitude."

"Why?"

"Because I believe he was the noblest ridder in Roberrus' army," she said with a smile. "When they came to the clearing where Reineshir now stands, many men fought over my possessions. That is, they each wanted me as a spoil of war. They were exhausted from the march and from fighting the people who lived here before them. One man was audacious enough to force himself upon me. And through him, through the portents I chose to accept, I later had my second child." She wandered into silence for a moment. Morley gripped at the hem of his tunic.

"Sir Gale found out and nearly killed the man—who duly fled after waking back to consciousness. And Gale did not leave my side for days after that, always sitting upright. Always with his sword drawn." She nodded to the old blade under her son's feet.

"I urged that such was unrequired of him, but he stayed nonetheless, telling me it was his duty to protect the weak. I urged him that I was not weak nor was I hurt, but he said nothing more. I reckon still that he desired me as all the other men did. His means of expressing it, however, were gentle. I grew quite fond of him anyway. Though not as fond as Roberrus was of me upon his arrival." Without mirth or glory, she chuckled under her breath. "He was infatuated. Even before he came under my spell."

The lad shook his head yet again. "So you repaid Gale by giving him one of your illimit—illigin...illegitimate sons? Is that right?"

"The pronunciation or the concept?" Morley said nothing. "Both are correct. And yes. There are too few men on this island whom I trust with the guardianship of my children. I knew Gale would protect you as he protected me. And if what you said about him is true, I am more than glad you were sent to live with him, to occupy his lonesome life.

"Who else would I send you to? Sir Baldwin of the Tree Farms? Sir Wortin of Hoerlog Tower? Certainly not your true father. Earl Laisroch is married to Mennia van Lattaholm. And the discovery of his adulterous actions would bring a bit of a strife to southern Bienvale, I am sure. Their wedlock was an assuagement that followed a feud between their two families. At least, that is what Michel told me after I sent him the message regarding your conception. I never pried further. You would have grown up to be a lech if he raised you."

Morley stopped listening after Gale left her discourse. Michel Laisroch was of no concern to him and probably never would be. Nothing, in fact, seemed to matter now—not his unnamed siblings, not even his intentions for coming to Wallenport. He needed isolation, preferably outside Sivliére Castle. Somewhere to sit and sift through all the implications at hand, all the things he wished to know. His stomach began to churn again, not because of the food he'd engorged earlier. He missed Egainshir and began to regret his departure from the place.

"Now," Ellemine spoke up, "I have answered a number of questions for your satisfaction. Could you do me the honor of answering one of my own?" Again, the lad hadn't been listening. He nodded all the same. "What are you doing here in Wallenport and why are you sneaking around my home? You know this part of the keep is forbidden, yes? If I had not found you first, the guardsmen would've crippled you."

Her son bobbed his head and gaped at the ground, then snapped up to address her. "Could you repeat that?" She did. Once he managed to reassemble a shard of concentration, his heart leapt. "Anae," he breathed

"You came to see my daughter-in-law. Why is that?"

"I mean to speak with her."

"About what?"

Foolishly, he hadn't expected her to continue pressing. "It's a private matter." The woman did not move. He proceeded with as much truth as he could spare: "I knew her when she lived in Reineshir. We were friends. Until Felix came and took her away. I never got to say goodbye or give her a farewell gift or anything. She was just gone."

Ellemine smiled warmly. "You wish to give her a gift?"

Morley glanced down at the blade beneath his heels. "No. I just wish to speak with her. That's all."

It was no lie: in conversing, they could plot their escape. Ellemine, much to his satisfaction, stood up. She roved through the crepuscular candlelit chamber toward the furthest wall and its enormous curtain—a wide quilt embroidered with bright florid designs and centered with a dark blue and silver icon, a dagger with antlers protruding from the hilt. It was the same symbol adorning the many banners around the castle, the same mark burnt onto the covering of his favorite childhood book.

She pulled out a loose string from a stitched daisy, then removed the flowery badge, revealing a small black compartment behind the quilt. She reached inside fluidly. After removing her hand, she cupped her other palm over it. Like a lost spirit, she glided back to her son.

"Tell me," she said, "what do you plan to do upon leaving this place?" The inquiry came as a surprise, but Morley believed he knew what she wanted to hear.

"Go back to Werplaus, I guess. Maybe stay a few days in Olford. A friend of mine lives there."

Ellemine's mouth twisted in disbelief. "You won't go to Westley, then?" she asked.

Morley narrowed his eyes and bit his lip. "Why would I go there?" The woman did not speak. "To meet my father?" She bowed her head. Morley hadn't yet thought about this. "Seems to me like a worthless trip. Why, would he wish to see me?"

"I do not know," she confessed. The words sounded strange coming from her.

The lad sighed away his confusion. "I have no reason to go there, then."

At this, Ellemine opened her hands: an abnormally large daisy head rested on her palms.

"Will you ever go there?" As she spoke, she covered over the flower again. Somehow. It had been large enough to stretch across both her hands. Now, not even a nail-span of petal poked out from under her fingers. There was no trace of it at all.

"I...maybe. Someday, I'm sure," he tried. The woman separated her hands, let them drift to her sides: the daisy was gone. Morley gaped.

"Do me another favor, my son," she said softly, slipping two fingers under his chin and prodding his head up. "This meeting of ours, this gift. Keep it to yourself. And I will do the same." With her other hand, she slipped two solid objects into the flap of his shirt. They chinked against his last nickel piece. She backed away. "And Anae will follow suite. I imagine I won't have to instruct her discretion."

At that, the door opened.

It was Anae. She slipped into the room and closed the postern without barring it. Her eyes fell on Morley. She stiffened with an intake of breath. Then she searched Damme Ellemine, almost pleadingly. Silence. And the whirring of candle flames.

"You knew he would come, dear," Ellemine cooed. "More than I, you expected him."

"No, I didn't," Anae replied, still staring at the halfelev. Her tone, lacking a quaver, insisted otherwise.

"Well, he wishes to speak with you." The woman looked over her son with a lofty jovial grin. Then she turned back to Anae. "Will you show him the way out whenever you finish your discussion?"

Dread took root in the lad's guts. After another bout of quietude, Anae issued her familiar subdued moan. "Yes, damme," she muttered. With that, Ellemine placed a hand on her son's shoulder and leaned down to kiss his forehead. Morley blankly allowed her to do so.

"Remember everything I have told you," she purred. And the lad realized, with some embarrassment, that most of her words had already left his mind. Without ceremony, his mother strutted out of the chamber and sealed the door behind her.

The two youths faced one another. The lad tried to smile; the girl tried to mirror him. And her smile wasn't her true smile. Morley could tell. It wasn't much of a smile at all, he thought. Only one side of her mouth was curved up, undimpled. Her eyes were dull and disinterested. Her hands were entwined at her waist. Perhaps worst of all, she did not move away from the door—she didn't charge forth to embrace him, didn't step lightly into his enveloping arms.

She stood. Waiting. And for what? Morley felt something congealing in his throat.

"Hello," she said. Then, as if she heard the insensitivity in her own voice, she blandly added, "Country boy."

"Anae," He took a step, kicking the cup he had set on the floor earlier. It hit a leg of the bed, cracked, and a chipped piece fell away from it. They stared at it until Morley bent down, taking up his sword.

"I…" He wanted to ask why she seemed so heedless, so despondent of his presence. "I've missed you."

"And I've missed you," she replied. She hadn't. He could tell. Or she had and was somehow being prevented from articulating such. What had the Sivliéres done to her, he thought—what had his mother done? He could no longer hold back his impatience.

"I thought you would be…I mean, I…Come closer," he said. Anae did so until she was within the reach of his arms, though only just.

He tossed the sword down onto the bed, clutched her head in his hands, and planted his lips on her own. She did not recoil and she did not cling to him. She stood with closed eyes and receptive lips. When they parted, Morley kept his hands, now lightly trembling, near the lobes of her ears. He eventually lowered them and cast down his head, embarrassed.

"Is that all you wanted?" she asked. Before he could say anything in response, she continued, "You know, if you were anyone else, I'd be compelled to call the garrison."

He didn't understand why she felt the need to say such and, by the teary sparkle that glazed over her eyes, she probably didn't either.

"Why are you here?"

Morley wanted nothing more than to tell her: He came to rescue her, to carry her away from the luxurious castle that was now her home—away from the servants, the delectable meals, her knave of a husband. He couldn't say it.

Was he the hero or the villain? Was he Sir Tornau or the Baron of Cornhal? He was neither, he decided, because they were both the silly dream-beings of some dead Bienvalian scribe, a man who heard a tale from another man who heard a similar tale. And when that tale reached the scribe in question, it was embossed upon a vellum, turned into an immortal lie—or merely an outdated truth. And the scribe sealed it away with his other dream-beings, all of whom were smashed between two leathern boards and squeezed into one united dream-being by the pressure of the book hinges. That *one* was the definition of Hero. It was a term Gale had so rarely used despite its frequency amidst the many pages. Outdated truth. Morley had realized it. There were no heroes and there were no villains.

Still, there were promises the book fulfilled. There were vodniks in the world, for one—he had seen them and smelled their noxious odors. They were not evil, though, no matter how ugly or vicious they might've been. There could still be jotuns, wicchas, goblins. All unaligned, yet doubtlessly spiteful.

There were also princesses and pretty women who were scooped up into the arms of decisive nobles, carried off to high towers and kept secluded from the foul realms without. Therein rested the problem, he decided. The stories took only an imitation of truth from the outer world. But stories did not live, not in any sense whatsoever. Stories had no agency, so their subjects had no agency. Characters were bound irreligiously to their maker's will; characters were useless reflections in the paramount Reality. To play the role of one was to live as a semblance of a semblance, an effigy of a near-truth.

Morley had vacantly resettled at the edge of Ellemine's bed. He'd said nothing after Anae's queries and thought he heard nothing from her, though she had been speaking, berating him. All the same, Anae was now sobbing softly by the stitched curtain.

He stepped over, afraid to touch her, to ignite the revulsion she surely felt. Instead, he muttered softly to her, "I can't tell you why I'm here. Both because I'm ashamed and because I don't know what spurned me. It was the voice I used to tell you about, if anything. The one which ordered me to kiss you back, up in the stables during our first night. The one I heard when Gale was fighting and when I stole from the Reineshir brewers on my way here." He paused, strangely uncertain about what exactly he was trying to say.

"I'm sorry," he said. "The blame can go to nothing else."

She turned to him; he saw that her tears had already dried. He puzzled over how much time might've passed since she entered. Five minutes? Ten?

"That's you, Morley," she asserted. "That's your voice, your own. It's the part of you that's been imprisoned since the day you learned self-control."

The lad thought back—or tried to think back beyond the limits of his memory, to the short period in which he ceased his post-infantile babblings for Gale's sake. The idea made sense, he thought. Or perhaps he was just too easily convinced.

"It's your volatile side. You've been holding it back for the good of those around you, as you think. We all have it—I have it, Felix has it, everybody. It compels us toward stupidity and passion and intense want." Morley still didn't believe her but kept his mouth shut. "It also keeps us from thinking ably. You're not here to join Felix's army, are you?" He shook his head at her. "You're here to see me. Then what?"

Never before in his life did he feel such immense idiocy. He confessed: "Then we escape together. Hide out in the wilderness. For however long it would take for your husband to stop searching for you."

"Then what?" she said again. No words came to him. "That's as far as you went, isn't it? Like something out of a chevalier tale." Morley blushed. The biting edge that dominated Anae's voice vanished then with a scoff.

"I don't even know if it's right of me to chastise you. You've seen so little of the world, yet you've read so much about its people. But did anyone ever tell you that writings are hardly more than the fantasies of the writer, that stories are the painted idylls of what the storyteller had once witnessed? When he was my teacher, Mester Alherde made sure to press this truth into me like a pin. I wished only to read from *Chevaliers of Bienvale* when I was younger, much like yourself. Only I learned to resent it after three years of living in Reineshir. After seeing how hideous the real world can be."

Morley chose not to share his opinion: Istain the Trader loved Reineshir while Yeva thought it was little more than a few roads surrounded by refuse; Arrin thought fish smelled and tasted worse than sheep piss while everyone else in Egainshir was fond of the flavor. Gale had seen so much in his lifetime, had so many withheld thoughts connected to its multitudinous events; Morley had lived most of his life in the barrenness of Werplaus and only occasionally chose to hide his feelings.

Experience—with all its quantities and qualities—was a fickle thing. Perspective, meanwhile, was the universal fibber, the force that convinced the beholder of *rightness*. But perhaps it was good that Anae still possessed this one naivety. Morley, in that significant moment, no longer had any yearning for her.

"—and though I might sound petty to you, I don't quite feel compelled to go from eating two full meals a day to living off mushrooms and rabbits for weeks at a time."

122

She'd been talking all the while, he assumed, but now her rant was coming to an end. Morley picked up his greatsword from the bed.

"I'm sorry," she concluded. "I'd warned you when we were still together, I'd told you countless times. This town, this castle. I have to be here."

"It's getting late," he said abruptly, clearing his throat, knowing well it was hardly the evening.

"The feast will be ending soon, if it hasn't already." She stared at Ellemine's broken cup, daring not to meet the lad's eyes. "Do you want me to show you out?" Morley did not reply. "IThere's a secret way. I'd rather not arouse suspicion. And I still trust you. As a loving friend." The halfelev nodded as Anae finally rested her troubled gaze on him. She allowed another quick smile.

"I'm ready whenever you are," Morley said laggardly. "Damme." Under better circumstances, they both would've felt the humor of his jest, he knew.

"Just 'Anae' will do."

She lifted her skirt and made for the door, opened it, entered the hallway observantly. She beckoned Morley to her. When he came into the corridor's fading light, he brought up his hood. The pecans he'd stored there fell over his face and onto the floor. They stood there in a brief, baffled silence as the nuts tittered over the hardwood.

Then Anae pressed a hand over her mouth to contain her quivering grin. "Still as full of surprises as ever," she said, bustling over to the downward stair, the one Morley had seen the aproned scullion dismounting earlier. Anae made her way down, staying several paces in front. At the bottom was a second hall, similarly designed and lit only by two oiled braziers.

She took his free hand—the bandaged one, which she otherwise ignored—and led him through one of the closer doors into a long kitchen filled with distracted cooks, all scrubbing their cutting boards and crockery. From there, they flew down another flight of steps into the castle buttery, a dark aisle of shelved kegs and casks. At the opposite end were two gigantic barrels resting in brackets of stone and timber; the lids of each were almost as tall as the baffled halfelev. Anae fiddled with a contraption locked into one of the foremost hoops; then, with astonishing ease, she pulled back the full head of the barrel. It was a door, the latches of which were set into the chime.

"This leads down to the beach," she said with a gesture. As Morley inched into the gaping passage, Anae stuck her arm around his nearest elbow. He wondered if she did so out of kind affection or safety, as the path forward was properly abysmal. Either way, they entered and halted at a soft and barely perceptible rail. Morley rested a hand on the wood and followed it to yet another stairwell, the most treacherous of them all.

"We're under the castle now," Anae said, "if you can believe that. Roberrus had hundreds of foundations and scaffolds built up against a giant pointy rock—what are they called, again?"

"Sea stacks," the lad muttered.

"That's right," she said. Her tone, Morley thought, reminded him of Amarta when she encouraged her child to stand up on his own. She went on: "Aethelings on the continent like to build their castles on big mounds of dirt. They're called moats, I think. But Roberrus wanted his to be higher than any other, so he piled up tiers of gravel and stone. And he kept this one shaft open for some reason, maybe as an escape route. I can only hope no one locks it back up behind me while we're down here. Or else I'll have to go through town and up the hill."

"You used to always go through town." A plank cracked under his heel.

"Well, Wallenport is different. I don't know many of the commoners here, but they all know me. I don't trust them yet." Cautious as ever, they continued down into the nebulous rumbling darkness.

"So…" she started, squeezing his arm tighter. "You're the son of Damme Ellemine. I'm sure she told you."

Quite bizarrely though somehow appropriately, Morley had already forgotten about his alleged mother. "Yeah," he answered her. "When did you find out?"

"When I stepped into her chamber and saw her kiss your head," she said, taking up that long-missed conversational tone the young man once fell in love with. She spoke now as if they were walking down a street in Reineshir. "But I pieced it together weeks ago. You and Felix are the only halfelvs I've ever met. And Ellemine told me Felix isn't her only child, that the rest of them are elsewhere. And since you never knew anything about your mother—what her name was, what she looked like—I guessed. It became somewhat obvious after a few conversations. She's an outlandish woman for certain, but Ellemine and I are very close already. I asked her one day about childbirth and whether or not she would ever

124

want to go through with it again. She said she couldn't even if she wanted to because she's already given birth four times. Did you know that purekin elev women can only ever have four children before their bodies—"

"I don't suppose I'll ever see her again," Morley interrupted. "It's strange. There are so many things I could've asked her if I was more prepared. Instead, I just listened to her talk about portents and stars and a load of other things I'll never understand. It's like I'm a character from a chevalier tale who wandered into the wrong story. I rarely thought about my parents over these past years. Then one of them found me and…"

He had a clear idea of what he wanted to say: "I don't think I care." As he considered his next words, another notion invaded his active thought. A detail of Anae's own curiosities.

She had been wondering about childbirth.

"Are you going to be a mother soon?" he asked. The young woman huffed.

"Maybe," she said. "Not soon, I don't think. I told Felix I'm not ready to go through with the struggle of bearing a child. He accepted that. He told me he wasn't ready to be a father." Somewhere under them, a beam whined and creaked. "He's very good to me, much better than I expected. Better than the princes and aethelings we used to read about."

"I saw you earlier at the banquet," he stated. "You didn't seem very happy." Anae paused awhile. "And I saw Felix lean over and say something to you. I thought he was unhappy with your attitude or…I dunno."

"He said, 'Try the sprat with lemon.' Or something like that."

"You didn't see me," the lad mumbled.

"I didn't need to. I knew it was you." Morley's face reddened at this and he nearly missed the edge of the next planked step. "I saw, out the corner of my eye, an aspirant coming to our table. I know your height, country boy. And I know the height of your sword. I didn't have to look right at you to know brave, brave Fitzmorley had come to rescue me."

Though the explanation was feasible, Morley didn't believe her: she must've looked right at him, then averted her scrutiny elsewhere. "Be careful here," she added. "Some of the steps wobble and are close to breaking." They surpassed the mentioned section of stairs in quietude. Sure enough, several of the boards beneath them faltered under their weight. "It'll be a very unpleasant day when those planks break under me. Or anyone, really."

Morley made no reply. He no longer had any desire to exchange words with her. To his own shock, he yearned for their separation. However, and as expected, the silence couldn't be maintained.

"What's next for you?" she asked, a touch of worry in her voice.

The lad summoned an easy lie. "I'm going back to Egainshir," he said. "Where else would I go?"

"The Stead? Laisroch County maybe? I wouldn't be surprised if Felix rode out to check on his aspirants before the year's end. I imagine he'll be looking for you, believe it or not. You're one of only four others he called to his table, you know. During all the previous banquets, he only bothered to make a short speech near the end. Then he dismissed everyone back to their homes. But anyway, desertion is a crime."

"Won't be the first one I've gotten away with, Bertriss girl. And I'm sure he won't search for me in Werplaus." At this, Anae grunted.

"Suit yourself." Then, as if intending to impress or provoke her old lover, she said, "Your father lives in Westley, you know."

Really, this statement bore only one small intrigue: the breadth of disclosure between Ellemine and her daughter-in-law.

"I know," Morley replied, "she told me. But I don't really care. Gale was a good enough father and Amarta a good enough mother. I'm sick of aethelings and dammes after this trip north."

The lie glistened with venom. He almost regretted making the comment the way he did. They passed through a small beam of scarlet light, a shimmering disk from the beach and its skyline. Many more rays, all of variant size and shape, lit the rest of the rotting stairwell. The young man fixed his eyes on his ever-descending feet, not daring to look over the face beside him.

"Very well," she muttered, all kindness leaving her. A twinge of compunction. If he were less kind, the conversation would've ended there. She would then abandon him on the beach and they would never meet again. Already, Morley knew he'd rather not live with that memory.

"I'm sorry," he said. "I often forget you're a damme of the court yourself. I never really thought of you in that manner, not even when we first met."

"I know what you meant." Their toes touched hard, gritty ground. An astonishingly confined tunnel was just ahead. "We'll have to squeeze through there. Come."

She continued sidewise into the tight stone burrow, immediately dirtying her gown. Morley followed, entering the space with less difficulty. Less than ten strides away was a lath of driftwood wedged between the rocks. Radiant needles pierced through its orifices. Then—partially reminding the lad of Yeva—Anae shoved her body twice into the makeshift door, loosening it with the second push. She removed it with both hands and continued on through the latter half of the egress. At its end, the infinite gloaming of the sea yawned before them, its tight bank covered over with giant khalfrey crabs, detritus, and globs of washed-up jellyfish. Anae placed the lath down against the sheer wall of green-grey stone behind them. Morley breathed the salt air, sticking his sword's point into the sand.

"You'll have no trouble climbing a few boulders up to the pier," Anae told him, pointing south along the strand to Wallenport's docks. "And you'll have even less trouble getting through the harbor area at this hour if you have your sword ready."

The lad nodded, rubbing the flat pommel with his thumb. Only the swishing of waves could be heard before a loud bell chimed out from the port. "Halfway to the hour of Tierles," Anae said. "I must hurry back." Regardless of the supposed urgency, they stared at one another, equally unsure.

This was the end, the fitting closure he'd wished for since the day of her abduction. Or the day of her betrothal.

"Must you?" he said. Anae forced a smile and approached him. She gently placed her hands against his jaw and kissed him. After separating her head from his, she inclined and kissed him again—less pleasant this time, as a bit of her flaxen hair had been windswept across her lips. She stepped back toward the hidden passageway.

"I won't forget about you, Morley," she avowed. "And I *will* always love you. You know that."

"I'm sure you will and I'm sure you won't," he answered uncertainly.

Then she was gone.

The halfelev traipsed along the beach.

He thought about the girl, of course, making the ascent back to the great hall. No, back to her bedroom. Back to her richly adorned husband, his half-brother. No, never mind all of that—Felix wasn't his brother. He had no brothers. And Felix wasn't richly adorned. He was naked, awaiting Anae under their bedsheets. She'd give him a real smile.

They'd talk awhile, conversations about their day, about the new recruits, about the state of the island—they had so many damn things to talk about. And they could lie in bed together, undressed, and call upon their staff if they so wanted. Servants could bring them food or wine if they wanted it.

Let them have their freedom. They're both happy with it. So why couldn't he be happy for them? Because there was nothing for him to be happy about. Because he was selfish, he thought. And why not?

For the first time in his life, Morley thought about ending his misery. He could run into the ocean and keep swimming until all land was out of sight. He could use the blade to slice open his neck, bleed to death on the beach. Then Anae would find him the next time she decided to go for a solitary walk.

Pale, limp body. She'd cry and cry and cry. She'd see what she'd done. She'd take the blade and do the same. Felix would be without a wife. Maybe he'd kill himself as well.

He remembered Anae's words from earlier: "That's you, Morley. That's your voice, your own." She was probably right, at least insofar as it was his *voice*. Whether or not it was motivated by stupidity or passion, that mystery had yet to be resolved. So little time in Wallenport and already she'd become such a wise woman.

She was fond of her new teacher, her mother-in-law, Damme Ellemine. But was Ellemine really wise? He tried to compare her to somebody else of sagely character. And no more than a minute later, Morley questioned wisdom itself.

What was it more akin to? Intelligence? Moderation? Who was wiser, Gale or Semhren—the man who said little or the man who said much? Perhaps it was the mean between the two: the individual who said enough. If that was so, then Sethan was wiser than the two, as was Elmaen, Istain, and Yeva. Yet, none of them had ever expressed much profundity. Maybe, Morley thought, he was himself the wisest person he knew.

If that was so, why was he contemplating self-destruction? Surely, that couldn't be a mark of wisdom. Although, he hadn't yet performed the fatal act. Why not? What prevented him? Ceridwen, ever devout, had once told him about the afterdays. If a person was good all throughout his or her life, then the spirit—"the part of the body that's *you*," as she always described it—is transported beyond earth and Reality, carried off to an endless mass of spirits, like a stormcloud formed up of all the experiences ever experienced, a nimbus of the world's knowledge.

This never interested Morley, so he didn't bother to believe in it—nor did he have a care to dedicate himself to its omnipotent overseer, the All-Being. Prayers and rituals were a waste of time, he thought, time that could be spent *not* thinking about death.

Why do you continue to live? All this pain is far worse than death. Get it all over with.

There was a simple answer, the young lad realized, a very simple answer. A life without faith was little more than a march to the grave, he agreed. But to surrender the self to an unrealistic deity—in the fashion of writers and the committal of their scrawlings—that was hardly different from shackling one wrist to a brick or log or something of like heft. Without the burden, life would be so much easier, so sinless, happier.

There it was. Happiness.

That was the only thing Morley needed to put his faith into: the prospect of happiness. His only love was out of reach, his parentage was superficial and driven only by a half-forgotten ardor—why continue on? Because there was so much more time left, so many more chances to attain satisfaction; because Egainshir was comfortable, filled with loving people; because his new friend awaited him in town and, with him, he could drink and laugh and rollick.

Sethan. He'd forgotten about the archer. The plan was to bring Anae down to the beach and spend the night there together, then meet him back at the inn. What a terrible plan, he thought. He'd not considered that Felix might note Anae's absence before morning. At the very least, if the young damme had been willing to escape with him, she would likely think up a much more suitable withdrawal—and it would no doubt exclude Seth. Reentering Wallenport to gather up some Olford bumpkin she'd never before met would be ill-advised.

Morley found a clear spot of sand and sat down for a time. He then reclined onto his side, then his back, staring up at the emergent stars, less visible above the warm light of the town. Much of the day was spent traveling, he remembered as his legs rejected the idea of standing back up. Seth had woken him at dawn and they'd tramped across five kalcubits of sand. After that, after their entry into Wallenport, after Morley's subsequent infiltration of the keep, there remained the onerous trial of…

He decided not to linger around it. He shut his eyes and strode his mind forward into the morning hours, when he would find Seth and plead for guidance to Westley—though preferably not by way of Sylvan again. He came up with a better route, a more cunning scheme before sleep dragged him down under the soft dust.

Ellemine was coming down the beach, dragging her dress through the ugly tidewaters. Here and there, she halted, picked up a dead khalfrey with one hand, set it back down. The critters sidled off, resurrected. She did this seven times before standing over her son. The elev woman kissed him on the forehead again and placed two solid pieces in his tunic flap. Then, she strode out to sea, out into the yawning ocean. Never to be seen again.

When he woke, the sun had preceded him by several hours. The sky was blue, the ships were drifting about, and the sounds of life had returned to the adjacent harbor. Instinctively, he gripped the forgotten flap: its contents were still there. He removed Ellemine's yet unseen gift.

Two coins, both the color of baked bread, both inscribed with 'Hugon IV' and an engraving of a robed man. They were heavier than copper, than nickel, than the silver piece Istain carried with him.

He replaced them in his flap. And remembered his mother's baffling trick with the daisy head. The lad stood, wiped the grit from Seth's cloak, then trotted off.

*   *   *

When Fitzmorley first learned about mothers and fathers—inordinately late into his life, of course—he had very little curiosity regarding the identity of his parents. Speculating on the behaviors of Tommas, Serryl, and Robi, as a matter of fact, made him care even less. They were just three housemates, as far as he could see, each more or less invested in the good of the community. If that were a proper family, there was hardly anything unique about it.

However, in watching Amarta tend to her infant child, he was stung by the sweetness of motherhood. If Tommas' relationship to Robi were any proof, Gale had essentially been a proper father—a better one than Tommas, even. Amarta was peculiar, almost mysterious. The two of them mourned Gale's death with equal passion on the day of his burial, and she was the first to offer Morley a place to stay, despite already sharing a bed with Ceridwen at the time. Thus, the lad treated her with a son's affection, visiting her whenever his woes crashed down on him.

One morning, hours after waking up between his goats—it had been a miserable night—Morley joined Amarta in her house and helped her bake wheat bread, his favorite. Her yet-unnamed baby slept on the bed opposite the oven. Morley kneaded the dough of their second loaf as Amarta watched the first, browning in the kiln mouth.

"I tried to talk to Yeva," he was saying, "but I just…I didn't know what to say."

"Well, what *did* you say to her?" the baker replied with seriousness. Morley shook his head over the dough, embarrassed. "You didn't say anything, did you? You know, that's worse than saying nothing. If she was crying, as you said, and if she knew you were there, then what would she be thinking?" Morley shook his head. The craft and concept of empathy, which Amarta had only recently introduced him to, was far out of his grasp.

"I guess she would be wondering why I was there still, watching her. Or maybe she wouldn't even be thinking about it. I don't know. I'm not a girl, I don't know what girls think."

Amarta frowned at him. "In the courts, as they say, the differences between men and women are woven into their speech, their habits—all that," she said, wrapping cloth around one hand and taking up the oven peel in the other. "Out here, where women and men share the workload, where drudgery isn't given just to men and handcrafts aren't left out for women to pick up, there's no reason to choke on differences. Think of Yeva as just another boy, if that helps. Trust me, she's tougher than both you and Arrin."

"If that's so, then why does she favor Arrin over me?" the lad grumbled.

"As I said before, you don't know that for certain. She could've just been jeering at him and Ceridwen last night because she wants what they share. But, to answer you, it could be for a dozen reasons—likeways, there could be a dozen reasons for why she doesn't approach you. Maybe she'd prefer a man who's tougher than her—maybe she'd prefer a woman. You only need to weigh what you know about her, then decide what's realest to you." With that, she steadily extracted the loaf from the oven and let it slide onto the table beside Morley's wad of dough. The lad stopped kneading.

"She isn't shy," he said.

"Right."

"So, if she did like me back, I think I'd know by now." Amarta hummed disagreement at this, then let him continue. "She isn't happy. Not often, anyway. She doesn't talk much, unless prompted to. The only thing I know she enjoys doing is making socks and scarves.

"What colors are they?" she asked.

Morley gave her a strange look. "Green and brown. You know that. It's the only yarn she ever uses."

"Is it the only yarn she ever has?" The boy shook his head, unknowing. "Green and brown dye is cheap in Reineshir, y'know. That's why Istain gets it. Maybe you can convince him to pick up different colors next time. Tell her it was your idea or, better still, present them to her yourself. You see, there's another difference between country and courtly folk. What do they say? 'A gift for a princess is received with a yawn; a gift for a peasant is received with a blessing, and a true one at that.' I think it's supposed to rhyme, but I can't remember the right words. Anyhow, show her she's in your thoughts."

"And what if she doesn't want to be in my thoughts?" he sighed. Amarta picked up his dough with another frown, set it on the peel, and thrust it into the oven.

"All I'm trying to say is it's worth a try. Right?" She set down the staff with a sigh. She then went to the bed across the room and sat on its footboard. Her child slept soundly on his belly.

"You know…" she stared into Morley then, "I knew Gale for five years before he said anything to me, before he even bothered to share his name. When I first moved out here, I only knew him as 'That Man.' He would come with a hood over his eyes and speak to no one but Elmaen, Istain, Reffen, and sometimes Semhren. Whenever he showed up, it didn't matter if I had bread burning or if the rains were picking up. I always stepped out to watch him there. I waited and waited and waited. I think sixteen or so seasons passed us before he chose to throw an eye my way. After that…yeah, it would take another year for him to speak. His visits increased, though. And he watched me every time he came."

Morley peered at his feet as Amarta spoke. He didn't believe her, but yearned to know more. When she paused, he looked up, waiting for her continue. The baker smiled curtly.

"While he was standing with Elmaen by the coops, one day, he pointed to me. They kept chatting for a while, then he left. And Elmaen came to me afterwards and told me 'That Man' thought I was pretty. All I could think was, 'Why didn't he come and tell me himself?' Right? Well, you lived with him all your life. Why do you think he walked away?"

Morley gulped at the thought of Gale, their past together, how it ended. He recollected himself swiftly. "Gale didn't like talking much," he murmured, still fixated on his shoes. "Trust me. It took years for us to have a conversation. And not just because I had to figure out how to speak all on my own through that time."

"And why is that?" the woman asked. "What was he afraid of?"

"Nothing," Morley said without thinking. "Gale feared nothing, not even death. He just wanted to be alone. Sometimes. I think." For the first time in over a year, the lad's mind returned to its most vilified question: Why? Why was Gale his guardian? Why did they live together? Who sent him to the hill-house?

He shook off the weight of the enigma. Nobody knew the answer and that was that. Yeva was the issue at hand, as was Amarta's story. "What did Gale say to you?" he asked. "I mean, when he finally decided to approach." The baker, now gazing over her child, made a strange face, as if she was either about to laugh or cry.

"'Fine kiln you have there. Did you build it yourself?'" She started to chuckle. "That was it. And I thought it was such an odd thing to ask. But I answered all the same. And we spoke awhile after that."

"What about?" He was drawn back to the thought of Yeva, standing alone at the hamlet's well.

"The only thing I knew we both had." She tapped at her temple with a pinky finger. "A distant past." Morley nodded. "Though I thought he was very handsome, I also thought he was the strangest man I'd ever met. I would say something, a long sentence or two, and...after I'd finished speaking, he would not reply. Whole moments passed us by. And he just stared at me. Then, out of nowhere, he'd mumble something else." She laughed again. "I thought he was broken."

Morley felt the caress of relief. It was an odd matter: this unsociable man, a chevalier of The Acquisition, had been the one to teach him language. Sociability. And yet, if Amarta's words sustained any truth, something troubled him. An abnormal internal force so often manipulated his will to show affection.

"Then, one day, he showed up here with a tiny elev boy," the baker continued, redirecting her eyes to Morley. "None of us had been to his house except Elmaen, a long, long while back. But we all knew one thing. He lived alone." She smiled. "Apparently not. Here he was with a wide-eyed lad, a boy who hid behind his guardian's cloak at the first sight of other people."

Morley remembered that first visit well. Never before had he felt so overwhelmed. "Did you think there was another woman in his life?" he asked.

Amarta stood back up and made her way to the oven. "I didn't know what to think," she said, checking the dough. "He handed you off to Elmaen and—"

"Reffen," he corrected her. "He gave me mint leaves. That was the first time I ever tried them. First time I was around anyone besides Gale, in fact."

"Such an odd life you've had," she said, crossing her arms and tilting her head. "Anyhow, he came over here and said your name was Fitzmorley. He said you lived with him. That's all. I asked if you were his son. He said no. And I wondered why he hadn't brought you over to my house, why we needed to be alone." She paused, rubbing her chin and taking a deep breath. "He…didn't want you to know about us. About whatever connection he thought we had. I…he wanted to keep things simple for you. Or he thought you were too young to know—I'm not sure why, really. But he cared about you in a very unregular way. That, I do know."

"I wouldn't have been concerned," the lad said after a pause. "I wouldn't have understood either. But, like most other things in life, I would've anticipated his explanation. Be that as it may…" The lad couldn't help but laugh. "Better for *you* to teach me about love." He smiled at the sleeping baby.

"So," she said the word after another deep sigh. "You're going to seek out Yeva tonight." Morley gulped. He'd already forgotten that she was the reason he came to Amarta in the first place. "And what are you going to say?"

"Nice kiln. Built it yourself?" Neither laughed at the joke.

"Try again," she said. The boy sighed. Amarta's advice from earlier didn't feel entirely helpful. And the interlude on Gale did little more than provide a previously unrevealed detail of the man's life. If that too was meant to be instructive, it chiefly concerned how *not* to approach a woman or girl, as he thought. Once again, Morley looked to the baker's little son.

"Want to go for a walk, Yeva?" he tried. Amarta nodded slowly at this proposal.

"And what will you talk about?"

"Sheep and grass, I guess. The only things we both have," he answered, trying not to sound disappointed with the situation.

He soon left the hamlet's bakery with dulled spirits. As he returned to sit with his goats, he rummaged through Amarta's brief account on meeting Gale. He thought over it until he was unsure of the precise words the woman used. The basic idea was still there, still strange as ever: Gale the Hermit Chevalier came to Egainshir one day, saw a woman he liked, and decided to talk to her—although he wouldn't get around to the last step for another year. When he did, the woman thought he was socially inept. However, she still liked him. Why? It was obvious now.

Women are unconditionally attracted to knights, Morley thought.

That night, the lad didn't bother talking to Yeva, not even after he watched her disappear into Amarta's house. It would've been the ideal place to approach her, he figured, but what was the use? Instead, as he stood by the well, hauling up its small skin for Elmaen's tea, he decided to start avoiding her as much as possible, or at least avoid talking to her if keeping distance was no option. And he did for a time, for as long as he could.

Then, one day, they were minding the sheep together and Morley let slip that his ears were cold. Three weeks later, she presented a woolen coif, made specially for him and his elevi ears. It was dull, mud-colored, and drooped at the back. But it was incredibly comfortable.

They became best friends overnight. And yet, the lad still wanted more.

*   *   *

There was a magnificent crowd gathered in the open area around the church in Wallenport. After dashing through the narrower streets and climbing over an occasional fence—and after losing his way in one or two dead ends—Morley found the beerhouse. To his agitation, Sethan wasn't present, though the barman they'd conversed with was.

"The Olford fellow?" he said in reply to Morley. "He had two more drinks after you left, then he was out the door himself. Didn't say a single

135

word. And he had this strange look in his eye, like he knew exactly what he was doing and had no good reason for doing it. That's all I can say, I'm afraid. Can I get you a pint or a double?" The halfelev kindly refused and left.

True enough, Morley thought, Sethan said he wasn't going to stay there for the rest of the night, but he did agree to return and meet with him—and Anae—in the morning. It was now almost noon, he figured. Did he get impatient? Did he get arrested? Did he simply decide to leave and go back home right after Morley climbed the hill? Mayhaps the cloak didn't mean so much to him after all.

Frustrated and saddened, the lad made his way to the mass outside St. Maguir's Church, where he awkwardly discovered he was one of the tallest men present. The others around him stared for a time—male youths and elders alike, all garbed in simple linens and mantles, some bearing walking sticks and bundles. Confining them, all around the perimeter of the immense courtyard, were women, similarly old and young, and a smattering of workmen. Altogether, it seemed the full populace of Wallenport was present.

A platform was set up before the entrance to the temple and, on it, there stood a line of dignitaries. Several bore familiar outlines; one of them was unmistakably Anae. Next to her was Felix. Next to him, wearing the same colors, was the gentleman called Iacob. Herman was there too, his hands behind his back.

Morley began to move forward through the crowd, which seemed to part before him—the tall, sword-bearing aspirant—without complaint. When close enough, he saw that the woman standing before the line of luminaries was wearing the same black and white robe as the 'priestess' he overheard the day prior, just before Ellemine opened her door and found him hiding in the niche.

Once close enough to hear her, he strained to understand her words. It took another moment for him to realize she was reciting a page from *The Divine Conjecture*—the one with two troublesome words at the bottom of the parchment.

"Oh, that Maker of all," she cried out in the common tongue, "has gifted unto my head and the oculi encased within it the glories and the potentialities of greater glories which Man has yet to pluck from the drifting flames, from the billowing sea, from the wriggling soil and the shivering gravel. And though it was only for an instant, like the dream in the midst of dreams, I knew at once that it was the Beyond. And so from then on I walked the forests slow, I swam the rivers and observed their beds, I climbed the mountains to see above the pines; you see, you see! I had learned to learn, I had come to relish the cognoscible and aesthetical!" And so on.

"Cog-nos-kibble," Morley slowly repeated to himself. "...Ess-tha-tickle." Still yet, he was unsure what either word meant. They escaped him in a flash, though, as he quickly apprehended Anae's empty stare.

They locked onto each other for a time, as the cleric rambled on to her flock. Anae did not smile and did not frown; Morley did his best to reflect her, to show that he'd given up, that he was bound for the old life. Though she did not show it, he knew this pleased her.

There was a vague train of commotion behind him, an incoming collective of "Hey!" and "Watch it!" and "Try it again!" The cleric continued her sermon despite it all. A hand suddenly gripped Morley's shoulder; its owner struggled to take his place at the lad's side. Of course, it was Sethan, complete with bow and quiver. His hair was bedraggled and his tunic was slightly torn across the chest.

"Cloak, please. Thank ye," he said, simultaneously unclasping the brooch and pulling away the hood. "No luck with the girl?" Morley shook his head, allowing his mate to remove the cloak.

"She, ehm...she didn't think it would work. Not so soon after the marriage, at least." He cleared his throat.

"Sorry to hear. We should be goin' afore this one finishes her god poem. May even have enough time fer a few ales, eh? Still got money enough." The halfelev resumed peering at Anae, though she'd directed her eyes elsewhere.

Morley then considered his coins, the paths out of Wallenport, his father and mother, his closest ally, the dangers he'd bested, the vile pit to the south, the jotuns of the coastal cliffs, his yet desired adventure...

"I need to get to Westley," he mumbled to Seth, who was adjusting the longbow back over his covered shoulders.

"Fine by me," the archer muttered back, somewhat to the lad's surprise. "So let's get moving."

"Well..." Morley started, adopting a newfound caution, "wouldn't it be safer to travel with the aspirants? At least as far as Chaisgott or The Stead?"

Seth shook his head. "Ye've forgotten what I told ye, haven't ye? Those roads're dangerous."

"More dangerous than Sylvan?" Seth tilted his head as if he were reluctant yet prepared to say yes. "How could it possibly be dangerous— we'd be hidden amidst an army of hundreds. And after we leave them, we can stalk through the woods if the need arises. And besides, we're both armed. How much more dangerous could it be than the swamplands?"

"My way's quicker." Neither spoke for a time. The cleric's sermon increased in volume.

"You don't have to come with me," Morley reminded. Seth deliberated wordlessly. "But I need to get to Westley. And I've had my fill of vodnik breath."

"Why d'ye need to get there?"

"I'll tell you later. But you'll have to come with me."

Again, Seth took time to speculate on the journey. "Fine, fine. Fine," he soon gave in. "I guess it's fair enough. But let's get a few drinks in us afore the crowd moves on out." Morley, holding up his sword before him, proceeded back toward the main gate with the archer. The aspirants allowed him space to move, just as he anticipated. Glancing down after a few strides, Morley saw that his companion now had a neat pair of shoes.

"I reckon it'll be two or three days to Chaisgott if these sprites're good marchers. Then, I dunno, a day and a half to the Laisroch border if we get ahead o' the asp'rants. Then four or five to Westley if we don't lose our way."

When they reached the end of the congregation, they paused to stretch their arms and legs, then headed off toward the castle's hill. They entered the inn's near-empty lounge and placed their orders for four double-pints—Morley using part of his nickel to pay, which he claimed to have stolen from the castle. The rest he expended on bread and fruit for the road and a late breakfast of boiled eggs and fish.

"By the way, where were you last night?" Morley inquired after the barman left the room. "What were ye gettin' up to?"

Seth didn't have to ponder his answer. "Don't rightly know." He put up his hood and rested his eyes.

"That so?"

"Ye ever try an uforian tincture?" His companion shrugged, though Seth didn't see. "Keep it that way, mate."

138

Chapter IV – Peripeteia

The march to Chaisgott Castle began that same day, just after
Aetheling Felix concluded the church service with a few words of good
fortune and great endurance. The army of aspirants then proceeded out
through the palisade gates and into the shaded lowlands.

Morley and Seth, having sped through the thick dregs of their double-
pints, deftly blended amidst their number. They weren't alone in
attempting this: several impromptu and decently hungover commoners
pursued them after they were over a thousand strides outside the city.
Others, meanwhile—largely ambitious stoneworkers—joined the rabble
just as it passed by the quarryland, few hours into the march.

By early evening, they had only made it as far as the lower slopes, the
northmost border of the Crouxwood. When the five-hundred-strong mob
of recruits was urged to halt for the night before light left the sky, Seth and
Morley bickered for a time—the former pressing his companion that they
should move on immediately. He was tamed when a familiar chubby-
necked man of middle age offered a bowl of potato soup with carrots and
leeks. They rested well.

The next day was rife with setbacks. An intense storm blew down from
the high coast, drenching the forest and muddying the forward trail. The
wheels of two supply carts were consumed by the earth; one of the leading
ridders was thrown head first to the ground when a crack of lightning
startled his horse. When they halted at a sprawling lumbermill—dedicated
to a certain Sir Baldwin—many of the younger men griped about the
weather, already sharing with each other their inaugural misgivings about
life in the military.

Morley, on the other hand, welcomed the clean rain, taking the
opportunity to wash some of the filth from his tunic, hair, and the wound
of his hand. It wasn't half as bad as traversing Sylvan, as Seth surprisingly
agreed.

The march stopped early in the evening so the men could take time in
setting up makeshift canopies or tents. Few succeeded. Others yet
ventured away from the main encampment to occupy a cluster of
abandoned rustic huts, so recently concealed by a wall of young pines.

Morley woke twice in the night's latest hours, believing he saw
movement further past the brush. Deluded by his restless mind, he

assumed the figures were vicious wilders returning to their homes, slaughtering all who slept within before bounding back into the woodwork. His only means of abating this little fear, oddly enough, was to remove one of the coins given to him by Ellemine and rub its rough surface until sleep overtook him again.

*　　　*　　　*

On the day Fitzmorley first saw the Crouxwood's border up close, the day he first helped Tommas with wood-gathering, he was introduced to something perhaps equally as alien as the forest.

At the end of that day, he bundled up his sticks and for a short time assisted in loading up the rest of the space in Istain's wagon. The older man had successfully sold away all his goods, acquiring fresh and dry meats, plenty of grain mash, feed for the animals, extra vegetables, three small barrels of beer, ingredients for Reffen, and some other supplies both necessary and unnecessary. They all headed back home.

"How're things in Reineshir?" Tommas asked as the last of the sun was drained from the fields. "You get to see Meggs or Bayette over there?" He added a nudge to this.

"Not with you two gents waitin' out here," the squat man replied. His voice always jiggled along with the skin under his chin. "They'd keep me in all night and you'd be forced to sleep out in the cold."

Fitzmorley, who was sitting uncomfortably against a bag of barley, piped up. "I think I could do that. It's nice in there—all the leaves make a nice sound when the wind passes through. Back in Egainshir, it just howls. Like it's hollow or something. It's got nothing to brush up against."

"Feels good to me, right Istain?" said Tommas. The trader shrugged and the yoked varken-ox moaned. "Nudd here thinks so. Anyway, I guess I've forgotten how far Reineshir is from us. Only been there once in my life, back when Serryl and I passed out of Olford." His stomach gurgled thunderously.

"Hey boy," Istain twisted his head back to the wagon bed, "that basket there, pass it on over to us. And take a bit for yourself, o' course."

Fitzmorley searched the stock around him until he found a familiar wicker basket, originally used to hold a mass of wildflowers for the Reineshir dyers. Inside was soft bread, a loaf of which had been previously cut, revealing a dough mixed with raisins. He took a hunk and passed the rest over to the men at the front, then began plucking out the beads of dry fruit.

Chewing away, he surveyed the filled wagon again: though the land's light was nearly gone now, it was easy enough to tell that there were more items than they left Egainshir with. Gale had taught him a bit about trading and how certain things were more valuable than others—a sheep, for instance, was much more valuable than a sack of wool—but this seemed more complicated. Perhaps the rules of trading were different in Reineshir. Regardless, he inquired.

"Ah, well," Istain began with a chuckle, "for one matter, they don't have too many sources for crab or salmon round town. And they've got very few sheep after Gertruda and I bought out the healthier yews way back. And their apothecarist doesn't have half o' Reffen's talent. A lot of their stock is given away cheap, like the lettuce and onions, since they have so many of them. Keep them around for too long and they rot away. The grain and feed they have in surplus, too. As for the rest…"

There was a vague jingling as the trader tossed a leather pouch over his shoulder. Fitzmorley caught it deftly and opened it: inside were small round pieces of metal. Most were of a brownish rusted hue; the rest were of a greyer sheen. One near the bottom was particularly shiny.

"That's Egainshir's treasury right there, you might say," Istain continued as the lad fingered through the pieces. "The pretty one is silver—you'll know that when you see it. They call it an argen on the continent. Wasn't hard-earned or anything, though. Found it outside the Bertriss manor, a tiny section of it pokin' out the dirt."

"Really?" Tommas sounded surprised. "Pass the bag on up here, I wanna see." Fitzmorley did as requested, resuming his dinner. Tommas found the coin and held it up to the dwindling light.

"True as the day, friends," Istain continued. "It'd been there a long while, someway. Guess the busybodies of Reineshir are too bemused in their work. Nobody has the time to watch their feet. Nowadays, I make sure to walk round the Bertriss gates every time I visit. Mayhaps I'll find a bit o' gold one of these days. A big fat aureon."

"Is that better than silver?" Fitzmorley asked.

Istain laughed. "It is, boy. One bit o' gold is worth twenty-five o' those silvers there. Usually only kings and high lords have gold."

"What can they do?" the youth pressed.

"Why, they can be used to buy things, o' course."

141

"Yes, but what can they *do*?" There was a hush. The lad went on: "You can make clothes with wool. You can eat fish and bread. You can treat sickness with medicines and make work easier with tools. But what do little bits of metal do?" Tommas looked over his mate beside him. Apparently, the lumberman didn't know the answer either.

"They buy things," Istain said again, as if an explanation was unneeded. "That's all. You can get anythin' with it, anythin' at all. Foods, favors. It never rots or sours. If you don't have stuff to trade, you use money." Tommas nodded, then ceased the movement abruptly. The varken-ox flatulated.

"What if," the lumberman began, pointing up with his finger in mimicry of Semhren, "a man has a sack o' lemons, but won't take yer money in exchange for it? He'll only take a sack of oranges, same in amount."

"Well, if you still want the lemons, go buy some oranges." The trader sniffed and coughed once.

"What if ye find an orange seller and he only takes sacks of lemons in exchange for his oranges? Nothin' more, nothin' less."

"Yeah," Fitzmorley jumped in. "And what if all the orange sellers in the world live somewhere far away?"

"Well, then lemons and oranges are unfortunately right outta your reach, then. Better yet, use your money to buy a ship and sail to Orangeland. Or Lemonland. Or trick the lemon seller with a bag o' fake oranges made from clay." He chuckled, but Tommas and Fitzmorley weren't finished.

"What if ye only have loads o' useless things that nobody wants to buy?" said Tommas.

"Well, if Semhren's available, get him to argue their value."

"What if you find yourself in Reineshir and have no items to begin with?" said Fitzmorley. "Nowhere to sleep, nothing to eat. Naught."

"Well, see if someone"ll take your service—whatever it is you do best."

"What if you have no talents and a broken leg?" the lad threw in.

"Well, then you're one unlucky pissant aren't you!?" he shouted. The three of them chuckled. "Might as well be a storyteller, eh?" Istain added.

*   *   *

By the morning hours, the previous day's downpour turned to a mist-heavy drizzle and the weather's increments of the proceeding hours were no worse than a dreary chilling fog.

Night fell and the commanding officers—twelve mounted ridders in all, each of whom made a show of never stripping off their chainmail—drove their torchlit army on into the darker hours, reaching the base of Chaisgott's hill before twilight. This was problematic for the archer and the halfelev, as they'd planned to depart from the company as soon as they reached the obscure ringed keep. Now, after a full day of marching without interruption, they were just as exhausted as all the others. Still, they resolved to move away from the rest of the aspirants, creeping off into the treeline until they escaped all possible illumination. They slept amidst the wet ferns and woke at dawn, then bounded onward until the road was again in sight.

That day, the pair mostly avoided the trail until Seth was sure they had surpassed The Stead, which he claimed was less than a kalcubit to the south or perhaps southeast. Relieved, they slowed for a few hours and the archer unfurled his new bundle, revealing a load of cheese, vegetables, and dried fish skins he'd stolen from the other aspirants during the exodus. They decided to rest up for the remaining day and treat themselves to a much-deserved though conservative supper.

At the start of the following day, the grassy path brought them to the limits of the Crouxwood, to the steady cant of Laisroch's highlands. It had taken four days to get out of Sivliére County.

During that same day, though, Morley began to question the guidance of his companion, who assured him their route was more than just an abandoned lane set down by the island's first Bienvalian visitors, the ridders who challenged the jotuns. Seth expressed his ignorance over this little outdated truth, so the halfelev shared the account as well as he could remember, though Gale had only recited the tale a handful of times. And his version was a secondhand retelling from Sir Chaisgott.

By dinnertime, Sethan seemed to have developed his own doubts in regards to the halfelev: as he put it, "How in hell did this Sir Gale know both Chaisgott and Roberrus and all the others? And who in hell sent ye to live with him?"

"I've told you already," he answered. "The Earl of Westley and Damme Ellemine. My parents. I only just found this out when we were in Wallenport."

"At what point? I thought ye said ye were caught and had to fight yer way out. Was that all afore or after ye found the cash ye stole?"

"I was caught first," the lad lied. "When running off, I ducked into a room and met my mother. She told me everything. And she redirected the guards when they showed up at her door. I took the nickels from her table while she spoke to them. Then she showed me a secret way out. Though I had to jump out a window."

It *was* all a bit unbelievable. But at least it was far less humiliating than the true event.

"Did ye really sneak inside Sivliére Castle? Or did ye just go fer the feast, then have a nice walk along the shore and make up more stories?" Seth questioned.

Morley grabbed for a quick escape. "Have you ever actually used that bow?" he retaliated. "Or do you just lug it around with you wherever you go and pretend to be fearsome?" This was ignored. "I don't need you to believe me—I barely believe it myself. But I need to find out if what she told me is true. Wouldn't you want to see your own father if you found out where he lives?" Sethan had told Morley of how his father left home when he was an infant. The archer again did not provide an answer.

That night, they helped themselves to half their remaining potatoes and slept under a lip of rock jutting from the cloud-capped hillside. Once he was sure Seth was asleep, Morley again removed one of his coins and held it up in the silver moonlight, contemplating its mysterious origin, its undiscovered applicability. Its value too, if it weren't one of the fabled aureons.

After leaving the faded path the next day and cresting almost a dozen hazy slopes, they spotted something sitting before the island's coastal cliffs, solid against the shrouds of the ocean: a tall black cylinder emanating fumes from its base and topmost crenels. Boulders and ebon contours littered the ground before it like acorns from a tree. Indeed, the visage was so mystifying that Morley first presumed it to be the source of all the surrounding fog. They stopped awhile to inspect it from their high vantage and, after some time, they discerned a collective of divagating bodies— ridders, Seth proposed, as they were all adorned in cloaks, tabards, and trousers. No armor, though, so perhaps he was mistaken.

"Think we should go down there, ask for a bit of food and drink to take south?" the lad asked. He then facetiously added, "Or will they notice you, the most wanted man on Sarcovy?"

"If they're ridders at all, they're ridders o' Laisroch," he explained. "Doubt they'd catch the notice. But just in case, here. Put on my cloak." He unbrooched his cape, twirled it off his shoulders, and flung the fabric over Morley's head. "Reckon if they know my name, they'll know my look. Fits ye better anyway, so they won't think ye stole it."

The lad didn't understand, though he didn't complain. He'd been shivering for the past two hours.

"Should we say we're aspirants from Wallenport?" he asked.

"Why would two asp'rants be out here in the middle o' the highlands?" said Seth, slipping the longbow back around his torso.

"We'll say we got lost…on our way to Westley. We're tryna deliver a message to Westley. How's that, eh?"

"What's the message?" They both drew up their justifications in silence. Seth was the first to speak: "We could say Felix sent us. He needed someone—or sometwo—to go speak with the earl. That's why ye wanted to get there, anyway. We're sent to tell Michel that his aetheling needs to see him and right quick. And so he sent us and we got lost."

"Fair start," Morley affirmed, pulling up the cloak's hood. "But why does Felix want to see him?"

"I don't know—why would they bother to ask that?" said Seth.

"Because they're tasked with watching over a wall of fog, that's why. They're bored out here, they must be. They'll sap us of everything we know about the happenings outside Laisroch. I would do it if I still lived in Werplaus and someone stopped by my house."

"And how d'ye know *they'll* do the same?" Seth seated himself on a stone buried in the soil.

"I don't," Morley said, "but I'm good at guessing. Besides, there's no harm in preparing ourselves for a case like that."

"Why don't we just tell them we didn't get the details o' the message. Or that it's none o' their business? It's a message fer the earl, not them."

"Because that's less believable, Seth." He stuck his sword in the ground. "And probably rude."

"It's duty is what it is," the archer retorted. "What'll a bunch o' ridders respect more? The pair of asp'rants who toss away their discretion or the pair of asp'rants who…" He trailed off, as if finally realizing he had nothing to lose. "Why did ye want to go down there again?"

"Food and drink." At this, Seth tossed a dismissive hand toward his mate.

"Plenty o' tarns to drink from out there. And plenty o' reindeer to throw some arrows at."

"I still have some money left," Morley pressed on. "Why bother risking a bad hunt when we can just buy what we need?"

"Why bother exposin' ourselves to a flock o' watchers when we could keep on our way to—"

He was hindered by a sharp whistle. Morley snapped his head to the tower: a man in a white coat was resting against a boulder near its steps. He was waving up at them. The archer and the halfelev searched one another.

"Still want to get moving?" Morley said.

The other sighed, getting up from his seat. "Too suspicious," he mumbled hurriedly. "Might as well head down. After you." At that, Morley threw a corner of the cape over his opposite shoulder, held it with the flat of his blade, then scampered down.

In their approach to the tower, the lad saw that many of the indistinguishable objects he'd spotted from above were naught more than emptied or sealed containers. A set of fresh barrels were huddled together near a cart; and closer to the cliff's edge was a graveyard of disused wagons and wheelbarrows, beside which was a lumber pile covered over with linens.

Eight men were present, as far as Morley could tell, and only one was active, splitting logs on a flat soil-consumed slab. The rest were gathered around elevated fire pits—repurposed cauldrons, he soon identified—conversing with cups at hand.

The man who had beckoned them was alone, closer to the tower's lambent entrance. Much like the others, he had on an undyed tabard with a hoodless cloak; unlike the others, he wore a blue liripipe over his head, the tail of which drooped down around his neck. He was unarmed, though his glower was enough to fend off a vodnik.

Once Seth and Morley were close enough, he ordered them to stop, soundlessly upraising one hand. He glared into both of them without speaking, without so much as glancing at their weapons. Seth prodded the halfelev with the tip of his bow.

"Hello," Morley started timidly, forgetting the bravado he so recently utilized outside Sivliére Castle. "I'm—We're…" He tried again. "My name is Morley van Werplaus, this here is Sethan van Olford. We're two ridder aspirants. And we bear a message. It's, um…It's for Aetheling Felix—er, it's *from* Aetheling Felix. And it's intended for Earl Michel." He stopped there. The man in white raised an eyebrow. Seth poked a second time. "And we're lost. We've lost our way there." Seth came in before he could continue.

"We're hopin' to buy some supplies fer the rest o' the journey there." He then unhelpfully included, "This one's got the cash fer it." Morley could hear Seth sniffing and rubbing his nose.

The man before them had waded through a variety of contemplative expressions since the halfelev started talking: he tightened and scrunched his lips, blinked sluggishly, knuckled his cleanshaven chin. At the mention of money, he took a deep breath.

"How much?" he said, his voice disarming and fair. Morley shrugged tiredly.

"Just a few coppers, nothing much.

"Then we don't have much to give you," the man said. "Aside from two loaves of bread and a cup you two can share." He traced a finger around his mouth, scrutinizing the pair. "What's this message you carry for Earl Michel? Or Aetheling Felix, or whomever you're carrying it to?"

Morley could feel Seth's expectant eyes burning through the hood and the mop of hair at the back of his head. He stuck with what he had, lowering the claymore's point back down to the ground.

"Aetheling Felix wants to meet with Earl Michel. He wants to talk about recruitment. And he wants to do it within his own keep."

"What about recruitment?" the man countered without so much as a blink. Morley faltered for an answer, juggling between Seth's preference for covertness and his own bid of authenticity.

"Well," he improvised, "The Stead has recently taken in about five hundred recruits from Wallenport. Of course, I didn't get the message right from Felix—*Aetheling* Felix…but from a ridder in his service. I believe the aetheling wants to speak with Earl Michel about getting men from Westley or, um, or the area around it."

He was relieved to see that the man in white was peering intensely at Seth. He could picture the archer behind him, pale, his eyes nervously swiveling about. Morley continued, now more confident.

"Not quite like the ridders of the old days, eh? I, ehm, I suppose Sarcovy doesn't have enough people for Aetheling Felix to do a conscription. He just wants to make ridders out of every able man he can reach." He unconsciously tapped his blade with a toe, pointing over his shoulder. "We were chosen to go because this one has a brother in

147

Westley, so he mostly knows the way there. But, you know. All this fog makes for hard navigating."

"What's your brother's name?" the ridder inquired, somewhat randomly. When Seth didn't say a word, his companion again filled in.

"Sieger. Another Olford fellow."

"I see. Who gave you the order, what was the ridder's name?"

Morley panicked and spoke too soon. "I…" He rifled through a list of names, but resolved to the safest answer. "We never received his name. He only said the message was from Felix—*Aetheling* Felix. But the man had a horse and armor, so he…I assumed he had the authority."

The man in white stared for a time, biting his lip. He then stood—revealing his substantial height—and began to slowly step away, back toward the firelit entrance to the tower.

"Wait here," he said. The tone he used made the lad's heart sink: he sounded unconvinced, even frustrated. Seth shuffled to his side.

"And now?" he muttered impatiently. "Should we just get outta here while he's gone? Nobody else heard us, they'll just think we've been dismissed—look." He nodded to a cloud now rolling along the base of the hill they descended earlier. "What d'ye say? Should we get? Eh?"

This time, Morley was the one to freeze up with indecision. Before he could even give so much as a delaying hum of hesitation, the ridder reappeared at the top of the tower's bricked stairs. Another man emerged, treading cautiously down the wet steps behind the first. He was vested in the same tabard but had on a heavy mantle of fur. He was greyer than the other, with a frosty beard and stubbly bald head—which proceeded to cover with a rabbit hide cap.

"Your names?" he asked while still walking in their direction. Morley repeated what he said to the first ridder without the slightest change of articulation. "Right. Can you describe this ridder who gave you the message?" Seth and Morley turned to each other—with a mutual realization of how conspicuous the motion made them seem. The archer, amusingly, was the first to speak up.

"He was helmeted—one of those ones that goes all the way down over the face but still shows the eyes and nose and mouth, yeah?"

The older ridder nodded. "A barbuta," the man suggested.

"Right, that. And he had black bushy eyebrows and a big nose. And there was a wart under the left nostril. And a scar at his jaw."

The first man in white moved closer. His associate, the older man, looked back at him. "Hear that?" he said to the glowering ridder, who gave no response. "Familiar?" The other shook his head and the speaking man readdressed the conspirators. "You sure you can't recall a name? Neither of you?"

"He gave none," Morley said. "Of that, I'm sure."

Then it was quiet. The wind cooed over the lapping of the cliffside waves; the men at their fires grumbled to one another. Then the ridder grunted with displeasure.

"A shame," the older man went on. "Which one of you was the brother of Sieger? You?" He gestured to an apprehensive Seth. "Must be you. Same nose. Give him our regards when you see him. I'm Sir Wortin, Kapitain of Hoerlog—that's the name of this tower, in case you weren't sure. Back there is Sir Willian, my second-in-command." The ridder in question did not move. Morley wracked his mind: where had he heard these names? In *Chevaliers*? "You need food?" the man asked. "Mead? A place to stay for the night?"

"Food will be enough," said the halfelev, "but—"

"We'll stay if ye can spare the space," Seth came in. "Sieger once told me ye have good drink here—might as well try some and settle fer a warm sleep. And might as well wait till the air clears up, eh? Can hardly see the sun through this stuff. Good with that, Morley?"

"Yes," he replied, unsure. "I am."

"Very good," said Wortin with a gentle smile. "One of the others can fetch you a cup and a few hunks of bread. Not much room in the barracks below. But feel free to sleep by the forge right in there." He pointed back at the tower door.

With that, he and Willian receded back inside, both glancing back at their guests. Once the ridders were out of view, Morley and Seth meandered to the refuse pile beside the stacks of wettened timber. The lad, now just as anxious as the archer had been minutes earlier, leaned against a rock and probed the area with his eyes: little had changed aside from the smogging of the upper tower.

"Did Sieger really tell you about this place?" he finally asked.

"Nah," the archer answered.

"I'm surprised you accepted their offer. I would've thought you'd want to get moving as soon as possible." At this, Seth tapped the side of his brow with a curled forefinger.

"Mead, my friend," he whispered with a smirk. "He said they have mead. That's worth a stay fer certain. Ye can do whatever ye want fer the next few hours of lazy light, mate. But I'm gonna have a search round, see where they keep it all, figure out how to get a bit more than we can afford. What d'ye think?"

Morley felt his face curl with disdain. "I think yer a goddamned idiot, Sethan. First you wanted to stay clear of this place, now you wanna risk your neck for some beer?"

"It's mead, not beer," he corrected, oddly taken aback. "And I'm not gonna just grab *some*. I'm gonna filch a full cask if I can." The halfelev gave an imploring cringe. "And again, I don't need yer help to get it—I stole these shoes in Wallenport, after all." He lifted and waggled a foot. "At least, I think I did. And I have no recollection of ever carryin' out the deed. So, go warm yer pink arse by the fire. Don't even think about what I'm up to, right?"

Before Morley could protest, Seth jogged up to the tower and disappeared inside. The lad's stomach twisted uneasily as he swept back the hood of Seth's cloak. A group of ridders around a nearby fire watched him. He moved out of their sight, climbing up several of the slippery rocks embanking the coastal bluffs. There, he sat for a while, trying to see the ocean below through the fog.

After an hour or so, his buttocks were wet and cold, and his confidence had meagerly returned. He got up, pulled the hood up again, and carried himself and his sword to the closest active fire. The men tending to it chatted about the greatsword without much regard for its owner; they only once asked him where he got it. And all the while, Seth circled the tower and the encompassing grounds like a fox around a chicken coop.

The evening sun fell and the ridders yet continued their conversations—all of which were anecdotes concerning other men on Sarcovy, dead or living: Sir Irwyn Briht, the earl's stout pet. Sir Amalic, son of the hertog and 'rooster of the field.' The only name he recognized was Sir Rolle, forefather of Westley.

Soon enough, Seth rejoined his friend and offered half a barley loaf, its open end smeared with honey.

"Got it all figured out," he muttered through a mouthful, choosing a moment when the others were rapt by some elder's tale of adultery and misfortune. "Gonna need to borrow yer sword, if ye don't mind—nothin' bad'll come of it, don't worry." His friend sighed and, without much deliberation, held forth the greatsword, its blade balanced on both his palms. Seth took it by the hilt. "When I get up, go oceanside." Morley narrowed his eyes, confused. "Oceanside o' the tower."

"If you say so," he grumbled.

That time soon came once the sky withered to a sapphirine dark. Seth got up, stretched, and carried the sword into the scarlet glowing mouth of Hoerlog Tower. Morley waited, then left the three remaining ridders around the pit and ventured back toward the lumber pile.

Climbing over it, he stumbled his way over the moist rock, hugging the lowest sides of the tower, planting his feet along the soft stripe of earth between the brickwork and the crags below. He suddenly slipped, gasped, and landed not a second later on a yet unseen outcropping, an ovular platform reaching out from the soil. The lad's heart thumped: he was reminded of the vodniks and the ladder, of the upper hall at Sivliére Castle and the passing interlocutors. And for the briefest wink of time, he again reflected on why he abandoned Egainshir for this misguided undertaking.

He lowered himself against the clinger weeds under the tower. A sodden flapping noise, like a rain-washed flag in the winds, resounded from above. The lad bent back his head to observe its origin. Sure enough, there it was: an inky banner with frayed edges, forgotten or neglected, hanging by a pole affixed beneath a slender window. A second sound then eked from the heavy fluttering of the first, this one more rhythmed and emanant.

"Mate?" came a hushed voice.

"Down here," he said back. Shortly after he gave the indication, Seth appeared above.

"Hope ye didn't fall," he said, stepping down cautiously, "but I *was* hopin' ye'd find this wee spot." Once he reached the bottom, he lifted himself against one foothold and reached up to where he'd been standing above, then pulled down something heavy. "Here's yer's," he grunted, handing over the claymore, its blade now wrapped up to the crossguard with a soft material. "And here's mine." He brought down a cask, exactly like the one Morley stole from Reineshir weeks before. Seth removed his bow and sat, then held the keg between his legs and pried open its loosened head. He sniffed the insides.

"Well?" said Morley.

"Smells like a dream." With that, he lightly tipped the barrel against his face and slurped. He hummed seconds later. "Tastes like a wish granted."

Here." He passed it over and Morley drank of it in the same messy fashion: it was thick, overwhelmingly sweet, and clotted with flavorless clumps that melted against his tongue. After it was all down his throat, a stickiness remained against the back corners of his teeth.

"I hate it," he said, handing it back.

Seth made a spitting noise. "More fer me then, ye bastard." A thoughtful quiet passed over them. "Sorry, didn't really mean that. Just a byword fer 'bugger.' Tough gain this was. The cellar's across from the guards' quarters and both're dug under the smithy. Had to distract the forgeman with this—" he tapped the claymore, "then had to rush down and get the right cask—needed to steal the key to the cellar *and* replace it in time. Then I needed to distract the forgeman again and, ech. Made it without a mess, though. That's the price of hours, I guess." He took another gulp. "The cloth cost a copper. Should keep ye from cuttin' yerself, at least."

"I appreciate it," Morley assured. A voice sounded out, but they disregarded it.

"I say we get to sleep soon and leave early in the mornin'. I'll try and finish the cask—wouldn't mind yer help at that either, though ye hate it— then I'll just throw it into the ocean, never to be seen again."

He gave the keg back to his friend. The lad took it and drank again. It was no better with the second draught, but he did have a feeling it would help him get to sleep or perhaps nudge away his passive melancholy, his surging homesickness.

The voice came nearer, snatching his attention again. It seemed to be floating closer to the mound of disheveled vehicles.

"I'd say it's four days to Westley from here," said Seth, "mayhaps even three if the lowlands have enough passage. The way to Wallenport from Sylvan took a while 'cause the whole way was sand." Still yet, the unknown speaker overhead became more and more lucid with every pause in Seth's speech. "In this case, it's the bastardly hills that make the way onward so tricky. That's about the same hassle as—"

"Do you hear that?" Morley stopped him at last. They both strained to listen: Sir Wortin. He was talking weakly, though audibly.

"And Nicholan will be the next one to drive for wood once Bedweir gets back with the horse. Mortglover will go after him, unless I send him to Reineshir first. If that's the case, Cowen will take the cart. Also, Smid is leaving for Wallenport within the next three weeks, whenever he runs out

152

of hilt pieces. Leather supply is fine, so says Bedweir. And that's all I need to hear from him." Whomever he was speaking to hawked and cleared his throat.

It was at this time that Morley finally began to wonder why the ever-complicated circumstances of his life always happened to place him near conversations that weren't his to hear. Not much ever came of it either, he noticed. And none of these surprise sessions would ever be as terrible or perplexing as the first—the discussion preceding Gale's death.

"Very well," said another voice beside Wortin's.

Seth angled his shadowy head towards his mate. "Willian?" he murmured. With that, Wortin resumed speaking.

"You sure you don't want to go with Smid when he heads out? He won't be staying anywhere near the castle, so he says. Besides, I doubt Felix would spot you. I hear he doesn't sleep around now that he's married. Hell, Hamm says Enriet hasn't been with him since the day Roberrus' corpse was brought ashore."

"Trust me, I have no desire to go back there." The voice definitely belonged to Willian.

"If you say so. Now, what were you telling me earlier? Something about last night? You didn't sleep well, I know that much. Hell, I'd say you slept worse than you did two nights before. Must not be drinking enough before bed." He huffed, shivering, and Willian came in again.

"I don't like drinking before bed, it gives me headaches in the morning. At least, mead and beer does. Chamomile's always been my preference. Not that it does much good anyway." He heaved a deep sigh. "It's the woman again. Or, you know, whatever it is. The thing that speaks and looks like a woman."

"In your dreams, you mean?" The thud of softwood against softwood echoed out into the endless cloud. "Same one from, what, two years back?"

"Three, I'd say. It's different now, but the same images are all there. Just warped, made more real if anything. They've been coming to me for a long time now, mind. Longer than I've known you. They go all the way back to my time with the Sivliéres. That's when it hit me the worst." He gave one spiteful laugh, as if he'd diverted a flood of unpleasant memories.

"Tell me," said Wortin kindly. "Maybe that'll help you sort it out. In a way." Seth tried to hand over the mead, but the halfelev pushed it back without a word.

"I'm no good at description, like I've said," Willian replied. "And I never know where to start, not even when I'm thinking about it on my own. I just get caught up in a mood and I can't attach it to a single exact...I don't know. Impression."

"Well, start with the place. Where are you in the dream?"

"Nowhere I've been before—yet at the same time, it's everywhere I've ever been. I suppose you want an example. It's like the clearing of Reineshir, except all those vile buildings are gone. And the road isn't so much a road as it is a line of barricades. Or it's just the same road, only raised from the ground. And it's made out of the same stonework as Hoerlog's steps. But also, the forestry goes up a steep hill much like the ones in the highlands. There's sometimes a fortress at its peak, a round one like Chaisgott. Often it's in flames but, last night, there was a giant standing inside of it with an enormous tattered sheet over his head. And it was on fire. I woke when he saw me but, when I drifted back to sleep, he was gone. And the fort was in ruins. That's just one of the things there, mind. All the while, my old mester is reading to me from the treetops, sitting there with...an old friend of mine. And there are sheep lying on their backs with legs upraised."

At this, Wortin began to chuckle. "I'm sorry," he said. "Go on."

"There's no use in saying more."

"But what about the woman? Rather, the woman-thing. What role does she play?" Willian did not speak for a moment.

"It used to be frightening," he eventually continued. "When I was a child. An emaciated black figure would be standing around a corner or at the end of a hall. It didn't matter what sort of dream I was having up until that point—she'd be there and I'd wake with a yelp. It was her face. There were only two white eyes, watching me through this slimy hair that dripped from her skull. She disappeared awhile, a few years."

"But now she's back?"

"I think. Except she's now clearer. As if she grew up with me. And she talks to me and I can never understand what she's saying. Or if I do, I forget the words as soon as I wake." He paused. "Hold on. I believe this is our man."

"Looks like it," Wortin strained to say, as if he were lifting himself from a seat. Seth turned to say something, but Morley shushed him after one syllable: he caught the plodding of hoofs and the unmistakable snort of a horse. The archer lifted the mead barrel and took four ludicrously deep gulps.

"Hamm," said one of the ridders, just before a jingling thump heralded the estimable size of the newcomer.

"Sir Willian, Sir Wortin." The voice was young, though its pitch was no higher or lower than the halfelev's own. "Everything still in order on this front?"

"Better than you'd believe, my boy," said Wortin.

"You go first," Willian came in. "What've you found?" There was a crash of hardware, as if the young man called Hamm had dropped a sack of iron rods. One of the ridders drew out a single piece from the metallic collective. "They work fast."

"Surprised me too," said Hamm. "We should have more than enough by mid-Hosten. Besides all of this, though, my sister deserves the most credit. She found the perfect place to hide out, right between Chaisgott and The Stead—and I mean *right between* them. She's been sweet now with a guard at Chaisgott and goes out to visit him every season. Sometimes they leave the keep to find privacy and end up walking westward for hours and hours. But anyway, it's a cave along the coast.

"Real hard to get into but it's too deep to pass up. Goes back underground for half a kalcubit, I'd say, and runs west toward the Lightrun's head. And it's got a big wide chamber filled with water—a huge, huge running reservoir! My sister and I call it the Jotun's Cave, though there's no way a jotun could ever fit down that tunnel." There was a brief hush. "Enriet wonders how you're feeling, Sir Willian, by the bye. She wonders when she'll get to see you again."

"Soon, I hope. You can tell her when you next meet that I'll be around in due time."

Seth propped his head against the grit under the hanging weeds; the halfelev did the same after pulling up the hood of the archer's cloak, leaving one ear exposed.

"So," Hamm resumed, "what's new?"

Wortin cleared his throat. "Two professed aspirants came here this afternoon bearing a message from one of Aetheling Felix's men—as they said. Apparently, Felix wants to host a meeting with Earl Michel." He muttered these words gravely. Or incredulously. Morley couldn't quite tell.

"What about?"

"More ridders," Willian said with a scoff. "Or more recruits. So, if it's true, we can all guess what's in store for Westley."

"He isn't going to ask for all of them…is he?" Hamm breathed with palpable shock. "Is he really that stupid? He just cleared out Wallenport a few days ago—how can he already want more men from the other counties? Really, does he know how many people live here? What does he expect, Westley's whole sodding garrison?"

"He's the aetheling, Hamm," said Willian with a critical edge. "If he wants it for his silly army, he gets it."

"All of this for a war against Taliorano, some say," Hamm added. "It's like something out of a story. Except everyone involved will die if Felix goes through with it. And they won't be romantic deaths." A pause.

Morley was prodded by a curious form of guilt: he had an unsettling feeling that his fib from earlier had fueled an already overwhelming fire. Seth twitched as if waking from a doze, then poured more of the mead down his throat.

"The deaths suffered during Roberrus' wars weren't romantic either, take my word for it," said Wortin. "And those fights were against Piikish islanders. Folk without steel, without proper cavalry." He cleared his throat. "Anyhow, there's something else. One of the aspirants claimed he was Sieger's brother." At this, Seth stiffened and placed the cask between his thighs. "I didn't know he had one, did you?"

"I did," Hamm replied. "But Sieger told me he lives back in Olford, watching over their mother or father or something. Maybe he heard about Felix's war and decided to join and become a *ridder.*" He sneered the last word.

"That's what I hoped. Don't see how he could know anything else. Must be some strange coincidence." Wortin moaned as if he were stretching. A clatter followed: someone picking up the metal rods—or blades. "Regardless, I want you to go with them. If they haven't already left, that is. Show them the quick way to Westley on foot. I'm sure they don't know it from here. Meet up with Sieger and Allesande. I'm going to go find our two visitors once I leave this with Smid." As he spoke on, Wortin began walking in the direction of the tower. The other two, Willian and Hamm, moved on at a slower pace.

"We'll talk more inside," Willian said. "You must be getting cold. So…tell me about this jotun cave near Chaisgott."

156

From then on, the voices could not be heard well. Morley listened until all he could hear was Seth's breathing. Reluctantly, he took up the mead between them and tipped it, misjudging the remaining volume. The thick juice splashed up his nose and he broke out in a fit of loud gags and coughs. Seth pulled away the barrel.

"Well done," he muttered.

Not long after, the archer decided that finishing the rest of the keg would be unreasonable, so he threw the rest into the ever-present fog before them and waited for the splash below. Then, together, they made their way back up to Hoerlog's green, where only two remaining men tended to a private fire. Morley and Seth dazedly joined with them and, minutes later, Wortin appeared with two blankets. The pair took them, thanked the generous ridder, then slept.

*   *   *

Before dawn, Seth tapped Morley awake: Willian, still wearing his long liripipe hat, was standing over them. Beside him was a young man. He was short, coated in heavy wool, had a shortsword sheathed at his hip, and wore what appeared to be his first moustache. He had a full pack at his feet.

"Hoped you two would be awake this early," the taller man said. "This is Hamm, my squire. Likewise, he has a message to take to Westley, so he'll be accompanying you. Objections?" Neither Seth nor Morley spoke. "Good. He would join with you anyway, even if you did object. Be safe out there. Watch for wolves." And with that, Willian smacked Hamm's shoulder and stomped off back to the tower.

The archer and halfelev proceeded to wipe the sleep from their eyes; the other lad watched them. "I'm ready whenever you two are," said the squire. They ignored him.

Less than an hour later, the trio was well on their way. They treaded single file down winding trails and up rock-heavy ridges, through soggy valleys and past the dens of unknown beasts. Morley watched his feet for most of the day, begrudgingly thinking about Anae, Ellemine, Felix, Gale, his father in Westley, the folk back in Egainshir, the treasure he carried. Seth, now recloaked, took to whistling. Hamm said nothing.

None of them spoke on the first day, in fact, though they stopped to rest once before settling down for the night. Hamm, who'd taken the lead, merely stopped and sat down on a rock, opened his pack, and pulled out a few strips of dried venison. With a suggestive look, he tossed two fillets over to Seth and Morley, and they all chewed in peace.

The same occurred several hours later: the squire halted at the top of a hillock and, in seeing that the way forward was far too obscured in darkness, threw down his gear. Again, he soundlessly shared his food after building a little fire out of twigs and dead grass.

At that time, Seth continuously cast his eyes over Morley, as if intending to convey something private. Morley, not wishing to engage with anyone outside of his own head, pretended not to understand the eventual gestures that followed—that is, until the archer stood with a growl and walked off. Hamm watched him go suspiciously.

After a minute, the halfelev followed without enthusiasm, avoiding the squire's stare. Seth was further down the hill, pissing off a low cliff, directing his stream with a cyclical motion. He was finished by the time Morley stumbled down to him.

"Dammit all—been tryna get yer attention all day. What's the matter with ye?" He was plainly frustrated, but something in his voice insinuated a sense of betrayal. Morley couldn't blame him.

"My mind's been on other things," he said.

"Like what?"

Rather than sharing all the sentiments concerning his lost love and controversial lineage and the delicate mystery of Ellemine's gift, he diverted the question by pointing over his shoulder.

"Our company," he said after realizing it was too dark for Seth to see his jutting thumb. "I'm not sure why, but I'm starting to dread whatever's just ahead of us. You heard the way the ridders were talking last night."

"Mostly. I was fallin' asleep durin' some of it, just afore they brought up Sieger."

"I think we've involved ourselves in something," the lad whispered. They traded places and Morley pulled down his trousers to urinate. "I don't know how, but...I don't know. I don't trust those Hoerlog men. They certainly didn't trust us."

"They're behind us now, there's nothin' to dread. And besides, we've been involved with danger long afore we met, mate," the archer said, watching for Hamm. "I'm still a wanted man, say what ye want. Ye see the way those Wallenport ridders were gawkin' at me when we were on the march?"

"No, I honestly didn't."

Seth sputtered at this but let it go. "So what should we do about our fellow traveler, eh?" he asked. Morley had no ideas. "Don't think I could kill him, not someone as young as him. Wouldn't be all that fair either, would it? Two against one? He's got things to hide, we've got things to hide. Let's leave him be, yeah?" Morley pulled up and corded his waistband, then the pair made their way back up to the squire's little flame.

"On second thought," Seth muttered, possibly to himself, "there shouldn't be any harm in broilin' our little friend tomorrow."

"Broiling him?" Morley mumbled back. "What the hell d'ye mean by that?"

"I'm gonna put him on edge. With words. Then see if I can't get him to let somethin' slip."

"About what?"

"About why he's with us, o' course," Seth said. "About why he needs to meet with my brother. Mayhaps about what they were gabbin' about last night. Ye get me?"

Sure enough, on the following day, they came upon the base of a sharp-cornered hill: one path at its side ran down to a tinkling crick, the other remained on their level of ground and seemed to wend its way east. Hamm, still at their front, took the downward trail.

"Uhm," Seth called out, startling the young man. "Why're ye goin' down that way?"

Hamm's face tightened, as if he were unassured and dually baffled. He played off his conviction nonetheless.

"Because it's the right way." The statement was muddled by a tremor in his voice, Morley thought.

"No," the archer contended. "Looks like it, but it'll just swoop down to another tarn and we won't be able to round it. Sheerness and all that."

The squire looked down his preferred way, then back. "I've made the journey before, many times. And I've always stayed with the lowlands."

"It's no faster, Hamm." Seth began stepping toward the alternate path. "Highlands only make the trip feel longer 'cause ye have to look out over the whole of yer remainin' distance. It's a mind-trick, is all. But hey, don't let me prevent ye—we'll go our way and you'll go yer's. Let's see who makes it to Westley first, eh?"

The archer moved on. Morley yoked his sword across his shoulders and tagged along, leaving the squire behind.

159

After no more than a hundred strides, Hamm jogged up behind them, huffing as though he'd never run before in his life.

"Ah, what's the matter, lad?" Seth continued as he walked. "Realize yer mistake?"

"Safety in numbers," he replied. "And Sir Willian wanted me to stay with you two, like it or not."

"Well, he's not here, is he? Who cares what he ordered—go yer own way if ye think it's faster." Seth didn't bother to peer back at the squire as he spoke.

"Good luck entering the ridderstaat with sensibilities like that."

"I dunno, Hamm. Felix seems keen enough to pass out the badge to just about anyone—least, that's what they're sayin' in Wallenport. At his rate, my mother'll be a ridder afore year's end." Morley smirked at this. "I'll bet yer the last squire this place'll ever host. I hear Felix is tossin' out that gloryful tradition. Hell, we're both of the same rank now, aren't we?"

Hamm let out a laugh. "Theoretically," he said, "though I don't consider it a matter of the aetheling's judgement. As Sir Wortin says, 'It's the man and the method, not the man and the merit.'"

They turned along a gravelly bend and saw a convenient though dubious crevice cutting downward through the hill, likely formed by a long-forgotten creek. Seth headed towards it.

"I give in," he said. "What's it mean?"

"It doesn't matter how honored you are," Hamm answered. "If you can hold your own in a scrape, any scrape at all, then you're worthy of a title. Even when nobody is willing to give you one."

"In that case, I'd say we're still even," the archer chuckled. Morley gulped. He unyoked his sword and held it at his side, preparing to give Seth a cautionary nudge.

"I doubt it," the squire incited. "Not too much you can do with a bow."

Morley subtly quickened his pace until he was within reach of his now stammering comrade.

"Oh, is that what ye think?" For once, he glanced behind him. "That's a nice cabbage cutter ye have at yer belt. I'd like to see ye pull that one out durin' a fight—ah! Is that why ye call them scrapes? 'Cause that's all yer little sword can do?" As they passed into the dried canal, Morley tapped Seth's shoulder with his pommel; he paid no mind.

160

"You'd be surprised what my 'cabbage cutter' can do," Hamm spoke. "It's far more useful than that greatsword your friend is lugging around, I assure you."

The lad sighed inwardly as Seth sputtered a second time. "Ye gonna let him disrespect Sir Gale's claymore, Fitzmorley?"

"I'm sure he has a point," the halfelev dismissed.

"Then how 'bout a spar once we get to open ground, Hammy?"

"How 'bout we don't have a spar?" Morley recommended.

"How 'bout ye lend me the blade and I'll do the spar?"

"No."

The trio hushed up for a time. The crevice soon opened up onto a steep slope, the bottom of which led down to the same lowlands Hamm had opted to take earlier. Seth's error was so blatant that it seemed the squire didn't bother to point it out. Still yet, as they slid their way down the crumbling sod, the archer aimed to preserve his dignity.

"Here's a situation fer ye. I just thought it—" He slipped, caught himself, and continued. "I just thought it up. Say I'm right there on that little bit o' rising rock." He pointed down into the widening highland valley: an abrupt plateau bulged from the side of the hill across from them, smoothly diverting the crick below. "And Morley and yerself are right over there..." Again, he pointed, this time closer up the roaming creek. "Now, say I'm up there loosin' some arrows down at ye. Meanwhile, the two o' ye are fightin' with yer swords and I'm shootin' over Morley's shoulder. What would ye do? And mind the rocks in the water, they're damn slippery."

Squire Hamm didn't waste a breath before offering his resolution.

"Given that the two of you were sufficiently trained," he said, "which I doubt, the method is very simple. Morley here—and no offense to you—is thin as a twig and couldn't swing that behemoth of his for more than five minutes, no matter how skilled he is at brandishing it. If it were just the two of us, I'd tire him out and finish him off." At this, the halfelev scratched at an ear uncomfortably, almost stumbling.

"But you're lobbing arrows at me," Hamm continued, "so there's a fair urgency at hand. If Morley is aggressive, then I'd keep away by six paces and use him as cover until I find the right time to strike. If he's keeping up a defense, then it'd be over quick. Vertical block, horizontal block, slant block—it doesn't matter. At the closest range, a greatsword can't do much. I'd grab it by the hilt with my free hand and cut his throat. One advantage of the shortsword.

"Thence, I'd have to deal with you up on your perch. So I'd keep Morley's body at hand, sheath my weapon, and bear him over my shoulders and head as I advance. Only trouble here, as you said, is watching my step along the rocks. But once I'd made it up to you, I'd get rid of the body, draw my weapon, and skirt the stone while keeping an eye on you, if possible. If you're in sight and an arrow is drawn, I'd wait for you to take the shot—which I'd avoid by sticking to my cover, just before making my assault. If you gave chase, then I suppose we would have a hunt."

A gust of wind gyrated through the hills when they reached the rivulet. Morley and Seth gave no reaction for the young squire's postulation; instead, they settled to catch their breath and sip palmfuls of water. Hamm took the vanguard once again. The duo followed after exchanging grimaces.

"I've got one for you, Seth," the squire offered once they gained on him.

"Go on."

"Say you're standing on a flat plain. There's another archer within range and a mounted ridder charging on you. You've got your longbow and enough arrows. What do you do?"

"Shoot the archer, then shoot the horse right between the nubs," Seth answered. "Then shoot the man who was ridin' it."

"You don't check the wind?" said Hamm.

"I'll check the wind by loosin' my first arrow."

"The horse would be on you by the time you made your third shot."

"Not with my speed," he claimed. Morley felt a migraine stirring in his head. "And if he was close enough, I'd just get the rider instead o' the horse."

"Not as easy as it sounds, you know."

"Sure it is, I've done it," Seth stated.

With that, the halfelev smacked the back of his mate's head.

"Have you?" Hamm replied, skeptically.

Seth scowled back at Morley. "No," he gave in. "But I could do an even harder target. I'll prove it, wherever and whenever."

They argued through the rest of the day. When they stopped for the night below the highest reaches of Laisroch, somewhere amidst a collective of hummocks and bushes, Hamm built up a cairn of five hand-sized stones. The two of them stood forty strides away from the delicate pile.

Hamm then tasked Seth with knocking away each of the rocks with only ten arrows, promptly betting against him; the loser of this wager would have to both retrieve the bolts and take first watch for the night.

Morley, very much annoyed with the now ceaselessly bickering duo, went off to be alone. When the squire and the archer came back, they were quiet: the result of their contest went unannounced. Morley awaited Seth as he returned to their unlit heap of sticks.

"Thought you were gonna put him on edge today," the lad groused.

"Looks like he put *you* on edge without having to plan on it."

The archer tossed up his hands nonchalantly. "I mistook him fer a coward, I guess. Didn't think he'd disrespect my art."

Within the hour, Morley, not wishing to sleep despite the soreness of his muscles, offered to take watch. The two others accepted and, seconds later, they were snoring. He thought of Anae again, whether or not she'd already forgotten their meeting; he thought of Westley ahead, of his negligent father. Why did he wish to meet the man? For some sort of closure, he decided, whatever that meant.

Perhaps more importantly, he speculated on how he would go about convening with the earl. Nobles were an inconstant breed. The Bertrisses wouldn't permit Morley to set foot on their estate, as Anae claimed. And yet, he was welcomed into Sivliére Castle without trouble—though the circumstances there were vastly different. If he could even manage to be admitted into Michel Laisroch's hall, could he plausibly entreat a meeting in confidence? The lad felt as if he needed to weep, then elected not to.

He was turning over one of the coins in his scarred hand, he noticed.

The next day went by slow but, since they surpassed the highlands, easygoing. The land was now a field of knolls and meadows, bobbing smoothly under a benign sky. Morley said no more than a few words during the daylit hours. Seth and Hamm, on the other hand, continued their series of sketches, debates, and boastings with a renewed vigor. The halfelev listened to every word, trying his best to ignore his own thoughts. By high noon, he was convinced the other two were now inadvertent friends. This had become evident once their conversations shifted away from successive brags to subjects of a more wholesome nature. This transpired when Hamm mentioned the remaining interval to Westley—six to seven hours without much pause.

"How's it that ye know my brother, exactly?" Seth asked. "Y'know, aside from bein' o' the same profession."

The squire took a long sip of tarn water from his skin before answering. "He was a squire when I became an aspirant," said Hamm. "Our ranks often intersect in the training field."

"Ah, Sieger's a proper ridder now?" Seth said without much surprise. "How long ago did that happen? He's been away from Olford fer only two or three years. I'd think it'd take longer to sweep up the rank."

"Not under Allesande." The squire hawked and spat. "And your brother is quite adept. I was an aspirant for twice as long as he was. Though in my defense, I chose to serve at Hoerlog under Sir Wortin so I could squire Sir Willian. They're men of older tradition, one could say."

"Hm," Seth grunted. "Sounds like Felix's tried to learn a few tricks from the Laisroch folk."

"So he may think," said Hamm. "Ridderstaat around here is still expensive, like it is on the continent. And it's still *ridderstaat* in the original sense of the word. Aetheling Felix is essentially levying a load of plebs with the promise that they'll gain the title of a ridder come wartime. No offense to you two." Morley recalled the barman they'd met in Wallenport.

"Then how did my brother afford it all?" Seth asked. "He left Olford with only two nickels. That can't be enough."

"Allesande's offers are reasonable. If you wish to become a ridder, you have to buy out land and pay tallage like everyone else in Westley. A nickel for a cottar's plot, I think. If you can't afford that, it's the garrison barracks for you—or under special circumstances, Allesande sends you to live as one of the earl's housecarls. Anyhow, and luckily enough for Sieger and his two nickels, rents are much cheaper for aspirants than they are for, say, craftsmen and farmers—those men have schedules to maintain. Aspirants lead different lives. They have to make money by whatever means necessary while also reporting to the training grounds. One only becomes a squire when a ridder offers a request of service. See, if an aspirant is worthy enough, he could become a squire within two weeks."

Morley half-expected Seth to make a jape over Hamm's own ineptitude at ascending the ranks. But the archer was strangely enthralled, as if his whole perspective of ridders had changed in a matter of seconds, singularly due to his brother's success.

"What's the catch fer the cheap rents?" he asked.

"When called to arms, a ridder has to have enough money—again, accrued by his own means—to rent or buy a horse, armor, weapons. Then, of course, they're expected to risk their lives in combat, if they're ever sent into it. Farmers just have to wake up and tend the furlong every day until Frysa when the fields are snowed over. It's a rare case that *they're* called to fight for their earl. Sounds like a fair trade to me."

They quietened. Morley repeated the name 'Allesande' in his head, trying to spell it out. Wortin had ordered Hamm to meet up with both Sieger and this other unknown person, a figure of evident prominence in Westley. To everyone's surprise—Morley's included—he inquired.

"Who is Allesande exactly?" he said.

The squire glimpsed over his shoulder. "Earl Michel's stewardess. And sister-in-law. She manages Westley's domestic preservation, as all stewards do. Which is to say she manages all the militia, the journeymen, the landed ridders. There's not much else to handle besides. You'll like her if you end up meeting her. She's very kind."

The halfelev hummed. If she were the earl's sister-in-law, a sibling to the lad's pseudo-stepmother, then were they related in some way? He tried to think if there were a term or phrase for such a familial tie. Then he realized he didn't really care.

Hamm continued his discourse on Westley, sometimes including short interludes about his early life in the town, how he first learned the laws, what sorts of ridders he knew. Neither Morley nor Seth listened with much interest, their minds now devoted to other matters. Indeed, if the squire's accounts bore any relevance to the true nature of the town, then Westley was bound to be an inordinately dull place.

Dull or not, though, the lad soon discovered that it was inarguably the nicest town on all of Sarcovy Isle.

Before sundown, they surmounted a high hill. Below, Westley stared back at them, waiting against the drop of the horizon, surrounded on all sides by hundreds of small hovels and acre upon acre of farmland. The town proper—an area encircled by a low stone wall—was a blanket of wattle-daub over a swelling of dry earth. Crowned at its mediocre peak was a long dark semicircle topped by an impressive thatched roof. He knew without asking that it was the house of his father. To the south of it all, a single dirt path cut through the golden expanse.

"Ah," Seth said fondly, "the road to Olford. I've missed that ugly strip."

"So have I," Morley agreed, though he'd never before traveled it: their overall journey hadn't involved too many roads, he realized.

The trio headed down to the beaten line, exhaling their relief for comparatively level ground. They continued on between the hordes of swaying stalks. Dusk had swept the sky by the time they reached the furthest houses, pens, and mills along the inner edge of the barley fields. Once deeper into the developed outskirts, Seth stopped and rested a hand on Morley's shoulder.

"This is our side route," he announced. "Sieger lives right round the barn there, see?" He pointed out a larger building of greyish planks.

"Then this is where we part for now," Hamm said. "I bear a message from Sir Wortin and need to deliver it before the longhall bars up for the night. Then I need to get some sleep lest I fall over." The other two nodded. "I'm sure we'll see each other tomorrow." With that, he brusquely marched off. Morley and Seth moved on, as well.

"He's all right, I suppose," the archer said, "for a cheeky bugger."

They passed by the barn and came to a development of squat uniform hovels. Many displayed subtle ornamentations at their doors: one had reindeer antlers affixed to the upper frame, another had a green and brown quilt draped over it. Sieger's, once they found it, had flat ford stones embedded in the ground before the entrance. Seth tapped the heels of his new shoes against them, knocked four times at the door, then pushed it open.

"Guess who!" he exclaimed, flinging himself inside. Sieger stood in plain view, wearing nothing but a pair of loose trousers. Excessively muscular, he made his brother look like a halfelev in comparison.

"Seth?" he said as Morley shuffled inside. An enormous wad of grey fur rested by the man's foot. It lifted its horned head.

"Geat?!" Morley cried, stiffening. On the bed against the opposite corner of the house, half of a figure rose up from the sheets.

"Morley?" Her short hair was tossed and she wore a simple tunic.

"Yeva?" Morley said.

Then there was silence, each of them waiting for one of the others to speak up.

*　　　*　　　*

The weather was the nicest it had been in many, many weeks: warm, bright, and windless. It was reflected in the abounding faces walking along Westley's inner lanes. The golden kempt hair of passing women hung in artful braids around their necks; the bronzed skin of farmer sons held a certain bold perfection under the candid sun. Everyone had a duty to fulfill and everyone appeared more than willing to carry it out at their desired speed.

The same very much applied to Morley, who tugged Geat along via a flaxen leash. The two of them, along with Yeva and Seth, were on their way to Michelhal, the house and court of the earl, an abode equally as magnificent as Castle Sivliére. And they were in no hurry whatsoever, preferring to wander across the town's acclivity from end to end.

"So, will you become the Aetheling of Sarcovy one of these days?" Yeva asked Morley as she passed him a handful of pecans from her satchel. Morley furrowed his brow, then clicked his tongue at Geat, urging him to follow.

"What makes you say that?" he replied, taking the nuts.

"Yer mum's the wife o' Roberrus," Seth answered, tossing up a pomegranate he'd pilfered from the market. "Or was. And yer father's the present Earl o' Laisroch. That all must mean somethin', eh?"

"No, I don't think so," Morley answered. "They had me illimita—illigen—what is it?" He tapped the side of his head. "Illegitimately. Which means I was born out of law, I think. And I guess an aetheling can't be born out of law." He nipped off the tip of a pecan. "I wouldn't want to do it even if I was allowed, though."

"I can understand that," said Seth. "Though I must say, yer description of Felix's banquet had me droolin', blunt as it was. I'd take up the lordship just fer the meals if I could."

"I don't think huge feasts like that are put out every day, though." He thought back to the conversation he overheard in the castle's upper hall, just before being discovered by Ellemine. "In fact, those three feasts may've been the nicest meals Felix himself ever had. He made them huge and elegant, just so he could show off to the aspirants and, y'know, show them he's a man worth serving."

Seth bit into his pomegranate, a fruit he had certainly never tried before. Disgust came over his face. He raised his arm in preparation to throw the fruit away, but Morley snatched it up and handed it over to Geat.

"Sanct's Bones, Morley!" Yeva laughed. "When I headed out to find you, I expected you'd be stranded at Olford, begging for scraps and building a little hut out of twigs and mud—I didn't think you'd make it all the way to Wallenport, let alone circle the entire island."

"Well," he murmured, "finding you in Sieger's bed was the last thing *I'd* imagined. Not that I'd imagined it at all, obviously."

It wasn't the most charming reunion when they stormed into Sieger's house the night before, but it was a welcome change of expectations. Naturally, Morley first believed their meeting to be some freakish accident or an immaculate proof of Fate or the All-Being. It was much too unbelievable, like the end of a pleasant dream that incites a longing in the wakened sleeper.

However, it was straightforward enough—a customary Yeva story:

"I was worried sick after you left Egainshir and disappeared out of Reineshir," she had said earlier as she cozied up next to Morley and Geat, both of whom sat on Sieger's floor. "Within the same week, I said to everyone that I'd be bounding out to find you and that I'd take the goat along—I thought he could persuade your homecoming just as easily as I could. And he's good company. But anyhow, Istain and Serryl tried to get me to stay, saying it was a dangerous enough road for you alone and it'd be especially dangerous for me—a 'supple young lady,' as Semhren said—but I tossed their words aside, took a fair share of coin from Istain—he owes me as much for all the scarves and caps and stockings I've made for his stock—and off I went with Geaty at my heels.

"First night, I stayed in Reineshir's inn and had a good long chat with the wench who owns it—second night, we rested inside a hollow tree—third night, I found an old hut far off the road. I was in Olford by the fourth day—would've been there quicker if Geat didn't have to stop for a rest every two hours." She knocked on his head between the horns, then continued her speedy story.

"Now, when I got there, I went around and asked the folk if they'd seen, y'know, a tall and scrawny halfelev with a mass of hazel hair. No one knew what I was talkin' about, but this tiny kid claimed he'd seen someone just as I'd described, only he had a giant sword over his shoulder, and he was 'friends with Seth' or something. So he pointed me to the right house and I went and knocked—then this older woman opened the door a crack and said a few words about Seth and Sieger being in Westley, so I went and asked someone else what it all meant once the woman closed the door on me."

She paused then and looked to Sieger, a brawny man who resembled Serryl more than Sethan. "That was your mother, yeah?" Yeva asked. He nodded. "What's wrong with her? She wouldn't show her face. And she almost fell backward when she opened the door up. Is she unwell?"

"Yeah, mum's had the swamp-sick fer a year now," Seth came in after slurping down the rest of his beer, a refreshing treat offered by his brother. "The woodland folk say it comes over from Sylvan and the vodniks. Mayhaps it crawls its way upstream or gets carried by the wind like a spirit. She'll live fer plenty more years, I'm sure, but she'll hafta spend them indoors lest her bellows shrivel up. Once they get the sick, they have to keep breathin' the sick, it's said. That's why she needs to stay inside our house fer the rest of her days. It's a sad sight, but at least she lives on, eh? Bit o' blood-lettin' or a sip of uforian now and again gets her feelin' better."

"Well, I wish her all the health in the world," Yeva continued. "As I was saying, Geat and I stayed the night in Olford, then took to the east road for another three days and, once we got here, I asked around for a Seth or a Sieger—sometimes threw in the description of Morley, but thought that if he was around he'd recognize Geat quicker than he'd recognize me.

"Soon enough, a guard in town said he knew Sieger well and led me over here. I waited a bit and he came back." The two of them eyed each other, as if dually recollecting an unmentionable plot. "A few weeks later, you lads showed up." Seth and Morley looked to each other and shrugged, each for different reasons. "Your turn, Morley."

He recounted everything. And strangely enough, Sieger was more intrigued than Yeva, demanding that he share everything Ellemine had conveyed to him with absolute honesty. It was easy enough to prove: his elevi features weren't so common on Sarcovy. And Yeva was there to support his claim of being born on the island, being raised under Sir Gale. Incredible as it all was, they couldn't help but believe the halfelev. When Morley finished his tale, Sieger sat carefully against a large straw drum. Its unseen contents rattled under his weight.

"It all makes sense," he said, as if to himself. "Surprisingly. Bizarrely. I come home from a spar and find a pretty young woman with her goat sittin' outside my door, askin' if I knew a lad named Fitzmorley. I didn't but invited her inside. Then, said Fitzmorley shows up a bit later with an impressive sword *and* my brother. And claims he's the bastard son of

169

Damme Sivliére and Earl Laisroch." He chuckled tiredly. "What am I supposed to make o' this?"

"Well, fer one thing," said Seth, "ye could try and get us an audience with the earl. That's the whole reason we're here and not back in Olford." His brother nodded again, deep in thought. "How soon could we get up there, eh?"

Sieger stood, then laid himself down in bed. "If the weather is favorable, so to speak, I can arrange a meeting of sorts tomorrow afternoon."

Not long after, they all retired for the evening: Sieger and Yeva shared the sheets and mat, Seth rested across the floor, and Morley—without objection—slept outside with Geat as his pillow. Sieger left to do his duties long before anyone else woke. Hours later, after the sun was high and vibrant, they shared a helping of old bacon and a jug of milk, then headed up to town, Morley and Seth leaving their weapons behind.

Noon encroached and a gurgling unease roiled the halfelev's stomach. Against the proposals of the others, he recommended that they continue exploring the town, just until the hour was right to knock on the door of Michelhal.

So, they wandered the avenues, entering workshops without aim, surveying items without the funds to make a purchase—Morley's gold coin being out of the question. Yeva toured every house and stall that held up the mark of the weaver—a simple strip or quilt with black weft and white warp threads—and studied their patterns with increasing interest. Seth, meanwhile, spent almost an hour at a apothecarist's laboratorium. Morley and Geat waited elsewhere on a slanted bench, watching the populace and hearing their cursory conversations. All were of a similar flavor: the weather, the crops, the wives and husbands, the cats and dormice. He rested his arm between Geat's horns.

"What d'you think?" the lad said. "Ready to meet my father?" The goat blinked. "Neither am I."

In truth, Morley wanted little more than to go back to Egainshir. What would he gain, he thought, by meeting with his true father? At best, a place within his household, the love of an unsought stranger. How was any of that better than the simple life in Werplaus? He knew his way around the island now; if he wanted to leave the south for a few weeks, he could do so. He looked down at the metal bits inside the flap of his tunic.

Yeva came up behind him then and slapped the back of his head. "Hey there," she said, seating herself next to Geat—who belched, much to their amusement. "Look at the twins here. All ye need, Morley, is a pair of horns to match his. I wouldn't be able to tell the difference."

Morley smiled, hung up on her sudden pronunciation of 'ye,' a slip of the Olford brothers' contagious manners. He did not realize until that very moment how much he'd missed her, how long it'd been since he was beside someone he could truly trust with his life. Of all the conveniences pitched upon him during his journey, encountering her was indomitably the greatest. There was something about her now. Something familiar but potent beyond recognition.

He searched about him: nobody else was near. "I need to show you something," he said, removing one of the coins and concealing it in his balled fist. He dropped it in her open palm. "Try not to let anyone else see it."

She cupped her other hand over it. "What is it?"

"I dunno," he murmured. "I was hoping you'd know. You're the first person I've shown it to, actually. My mother…Ellemine Sivliére gave two of them to me. For some reason."

Promptly, Yeva handed the piece back to Morley with surprising disinterest. And all of a sudden, the value he'd given to the coins faded like a mid-morning vapor. He hid it away, back in the flap of his tunic.

"It looks like it should be attached to a pin or a string, like a necklace." She smiled handsomely at him. His heart whirred and he gulped. "You should ask Istain what it is next time ye see him, he might know. He knows a lot about little objects like that." She turned, facing him, and sat with her legs at either side of the bench, her eyes panning over everything around them. "Where's Seth?" she asked.

"Apothecarist," he answered, clearing his throat. "You buy anything from the clothiers?"

"Nothing, but I inspected everything I liked—ever hear of a herringbone weave?" The lad shook his head. "I hadn't either, it's beautiful—the threads go up and down in sharp lines. Whenever we get back home, I'll try and recreate the pattern as best I can." Morley smiled at this.

"Speaking of which, when do we go back?" he asked.

Yeva tilted her head. "I was thinking of staying with Sieger for a few more weeks. You don't have to wait up for me, of course, you can just go

171

back to Olford with Seth, then head down to Werplaus with Geaty. Unless the earl gives you a special room of your own."

The lad blinked, just as Geat had a moment before. "You really like him, don't you?" he asked. She stretched and stuck one leg under the other. She wore trousers as usual, though the hems were rolled up to her knees.

"I like him enough to stay until I get sick of him," she chuckled. "He knows I'm not going to stay with him and I know he's not ready to settle down and take a wife. He treats the ridderstaat very, very seriously. Whenever one of his mates interrupted us, he'd answer the door as he was, say a few words—very few words—get dressed, then off he'd go without much explaining. I could never stay with a man like that."

The halfelev's heart skipped a beat. He clutched the coins in his tunic, slightly concerned by the sensation. "What sort of man do you want, then?"

"I'm not sure, but certainly someone just a slight bit like Sieger. At least someone handsome and strong and enduring." Morley blushed and rubbed his face with the side of an elbow, attempting to hide the color. "What I'd give to live in a mound-house—like the one you lived in with Gale—and share my days with a ridder out of service. They're the best lovers in the whole world, I think."

"I wouldn't know," said Morley dismissively. Then, already partly regretting the statement, he said, "My only lover was the Damme of Sarcovy."

"Like your father before you," she laughed.

Then, they were quiet for a moment. And something was amiss. Not particularly between them, but in the whole of Westley. The purring of bystanders and passing workers was reduced. It were as if no echo succeeded the drone, as if all the citizenry were crammed into one room.

A man was rushing down the hill toward the lower palisade. He passed by the seated pair. Morley saw that this man, singularly, had a worried face, an aura of tempered fortitude. And yet, he was dressed as all other men were—tunic and trousers, dirtied at the knees and across the chest. Morley spied on him until he was out of sight, then observed the upward lane of tiered steps, the direction the man had been charging from. Others were rushing about, making their way up the hill to Michelhal.

"—but at least you tried, right?" Yeva had been speaking all the while, he realized. "I understand why you went after her, trust me—there's

172

something about love that makes ye do foolhardy things. Like ye have a little ribbon of hope and even though it's smaller than a mite it's the only thing you're willing to hold onto. I had it when I first came to this island. I thought I'd find my father and sister again, one of these days. And I still feel it in me whenever—"

Another crowd was gathering on the hilltop: Morley could see it shifting between the houses, a billet, a chapel. This was a crowd of collective purpose, swarming under the half-dome of the longhouse. There was a shout, an order followed by series of loud compliances.

"—back there someday. Though, I wonder if anyone still lives on those beaches after everything that—"

"I think there's something going on up there," Morley interrupted, standing up on the bench. He had no intention of getting any closer, but tried to angle a clearer view for himself. Geat stepped down onto the ground and ambled his way upward. "Leave it, Geat. We're staying right here."

He hopped down and swept up the leash before it was out of his reach. Upon lifting his head, he heard a whinny and a sudden mass of protests. And a rider appeared ahead, cantering swiftly down the hill. He was dressed in full: a white tabard over a shirt of mail, metal greaves and gloves, a faceless frog-mouthed helm over his shoulders and head. His courser was bay with thick antler nubs; and after slowing for an instant, it raced straight down toward them.

Morley backed away, preparing to run without really knowing why, and tripped over the bench. The ridder and his steed rumbled down and halted before them, a cloud of dust in their wake. The towering blunt head settled its slit-eye on the downed halfelev.

"Come with me," it said, the voice a metallic muffle. Morley didn't move. "Now."

Before the lad could attempt to stand back up, the ridder swung down from his horse. He gripped Morley by the tunic and heaved him to his feet, then clamped a rough iron hand around the back of his neck, leading him over to the stomping courser.

"What are you doing?!" he heard Yeva roar.

"Climb up," the ridder ordered. Morley gawked at the fervid horse. "Eh," he said. "H-how?"

"Foot in the stirrup, other leg over the other side." Morley tried. "Wrong foot." He tried again. "You have to leap up." He didn't bother trying a third time. The man suspired inside his helmet. "Forget the stirrup, step onto my hands."

With this assist, Morley made it up onto the steed's back. The armored stranger surged deftly onto the beast, took up the reins, and kicked. They charged back up the hill.

"Hey!" Yeva cried out. "Stop! What're you doing?!" Her voice faded behind them.

Morley, too terrified to realize he was terrified, watched the horse's jerking head as it scaled the hill, as it brushed aside the hindering crowd of tool-bearing or empty-handed spectators, and delivered them onto the stone-tiled courtyard of Michelhal. It all happened in a flash of a hundred heartbeats.

In the time it took for the ridder to dismount, the lad tried his best to make an assessment: the hall's main door, ornately carved into a diptych of twin warriors, was smashed inwardly at its center. A group of guards were braced behind them at the edge of the courtyard, watching the innocuous gathering behind the earl's cobbled shrubbery. Six cloaked men were resting over the disheveled flower patches.

No. They were dead.

The armored man gripped Morley by the shirt again and brought him down irritably. He then directed him through the beaten doors, one fist at the scruff of his neck.

Though the lad could do little more than move his eyes, he could tell immediately that the main court was cramped—perhaps half the width of Felix's—but considerably high-reaching. The ample skylights burned down on the wrecked room, illuminating swarms of divagating dust. The floors, aside from the elongated firepit down its center, were of the same tiled stone as the yard; all the rest was of wood and irregular black bindings. Everything—the overturned table, the six pine trunk pillars, the seats of the earl and his wife, the scattered housewares—was patterned with the same repetitive swirls and antlerlike designs that pervaded all of Westley.

The hall was empty aside from Morley and his aggressive captor, though voices crawled in through the wide doorways on either side of them. The lad couldn't see very well, but the seemingly identical chambers beyond each opening were lined at the walls with leveled boards—beds, he presumed—between which were other extended firepits. The ridder gave him no time to take in his surroundings further.

He was shoved through the curtain at the other end of the hall, just behind the earl's chair: a bedchamber packed with murmuring people—a young woman weeping, somewhere beside the bed—cloaked and helmeted ridders...

A woman as tall as Ellemine was standing in front of something. She turned as they entered, backed away from the foot of the bed. An older man kneeled there, prostrate, his hands over his grey head.

The space fell into quietude as Morley and his escort stopped. Almost everyone's eyes were on them. Morley could feel his face reddening again. Without a word, the tall woman—her face stern and wolfish, her hair straight, brown, and unbraided—stomped over to him and brushed away a side of his own hair. He flinched as she did so.

"Right," she said to him, backing away again. "What is your name, boy?"

His throat tightened and his hands began to shake. "Fi-Fitzmorley," he said. The woman, puzzled, looked over the kneeling man near her feet. In turning back to Morley, she glared unsurely at the ridder behind him.

"Who was your mother?" she said to the lad. "And what did she look like?" Her voice was astoundingly deep.

Dumbfounded, he did not react. The other helmed ridders watched him like expressionless automata, like the fabled goelems of Bienvale's coastal caves. He tried to breath out an "um" and his voice cracked.

"Speak," said the man behind him. "Don't think." Though the words were sparse and hard to hear, the voice had a familiar intonation. Morley tried to gulp but found he was too parched to do so.

"Um," he tried again. "T-tall, like you. With white hair. But not like an elder's. And sh-she was an elev. With silver eyes, slim like mine. Pointed nose. She speaks softly and kindly..." They all waited for him to continue. The man on the floor quivered. "I don't know what else to say about her. Sh-she was Roberrus' wife. Damme Ellemine Sivliére."

The woman before him continued studying his features imperatively. The groveling man beneath her froze and cautiously separated his fingers for a moment; two pale eyes were briefly visible behind them.

"And who begot you?" the woman proceeded.

"Eh, s-sorry?" The word was new to him.

"Who is your father?" He knew exactly what to say and how to say it. But a different impulse dominated him.

Gale, say it was Gale, say he's your father. Get yourself out of this—say what you believe, what you want to believe.

But what would that accomplish, he wondered. He was already in the thick of this flourishing incident—what good would lying do? Would they let him go without further harassment?

Look around—they're going to harm you.

"Speak," ordered the ridder, prodding at his neck.

"I…"

He needed to negotiate, needed to run, needed to beg for mercy. He needed to know what was going on.

"A-are you going to hurt me?" he peeped, embracing his cowardice.

At this, the other men in the chamber glanced back and forth at one another. And the woman's tough features relented, giving way to pity. She lifted one side of her skirt and planted a foot on the fawning man's back. He quaked, hiding his head in his arms.

"All of you, leave us." she demanded. The armored men, including the ridder who brought him there, filed out through the draped entrance. One of them led a sobbing handmaiden by the elbow. After a moment, there was nobody else but the woman and her two prisoners.

"Go on," she urged. Morley felt ready to collapse.

"W-well," he started, his voice stumbling again, "I-I was raised by a chevalier. Sir Gale was his name. He—we lived out in the middle of Werplaus. He didn't speak much. Not until I was older." He cleared his dry throat. The older man began raising his head. "I met my mother not two weeks past. And she told me about my father and…I-I don't know if she was serious or mistaken, but—I—"

"Let's do this the easy way," the woman interfered. "Late last night, one of my men came to my door to tell me that the bastard son of Ellemine Sivliére and Michel Laisroch was residing at his house. He was convinced this was the truth. He swore his life on it. And though he didn't know it at the time, this truth confirms a suspicion I've kept for years. I'm very trusting of my men—him especially. *Very* trusting. Was he telling the truth? Or did he make an outrageous mistake by believing the lies of a young stranger?"

By now, the man under her leathery shoe had almost fully raised his head. The halfelev could not bring himself to stare back into that sullen face, tear-streaked and smitten with confused guilt. Morley took a deep breath, then another, then a third.

"I only know what Ellemine told me," he pressed. "She said she was my mother and that my father is Michel Laisroch. I was sneaking through Sivliére Castle. And she found me hiding outside her door. It was all a strange accident, really. I wasn't seeking her, but she found me. She said I couldn't be kept around Wallenport when I was born, so she sent me to live with Gale. As a favor to him, she said. I only went back there now to find...someone else. But I couldn't. So now I'm here."

"To find your father," she said. "Is that right?" Morley didn't know how to answer. "Well, here he is." She nudged the man onto his side with her toes then stepped over to the lad. "Get up now, Michel."

As if the bulk of his dignity had been restored to him, the man rose carelessly from the ground, brushing his padded arms and breeched thighs. An eyelid was swollen, darkening into a bruise, one of several such blemishes: his lower lip was split and glazed with dried blood, as was a small section of his trimmed brown hair. Once he'd collected himself, he peered straight at the woman.

"You finally did it, Allesande," he muttered, touching the colored wounds on his face with one hand. "But you didn't have to hit me so many times."

"You know it was deserved," she spat.

"Do I?" he said.

The woman—Allesande—moved a pace forward. Michel shied away and sat down against his bedpost, pretending he hadn't winced. The woman returned to Morley's side and crossed her arms. The earl gawked down at the floor.

"Well?" said Allesande.

"Well what?" he replied bitterly.

"Is the boy here lying?"

Morley joined his supposed father in observing the floor tiles. 'Boy,' the woman called him. He'd lived for two decades, at least—and he was taller than most folk. And yet people still called him 'boy.' Was it just one of those words, he thought, like 'lad' or 'mate,' used so often that its meaning evaporated like yesteryear's rainwater? Or was there some unconscious quirk, some irreflexive aspect that indicated his endless youth? So to speak, was it *him* or was it *them*? Did Anae refuse to come with him because she doubted his ability to protect? Did Sethan choose to become his companion because he seemed impressionable, prone to believe his lies?

He examined his father, his yellow garments stained with blood, his mind surely on other matters as well, indifferent of his bastard son. Morley grew pale and nauseous.

"No," the man finally said. "He is not lying." Allesande gave a muted heave of relief.

"Then that is why we haven't yet rebelled," she resolved with biting disgust. Michel narrowed his eyes as if in disbelief. And in that scant instant, Morley saw himself in the man's face. "Isn't it? That is why you oppose action. We have the means, enough supplies, the dedication of many—but you, eminent Earl Laisroch, serve Damme Ellemine as a mistress. And you would never compromise that little love, would you? Not even for your people."

"I haven't thought about that bloody elev for over twenty years," he hissed. "Really, do you hear yourself? Mennia is the only woman I've ever loved, you know that. Ellemine is—was nothing more than a faery temptress. She drew me in, forced me to betray both Roberrus and your sister. She said nothing would come of it—that it was only an urge led on by a dream."

"If she means so little, then why haven't you decided to stand against Felix. Your incompetent son-out-of-law?" Mouth agape, he floundered about for words. "You know just as well as everyone else that he'll lead us all to ruin," she went on. "You know his outrageous demands, his plans for war. And you know I'm the only one with the will to prevent it all. Why not let me? What have you to lose?"

After a time, he gave in.

"Spare me from another one of your confused, paranoid rants," he moaned. "I just want peace, Allesande."

"You want peace for yourself," she growled, stepping forward. "The boys of Westley can ride off to fight for their aetheling and die in some squabble. But as long as you can idle here and play your dulcimer and feed your falcons, all is well in Michel's demesne."

The earl shook his head. "And nobody will die if I start a rebellion here?"

"Under my lead," the woman attested, "nobody will die. Felix will be ousted before the year is over. And someone else will be the Aetheling of Sarcovy."

"You?" Michel sputtered, hiding a laugh.

As Allesande stomped forward and grabbed the earl by the fur-lined tufts of his collar, Morley left the room. Neither of the other two noticed. He marched to the other end of the hall absently and pulled open the battered door. Outside, nothing had changed: eight more ridders were guarding the courtyard against an ever-widening crowd. He stepped up to one of the armored men and tapped him on the shoulder. When the man whirled about, Morley made a motion, brushing his hand in the air as if to shoo the rabble away. The helmeted ridder nodded once upon receiving a wave of approval from his mounted official—Morley's recent captor. He then gestured to a nearby compatriot and led the lad down the hill, the second man shouting for the drove to clear a path. After minutes of struggle, they pushed their way through to the open air which, by now, was right near the bench he had rested on earlier. Geat and Yeva were absent.

Morley went down the hill, out of the city, into Sieger's house. There, he found the trio. They ceased their murmurings as the door swung open.

"There ye are!" Seth exclaimed. "What's goin' on—where've ye been?! Yeva says ye were snatched by some iron-man on horseback." Morley picked up the goat's leash, still attached to his neckband.

"What happened?" said Yeva. "What did they do to you?" He remained silent as he sidled past her to the bed, where his claymore was laid out over the mat. He lugged it up, resting the flat of the blade against his shoulder.

"Aye!" the archer exerted. "Ye hear us?"

Without a reply, Morley exited the house, tugging Geat after him, and set out for the uncrowded eastward road. He heard the other two following behind him, throwing the same set of questions over his head. They all walked on.

Bugger them. Bugger Ellemine, bugger Michel, bugger everyone else behind it—Sieger, Hamm, Allesande, Willian, Wortin, Felix. Bugger Yeva and bugger Seth, too. Everything. Anae—bugger her. All a waste of time. Nothing is right. Nothing. Adventures aren't real. Stories aren't real, heroes aren't real. The way things are told—all lies. Nothing is right.

A hand grabbed his unburdened shoulder, stopping him. Once it was removed, he turned to face his unwanted companions: Yeva was several more strides away, her hands curled into fists at her side, her face abandoning concern for annoyance. Seth's, on the other hand, was arched with sudden worry.

"Please, mate," he said. "Say somethin'. Anythin', really. Tell us what's happenin', what's wrong."

Morley blinked away a tear. "I'm going home."

With that, he proceeded down the road to Olford with Geat. And his friends did not follow.

Part II

Chapter V – The Omphalos

The pond scum parted beneath them, ripping as gently and soundlessly as an edge across skin. The crickets chanted with metronomic rigor, finer than any drum beat, finer than water ticking from a suspended clepsydra. The black claws of vodniks emerged from the filth and reached up to the boat's tip, only to submerge again without a sound. A timid wordless mitigation.

The boat stilled beneath a black house, its sides squeezed between the bodies of two feeble trees, its deck accessible via a ladder of entwined twigs.

The passengers were ready. The trio of satyrs crowded behind their matriarch impatiently, though their boat did not tip or shiver. Birgir rested his muzzle over the woman's shoulder. She rubbed his forehead between the stubs of his sawn horns. The two others—whose horns were yet intact—growled lowly.

"Test it, love," she ordered.

The beast gripped the ladder's brambly rails together in one grey-white hand, then tugged it down: the whole of it collapsed into the slough. The glowing eyes of the vodniks reappeared, watching from a safe distance. Viggdis growled quietly at them and they shrunk back into the untouched morass.

"The pack, Signy," the woman said to the third satyr.

The leather bag dropped before her, dangling from a furry arm. Without taking it, she lifted its flap and removed a black box. She took from it a thorny leaf of red aeker and a pinch of drabber, then put it away. Signy withdrew the pack.

The woman rubbed the brown drabber powder across her fingertips and sniffed heavily at its pungency, shuddering as her skin horripilated down from the back of her neck to her bare ankles. She held out her hands. An unnatural hush fell over the swampland, as if all the crickets and cicadas had fallen dead from their boughs, as if a casing of ice had snapped over the flesh of grunting toads. A moment later, the two trees before them, the frame of the elevated house, began to creak and moan— seemingly the only sound within a league. They bent away, parted from the shingled dwelling.

The house loudly scraped its way down the twin trunks, slanting this way and that, the shards of its exterior crumbling into the waters. They could hear from within the smashing of pottery, the toppling of furnishings, and the hollow banging of a metal pot, its belly tumbling across the floor. By the time the house's broken porch was within their reach, it had been rent down the middle and the trees had grated through the outer walls. And after the last dislodged plank of the covering had rattled to the floors inside, the quiet returned to them.

"Birgir? Signy?" the woman muttered. "The door."

The two satyrs grumbled and took up their weapons from the pointed stern. Birgir clutched his warped cudgel in both hands and stepped up onto the house's toppling deck, his hooves sundering the softwood beneath him. He kicked the door from its hinges, disappeared into the darkness. Signy followed behind with one of her javelins.

"Viggdis, my beauty…"

The final coal-black creature took up her shotel staff, scratching at the scar over her eye. With one hoof against the deck, she leapt like a mountain goat up onto the disheveled roof and burst down into the interior. There was a brief tumult inside. The satyrs bleated their show of fury.

It was all excessive, she knew, but well worth it. Sjaman was worth it.

She rubbed at the brownleaf leaves beneath her tongue, then let go of the water's grip around her boat, allowing it to waft about freely. She then held her middle finger and thumb close together, conjuring a spark of flame between them. Widening their gap, the fire expanded. By the time her fingers were stretched out, palm up, muscles quivering, the flame was an orb the size of a melon. All the while, she squeezed the prickled leaf of red aeker in her other hand, drawing from its inscrutable properties. At the appropriate moment, she ushered the fiery sphere in through the open doorway, engulfing herself again in the night's obscurity. And from this evil shade, from this absence of light, she braced another power.

A shadowed mist enveloped her from the head down, draping her body in a veil that flooded the burden boards and poured over the rowboat's sides.

As the orb's glow floated through the innards of the house, cutting through its splintered apertures and piercing the air around her, she flew up onto the porch. Her toes slid against its surface, the aural veil dissipating around her like steam. She entered the house with a bearing of menace, one which she spent many weeks practicing on the villagers back home—they, however, were susceptible. Sjaman would be harder to frighten, perhaps. Though, many years had passed them over.

The inside was utterly destroyed: fragments of wood were spread over the floors, hanging ornaments were smashed or buried under the rubble, potted plants were freed and splattered across the ground. A second, smaller room—perhaps the studio for Sjaman's concoctions—was in worse condition, as the once supportive tree had surged through its wall and obliterated the woodwork within.

From this room the ball of fire hovered, shedding light on the satyrs and their captive, his shriveled body held against the other intruding trunk at the opposite end of the house. The flame drifted to his face for a span of seconds, nearly burning the hairs of his wool-white beard before retreating back to the hand of its creator. As it left him, he saw the billowing wraith at his door.

She outstretched one of her arms from the adumbral cloak, extending her fingers into black glimmering blades. With them she caged the spherical fire, heightening herself and bending grotesquely over it, sapping its heat. The house dimmed with the dying blaze, drowning them for a time. Then the bones of her hand gleamed bright blue through the veil about her body. From there the light spread along each arm, up to the shoulders, across her collar, down the spine. The rest of her bones were left unilluminated as, at last, her skull burst into a near blinding radiance. She whisked closer to the elder and Viggdis set her shotel against the hair under his neck.

"Death comes with a guard o' satyrs," Sjaman croaked dryly. "I naught ever would've foresaw such. Or are ye merely the Death of the south islanders, who comes to Sarcovy outta the need to fetch me, an ole, ole enemy." He cackled at this.

"You are not far from the truth, Sjaman of Kamenin," she answered him, twisting her voice into that of a daemon's.

He grinned with a predictable toothlessness. "That's Sylvain o' Sylvan. I lord o'er this land now. And I leave it without an heir. I suppose the vodniks'll have my things and my house from here on." He laughed again. "Ye can have it if ye take it first. Foul dark."

She glided closer to him, holding her glittering hands at either side of his head. He did not avert his gaze from the blinding skull above him.

"What will ye show me?" he asked.

The memories had almost been lost to her. She discovered over the past week, as she and her satyrs drifted across the open sea, that remembering was much more difficult than any sorcery. Not just remembering the correct words or the correct progression of events, but the correct feelings—above all, as they were felt at the time. Without words, she realized, feelings would be impossible to recall. They could resurface under the right conditions, though to do so would be to conduct a ritual much like the Rite of the Mavrosii. Words, though largely impotent, could be arranged into spells, complex questions and statements that perspired the needed emotions. As she knew.

The beltreres tear she had consumed earlier burned in her throat. She was ready.

I do hope to see her again, came the voice of her father. *And her gardens and all those beautiful servants. You know, she spoke to me about leaving her island once, not so long before the big men invaded. I told her about staying—staying with her myself and waiting for you to be born. She allowed it. But then...then she forced us out, you and I. And that was forever the end of it. Do you hope to meet her someday?*

She gave him the memories and sought his own, melding the two together into what might have resembled Reality. Time and motion beyond the apprehended. They were both there, as was the third. But foremost, there was the image of the twins of two ova, playing over the high cliffs of Kamenin, building their cairns—one by hand, the other by force of air. And there was joy, hope, the warmth of nostalgia. Sjaman felt it, she could tell, as a smile had returned to his empty face. There followed the diminishing dread of the rite, conducted over and over until it lost its meaning to her.

It was required of her to taint the fair girl, the prettiest virgin of Mavros. She was the very first and, after her, there was already a hidden loathing for the young sorceress, one that would not vanish for years to come—when the spell was practiced on a chieftainess of the enemy. They cheered her name after that one. She made sure Sjaman could hear it. The last time, before she was cast away from the village and again sent up to the cold bluffs, she had depraved a recent lover. Still yet, he followed her at once, caught her meals and gathered her additives.

This was what she wanted from the start. A quiet place to practice. Though, something was missing. A tear rolled from Sjaman's eye: fear, habit, shame, comfort, longing.

185

Her sister wasn't there when she came down from her mountain. And she burned the chieftain's village as if urged by that overlord, the savage Roberrus Sivliére. She left. And when her sister escaped the Mavrosii, returned to find the burnt bodies of the serviles, Sjaman waited for her. They stole six pheasants and fled west. Over waves and under storms. And then they found Sarcovy and called their new land Sylvan. At least, he did.

The house took two terrible years to build. There was a man named Tommas and another called Elmaen. They set the deck, they raised the walls. Sjaman was the one to exude all his strength in lifting it. Pain and illness. No wonder he never used crafts again.

But what of her sister? And where did the rest go? After all that effort, she disappeared to a place called Egain. Barren fields and brush, below a vast wilderland. No difficulty in finding that.

Do you know what I have been through? she echoed in his head. *From Etmarna to Delisinin to Undramon I have searched, both for her and for myself. What did I find? To show you would take far too long. And I mean to leave now. Do you see the burning reeds, the shackled children, the boxes of silver pieces? They are spreading their bile over the sea, unto the Piikish shores, returning from whence they came. Here. I saw it through my father's eyes as he lay dying under my protection. You see? I have three tasks at hand. By year's end, I will be finished. I plan to be finished.*

She released him, casting off the coat of shadow and the effervescence of her limbs. Sjaman now gazed over the hairless girl above him.

"Feofan," he muttered. "My only pupil."

As if waking from a nightmare, he looked on the goat-beasts that held him in place, recognition swaying in his eyes. "The vestal Signy. The adulterous Birgir. The conquered Viggdis." The lattermost rumbled and pressed her blade further into his powdery beard. "I was wonderin' when ye would come fer the fourth."

Feofan kicked the man's stomach.

"That is why you stole her away?" she said through clenched teeth. "You thought I would respect the rite over my own sister?"

"I can see now. I was wrong. Ye wouldn't ever do that, would ye? Not even if yer own life was at risk fer it."

The woman almost laughed.

"My own life is never at risk, old man."

By first light, the house was stripped of its valuables and buried under the mud of the swamp. Sjaman, naked and with hands bound by a hundred strings, was hung by his beard from a high branch, left for the vodniks to taunt. Feofan and the satyrs were gone.

*　　*　　*

Frysa came to Sarcovy like a ghost stirred from its sepulcher. At the start of its first quarter, Damme Anae and Aetheling Felix padded aboard their flagship, the *Albatros*, and sailed with all their retinue around the northern coast of their island. Two days later, they docked at Aubin, the Traders' Islet, and were led into its only town, Leuwdorp, the home of Eren Pourtmann.

This was Anae's first time on Aubin, much to Felix's surprise. Having lived in Reineshir, she had been closer to the ferry of Rolle's Channel than anyone else in her new household. With a fast horse and a fair set of sails, she could have crossed over to the island within a day. She addressed her husband's unwitting criticism with the usual excuse: "I had no reason to leave Reineshir," as she said. "Everything I ever wanted was brought to me." Oddly, Felix always appreciated this answer.

Leuwdorp was a charming enough place, she thought—as a matter of fact, it was much larger than Wallenport and evidently better connected with the lands beyond humble Sarcovy. Its markets teemed with foreign trinkets and charms, and its streets were crammed to the walls with busied journeymen. Its garrison was lightly armed and unapparent, yet ever-present within the crowds. Even the children were plainly a product of their haunt, pickpocketing all their wares and selling them from secluded corners.

Best of all, nobody seemed daunted by the disruptive line of nobles parading down their main avenue, Anae and Felix at its fore. All merely sidled past and hurried onward to their desired confluences. This was a place she could retire to in her old age, Anae thought.

Handelhaus, the Pourtmanns' peculiar manse atop Leuwdorp's plateau, was built up entirely of imported red brick and, as Anae estimated, it was twice the size of Sivliére Castle. From its eyrie terrace, she could see the full breadth of the islet, every ell of coastline: with the exception of one untouched tract of sand and trees, the whole of Aubin's seaboard was compacted with piers and docks. Ships of all sizes and designs surrounded them—slender cruisers with triangular sails, robust cogs from Triume's

187

coast, double-hulled transports of the far west and east. The night's overture had draped the sky before she could tell apart the rest.

"How much longer are they going to make us wait?" Iacob asked behind them. "Hells, I haven't eaten since this morning."

"I'm sure they have some dainties downstairs you can chew on until supper," said Felix moodily. He and Anae stood side by side at the balustrade, waiting for the stars to appear.

Iacob impatiently changed the subject. "Do you think Eren seemed bothered by us? When we first arrived, I mean. Maybe that's why he's having us wait so long."

Felix shook his head. "I already went over this," he said. "Of course he's bothered by us. This isn't just a customary hallmote, despite what he might say. It's a damned public scorning."

Anae rested her hand over his, half expecting him to jerk it away as he did on the night of their departure. He didn't move.

"Well, you've got me at your right hand, don't you worry," Iacob affirmed. "These islet folks are brittle as shaved steel. And a plus—did you see the garrison as we passed through? Our aspirants had tougher garb than these fools. They might as well slap a cut of parchment over their hearts. Wouldn't come as cheap though."

At this, Felix slid his hand away, joined it with the other. "Edma," he muttered impersonally, "I wish to speak with my wife alone." He added no more. A moment passed. Then there was a rasp, a leather sole pivoting on stone, and a recession of footfalls. The aetheling and his damme were alone.

"What is it?" Anae asked.

"I once had a dream I was up here," he said. "Nothing was different. It had the same color, I could see the same number of ships. The sky and clouds were probably just as they are now." He waited for a reply, Anae figured.

"What else happened?"

"Wish I could remember," he grumbled. "Probably one of the two other things that reoccur. Either I was chased back downstairs by a devil or I saw my brother or father undressing another man in the distance. *Ach!*" He spat his distaste. "Look at me—talking to my wife as if she's my mother. Nobody else wants to hear about dreams, do they?"

"I like to hear about them," she said, sidling up to him. Ellemine did indeed have an otherworldly fascination with dreams. More so now than ever before, in fact. Anae wondered if that were partly why Felix recommended her to stay back in Wallenport. Otherwise, she knew precisely why he didn't want his mother to come along, to ride beside him, to endure the same silent derision he was about to endure.

"I swear, if I'm forced to suffer any of Eren's children…" He breathed, balled his fist, stretched his fingers.

"Would that really be the worst of it, Felix?"

"You've never met them. They came to Wallenport on St. Fergus Day last year—just them, not their parents. Brats strutted like gulls around my castle. One of them stole from the buttery and carved his name on a cask after he and his brother emptied it. 'Alfes' or 'Aflen' or something. And the girls kept asking me if I had this or that, kept saying it was too dark in the gallery and the court, kept spying on me in my room."

"They fancied you," Anae tried with lacking humor.

"So, I made some comment about their dead sister and they let me be after that." He sighed again. "She didn't really die, she just went missing. But they all assume as much." He clicked his tongue. "Hopefully those girls have been married off by now. Married off and sent far away."

"Felix," Anae hummed. They watched each other for a quiet spell, each waiting for the other to continue. Neither said anything. They merely recollected themselves in each other's eyes. It was a new ritual of theirs, Anae noticed, first employed on the day they received the news from Westley.

Not long after, she and Felix were summoned to court.

*   *   *

Still yet, the Pourtmanns outdid them: instead of a great hall, their house contained an open-air canopied cloister at its center. A large dormant table with an open space in the middle was set over the grassy quadrangle. Even better, in Felix's professed opinion, the table was lined with several dozen chairs, enough to seat all his advisors and all the needed confidants of Hertog Pourtmann. Anae situated herself to the right of her husband and requested Curator Arnaul sit on her other side—primarily so he could explain the proceedings. He assured her, however, that the meeting would be elementary.

"This should be an interesting one," he grumbled to her while Felix and Iacob washed their hands in the cloister's lane.

"Because of the uprising?" she said.

"That will be the brunt of it, yes. Hertogs tend to be amused by rebellions and feudal wars. I told Felix as much, though I doubt he was paying any attention at the time. Be a dear and remind him to keep his head if you think he's about to lose it. This is his first hallmote, you know."

She didn't know, much to her surprise.

"He'll be fine," she assured. A blatantly unhappy man slumped down next to Arnaul, but the curator paid no mind.

"Why does Sarcovy even have a hertog?" she asked.

"Roberrus wanted one," said Arnaul. "He was always warring elsewhere and needed someone to hold council with his two earls, his castellan, and the men and women of his household staff. That is, the ones who didn't join him abroad. Like myself. And Damme Ellemine."

Anae bit her lip. She hated public speaking, though she'd never tried it. Ideally, the Pourtmanns would have plenty to discuss; ideally, they were pompous enough to ignore their new damme.

Others were now entering the lanes and selecting their seats. A servant crawled under the table into the interior square and planted four tall torches at each corner. Once ignited, the staves illuminated the overlays of colored tarps above—which in turn lent a more glamorous hue to the cloister. This was soon accentuated by the delivery of the evening's meal, an exhibition of fare both common and exotic. The hertog's chaplain led them all in prayer, an appropriately brief invocation, and the feast began.

Though Anae was fascinated by many of the unidentified dishes passing by, she did very little experimenting. At the end of the plate rotation, her board was covered over with roast canary, bread pudding, black and green olives, long grain rice, sour cabbage, and a lemon. It was consorted with a very dry blood-red wine.

She ate slowly, scrutinizing the feasters around her, deducing which ones belonged to the Pourtmann family. The hertog, obviously, was the man across from them, as he was installed in the largest chair. A woman and a young man with wheat-colored hair sat on either side of him, their own seats of relative size. Eren Pourtmann—if that were really him—was heavily vested and embellished with the common colors of mercantilism: thus, all the colors he could obtain. Aside from his gratuitous layers and the outlandish violet that he donned, his grey features were ordinary.

He and the lad beside him stood once most of the food was devoured. He outspread his hands, calling for silence, and the young man stepped over the table's surface and down onto the turf. Felix huffed and dropped his knife loudly.

"Could I procure your attention, please, all of you?" he called. Everyone ceased their conversations. He placed his hand behind the neck of the woman beside him.

"'Glowing in the whitest raiment, they came into the oubliette of our time, bearing naught more than those words I had sought.' So spake our Divine Scribe. Such a monumental occasion this is. Damme Jessa and I thank all of you for coming, for encircling my table, for enflaming cheer despite the tribulations of this dying year. Not only are we graced by the attendance of our esteemed aetheling, Felix Sivliére, but we have also been granted the privilege of beholding his resplendent wife. The fair Damme Anae."

The young woman smiled at the hertog, eschewing the drove of leaning spectators.

"A monumental night, indeed. I can only hope that the flavors of our evening's supper were not too bitter nor too sweet, and that all of you were pleased by the display. Now, where was I...'When they spoke as All, I knew life's absolution. When they touched me, I knew it was my demise, the dissolution of my earthen spirit, the foremost bereavement of my flesh. And yet I could not see that beatific spectre through the dark of my cell of clay. It has become me, they said, or I have become them or All has subsumed me'..."

Once it was clear he had finished, his audience gave a mixture of reactions: the more learned or pious of the group interjected with "Patta Merr," while the rest—Felix, Iacob, and few others—gave a hum of feigned understanding.

"The passage is, of course, from the finest and final work by our beloved prophet. I utter it here only as a devotion, an exordium for my son here. Gentle Alfons has for us a composition. The muse thereto came into his baldachin, not one week past. It was a divine act, I believe, a sign that his sibling, my son, worthy Amalic, is safe from all harm in Westley, where our enemy holds him captive. It is his gift to you, my exquisite guests."

Eren Pourtmann sat back down, his hand still caressing the shoulders of the woman beside him—the Damme Jessa, presumably.

His son, meanwhile, paced around the inner confines of the table, his hands behind his back, his lips curled up into a smug grin, eyes downcast. Felix made a soft sound, as if he were exhaling without releasing air. He

191

was officially unamused, Anae could tell. It was the same sound he made whenever they were lying in bed together and someone knocked at the door, insisting he answer himself. It was usually Iacob the Edma, inviting his mate out to a hunt. Felix usually declined and returned to the sheets.

"Hear it!" commanded Alfons Pourtmann, sweeping his hands about like a pantomimist. "Heed now the heart-song of Aubin the Able and Larenta the Lovely of Loren's old lake; but first will I furnish the forebear's flight, whence Wallen strode strong on his steed…"

Already, Anae was repulsed.

A quarter of an hour dripped away and the Pourtmann son had not yet made it to the second act, the part of the story where Aubin leaves to join the Conquest of Sarcovy. Anae knew the legend from *Chevaliers of Bienvale*—or so she thought. It was possible she was confusing it with another tale—they were all so similar, after all.

"So aboard Aubin's ship did Larenta lie low and sleep under sails of pale scarlet. The orbs of Ophinan she plainly observed while the wild winds frothed forth the foam…"

"Is this a regular feature of the hallmote?" she muttered to Arnaul, who leaned over to receive her. Neither took their eyes off Alfons or his father.

"It became one after the lad learned how to write," the curator grumbled through a corner of his mouth.

"Are you sure you don't mean 'when he started to write'?"

Arnaul sat back in his chair and cleared his throat, ignoring Anae's jest. It was probably best that he didn't laugh, the girl resigned, as it would have disturbed the performance—and the curator had a tendency to do just that, particularly when he snored during church services. Felix, meanwhile, had begun anxiously shifting in his seat. Anae placed a hand on his leg.

"And the stars of Synesti thus glowered and glowed while Haem's holy halo hooked round the moons. Here Larenta laid lonesome on long planks of lumber, wandering through worlds undemised and undarkened…"

Felix moaned. It was loud enough for a whitebeard at another side of the table to hear: the elder turned his head and frowned in their direction. Damme Anae squeezed the topmost portion of her husband's thigh and angled closer to his ear.

"I know," she whispered, "your verses are much better. And shorter."

Felix shook his head acutely. Others around the table began noting his impatience, Anae saw, though Alfons was still lost in his composition. She clenched her teeth, digging her fingernails into the side of his breeches.

192

"It's enough to avert anyone from the art," he said to her; then slightly louder, "Hear that? Now he has me alliterating."

Anae shushed him. Two young women next to Damme Jessa tightened their lips and peered over. One, a freckled youth, crossed her arms and held her sides.

"This is not the place and most definitely not the time, Felix," she pressed as quietly as she could. "Remember we have a favor to ask." Felix sighed through his nose. "It can't go on for too much longer."

Half an hour passed.

"Then Rien came and ravaged the coven's copious clearing as the barbuted brothers had a bout for its best: the taller took victory, quite a contest tempestuous, and his challenger in chains left the lady her life…"

Neither Aubin nor Larenta had been in the story for hundreds of verses. Iacob began drumming his fingers along the table's edge; it was audible whenever Alfons paused at the end of a stanza or lowered his voice to magnify the tension. Anae kicked her husband's foot: he was presently slouching with two fingers against his temple, as if focused on the beating of his heart, the passage of blood to his brain. He glanced at Anae, then at Iacob, then booted the edma's heel. Iacob stopped his drumming.

Felix began tracing the outlines of his long ears—another show of sever apathy. On the girl's opposite side, Arnaul's head began to gradually droop forward. He purred smoothly, like the cats she used to play with back in Reineshir. She gave the man a similar treatment and he jolted to life as if roused by a thunderclap. Anae began to worry: what if other, out-of-view members of the Sivliére staff were dozing?

Another quarter of an hour melted away.

"Larenta's tears twice filled the jetted jail till in torrents they tumbled the towering trees; Aubin beat his breast and bawled as a beast when the waters white parted his peaceable purpose…"

"I need to take a piss," Felix mumbled.

"It's almost over, it has to be," Anae whispered back. "The story ends with the Lightrun parting and Larenta drowning and so on. You can wait."

"We came here to talk about the state of my goddamned demesne," the aetheling persisted, "not to listen to this over-inspired balladmonger dross."

"Just let him speak. He must not get much attention otherwise. His family is made up of merchants, not minstrels." She paused. "God, his rhythms really are infectious."

193

As she muttered these words, the guests began clapping; the applause reverberated through the cloister, granting the illusion of a more impressive ovation. The two of them joined in. Alfons bowed pronouncedly to each side of the table, then retreated over the boards, kissed his father's head, and raced off.

"About bloody time," Felix said privately, straightening himself. He got up, outstretching his hands to Hertog Pourtmann. The man wrinkled his brow as if expecting an offense. Damme Jessa slanted over to him, imparted a few words. He nodded as she withdrew. Anae chewed at her lip as she observed this exchange.

"Thank you for the..." Aetheling Felix twirled his hand at the wrist and an unfriendly hush fell over them all. "Poetry. It, ehm, it's been a long time since I heard a proper chanson. Your son will have to teach me some of his methods."

Nobody spoke. Arnaul cleared his throat inopportunely. The whitebeard, the first man to notice Felix's recent displeasure, hacked into a sleeve.

"Now, we've all been fed," Feliz went on, "we've all tasted the lyrical artistry of the Pourtmann clan. I think it's time to move on to—" He choked on the word as if he finally realized the floor was his, as if someone had just spat in his face. "Domestic matters."

The hertog bowed his head in agreement and massaged his chin with a thumb. Another pang of quietude. At its end, Felix sank back down into his chair.

"Yes," Eren conceded. The aetheling awkwardly pushed himself back up. "No use in prolonging our talk of disharmony. We have an uprising at hand—perhaps a long anticipated one, at that. And I believe every one of us is prepared to exchange solutions, propositions of action, plans for domiciliary relief. I will call upon each suitable sojourner when I feel it is their time to speak—as my station permits, good Aetheling Felix. Do stand as the others speak. And interrogate them as you see fit."

Felix smoothed down the hairs of his short beard.

"I shall," he began, wringing his hands, stretching and bending each joint as he so often did. "As you all know by now, ehm..." Already, he fumbled for the right words—or as Anae soon guessed, more eloquent words. He gave in before the bland caesura could undermine him.

"Our island has been disunited," he began again. "Nearly a season ago, the ridders of Laisroch County launched a coup against their earl. This, eh, started in Westley, of course, though the men of Hoerlog Tower are possibly in league with them, as I have heard nothing from their post. That said, the tidings are scant in regards to this rebellion. Little over a week after it commenced, my Westley informant—he was positioned as one of Rolle Laisroch's gardeners, I think—arrived at my court. He told me that a band of ridders stormed the earl's courtyard and slew all of his men before raiding the hall. My informant did not stay long, he admitted. He'd raced out of town at the first sign of danger.

"Four weeks after that, I was given a letter. It, eh, it came from Rolle Laisroch. Who, as he claimed, fled here to Aubin after being usurped by his stewardess and war-mester. This reminded me of the aspirants I sent to The Stead not long ago. More weeks passed, the Hosten season came to an end, and I have still not heard from the men there. I had only heard from Count Bertram here, who disclosed that no more than forty ridders—some wounded—were received at the gates of Castle Chaisgott. They announced that all the lands west of the keep were, uh, have been lost to the unnamed rebels." Hertog Pourtmann held up his hand and Felix discontinued his speech.

"Before you proceed," he said, "I would have further details divulged by other members of the party." He directed his hand to the man seated beside Arnaul. Anae only partly caught onto this signal, as she was once again distracted by the lemon on her plate. And by the involvement of the ex-Earl of Laisroch, Morley's father. And by her husband's error in calling him 'Rolle.'

It was all a coincidence, she knew. There was no way Morley was capable of kindling a revolt.

She perked up when the hertog trumpeted the new speaker's name: "Michel Laisroch." She examined the man's profile. He had the same umber hair as his son and a vaguely similar mouth and nose. Anae further confirmed the kinship when he turned his head to Felix.

"If I may correct you, aetheling," he said, "Rolle was my father, the first earl. He had no gardeners, to that point." Felix opened his mouth to apologize for his mistake, but Michel pressed on, turning himself back to the hertog.

"I had included other, yet unmentioned particularities in the letter I sent to Wallenport. And there was another aspect I omitted. I'll share everything here but, first, let it be well and widely explicated that my stewardess, Allesande van Lattaholm—who didn't *quite* usurp me as much as dismantle my function—is indeed my sister-in-law. In starting this insurrection, she has not only betrayed me, the only remaining agnate of the Laisroch name, but she has also acted against the best interests of her own family. The Meerholzes, if you are unfamiliar. They have no confidence that she may succeed in supplanting the Aetheling of Sarcovy. So, they have agreed to assist our cause."

"They, eh, they've reassured me of this, as well," said Felix. "Their messenger arrived at my door not two weeks ago." Then, as if he'd been reading Anae's mind, Eren spoke up.

"You would do best in maintaining the pretense of your chances, then," he suggested. "Unless I am deaf of ear or reason-blind: if you have lost your primary cantonment and all the lands west of it, then the odds are against you. Your best choice is to seek continental aid. And hope the enemy doesn't call on them first." Anae could hear her husband quiver as he breathed.

"Continue," Eren said to the ex-earl.

Michel did so. "They cannot offer much—maybe four hundred men-at-arms. If you, Aetheling Felix, wish to appeal to the earls of Garm or Nelborg or Knowlshir, I could act as your envoy. Your father hasn't been forgotten in those places, believe me." Felix tried a warm satisfied smile: the result made him look queasy.

"Now, to return to the subject of my county," Michel went on. "The contents of my letter to Aetheling Sivliére also provided a full report of Westley's biennial yield—namely, cash revenues, livestock, and crop. I have it written here for anyone who wishes to review it." He limply held up a piece of parchment, then set it back down. "The livestock and harvest yields of Westley, as you all know, feed over half of our island's population. Which is to say, it sates *everyone* in Westley…and a considerable fraction of Wallenport's citizenry."

I knew it, Anae thought. The banquets, the three feasts for the aspirants. It was just as Arnaul feared. They were much too decadent. The price of fish had nearly doubled since then. What would the price of bread be once the rebels took the farmland near Reineshir? Wallenport had no fields, just the sea, the quarryland, and most of the Crouxwood. The rest of Frysa was bound to be miserable—and not just for the commoners.

As Michel prattled on about other losses, Anae stayed transfixed on the idea. Widespread hunger. The alternatives for cultivation. Was seaweed edible? What about barnacles? Could they set up crab farms along the east coast?

Her immersion in the hallmote was restored once Michel concluded his summary. Felix then brought back the topic of the assault on the ex-earl's house.

"Ah, that's right," Michel said. He pinched at his lip and stared down at the grass for a time. "Well, I have since concluded that Allesande's been plotting against me for as long as you've held the lordship, aetheling. Whether or not your ascendancy was the first mover, I am still unsure. What I do know is that she had been dipping into Westley's coffers— which were under her management at the time—and was thus using the stolen funds to bribe the best ridders in my service." He blinked twice. "*Her* service, I should say. She also managed the garrison…and the chevalerie."

Several men close to the hertog began murmuring to each other. Michel started to sweat.

"The ridders she bribed were given the task of sowing dissent among the aspirants and squires, I believe. They did so. Proficiently. Some ridders, however, she knew were incorruptible, as they once served me in my household and know—*knew* how honest a man I am. So, she promoted each of them to the rank of 'housecarl,' a position which hadn't yet been oriented in Westley. These promotions were assigned earlier this year, during Hetta.

"The men were slain while I was alone in my bedchamber. I heard shouts from the courtyard, then a forced entry. Allesande came in, told me that Mennia here—my wife, her sister—was locked away elsewhere. And…" He became pensive again for a moment. "I'm unsure why they chose to strike at the time they did. She likely underestimated your ability, Aetheling Felix, to organize a retaliation within the remainder of Hosten— or else, she was confident she could ward off whatever you sent her way. Moreover, she must have predicted that neither you nor your army of aspirants would be motivated to launch a counteraction during Frysa, as the conditions can—"

"Oh, Sanct's Bones!" came a woman's voice. Everyone's eyes shot to the seat beside Michel, whose face was now glistening despite the cool air. "Will you tell the bloody truth for once in your life—for once in your pathetic perverted life?!"

Silence followed. Damme Jessa's jeweled hand covered her mouth; her husband looked more intrigued than infuriated. At the end of the stillness, there was a light swishing sound: chair legs being pushed over turf. Then, from the other side of the standing ex-earl, a woman stumbled off into the cloister's perimetrical hall. She soon disappeared. And the murmurings proceeded in full.

"Care to explain?" Eren casually said over his droning guests. Michel sighed as the voices receded. Anae scanned the table and saw that most on the opposite ends were leaning forward. Michel respired a second time.

"It was a false accusation Allesande thrust upon me," he said. "Believe that if nothing else. I didn't mention it because I thought it inappropriate. But it cannot be avoided now, I suppose. Please pardon my wife for the outburst. For her, the rebellion has been quite taxing." Once again, he released a hot breath and wiped the sweat from his face. "While I was restrained in my chamber, one of the traitors brought in a young man. A halfelev."

Upon hearing that single coupling of words, Anae felt her heart, lungs, and stomach heave up into her throat. She instinctually raised a hand to her chin, as if to catch the organs as they spilled out.

"Allesande then interrogated him, asking him about his origins," Michel continued. "Who his mother was, for example, and...who his father was." Some, the hertog included, bobbed their heads. They knew exactly what he was insinuating. "The boy claimed that, ehm, well, he said I had—had an affair of sorts with..."

Anae glanced up at her husband. He was pale as a corpse.

"Our damme. Our aetheling's mother. Ellemine." As before, the mumbling resumed. This time, Michel was determined to combat it. "B-but I didn't do it, I swear it!" Nobody paid him any mind. "The boy was born off the island, didn't even know what he was doing in my hall! Nobody knows where he went after that either—it was all a play, a show, a—"

"That's enough, that's enough," said Eren Pourtmann, both to Michel and his guests. He dragged his seat closer to the table and set down his elbows, fingers knitted. "Now, pardon my misapprehension, but what does this have to do with Allesande? What were her reasons for launching the insurrection at the time that she did?" Everyone calmed and waited for the ex-earl to continue. Anae, on the other hand, had strayed from Reality.

Fitzmorley, you blundering idiot, she thought, you've really done it now. Sneaking into Castle Silviére and attempting to rescue her from a life she didn't wish to leave—that was bad enough. Sparking a small war: this was unforgivable.

What was it that Morley had said as they walked down the black steps beneath the castle? "I'm sick of aethelings and dammes." Was he lying? No, no, no—Anae could always tell when he was lying. Really, he *never* lied. So then why did he decide to travel off to Westley? Was it *not* Morley after all? Was it some other halfelev? Of course not. Ellemine did have other misbegotten scions out in the world. But besides Felix, Morley was the only one who could accurately be called a 'boy.'

She pulled her speculations away from the silly halfelev and cast them unto her mother-in-law. Who else knew the truth of her adulteries? She shared the anecdotes with Anae as a demonstration of her trust—or so she said—and also because they ostensibly weren't heavy truths to her.

She was an elev, a purekin. The conventions of humble naemas never concerned her. In fact, nothing whatsoever seemed to matter to her. She could be buried alive and not so much as cough. If Felix was to approach her with Michel's account, would she admit the truth to him? Did he already bloody know it? Roberrus had known the truth. He concealed the scandals without care and sailed off to murder more Piikish tribes. Would Felix be so callous? Again, she tugged her thoughts away...

And, in returning to Morley, she realized something else: "Your father lives in Westley," she'd said to him. She would've readily told him more if he expressed interest. Or if he hadn't already known the truth.

"—found him in passing and, thinking that he'd leave Westley at any hour, they abducted him, gave him a faux testimony about his lineage and—and used him as a threat to my authority. Allesande said I could keep my title if I publicly admitted the lie was true. But I could never do such a thing. If I did, then Allesande could have convinced my people that this— this halfelev from nowhere has a claim to the lordship, being a son of both Laisroch and Silviére blood. B-but as I said, the boy's gone, vanished. It was all a show. Allesande couldn't get what she wanted the way she wanted it, so she dispensed with idea, let the boy go. And threw me out of my own home."

The cloister still rumbled with private discussions, each of which began during Michel's explanation of his stewardess's plot. The hertog raised a stifling hand.

"I believe we have heard enough on this matter, Michel. You may sit down." The earl did so, heavily. Anae looked back up at Felix: color had returned to his face, but he was still vexed.

"With all uncertainties aside, here is my conclusion," announced Eren. "If Laisroch County—or Rebels' County, one might call it—is not brought back into Aetheling Felix's demesne or if Allesande's yet undefined demands are not met in due time, then many will starve in Wallenport and Sarcovy will inevitably be lost to you. Aetheling Felix, your best hope is to call upon the noble families of the continental coast, request an army, and offer sumptuous compensation."

"Yes," Felix squeaked, clearing his throat to cover the dissonance in his voice. "In that same vein, Hertog Pourtmann, I have another request that I would—"

"Before we discuss that," Eren interrupted, pointing further along Felix's side of the table, "I wish to have the others speak first. Count Bertram."

Three seats down from Iacob, the middle-aged castellan stood up with the usual gravitas. Whenever he attended Felix's court, Bertram made sure he was the best dressed—silk-laced tunics and skirts with the finest embroideries Anae had ever seen. Here, he wore a mundane black cloak.

"You have recently received a number of troops at Castle Chaisgott, is that true?" Eren asked. Bertram confirmed. "What have they told you?"

"Nothing that has not already been implied, Hertog Pourtmann," he said, his voice hoarse. He was probably recovering from a late Hosten fever, considering the pallor of his face. "Nine and thirty men called for me to raise the portcullis on that morning. Of their number…" He drew out a strip of paper from his sleeve, peeked at it, then crumpled it up.

"Ten were aspirants—five youths among that lot—twelve were ridders, eight were arbalesters, six were avantgardes, two were bijl-ridders, and one was a squire. Between all of them, they had only eighteen horses. They all claimed to have retreated from The Stead, which was encircled by the rebels. How they managed to flee from the scene is unknown, though they say many others escaped into the Crouxwood.

"They explained that, at the start of it, the enemy was hidden all around the edge of the glade but, with a few arrows, they announced their presence. The ridders rode out to expose them but none came back. They say a full night passed before the rebels made an advance and, when that time came, cacophony ensued.

"The Stead was emptied. That is to say the aspirants were largely unhindered, so far as the survivors could tell. They were likely captured and dragged off somewhere. Needless to mention, that tract and all the lands around it are occupied. Before I left Chaisgott to join Aetheling Felix on his voyage here, three of the men—specifically, two avantgardes and the squire—ventured out to confirm the loss of that land. I'm sure they have returned to Chaisgott by now."

Felix hummed, slowly twisting toward the count. "Excuse me for not asking sooner. But who is attending the castle in your place?" All eyes went to Bertram.

"My nephew," he answered. "Sir Matten. He has acted as overseer before. Does the job well despite having only one eye." Few chortled, thinking the comment a joke. Bertram seated himself with a grimace.

"Very well," Eren grunted. "If these rumors reflect their verity, then the dissenters have a different goal in mind. And it might be the case that these men have no intent to terrorize or harm those who serve you, Aetheling Felix. Be that as it may, Castle Chaisgott could be Wallenport's final bulwark. Unless…" He beckoned to yet another figure, this one closer to Iacob.

"Mester Alherde?" he said.

Again, Anae's heart leapt. Why was her old teacher here, she wondered—and at that, why weren't her parents in his place if Debois County was obliged to send a representative? And most of all, how did she not notice him—how did *he* not notice *her*? Was he ignoring her?

Anae resolved the question before the man could stand: she had been his worst student, as he used to regularly remind her. An insufferable pupil. Unless he was forced to, why would he ever bother to say hello?

She examined him as best she could from her place at the table: he appeared to have aged backwards.

"What can you tell us of Olford and the rest of Debois County?" the hertog queried as Alherde swept crumbs from his robe.

"Only that we've seen very little cartage from beyond the Lightrun's borderline," he said. "On top of that, there has been a decline of transit within the county itself. Normally in the course of, say, five weeks during Hosten, we receive in Reineshir more or less than ten cartloads of miscellaneous goods, a majority of which come via the northward roads between us and Olford. Those shipments largely carry flour, cheeses, butter, raw grain, sometimes surfeit breads—all of it comes from Westley's and our farmlands. During the latter half of this previous Hosten, however, we received no more than eight carts, the supplies of which were stripped of all their foodstuffs. But—"

"That makes no sense," Felix interrupted. "If the rebels are centered in Laisroch, they should have all the food they need. Why would they bother to steal more?"

Alherde snorted with placid irritation. Anae began to feel drowsy, tired, and disgusted. "I was getting to that, Aetheling Felix," said the scholar. "The Bertrisses have a hymeneal tie to your own family so, if a rebel force were to move onto their property or offend their lord, they, more than anyone else, would be compelled to assist you in quelling them however they can. They have many impressive allies back in Bienvale, you know. And a number of them owe favors.

"But since the Bertrisses sailed back to their manse in Oxhead, that threat is now almost irrelevant to the Westleyans. Imagine how long it would take for someone to get them the message, for them to muster their allies, for their allies to sail through the cold. The island will be lost by then. My idea is that the rebels want to clear out Reineshir, indirectly force its populace to move off to Westley or Wallenport, and then move in and repurpose the town for their own needs before you can do so yourself."

This time, Anae's heart sank down into her belly. Her mother and father, Fruela and Lammert Bertriss. They left her behind. Left her on Sarcovy to fulfill her duties to Aetheling Felix, her lord husband, their lord son-in-law.

Not a letter? Not one note to their daughter: "Beloved Anae, we are returning home. Please, come and see us if you can. Our door is always open, as you know. Our love is always yours." Nothing of the sort.

She had been spiteful at times, she knew that well enough. Her father adored her. He'd wept to the point of fatigue on the day Felix came. He must've sent a message before they left. Someone, a creature or a thief, had to have taken the parcel. Or slew the courier on the road. So then how did everyone obtain the summons sent by the hertog, the call to council on the Rock of Aubin? The meeting of utmost importance.

Who, then, would steal the words of an adoring father?

Arnaul discerned it first: she was crying. Rather, tears were cascading down her face, dripping onto a soggy patch in her skirt. But Anae, thrown again from the fringes of Reality, perceived nothing until the good curator dabbed her jaw and cheek bones with a kerchief. She took it from him, placed it under her nose. The girls next to Damme Jessa were whispering to each other, pointing her out to their matron.

"What could Reineshir possibly have that Westley doesn't?" Felix finished. Alherde huffed and lowered himself down into his chair.

"From that," said the hertog, "it is clear to me that the County of Debois may already be in the hands of our opponents, at least as far as the farmlands. If the roads from Wallenport to Olford are lost, then Chaisgott will follow. And a besiegement of Wallenport will not be far behind." He adjusted himself and held out his hands to Felix. "So, you have a request, aetheling?" Anae could hear him taking a deep breath. She took one herself.

"Yes, Hertog Pourtmann," he started. "If Michel succeeds in coaxing our allies to support us in full, they will need transportation across the Daarkan Sea. So…well…" He buckled under Eren's stare. "You have many ships from many coasts of Triume. Some are under your possession, others could be temporarily coaxed into your custody. All I ask is that—"

"You want me to lend you a fleet of ships," Eren concluded for him. Felix did not speak. "You want me to impede the commerce of Aubin, the only source of profit for my family and the entirety of my vassalage, all for the sake of supporting your conflict against an insubordinate stewardess. You think that the earls of the Bienvalian coast will find your terms unnegotiable if you urge *them* to send off their own ships. In that regard, you are right, as the Frysa winds make for treacherous sailing. So, since the risk is too great, you might as well ask me, one of your father's many thralls, as I have more ships than anyone else within a hundred kalcubits. And since I am nothing more than a thrall, the risk of sending my ships back and forth from here to the continent is entirely insubstantial. Therefore, Hertog Pourtmann should surrender his useless vessels to his all-conquering invulnerable aetheling."

Felix was still at a loss for words, more so now that everyone was watching him again, waiting for him to convey his weakness. Anae stared back at the men and women, as if to challenge them. They saw humor in this exchange—she could tell by the way they smirked—a wicked and satisfying humor that she was no stranger to.

Back in Reineshir, whenever Mester Alherde was corrected or dismissed by another member of the house's staff, Anae always had to gloat cruelly at the man's defeat. Why? Abrupt glory, victory through the defeat of a competitor—but what was the competition? That was obvious.

Everyone in the cloister was playing at it, some with more ambition than the others: Pourtmann had just realized he was in the lead, that the hierarchy of the land was out of balance, that the future of Sarcovy's leadership was completely in his hands. He'd been waiting for a moment such as this for some time, at least since Felix became his true superior.

As for the others, it was no doubt pleasing for them to watch the shift. Would nobody stand and defend their aetheling's mistakes? Not the edma, not the war-mester, not the curator?

There soon came the dreaded question: "Why would I ever do that?" the hertog asked.

Anae stood.

"Because he *is* your aetheling!" she cried out. "Why did you bother to call us all here?! To insult us, to undermine us? Is this some sort of joke to you? Sarcovy can burn and smolder but, as long as you're here warming your hands, it's all worth a laugh! Isn't it? Where is your loyalty?! Where is your respect, your generosity?! He's the bloody aetheling!"

Mutterings ensued, but they were swiftly abated as Eren gave his answer.

"The way I see it, Damme Anae, he won't be for much longer. I'm confronted with a crucial choice: lend my advocacy to a doomed associate or save such an endowment for the next regime. It isn't a case of favor, mind you, it's a case of reliability. It's a business choice. An investment. Never mind the invisible laws of faith, I seek only the wellbeing of my family."

"If you're so quick to cast aside your devotion to Felix," Anae pressed, "why should his supposed replacement find any use in you?"

The hertog grinned. "They're welcome to remove me from my islet. But they must do so at their own risk. I have more friends than you might expect—and each is owed something, sometimes perpetually. If that sum isn't paid or repaid, I won't be the one to face retribution. I am a man of my word. And I am a man of mighty favors. The whole southern coastline of Triume knows this."

Felix cleared his throat. "We mean no offense or disrespect," he rejoined with some confidence. One of his hands floated to the small of Anae's back. "I know of your capabilities and assets. That is why I've come to you today. Ten ships, that's all I ask for—we won't have them for more than a half-season."

Eren snorted at the demand. Anae knew it was a genuine reaction, as ten really was an exorbitant number.

"The ships docked at Wallenport are low-decked fishing yawls," she clarified for all. "Even if they could carry fifty men each, we still need them to haul in our food every single day. If we lose even one, families will go hungry, start begging at our doors." Anae felt tears welling again in her eyes. She leaned forward, her fists on the table's surface. "If you lend us ships, the coastal Biens will see that we have your patronage. They know how powerful you are, just as you say. If they won't fight for *us*, they'll fight for the side that has the backing of the Pourtmanns."

She could feel Felix peering over her, either proud of his wife's impertinence or—if he truly were an absentminded statesman— disappointed that she would so readily admit their weaknesses. Hopefully, it was the former, as she was prepared to speak the castrating words.

"We are at your mercy."

More mumblings. This time, Eren allowed them to endure. Damme Anae sat down, expecting either Felix or Arnaul to speak with her. However, it were as if she hadn't said anything at all. Despite the succeeding proof that she had indeed been heard.

"Two cogs," the hertog announced through the soft din. "I will lend you two cogs, due back here by Mid-Skonhet." Felix loosened, relieved or defeated. "My only offer. See the mester of the east dock when you leave tomorrow. Now, the table is open to all. Aside from Aetheling Felix, those who wish to dismiss themselves may do so."

With that, the scowling old man she spotted earlier struggled to his feet and offered a question to the hertog, though the words were lost. The conversations around them increased in volume as couples and individuals removed themselves promptly. Though she wished to stay by her husband's side, to comfort him and catch him if he were to stumble again, Anae saw Mester Alherde leaving through one of the lanes. She squeezed Felix's hand once.

"Give me a moment," she said. "I'll be back." She kissed his head and raced off.

Alherde—or the outline of a man with a comparable frame—was advancing through a long tunnel at the perimeter's corner, one which led to the outer courtyards of Handelhaus. Anae followed as best she could, though two others had entered the passage before her and obstructed the way forward; they were discussing Michel Laisroch's excuses, sniggering back and forth. She gave them time to heed her but ultimately shoved past and rushed into the open air.

Alherde was nowhere in sight—really, nobody was in sight, as night had fully settled over Leuwdorp. There were only shadows shifting over the scant flecks of light in the town below. Anae stood against one of the many bald columns surrounding Handelhaus, her hair grimy in the blowing salt-wind.

What had been longer? Alfons' epic or the banter afterwards, the main body of the meeting? Such a flurry of emotion, such an incompatible progression of feeling. It had begun with levity, diminished into boredom, simmered to distress, boiled into reserved rage and shock, then snap froze into sorrow, and so on. By the time she got up to defend Felix, there was no feeling left. No coyness, no worriment. As much as she hated to admit it, it made her feel like a true leader.

There was a goal at hand. But enfolded within it was every affection she ever felt. To pick out any one or two of them would be to dispense with the grand end, to focus all desire on a constituent achievement. The satiation of Wallenport's populace, the defeat of the rebels, the absolution of all debts. These were all secondary, all distractions from their totality.

To be a great ruler was to be cold. The great ruler was inconsiderate of his friends; the great ruler afforded no respect for his smaller subjects. And yet at the same time, the great ruler was the greatest servant to all.

"Damme Bertriss." The voice drifted to her from near one of the other columns. She looked to the dark lineament smoothly, as if pretending not to have expected its presence.

"Alherde," she said. "How have you been?"

He came to her side. "Fickle as always," he replied. "I almost didn't come for tonight's gathering. Still not sure if I should've." Anae didn't know what he meant by this and didn't bother with asking.

"Who's watching over Reineshir in your absence?" she asked.

Alherde laughed once. "Does anyone need to? Between Amstudt and Maud, I think they'll be fine. I see you've adapted to life in Sivliére Castle. Your words tonight were unexpected, very unexpected. You've got more brawn than your husband, it seems. Just like your..." He paused. Anae scraped her heel against the ground.

"With you by his side," he continued, "the rebels might have something to fear. And if Aetheling Felix's retinue is practically the same as Roberrus', the rebels have *much* to fear. I thought I recognized their familiar faces tonight. Herman, Arnaul. Can't speak much for the edma, but—"

"My parents," she said. The scholar said nothing. She turned to him. "What about them, my dear?" he said. Still, she stared through the night. "They moved back to Oxhead some time ago. I thought you knew. I thought your father wrote to you." Anae shook her head. "Well, surely it isn't a stupendous matter. They're not so far off—they're just across the sea. A courier could reach them and be back to you within the season." The girl did not speak.

"You were very brave tonight, Anae," he said earnestly.

The girl's face curled. "They could have told me they were leaving," she whimpered. "They could have visited me, could have invited me to come see them before they left. Why didn't they do any of those things, Alherde? Do they ever plan to speak with me again? Have I been forgotten already?"

She felt her throat tightening, her eyelids twitching. Seconds later, tears began rolling out again.

"Please, Alherde. Justify this. Tell me why they left, tell me anything, please…"

As she sobbed through her words, Alherde put an arm around her. She collapsed against him and sobbed into the fabric of his robe.

"I want to leave now. I don't want to be here. I want to go home."

Chapter VI – Friends, Old and New

The cave's egress was just ahead, so Willian took up the oar and dipped it in the water, veering to the only raised bank of stone, a slippery mess concealed by locks of frozen hanging lichen. It wasn't until the bow of his vessel knocked against the rocky shelf that he realized there was nothing to tie it in place. He clambered out anyway, holding onto the stubby bowsprit and parting the curtain of wet lichen with his other hand. He dragged the rowboat along to the edge of the bright icicled maw ahead.

Beyond it, the Crouxwood stepped down the hill with the swishing watercourse, concealing the level head of the Lightrun below. There was movement through the white foliage—brown hair, now black, tamed and curtly waving.

Willian decided to improvise, something he did particularly well: he bunched together the hairs of lichen in his fist, found the rope tied to the yoking thwart, and knotted its free end to the hanging braid. Pushing the craft away lightly, he watched and waited to see if the line would hold. It did.

He passed into the lighted world, stuck on his liripipe, and trotted ably down the descent, sliding here and there on skins of ice. The water accumulated in a large pond just past the threshold of the thickening treeline, then pattered away in its foremost runnel.

Hamm was waiting by this stream with two horses, both of whom were dipping their muzzles in the water.

"All-Being above!" he exclaimed. "Your timing is flawless as always, Sir Willian. I only got here a minute ago."

"I have a penchant for meeting coincidences," Willian reminded him. "Or else it's the other way around." He was ready to mount up but let his preferred steed drink her fill. "Chaisgott?"

"Is wide open," the squire answered. "As you can see, one of our own is already taking charge of the stables." He shook the reins of each horse. "Bertram came back from Aubin three weeks ago, before we could grind into Matten more. He's an adamant one, but the men under him are susceptible enough. They strike me as mutinous types."

"What was Bertram doing in Aubin?"

"Oh, he was at the hallmote—that's where he said he was going, anyway. Felix and all his staff went, from what I hear." Hamm climbed onto his horse, the one with the larger antler nubs. The beast continued to drink from the rivulet.

"Allesande wasn't invited, I guess," Willian joked lazily. "Eren Pourtmann is bold but not stupidly so. I reckon his family will be unscathed when all this is done and over with. Unless his son falls off a horse or sprains an ankle." The ridder mounted as he spoke. The horse raised his head from the creek. "Hear anything from Bertram? About the gathering, I mean."

"I'll tell you when we get on our way but, unfortunately, I only have a secondhand account from Matten, his nephew. And he—well, he isn't all that intelligent." Hamm climbed into his saddle and prodded his ride's haunch. The mare grunted, breaking from the stream.

"Neither am I," Willian added. "But I've got time to dwell on what I hear. We'll talk on the way. I've got my own words to share about our shelter."

Soon enough, they were cantering through the flat taupe wood, hooves cromping over the thin snow. The men spoke freely and firmly.

The council at Aubin—according to Matten, a cynical brute for sure—had been a humiliating and hopeless ordeal for Felix. As was recounted, he indelibly insulted the hertog's family before the exchange began: a son of the Pourtmanns was reciting a long-practiced poem of sorts and Felix, surely jealous of its craft, had openly expressed his displeasure.

Michel Laisroch had given an inconsequent sketch of Westley's condition, then offered his service as a continental diplomat, then recounted the day of his removal—and denied his infidelity with Damme Ellemine, of course. Alherde was there too, making things up. At the very end, Felix asked the hertog if he could borrow ships to transport a potential army across the Daarkan Sea—an unlikely prospect. He was permitted two vessels after his wife, Anae, berated Eren Pourtmann for his disloyalty.

This was the best news by far. Allesande, in many different senses, had much more to offer than Felix. If they wanted the hertog's help in trapping the young aetheling, they could get it in half a week's time. Eren's needs could be included in their ever-broadening list of stipulations and Felix would be forced to cooperate. Even if he managed to lug an entire army of Biens onto their shores, they could have Wallenport blockaded before the last ship made it to the docks.

The fate of the Sivliéres hung by a thread of spider silk.

They rode on for six hours with intermittent stops. Willian described the rebels' cavern barracks—the Jotun Cave, as they called it—and Hamm shared his version of the attack on The Stead. He subsequently gave details on his time in Castle Chaisgott, strolling amidst the enemy front.

"I still don't see how this is better," he was saying. "I'm forced to listen to them at night, whenever I try to get a wink of sleep. They think we're all gutless! They refer to us as 'Laisroch laggards' and 'forest rats.' They truly think Felix will pull through, only because he's the son of Roberrus. It's ridiculous! I keep saying to myself, 'We have the means and we have the right leadership, don't start any damning arguments.' But day after day, taunt after taunt, I have to excuse myself from the keep. I just don't see why we need to wait in the cold like this."

"As I've told you before," Willian answered as he wrapped the elongated tail of his hat around his neck, "Wortin says we're not trying to dispose of him. We're not even trying to shed blood here. They know we're on the winning side—they'd have to be idiots not to see that. I imagine words of encouragement are all they have left. You know? Let them revel while they can."

"I'd honestly rather hack them into bloody chunks, Willian. They'd just as quickly do so to me if given permission."

"Believe it or not, that's part of my point." Two red canaries landed in the snow ahead, then fluttered off into the dunness. "Give it five years after our success, you'll see what I mean. Unless you decide to sail off to the continent with the rest of them."

"The rest of them?" the squire asked, tightening his hood.

"The fools who want a good fight. Or any fight, with or without Felix. Mark me, put a sharp sword in someone's hand and note how long it takes before they want to use it." He squinted up at the sun to approximate the time. They would arrive at The Stead just before dark.

"That reminds me," said Hamm, "what are we going to do about the army?"

"That's up to Allesande. If she wants to build one, that's her prerogative. As for you and me—"

"No, no, I meant Felix's army. What if he gets one from Bienvale and manages to bring it here?" Willian furrowed his brow at the young man quizzically. "I'm just saying, what if? What if we can't do anything to prevent them from landing? What if they march to Westley without delay?"

The ridder knew his companion's point was valid, though unconvincing. He thumbed through some recusant notions.

"How do you feed a thousand men during a food shortage, even a minor one?" he countered. "Remember they're running out of bread and beer in Wallenport."

"They'll bring their own food maybe. Unless Felix is so desperate to maintain his reputation, I'm sure he'd tell the continentals about his people's plight." A permissible idea.

"Trust me, I wouldn't put it past him to conceal the situation," came the second retort. "He'd think that asking the Biens to self-provide is too heavy a request. They're already doing him a favor by sending men to fight for his land's security, so why should they continue to bother if he demands them to bring their own rations? Think of that—pretend you're an aetheling of the coast. Some incompetent boy, leagues and leagues to the south, is asking you and your ritters to sail through Frysa storms in order to help him right one of his own wrongs. Oh, and by the way, bring your own yields, all we have is fish around here. And not enough to go around, at that." He snorted punctually.

"I don't know, Willian. Remember they have a lot of wheat in Bienvale. And wheat is the soldier's crop. They mash the ears up in a big pot and boil it. If they're lucky, they'll have fruit they can toss in or honey to drizzle over it."

Willian was impressed by his mate's argument—even more so once a yet undisclosed outlook came to mind: What if the Biens really did agree to sail over to Sarcovy, but only to deceive Felix and establish their own foundation on the island, thus threatening both parties? Honor and reliance were only viable on the mainland because of all the interweaved clans and independent players, each duty-bound to uphold this or that treaty, truce, convention…

If Lord Alec was bound to both Lord Ben and Lord Cam, but the latter two were engaged in a contest of arms, Lord Al's best choice was to send his men to the aid of both, instead of betraying the trust of one for the other—though both had to promise not to pit Lord Al's men against each other in the field, else all others in the king's high society would label Lords Ben and Cam as misers, open targets for lords of higher trust and ambition.

If a serf under Lord Natt battered a serf under Lord Marke, then Lord Natt had a debt to pay to his neighbor, never mind how small the price.

And if a man under Lord Marke later stole a sheep from a man under Lord Natt, then Lord Marke still yet had to pay the new debt—it would never do to simply assert, "Well, I think we're even after that battering last week." Such would burn Lord Marke with the brand of stinginess, implicating—in the extreme—the right for all neighboring lords to ransack that territory if they should so choose.

Men had gone to war for much less, after all: two Bienvalian counts once devastated each other's lands because a man of one district had knocked down two trees within the other district, and recompense was refused.

There was only one absolute, one ground that commenced this feared free-for-all: perfidy.

But Sarcovy was isolated, a tree-covered rock often mistaken for an island of the Piikish archipelago. Roberrus was the only icon to inhabit it and he was already a fading memory. Merchant families—the Pourtmanns, the Bertrisses, the Meerholzes—they were the true rulers of Sarcovy now. Merchant families only fought with hirelings, if they were to fight at all. Merchant families, in the eyes of nobler kin, were therefore exempt from the creeds of honor.

Which was to say, merchant families were fair game. As were incompetent boys, like Felix.

"That sounds scrumptious," Willian replied to Hamm's wheat statement. "Hand the pack over, will you? You mentioned salt beef?"

"It's in there," the squire confirmed.

For the next few hours, they spoke less, occasionally stopping to debate the right direction. There were no considerable setbacks, however, and they entered The Stead's circumference before the sun retired.

What the men of Hoerlog and Westley left standing there, the Frysa snows had further dismantled: a crude fence of twigs and branches, propped up between the trees in some places, once circled the whole of the glade, but now drooped irreparably or rested flat under the oppressing powder. Few lines of tents miraculously still stood under their burdens of ice and two makeshift huts huddled together at the center. Four rudimentary watchtowers used to stretch up at intervals, he remembered; one yet inhabited the southern end, but the others had since fallen. Two had been burned down during the assault, as Hamm pointed out.

The squire also showed his mate to the graves of twelve ridders, the only men who perished in defense of the camp. Each mound was overlaid with clothing and armor. And snow.

"The first was struck while the archers were up in the trees," Hamm explained. "Didn't die quickly either. Someone got him under the shoulder by accident and, well, the whole place was emptied by the end of the night. So the poor fellow didn't get treated."

At the start of the attack, the squire reported, three dozen Westleyan archers climbed to the treetops surrounding the camp, then loosed down on the aspirants and their team of overseers. The purpose, of course, was not to pick off their numbers at range, but to startle the new recruits, force them to overtake their instructors and retreat into the wilderness.

"What about the other eleven deaths?" Willian inquired.

"Can't speak for most of them. But I remember one very well. He joined with the avantgardes when they rode out to find us, though he didn't have a horse. Most were captured within minutes but, since he was apart from the riders, he couldn't be netted. He came charging at a group of seven, an axe and a broadsword in either hand—and he kept on swinging, even when circled! He might've cut one or two of us badly at one instance, so someone gave in and stuck a dagger in his back or neck or somewhere. Fatal jab, that was that. Most of the other deaths were probably similar. And I think one or two others fell off their horses. Or knocked into a tree while toppling from the saddle."

"Where were the others found?"

"Never asked. I only saw them when they were laid out. And I didn't ask how they died. Two or three were hit with arrows."

"I see." Willian heaved hot air into his cupped hands. "I meant to ask earlier: there were around five hundred aspirants, right? You figured about three or four hundred passed by or knocked at Chaisgott's gate on their way back to Wallenport over the following weeks. And Cowen and Nicholan claim to have seen only about three hundred passing the Jotun Cave. That leaves another near-hundred or so, uncounted. Where do you think they went?"

Hamm shook his head. "I doubt they're still out here in the Crouxwood. Maybe some went to Westley or Olford. Not so many lived outside Wallenport, from what I hear. If any avoided detection on the way back there, though, it's because they were in small groups. Or alone. Your guess is better than mine, I'm sure."

"Don't be," Willian said.

Not long after they concluded their exchange, Hamm built a fire in one of the central huts and Willian used the flame to heat up a clay kettle he found near the last watchtower. They slept together in the adjacent hovel.

Willian dreamed as he did every night: he succumbed to the tricks of false Reality, only to wake and again pardon his error. Typically, he retained unbraided ribbons of his dream until the night of the following day, when the process was repeated with the usual variations. The version he conceived at The Stead felt cramped—the presence of Hamm's adjacent body might've been the source. Regardless of this, the night's vagary subscribed to the same unbroken illustration that had been dogging him for years.

It began in the Jotun Cave, as it had been lately…

He was in the stock chamber with few others, it seemed. Bruiner was talking, either to Willian himself or another member of their crew, but he was recounting a predicament in which Felix, ten years old and not yet the aetheling, was chasing him through castle stables with the hilted shard of a blade. But Bruiner was speaking of the event as if it had happened to *him*.

In summoning the images, the dream carried Willian to The Stead's tract instead of the Sivliére stables—and the land was bare, treeless. And Felix had disappeared. Now he saw that he was actually floating over the furthest, deepest pools of the Jotun Cave, forebodingly black, the grave of giant bones. Or the habitation of evil serpents. But no, perhaps not: there were sheep swimming about, their wool ragged and wet. Unless they were goats. Or strangely furry dogs.

Outside, the woman was waiting, a black stubble over her head. He marched past her, as if irked or weary, though endlessly expectant. She followed him, he thought, speaking her nonsense. The detached voice hovered behind him all the way to Werplaus, which the unseen and unheard locals had begun to call 'Semhren's House.'

It was much smaller than he expected: just past the treeline of Reineshir, now smoldering, there was nothing more than a pocket of grass and weeds before the sand bluffs, the crab-covered beach, the ocean. Five fingerlike sea stacks surrounded the place, as if the hand of a titan supported the floating isle from its one end.

Disinterested and physically unable to continue on, he decided to go back to the town behind him as the woman, the unwavering spirit, pressed on to the edge. But Reineshir was Olford—and Werplaus was gone entirely. There was nothing but an unportrayable slate waiting behind the trees, like the light of the world through closed eyes. Somewhere else, though, the woods were burning, smoking, bleaching to ash...

Then he woke up in time to see the squire ducking through the door of their shelter. The sun was not yet fully risen. This was perfect, Willian thought, as they had a long day of travel ahead of them. An hour later, breakfast was prepared: bread, half hard and half soggy, with leftover cheese from Chaisgott.

They left The Stead behind without delay, travelling southeast toward the road to Olford. Conversation became sparse once they set hoof on the wheel-imprinted trail just before noon but, for the bulk of their morning, they exchanged personal trivialities.

Hamm brought up the correspondences with his sister in Wallenport, mentioning the wellbeing of his family and neighborhood friends. This led into a discourse of their mutual comrades, both in the Jotun Cave and in Chaisgott, which led into a session of theorization: Who would stay in Sarcovy after the troubles blew over, what would they end up doing, how much wealth would they muster? When they ran out of ideas, Willian shared a recollection of his dream from the night before. Hamm had no comments, as usual.

On the road proper, they pressed on at a temperate speed, stopping only once to investigate an abrupt, almost violent sound from the thickness—a noise like an uneased boar or reindeer. Nothing was spotted and they continued on, reaching the dorp of Olford before dusk.

They were greeted by a boy, the only villager in sight, who introduced himself as Tomak. He led them to the inn at the other side of the ford, where they were attended by a middle-aged woman named Marion. She served them cabbage stew, offered ample volumes of ale, then showed them to their room, a damp space with a leaking ceiling. All of this was suitably paid for by Squire Hamm.

Rather than going right to sleep, the duo sat out in snow, listening to the passing dribble of the Lightrun, waiting to see if any more residents would show their faces. Nobody. Not even the archer lad who accompanied Morley van Werplaus. Reminded of that curious circumstance, Hamm again described the journey from Hoerlog to Westley, days before the removal of Earl Laisroch—the third time Willian heard his recounting.

"You'd think the archer would be the one to stir up all this trouble," Hamm was saying. "Seemed the type anyway. But no. Who'd believe that his silent companion was to be Allesande's long-sought kindling? To think she bloody believed it—she must not be lied to all that often. All it took was Sieger's and my account and, all of a sudden, she was up in arms with all her men behind her—didn't even give them a chance to have second thoughts. I suppose that was wise." Willian nodded, only partly listening. His mind had wandered ahead of him, down the road to Reineshir. Hamm went on.

"Do you think the lad really was Michel's bastard? Allesande said the old earl confirmed the truth for her. But nobody else was there to hear it. All that seems to matter is he was a halfelev—which, by the way, did you even notice when he was at Hoerlog? That he was a halfelev? I surely didn't and I was with him for days after."

"I didn't notice either," said Willian. They sat in near silence. Hamm, warmed by his four pints, hummed and sucked at his lip. Few times, he breathed in peculiarly, as if he were preparing to ask a question then deciding against it at the last second.

"Sir Willian," he said eventually, "might I ask—and I've been wondering all this while…when Bruiner came and gave me your message, he said you were heading down to Reineshir. Why?"

"I'm meeting its steward, Mester Alherde," he said honestly. "Just as you're meeting with Wortin and Allesande in Westley. We're just giving and getting reports, that's all."

"And you were chosen for the task, as I was?"

"No. I elected to carry it out."

"I see," murmured the squire. "Did you ever meet Sieger's girl? His recent one?"

"I haven't."

"Well…she knew the halfelev very well, it turns out. She claims they grew up together in Werplaus, from what I heard. And you know, she wouldn't tell Sieger or anybody where he went after he left Westley." He let the implication breathe. "If he's not here, do you think he went back?"

"Maybe. Or he's in Reineshir. Or he's out living as a wilder. He's none of our concern anymore."

"Well, maybe you can take a day or two to try and find him," the younger man continued. "It's all a bit tense over in Westley. Allesande wants to know why Sieger supported the truth of Michel's adultery so

216

firmly. But he wouldn't say a word about the girl, about how she was able to verify certain parts of Morley's story because they grew up together. Allesande sees them together, I hear—or at least her spies see them together. But Sieger won't let anyone near her. Maybe he's being overprotective, maybe he's embarrassed because she's of Piikish origin. Either way, Allesande is suspicious. And preoccupied."

"Yeah. I'm going to bed now," said Willian, realizing his mate could go on for the rest of the night. "I'll see you at the breakfast table." He retired to their room, leaving Hamm out by the river.

*   *   *

Morning slithered up and the two men parted ways, the squire riding west with both horses, the ridder roving further south on foot. As much as he liked young Hamm and his company, a day of lonesome drifting was needed—and preferably one which didn't involve boating over an underground river.

Thus, he walked on through windless air, whistling to the birdsongs and chatting with imaginary passersby. He stopped early after spotting the hollowed base of a tree: he always wanted to sleep in one, ever since his old mester told him the tale of Roberrus and Leafeye's Tree of Transformation. He recited the legend while curled up in his cloak, shortsword held to his breast. And he avoided thinking about the coming day, though his nerves could not be abated.

In the morning, he stopped before a plain towerless chapel at the side of the road, a structure he recognized from his most recent dream. Its door had an etching across the midsection with the name of St. Berthe, Matron of...the last words were scratched away, though the edges were carved over with twined buttercups. The matron of gardening or gentle flora, perhaps.

Before he could move on, a man robed in a black and white habit stepped around a corner, a basket hanging by his elbow. Cheerily, he offered the ridder some hard bread with honey. Willian accepted and broke his fast before the locked doors of the church. According to the robed man, Berthe was the patron of flowerbeds and sibling love.

By noon, he reached Reineshir. Though he'd been living on the island all his life, Willian had never been so far south. He'd been to Olford before but, like Hamm on the previous morn, he only ever took the westward road into Laisroch County.

Reineshir was bleak, as expected. On one side of the road, the Bertriss manse sat behind a high crumbling wall, its gates thrown open to the populace, its interior toft littered with broken clayware and other refuse. On the opposite side of the road, the eastern end, the whole rest of the town sat in a grumbling monotone.

The foremost structure was an inn, as indicated by the tavern sign nailed to the door. It was an unrefined picture of a tankard—a rectangle with the three sides of a smaller rectangle protruding from its body. The cellar door flew open as he passed and an acrid stench wandered out, followed by a bitter-faced woman in an apron. She carried a blackwood tray, its surface covered over with a line of slimy brownish stems. The woman did not take her eyes off Willian as she hobbled in through the front door of her establishment. The ridder carried on.

He halted before the gates of the manor and gazed down the avenue running into the town's bowels. He hadn't expected a numerous population, but the sum he *did* expect was in clear view from where he stood.

The buildings, their bases and balconies, were lined with groups of idlers, all drinking from their own cups, some passing tapers to relight their pipes. The day of rest and 'worship' was on every other Fimmday—and today was Triday, Willian thought, if he weren't mistaken. Many of the seated plebs were pointing in his direction; few even got up and disappeared around the corner of the largest edifice, bringing their drinks with them.

Already, Willian was judging if this place were better or worse than bashful Olford. He treaded onto the grounds of the Bertriss estate while thinking it over—and before a decision could take root, the manse's front entrance opened.

As if by the meddling of fate, Alherde came out and hurried in his direction, eyes downcast, a framed wax tablet underarm. Though hardly any older than the ridder, his hair was beginning to grey. Willian recalled the afternoon, years and years earlier, when he pointed out the first colorless lock at the side of the young man's head. It remained a subject of mockery for some time after, a humorous divination of Alherde's future as a scholar.

The ridder announced his presence: "Finally stopped staring at the clouds, I see."

The scholar swung his head up and froze. A stylus jutted from his mouth, then tumbled to the dirt as he dropped his jaw and his wax. It had been six years since they were last together, six years since they last embraced.

"Fitz?" he breathed. Willian curled a corner of his mouth.

"How long's it been, Al?" he asked, though the answer was known. Alherde scurried over to his mate, throwing his arms around him.

"At least eight bloody years!" he said into the cloth of Willian's tabard. "But too long anyway."

They detached—perhaps too swiftly—and Alherde moved back to retrieve his kit. Already, the ridder could tell something was off.

"How has life fared?" Al continued. "What've you been doing? What brings you down to Reineshir?" He asked each in quick succession and with a practiced measure. He always was steady-minded, Willian remembered—it was what got them out of trouble as children. And as young men.

"I came for you," he replied. "For more than one reason, at that. Then I'm off to Werplaus."

"Werplaus!" he exclaimed, taking up his dropped materials. "Surprises abounding! What's in Werplaus? How long will you be staying? Will you be residing here or—"

"Here, one night," Willian laughed. "Now let's talk slower. I'm not going to vanish without warning come dawn again." Alherde did not speak then, acquiescent of the ridder's call for patience. Willian chuckled again. "More than one hearsay has led me down this route, believe it or not. Maybe you know a thing or two about what I'm after."

The scholar made an uncertain face—an expression he probably picked up from the Bertrisses. "Well, can't say much about Werplaus. It's an ungoverned county—I mean to say there are people who live there, though they have no lord. Roberrus gave pieces of the land to a group of chevaliers after the island was—oh, but you know all this! Look at me, treating you like just another damn ridder." He hugged the wax board close to his chest. "Haven't been in town for long, have you?" Willian shook his head. "Good, good, I'll show you around. I've some records to fabricate for the Wallenport seneschals. If ever they show up." They strode through the gate and off the toft, Alherde leading.

Willian couldn't help but notice his old friend's fleeting glances, his reluctance to stare fondly at his mate. They were already on the move, as well. Why could they not stand and speak awhile, or lounge about like the rest of the townsfolk? It had been years, as they both knew.

"So tell, tell!" Alherde went on. "What've you been getting up to through all this time? Didn't get to give you a proper goodbye on the morning you left—was too head-sore from the night previous and couldn't force myself out of my bed."

"Understandable, if I'm not mistaking that eve." Of course, he could never forget a night like that one. He warmed at the thought of it. "I think I gave up drinking afterwards. But as for what I've been doing since, nothing incredible. Typical duties of the ridderstaat, typical duties of Hoerlog. In other words, I've been watching the sea for years on end. Till now, that is."

"You must be thankful for the change, then. Is that where you're coming from? Hoerlog?"

"No. Many of us have relocated to another spot on the north coast," Willian said with a lowered tone. Seven men occupied a balcony above them; and they had all been laughing raucously until Willian was in view. Alherde motioned his hand at them, erecting his small finger and pointing to his lips with his thumb. Two of the men moaned understandingly, then twisted to their compatriots as if to explain the gesture.

"Don't take this the wrong way," said Willian. "The demeanor of your folk doesn't match their surroundings."

The scholar buzzed. "Is that a slight against the people or against their home?"

"Wasn't meant as a slight at all. Though I suppose it sounds like one, now that I think about it." The ridder heard a soft sound from one of the stinking alleys: a group of three variously colored cats were digging into a bloodstained crate, swiping and gnawing at a mushy substance within— animal flesh from the tannery, he determined from the sour smell.

"What I was trying to say is that the townspeople aren't doing much to maintain the—" He coughed when the sour smell overtook him. "Charm of their homestead," he finished.

"On the contrary, my dear lovely Willian, they prefer it this way. Ah, but you must be referring to the manorial grounds." He chortled, glancing back. "It's looked that way since the morning the Bertrisses left. Fruela and Lammert never allowed anyone onto their property, aside from the staff and guests of distinction. I prefer to do what our ancestors did: my home is their home if they want it. Naught but wood floors for them. And Amstudt—that's the chef—Amstudt keeps his grip on the cellar key, though I don't keep the place half as stocked as it was a year ago. But anyway, if the Bertrisses come back for a visit, the smallfolk need to clear out. And clean up."

"I heard a fascinating rumor about Earl Lammert and Damme Fruela," said Willian as they reached the end of the road. They stood before a stretch of broken stalls, not one of which held salable goods.

"Which one is that?" asked the scholar. "I heard one myself the other day. And I'm not so sure how it could've gotten to the ridder who brought it to me. Since word got out about Michel's infidelity with Damme Ellemine, I hear Fruela's been trying to dissuade certain families of the Bienvalian south from interfering with our *troubles*."

"That's good, I suppose," said Willian. "No, that's not the rumor I heard."

"It's not exactly as good as it sounds." They were walking along the stone base of the town's largest building toward a small open entrance in its side. An extensive pen of pigs, chickens, goats, and cows stretched away into the forest ahead.

"See, the Bertrisses are a merchant family, as you know," Alherde went on. "All merchants are schemers and all merchants know that their counterparts and enemies are schemers. Thus, if the Bertrisses are trying to dissuade non-mercantilist nobles from a certain action, anyone who catches wind of such will investigate. Or worse, take initiative to interfere—and without proper surveillance. If anyone on the continent takes foolhardy risks, it's a merchant of Bienvale."

"I must be honest," said Willian, "I have no idea what you're talking about."

They ducked through the doorway. Inside, there were barrel racks against the lengthwise walls and a sporadic stockpile of boxes, many of which were badly aged and empty, all across the main floor. The only light crept in through two high windows on either end. Alherde stood at the center of the nearest rack and began counting the casks, flicking his stylus at each as he addressed his colleague.

"Fair enough," said Alherde. "It's only a guess I've fostered during my half-decade of serving them as a chamberlain and curator. But I think the Bertrisses want more of Sarcovy than they've bought, to put it directly."

And they hope to get it through the most passive methods possible. What was this rumor *you* heard, then?"

"I only heard it from my squire," said Willian, "who heard it from a man in Chaisgott, who yet heard it from another. That the earl and damme left the island without informing their daughter. Normally that'd be a trifle, but I hear she and Felix have soured. And her parents' departure helped fuel it. Count Bertram apparently witnessed it all aboard their ship on the voyage back from Aubin. Felix scolded her for speaking out during the moot, she scolded him in return, and so on. Eventually, she accused *him* of stealing her away from her family. I suppose it's a bit ridiculous, but I can understand her. You were at the meeting as well?"

"Bloody mess, it was. Damme Anae found me afterwards." He paused. "To wit, I could be the involuntary seed of that rumor. I am shocked she received no letter from her mother, but it's easy enough to assume that, if one were written, it simply never reached her. They sent one of their ridders to Wallenport, but I don't know if he carried any message. I assumed they were sending the man off to enter the Sivliéres' service or something.

"Normally, I'd be required to make a record of such, but the Bertrisses had me preoccupied with their mattresses and reliquaries and all the other chattels. It's a big manor. And it was packed to the walls. You'll see what I mean tonight. Either way, it was rather difficult confirming their retirement to Anae and hiding the other details. More difficult than standing before the council and delivering a part-spontaneous string of nonsense."

"What was that?" Willian asked with diminishing interest.

Alherde made a few scratches on his tablet, then navigated his way to the shelves across the room, sidling between boxes. "My words to the hertog and the rest? Being's Breath, I'm not sure if I remember. Part of it was true, I think. There were a few inconsequent words about reduced cartage. Then I touched upon the condition of Reineshir and how it's been largely ignored by the rebels. Or tried my best to. Felix was a little suspicious, so I broke off my explanation and let Eren Pourtmann steal the floor. When we were allowed egress, I left quick. That's when Anae caught up with me."

Willian drifted into the nimbus of his thoughts. Alherde—always modest at heart, though once a ruffian of Wallenport's streets—had inexplicably clambered up the hierarchy. And surely, he had done so without watching his step. Had he even recognized how far his path carried him?

When they first met, Alherde was a boy of the builders' guild. He organized his father's sketches and records, carried messages from the harbor to the growing motte and, when came the time for leisure, he drank as copiously as the adults surrounding him. He later fell in with Mester Semhren when the keep was finished, becoming the court scribe's assistant—the last of that line, potentially. Few years after the mester fled, he followed suite: the Sivliéres gave him to the Bertrisses, with whom he was given the duty of instructing the youngest of their name, Anae. Six or seven years passed. Now he was the steward of Reineshir and all the County of Debois.

Willian remembered their first meeting, well over twenty years prior— back when his mother still showed her face in public. He and the woman were riding together, somehow invisible to the undisturbed and unmannered masons, past the various skeletal constructions of St. Maguir's Court. Little Fitzwillian then spotted a boy, a regular naema who was playing in the sand closer to the uncovered beach. He asked his mother if he could join the child. With a smile, she lowered him to the street stones and, as he remembered it, she vanished.

The playing child was named Al. He had with him a lone khalfrey crab called Lestor. The two spent hours together, just following Lestor back to the sea.

Years and years later, through Willian's favor, Alherde was welcomed into the Sivliéres' castle as a practicing scribe, a potential retainer to Roberrus' potential son. None of that was important, obviously. All that mattered was the drove of fine memories and provocative images: the fogged scarlet light of Motte-side Inn's private room, the twirled scraps of finger-length parchment, the speckled beams under their heavy blanket.

"Anae Bertriss, Damme of Sarcovy," Willian finally echoed. "One-time student to the great Mester Alherde." The other man kept counting the barrels. "What did you tell her?"

"Bloody abhorrent student, if you ask me. I didn't tell her about her parents' hopes of the Sivliére downfall. I'd never liked her, but—ah. She was crying. Deceiving her at that moment felt like low thievery. Hopefully, the truth doesn't pain her when she learns it." He marked down another figure in the wax. "What was this about a squire? You have a squire now?" Willian smiled and told him everything about Hamm.

For hours hence, their conversation leapt about. Every small detail, every inexplicit word shared between them was elaborated as they carried on through Reineshir. After roving through the old vendors' field, checking on the chapel's inebriated cleric, and returning to the manse, they sat in the gazebo of the estate's croft. And before Willian could bring up his most delicate question, the cook—aforementioned Amstudt—brought out warm pork with bean sprouts, boiled onions, and eggs. He joined them in their feast after hauling out a case of wine, an import of Taliorano.

Once they were sufficiently drunk, they strayed off the manorial grounds and entered the inn across the road. Alherde preferred this den, as he said, to the brewery just up the street, as the more intelligible of his populace tended to gather in the gloom of its hearth.

Willian was introduced to them all. There was Byraon, a goatherder from Westley who seemed to know of every unturned rock in a radius of a hundred leagues. Ulfred Pakker, the town rope-maker, who vowed he could trace his lineage back to Daar the Conqueror; he persisted with a demonstration of this knowledge until another hushed him up. Lydia Ornhatter, the eldest daughter of the storehouse's owner, could recite the plot of any chevalier tale thrown her way—no wonder, as Willian thought, considering how snug she looked on Alherde's lap.

The ridder drank on, avoiding the sight.

The most mysterious and impressive of all the gathered patrons, however, was the keeper herself, Maud. Over and over, as she ascended from her cellar bearing a new cask of Reineshir brown, the seated discussants asked her to resolve their arguments.

The first of these was between Alherde and Gerard, a lumberman, as they debated the accomplishments of Aetheling Sarkoff Sivliére, father to Roberrus. As Maud came up the steps from her musty enclosure, Gerard tapped her: Did Sarkoff van Woodwar aid King Hugon in his war against the north wildmen?

She nodded at the inquisitive request, assuring them all that she'd think heavily on the matter, then disappeared down into her basement. When she resurfaced, the verdict was in her hands: Yes he had, she delivered without care, though he did not fight *in propria persona*. Alherde was correct again. Maud refilled their cups and subsided. After her third validation, accepted as infallible by the local tipplers, Willian was piqued.

He murmured his curiosity to Alherde but, as had been the case all day long, the steward was sidetracked again and again by the interruptions of

224

his other mates. The best, albeit vague explanation he could offer was that Maud had a dungeon of memories locked away in her head, a bottomless katabasis of the world's insights, its pasts and unreachable futures—whatever that really meant.

It took Willian until the next morning to realize his friend was joking. Although, the peculiar stench of her cellar had stuck to him—literally, as he could still smell it in the soft wool of his hat. It reminded him of inedible mushrooms.

Just after their session in the inn, however, as they stumbled the short distance back to the manse's toft, Willian watched his old mate and the young woman under his arm. He did not say a word, though he pondered a great many. Even after the pair retired to a private chamber on the second floor, Willian waited against the framed entry to his own quarters, waited for Al to emerge on his own. Nothing.

Again, he ran through his questions, never to be asked: How long have you known her? How long have you been together? How long did it take for you to forget me and everything we shared? Have you forgotten? Will you forget again once I'm gone? Surely. There are many more matters of heavier import, burdens of the steward's station and duties over the populace. I was merely passing through, hoping to see the man who once freed me from confusion.

An hour passed before the ridder decided to lie down on his mat of cold straw. He dreamed as he did every night, though the images were forgotten by the grey morning. And before he left Reineshir for the south, he ate again with Alherde and Amstudt in the main hall, stuffing his mouth with fresh barley bread, green apples, bangers, and more boiled eggs—enough to prevent him from conversing with the pair across from him.

After breakfast, he strode through the manor's wetted gates, promising his return within the next two or three days, hopefully with another guest in tow.

Willian marched on through the border of Werplaus, a thinning of pines that quickly became an open-air expanse lipped by a strand of split stumps. An hour later, the Crouxwood was a rising blur of white and black land behind him. After another hour, he was again stricken with a sense of desperate loneliness, another transitory impression of his fears. Though the forest he surpassed had its stretches of emptiness, it was never soundless. Here on this brushy moor, this space of cold salt-rich wind, he was more than once tempted to turn back. There was seemingly nothing ahead and, soon enough, there would be nothing behind.

After the third hour, he spotted to the southeast an unnatural block in the terrain. He soon found it was a house of stones and logs. More than half of it was collapsed beside the front door, covered in frost like all the rest of the county's shrubbery. Around it were the shards and tangles of a fence, scattered over bald muddy soil.

Inside, the standing end of the wall held a coffer-sized hearth. Its upper section was decked with a bar of wood, laden with hooks and bereft of devices. Resting himself on the pile of stone and wood opposite, he nudged away as many loose chunks of debris as he could, attempting to dig deeper into the innocuous puzzle beneath him.

Who lived here before, he wondered: why did they leave, why do I care, why am I still here? To the latest, he agreed it was only exhaustion from this end-to-end journey he'd been undertaking for the past week. And he wanted to block away the chilly gusts for a few moments.

But there was something else. Despite being a load of rubble, this place was cozy. There was a rarely recurring part of his dreams where he lived in such a place, slept close to its fire-niche after warming a pan of milk. Then a knock at the door would wake him. Willian thought of recreating the sound with a rock. In moving one stone by his knee, he spotted the eaten remains of bedding wrapped in an embroidered blanket, sewn with the lightning sigil of the Sivliéres.

A landed ridder's homestead once, he reasoned. Appropriate.

Noon had flown overhead by the time he walked away from the now twice-abandoned house and, by then, a touch of warmth was floating to the earth.

Far ahead was another settlement, a dorp much like Olford. Someone was splitting wood, he heard. Another was seated in a chair, watching the north. Upon veering into the second's line of vision, he saw that it was a woman, broad of body, hooded and adorned in flocculent cloaks. She stood, taking up a quarterstaff as she did so. She then called out to him, her hand cupped beside her mouth. He couldn't catch a word until her face was more than an inexpressive blot in the near distance.

"Ho there!" she cried again. The chopping nearby ceased. Willian stopped. He gave her a few seconds to add to her exclamation, but nothing followed. He introduced himself and removed his sword belt.

"Gertruda," she responded. "You can come closer, lad—I won't thwack you unless I need to."

The ridder did so. "Does this place have a name?" he said.

"Yeah. Egainshir. Welcome." Gertruda lowered herself back into her red oak chair, setting the staff down across her knees. "Not often we get two guests in one day. Folk who come round usually stay for life, see. That why you're here? Lovely hat, by the bye." Willian blinked at her, believing he misheard or misunderstood her. "What brings you here, lad?"

"I, eh—I came looking for someone. Really, I'm not doing much more than chasing a rumor."

"Rumors don't often come out this far. Neither do someones, at that."

"Fitzmorley van Werplaus?"

The watchwoman guffawed. To his own wonderment, the ridder struggled against chuckling along with her.

"Now, that makes sense. What'd the poor boy do? Lord-lady of Sarcovy wasn't with him when he came back so, if it's the girl you're seeking, seek elsewhere. If he committed any crimes, lad, he didn't know they were crimes firstly."

"He isn't in trouble, I promise you that," he attested, simmering slightly over the repetition of the word 'lad.' He was almost a thirty-year-old man.

"Fine. Why d'you want him?" the woman pressed.

"I only wish to speak with him. We met before at Hoerlog." Gertruda raised an eyebrow. "That's, eh, that's a watchtower on the coast. I was stationed there."

"Ah! Fellow watcherman!"

"Yes," said Willian, again misconstruing the nature of her statements.

"Didn't know our little elev went *that* far!" she bellowed before the ridder could continue.

His heart skipped a beat. "He is here, then?"

"Nah," she said. "Well, depends what you mean by 'here,' see. He's not here in Egainshir, as he doesn't live with Elmaen anymore. But he is here in Werplaus."

"Where?" At this, the woman pointed northeast without glancing away from Willian.

"Due that way for two or three kalcubits. You'll see a mound—maybe a garden first. That's where he lives now." The ridder's first thought was that Fitzmorley somehow subsisted on a barren hilltop, much like the fabled moormen of Bienvale's wetlands.

227

Before this could be elucidated, though, Gertruda said, "Gulp of chamomile before heading out? I'm sure a couple of the others would like to meet you." She pushed herself up. "One of us—that's Elmaen—used to be a horseman before he raised this little hamlet. Come, come. I'm sure Semhren has a pinch of hot water left."

For a third time, Willian was unsure of himself: did he hear her correctly? She had stridden ahead of him before he could deliver any audible pleas for clarification.

Egainshir's houses and pens were set up in a circle like a courtyard sundial, the gnomon of which was a well. To the southwest, a shepherd walked amidst a rambling white pool of sheep. He'd never seen a sheep in person before—plenty of wool clothes and one quaint manuscript illustration but no living, breathing, baaing sheep.

Eastward, a man and an adolescent labored beside a lean-to: the former was cleaving logs into kindling strips as his assistant carried the pieces over to a timeworn barrel. The boy froze in his tracks upon noticing the ridder.

Gertruda began to whistle, knocking on the door of an adjacent house. Willian peered at her just as the door opened.

"Yes?" said the man inside.

The ridder dropped his sword and belt. Once again, his dreams pervaded the wakened world.

"Mester Semhren?" he said. He wanted to bark the words, but they came out in a repressed murmur. The elder paid no mind.

"Anything left in the kettle?" the watchwoman was saying. "We've got ourselves another guest." Semhren leaned to see past her. "And I'll bet Reffen's poured the last of his cham for the girl, whatever it is they—"

"You there," said the man, squinting, recognizing.

"Mester Semhren. It's me," said the ridder, hardly any louder. Finally, he pulled off his liripipe hat. "Willian. Fitzwillian."

The scholar—the *ex*-scholar did what he could to push aside Gertruda. Instead, she compliantly moved away, wearing a scowl. Semhren visored his brow with a wrinkled hand, though the afternoon sun was behind him, buried by the clouds.

"Fitzwillian," the man breathed, holding out his other hand. "Fitzwillian?" The ridder prepared to clutch his old teacher's veiny palm. Semhren stopped several inopportune paces out of reach. He was confused, searching about him as if to verify that he was awake. Willian did the same: everyone was watching. The ridder tried a tender smile. Gradually, Semhren reflected it.

"I'm really here," Willian mentioned, louder.

"Sanct's Bones," said the elder, slapping a firm hand against the ridder's upper arm. "Never thought I'd see this boy again. Fitzwillian. What? How?"

"It's a long story. When it's unabridged, that is," Willian remarked. The ex-scholar laughed peacefully. "Just be glad you're not still with the Sivliéres, writing it all down."

Semhren gawked around again, then shuffled backwards to Gertruda and the open door of his home. "Let's talk inside, yes? It's chilly out here. And I've got a splash of cham left over." He rushed the suggestion. "Thank you, Gertruda, I'll take over from here." The woman grimaced as the pair moved by: the ridder perceived it as he entered the book-crowded stead, just before Semhren could shut his door—and through the ever-dwindling egress, when the opening was no wider than an ell's reach, he spotted a bald young man, heavily dressed, strafing to see them. The iron bar clunked down into place.

"They don't really know me," the elder whispered with a mischievous grin. "They know my name and they know my old occupation. But they know nothing else, *heh heh*."

He fiddled with his hearth coals and removed a kettle hanging above them. The ridder sat up straight: most of the house's space was taken up by a large table, cluttered over with wax parchment, vellum sheets, and script-writing utensils of all sorts.

"I'm not one to judge," grumbled Willian, still somewhat distracted by that fleeting visage beyond the door. "So, you left the Sivliére keep behind for the flats of Werplaus? I thought you'd sailed off to the continent. That's what the marshal said, if I remember right."

"Nay," Semhren grumbled. "Continent's too dangerous a place. Has been and always will be. And of course the marshal told you that, he was the one who helped me steal a horse. You remember how close we were, you must. Hmm…" He filled up two wood cups with a dark liquid. "He didn't get into much trouble for that, did he?"

In truth, the man in question was released from his aetheling's service because of this particular insubordination. He was replaced by a feeble groomer.

"He was still there before I was dismissed," Willian said. "I imagine he's been replaced by now, though."

"You were dismissed? What do you mean? And when was that exactly?"

"Six or seven years ago, I'd say. They collared me with a ridderstaat and sent me out to Hoerlog Tower. It was…"

He wanted to say that the act had been injurious to his sense of belonging, to his general outlook on family, community, and secularist conduct. But that was only partly true. And it wasn't a subject he had any desire to delve into. Not now, not so soon after their unexpected reunion.

"Unceremonious," he punctuated.

"Why did they do it?"

"I'm not sure," he lied again. "It had something to do with the Bertrisses and a land auction. It wasn't any of my concern. They expected I'd be happy enough in bypassing the squire's rank, but I couldn't have cared less about that. I just wanted to stay in the keep."

He avoided mentioning Alherde as he sipped at the warming chamomile. He could almost feel the snowdust melting along his shoulders as the fluid flowed down into the cauldron of his stomach. It was a refreshing sensation, though the leaves steeping in the cup were mediocre.

"I'll bet it had to do with your birth and nothing more," Semhren suggested.

Willian nodded. "What about you?"

"What about me?" As the elder uttered the last word, there was a knock at the door. He struggled to his feet with a muttered curse. "Who's it now? Alherde? Ellemine?" Willian snorted, amused.

"I was going to ask why you left Wallenport when you did. My mother was rather upset to see you leave. You know, she—" Semhren had opened the door.

The girl was poised there.

The girl. The woman from his dreams. All of his dreams. There was naught but a black stubble covering her head. And the rest of her body was layered with drab cloaks and furs. Stranger yet were her ears.

"Yes?" the elder inquired.

"Reffen pointed me this way," she spoke. The voice was deep, articulate. The voice in his dreams was comprised of four separate intonations, each rambling in a different tongue or dialect. "He said I could buy a kind of uforian from you?"

"Oofor-what?" he questioned, turning his ear to her.

The woman blinked slowly. "Chamomile."

"Oh, eh…" Semhren slid behind the door, permitting her entry. "Yes, I have a small heap of such petals. Come in, if you wish." The woman hesitated, then shifted through the stone and wood frame with one long step. The ex-scholar closed the door. "Really, if you only want five or so leaves, there's no need to—"

"I will take half of however much you possess. Will this do?" As if she'd been trained by a court illusionist, two nickel pieces appeared between her middle, index, and ring fingers. Semhren leaned forward with his now idiosyncratic squint. His eyes widened, then immediately relaxed.

"W-well, certainly. Do you need a container or a—"

"I have my own," she said, pulling out a flat ornate casket of polished blackwood; she'd removed it from somewhere inside the abyss of her superfluous clothing. Willian stared. Seconds later, he saw she was watching him back. He snapped his head away.

Dark eyes, he thought. Those are the eyes of the dream girl. My eyes, the ridder thought. At this, he was tempted to reinvestigate. But he couldn't. One flash of contact, one instance of connection—that was enough. Willian crossed his legs and focused on the burning coals.

The dual chime of coinage rang out at his table. Out the corner of his eye, he could see Semhren holding forth his bony fist. The girl held out her opened box and pointed downward into it. Willian stole a glimpse of the casket: its interior was bracketed into sections, each holding a different substance—dried stems, brown dust, a serrated leaf blade of blood-red hue.

She shut the case and whirled about. At the same time, Willian swung his head back to the hearth. But the girl was not moving. He didn't dare to look. Not even when he could feel her probing eyes again.

"Will that be all, my dear?" he heard Semhren say. "Eh, let me get the door for you." Still yet, she was solid as a statue.

"You are not from around here," she spoke, her voice wafting over the ridder. A coal flared. "Are you?" Willian raised his head to the girl. Her irises were dark, maybe black. "You have elevi blood. Like me. But I *am* from around here. Originally."

At that, she reached for the side of his head. His first instinct was to snatch her by the wrist. He once tried such in a dream, a recent one, and instead found himself throttling the throat of an enormous serpent. Before he could move a muscle, the girl stayed her hand and smirked. Semhren was opening the door.

"Try to stay warm out there," urged the elder.

The bald woman gave a pompous sniff, then strode away. "See you on the road," she said invitingly, disappearing out the door. Semhren closed it. Willian shivered and felt the pulse of his heart through his surcoat.

"Two bloody nickels!" Semhren chattered. "For a bit of flower! *Ha*! Seems *she's* the one who isn't from around here." He laughed back to his seat behind the table and savored his cup of chamomile. Willian looked into the hearth, suddenly afraid to leave the dark hovel.

"You hear me?" said Semhren.

The ridder fell back into the world: his old mester's house was warm, filled with litter. Semhren cupped his beverage in both hands. "No," Willian replied with honesty. "I'm sorry, what did you say?"

"I asked you what we were just talking about." They both ruminated, though Willian knew the answer. At the chosen moment, he reignited their dialogue.

"I asked why you left Wallenport," he queried again. "I didn't think men in your line of work retired so early in life, if ever. You were around my age when you rode off, perhaps a few years older." The elder put down his cup and cleared his throat.

"I wanted to finish my manuscript," he said with an inflection of regret. "But only for myself, see. It's not a work that should endure through the ages. It's just a silly youth's dream. Ehh, you said something, mentioned something just as I pulled open the door for that young woman. Something about your mother?" Willian nodded. "Yes. How is she? No, no, don't answer that yet, I don't want to forget my place. The book. Remind me, when I adopted you and Alherde as my pupils, what were your respective crafts? If you can bethink them."

"Well, Alherde already knew how to read and write, so he set about copying down your text, cutting parchment, binding. As for me, I was fresh as a Hosten apple, so you taught me letters and grammar. Never really mastered writing." He was prepared to add that it was because Semhren had left after so few years of tutorship. He deemed the statement tasteless. "Ellemine tried her best to teach me but, to be honest, I don't think she ever learned the letters herself. Thank the All-Being for elevi intuition."

Another image of the bald woman flashed in his mind: he imagined she was still standing right outside the door, listening. He shook his head. "I think she got Alherde to teach Felix when he was of the right age. Would've worked out fine if the brat was a better student. Or if Al knew how to discipline unruly children."

Behind the table, Semhren gulped. "I've heard about this Felix boy," he said. "New aetheling over Sarcovy and all that. He's a 'brat,' you say?"

Willian shrugged. "Only knew him into his late childhood. Barely came of age before I left for Hoerlog. Maybe he grew up since. Maybe Damme Anae Bertriss helped speed up the process."

Semhren ran a hand through his diminishing hair. "He's the, ehm, first son of Roberrus, isn't he?" he asked softly.

"I don't think so," Willian admitted. "My mother said she was pregnant before Roberrus returned from one of his campaigns. Wasn't all too angry about the situation, believe it or not. Ellemine has a way of calming the wicked." Yet again, he was reminded of their recent dark-eyed intruder, how she apparently possessed an antithetical power.

"I believe I left at the same time as Aetheling Roberrus. Who do you suppose is the father?" Semhren asked.

Willian dismissively waved his hand. "Never thought about it. Remember, I was only seven years of age when it happened."

"Of course, of course, you and Alherde both. My first and youngest pupils, brightest little bugs on all the island. I think." He rested back in his chair and shut his eyes comfortably. "Where is the other lad nowadays?"

Willian recounted nearly everything about his visit to Reineshir—which collapsed into talk of Alherde's social ascension, his tutelage of Damme Anae, and the rebellion he was privately aiding. By the end, Semhren's wrinkled face had drooped in wholesome surprise.

"Sounds like I've missed much," he said. "Can't say I'm disappointed to be away from it all, though." Despite the claim, the ridder couldn't help but hear a reverberation of longing. "So, you will be passing again through Reineshir on your way back to…wherever you're going. Is that right?"

"I hope so." He humored the idea that the dark woman was waiting out on the snowy flats of Werplaus like an ice viper.

"In that case," the elder said, standing and reaching to a shelf above the hearth, "might as well bring him back a memento." He took down a heavy book, wiped down the cover with a sleeve, carried it to his old friend.

Willian took it in his hands and rotated it right-side up: the Bienvalian sigil. The Crossed Bolts.

"It's been finished, then?"

"Has been for years and years, yes," Semhren hummed. "When I came here, a fellow—actually a ridder who fought in The Acquisition—he helped me build all this." He raised his hands, signifying the cottage itself. "I gave the book to him as a gift when he was finished. He, ehm, he passed away a few years ago, so it went to his foster son. The lad has since given it back to me. So, now that it's been returned, it's my right to pass it right along. Mayhaps Alherde still has his own draft."

"I'll bring it to him," Willian assured, opening to a random page: The Tale of Sir Olivien and the Grouse Hunt. He closed the tome.

"What, eh," the elder began, "what *are* you doing out here anyway?" The ridder did not hesitate to tell the truth.

"Did *you* know he was the Damme's son?" Willian asked finally, after all had been divulged.

"I had suspicions," Semhren whispered. "But I let them be. It never bothered him. And it wasn't my place to encourage him to go searching. Your mother is none of my business now."

He wiped his eyes with the same sleeve he used to clean the cover of *Chevaliers of Bienvale.*

For an hour or two afterward, they exchanged much: habits of life, diets, dreams, and the many intriguing events that consumed the island over the recent season—none of which had yet reached Semhren's ears. They left the house when a woman named Amarta beckoned all to come get their dinner. She'd prepared fresh maslin bread, and her young assistant offered a hunk to Willian with a coy glance. Another woman, Serryl, made a stew with crabmeat and legumes, which the ridder took in the same cup he'd sipped his cham out of. Upon finishing, his belly gurgled, unsated. This was likely the result of eating two hearty meals in a row, not a day prior.

Just after the noon hour, Willian set out again. The villagers of Egainshir, largely disappointed that he was leaving so soon, bid him farewell. He guaranteed his return, either much later that night or the following morning. And he hoped such was the truth.

*   *   *

234

Indefinite hours passed before the mound was in sight: a monticule of dirtied snow with an angular rise at its peak, solitary under the sky's soft dusky pink. There was no garden, contrary to what Gertruda suggested, but a span of weeds incongruent with its surroundings. As anyone else surely would, Willian toyed with the suspicion that all this was nothing more than an anomaly, a naturally formed cumulation—perhaps even one of the buried hill forts of antiquity. But regardless of any doubt, the ridder marched on.

Then a goat came over the top of the hill, a horned shape with twitching ears. It bleated dismissively before trotting away.

Near the foot of the ascent, he paused, then rounded it along the base to its front. He saw almost immediately that the earthen rise ceased before the peak and that this was indeed a proper house—cloaked down the back, as it were, with a drapery of turf. The hill-house had two entrances: a gapped wall of flat stacked stones and sod lining the ground level, and a gable of white blocks above, against which the goat reclined. The bottom entry had a door of driftwood, the upper a curtain of thick colorless fabric.

And there in front of it all, *he* squatted over a patch of grass brushed clear of hoarfrost. He was wrapped up to the chin in a shepherd's cloak, arms crossed, one hand holding a bitten radish. His hair was cut short, his elevi ears now salient.

Fitzmorley van Werplaus. The hidden icon of Allesande's uprising.

The lad watched Willian with dull patience. He bit into the rest of his radish, chewed, picked at his gums with a finger, threw the greens up to his goat. The beast, without getting back up, stretched his head to the remains and snagged them with his jutting teeth. The lad below proceeded to take up a leek stalk from a pile of raw vegetables near his rump, sticking the soft end into his mouth.

Though neither of them spoke, the ridder was at a loss for words. Declaratively, he settled with saying, "Fitzmorley?" The word precipitously wafted away.

"Nah," the young man responded, pulling the leek over to a corner of his mouth. "Just Morley." The goat made a belching sound. "That's Geat." Willian waved at the animal to lighten the mood. Still, he wasn't sure where to start. "You're far from the coast, Sir Willian," Morley continued, to the ridder's relief. "You here to recruit me?"

"Well," Willian said, clearing his throat, "that wasn't my intention, no. I, er…"

Yet again, all words left him, the purpose of his journey fumbled out of his hands and vanished under the stiff grass. Morley waited steadily, finishing off the remainder of his leek bulb. He smacked his lips and scraped tiny fragments of the leaf base from his tongue. Willian started again, slower.

"I was still at the tower when I heard about what happened in Westley. Of course, it was Hamm who brought me the news."

"Of course."

"He was excited as can be. Very, very excited. It took him three tries to make his story coherent to the other watchmen. For me, I'd say it took five tries. I thought he was confusing the details, at first. Still didn't believe parts of it, not until the other ridders showed up at Hoerlog weeks later. Eight of them upheld the squire's account." He wandered closer to the hill-house as he talked, inspecting his feet as he did so. "You're, eh…" He met the lad's eyes. "Is it true, then?"

Morley tilted his head. "Is what true?"

"What Allesande did—what she said?"

Morley tilted his head even more, protruding his neck forward. "Go on," he requested.

Willian sighed inwardly. "That you're the son of Michel Laisroch? And Ellemine?" At this, Morley relaxed back.

"That's what she told me, yeah," he said, sitting and stretching his legs. "Ellemine, I meant. Not Allesande."

"That eliminates *that* rumor, then," Willian said aloud. "Few others think you're just a boy plucked from the street. A, uh—a trick justification for the rebellion."

Morley puffed his nigh-amusement. "One with wax ears, I guess."

"Far-fetched maybe, I know." There was sharp breeze. Willian turned his back to it. "Still, I'm surprised she let you go."

"She didn't," he hummed. "And I'm sure she would've held me if I'd waited. Left at the opportune moment, I think. All the ridders let me through. And nobody came after me." He gave a throaty burp. "Until you."

"Why?" questioned the ridder, pulling down a side of his hat over an exposed earlobe.

"Why what?"

"Why did you leave?" Morley said nothing. "It's just, I'd think anyone—boy or girl, man or woman—I'd think anyone would appreciate such, eh, attention. If you remained behind, the people of Westley would've praised you as a..."

He juggled words: nothing too banal, nothing too grandiose. Hero? Icon?

"As a ridder?" the lad asked. Willian could conjure no reply. Morley hugged his legs to his chest. "They'd toss that aside fast, trust me. But anyway, I left because it was the best choice. Leaving *here* in the first place was one of the worst blunders I ever made. The weeks that followed were riddled with missteps and oversights. I don't regret all of it. But the purpose behind the trip was boyish. Silly, you know? The idea stung me like a nettle or something. And before I could dress it, I was on my way to Wallenport with a stolen cask of beer underarm." He watched the grass and slowly drummed his fingers against his elbows as he spoke.

"You weren't alone," said Willian. "Hundreds of others went up to Castle Sivliére to join Felix's failed army, as you must know."

There was a twinkle of misconception in Morley's face—a flaring of nostrils and a wrinkling of the brow. It dawned on Willian then: if the lad had been living in Werplaus for all his life, it would've been impossible for him to know about Felix's campaign, his mass recruitment for the war against the Taliorans, unless he began his travels north for other reasons. His intention for going to Wallenport had to be discrete: the alleged circumstances that led him and the archer to Hoerlog were contrived.

"You were never really an aspirant, were you?" Willian asked. Morley shook his head, resting his chin over his knees. "I see. What brought you to Wallenport, then?"

"I don't really wanna talk about it." The wind died down. "But while we're on the subject, what brings you to Werplaus?"

The ridder's heart seemed to inflate. He'd been shrinking from the expectation of the question for as long as the hill-house was in sight. A part of him hoped Morley's apathy would waive all interests aside. Upon reflecting, though, Willian became uncertain of himself: what was it? What *really* drew him southward to the reclusive plain? In other words, he knew precisely what to say to the lad—but why did he want to say it? He thought of Felix, of the year when the child learned that he could do just about anything with impunity. Then, without impetus, the dark woman penetrated his mind.

Willian gave a grunt, pinching the tip of his hat and dragging it off his skull. He rolled it up and ran a hand through his short blond hair. Morley was staring again, still blankly, his pupils gliding back and forth between the ridder's pointed ears. He gave an understanding nod.

"I believe we're brothers," said Willian. "Half-brothers."

Morley picked up another radish. "Fine." He bit into the vegetable.

The ridder's face flushed. The air became twice as cold as it had been throughout the day. That was all: Fine. No surprise, no joy, not a jolt of amusement. Just "fine."

Morley, surely seeing his disdain, swallowing the bit of radish and continued with, "Is that it?"

"I suppose…" A moment passed. The sky darkened to a clouded violet. "I expected you to be more startled. Or surprised."

As he'd done earlier, Morley crunched down on the last of his radish and threw the rest up to Geat. This time, the goat stood to fetch the remains; and his owner mirrored him, straightening up onto his feet, bending backward to stretch his muscles.

"Let me tell you about my year, Willian," he said, picking up the remaining leeks. "You'll be the first one in Werplaus to hear it. But come inside, I'll warm us up."

They entered the mound: there was a bed, a stone pit of ashes and smoldering logs, a ladderlike set of stairs to the loft, and an opaque compartment at the furthest end. All of it was held together by thick panels of wood, the edges of which were beginning to part against the weight of the earth.

After shutting and barring the door, Morley took up a clay kettle, wobbled it to check the volume of water left, and placed it down on the pit's rim. He prodded the embers with an iron bar and gestured for Willian to take a seat on the bed. The ridder did so, resting next to a messy compendium much like the one he left at Semhren's—the copy of *Chevaliers of Bienvale*. This book, however, was larger, propped open by something tiny and solid like a pebble, hidden under the mass of pages. He curiously lifted the front board: the title was *Treatises on the Soldier of Sea and Land*. Certainly one of Semhren's. He continued, raising half the comprising parchment—then swiftly lowered it back down. It was no pebble beneath the pages. Far, far from it.

The lad began with a deep introductory sigh.

"Before I begin, there's only one thing I wish to make clear: I'm not smart. I grew up here under the guardianship of a man called Sir Gale. He taught me nothing more than the sounds of the letters—from which I taught myself how to read the words in our two books—and he showed me the value of labor. And the pliableness of truth. When he was gone, I went and lived in Egainshir, stayed there for years more. Really, my first excursion out of Werplaus and into Reineshir was just last year.

"On that first visit, I met Anae Bertriss, who, bored as can be, was trying to play some weird prank on me. Had a cat and a ball of yarn and— anyway, I'm not sure what she was trying to do, but it worked. I'd never seen a cat up until then. Prank or no prank, the two of us spent the day together and became friends." He'd placed the kettle down into the hot bed of coals and taken up a wooden mortar, a pestle, and a box close by.

"Earlier this year, Felix—y'know, *our* half-brother, as you might insist—he became the aetheling and took Anae as his wife. So, at the time, I was convinced my friendship with her was over and done with. But I wasn't ready to accept that. I planned to steal her back. I left Egainshir and went up to Olford, where I met Sethan. He led me through the swamplands, where I almost died at the hands of toadmen. Eventually, we got to Wallenport. I snuck into the Sivliéres' keep, posing as an aspirant. Worked out well, see, since I had Gale's sword. Maybe even too well. Felix asked to meet me and see the sword, so I complied and met one of my half-brothers without knowing he was my half-brother." Morley was now mashing up what appeared to be tiny shards of wood, soft as roasted apples, inside the mortar. Willian, meanwhile, was attempting to locate the sword from his vantage by the bed.

"Anyhow, while I was stepping through the castle's upper hall, I happened to hide right in front of Ellemine's bedroom door. And Ellemine just happened to open it at that instance. And in somehow seeing that I was her son, she told me straightaway. Without passion. Thereon, she told me everything about my life that I yet didn't know, gave me money, then left me alone with Anae as per my request. I'll let you guess how that turned out.

"When I found Sethan, we left with the aspirants and traveled with them as far as Chaisgott, then made our way to your tower where, yet unbeknownst to me, I was introduced to another half-brother—ah, I forgot to mention. We were on our way through Laisroch County because I truly did need to get out to Westley and speak with its earl, but not for the reasons I shared with you. Rather, I planned to confront him as his son. Or thought I was planning such. I think now I was only playing with the idea but had no willpower to see it through. Already, I was fed up with disappointment.

"There were still yet other surprises on that route," he said, dumping out the mortar's contents onto a board, taking a knife to the squashed-up chips. "When we got to Sieger's house, a girl I grew up with was there with Geat, my goat. She'd set out to find me not long after I headed off for Wallenport but, when she arrived at Olford, someone pointed her off to Westley, where she found Seth's brother. And decided to stay for a while. The day after we were all brought together, I was taken away to Michelhal." He took up the kettle, removed its lid, hovered his chin above the opening.

"Good enough," he said, proffering a cup much like the mortar he'd used. He dropped a fistful of the chopped substance into the basin, added the gently steaming water. Geat clomped inside via the loft's entrance as Morley tossed the remainder of the stuff back into the mortar. He emptied the kettle into it and inhaled the drink's fumes. Willian did the same. The smell reminded him of Reineshir, though he couldn't specify which part. The warehouse? The manor? Morley sat along the fire pit's wall, right across from the ridder.

"What happened next?" Willian inquired.

"You already know. Allesande used me, the stupid rebellion started, and I came back here. Beyond that, you know more than I." Geat slumped down above them with a thud. "And you understand now why I wasn't knocked off my feet when you told me we're brothers, yeah?"

Willian, who was raising the cup to his lips, glanced at Morley in response. He took a sip without letting any of the brownish white gobs into his mouth. The drink had a robust offbeat flavor much different from the cham he was so accustomed to.

"What kind is this?" he asked.

"Simon's hat, it's called." Morley took a drought himself, then started to chew. "Istain back in Egainshir gets it when trading." Willian drank again, this time trying out the additives. They tasted faintly like nuts, though they had the consistency of overcooked meat.

They sat in silence for a long while. Willian began picking apart his half-brother's outlandish personality as he drank the ever-abhorrent beverage. Questions cropped up and were acutely reaped away. He felt as though he'd tracked down a twin, long since disguised by the passing days. If Morley's life were spent out in the fields of Werplaus, how did he learn to speak so decently—and with such a fair vocabulary? The answer, crouching behind him, poked at the back of his head: Semhren, of course. Or this unknown ridder who raised him.

More difficult to solve was the question of Morley's honesty. What if his alleged companionship with Anae were made up? What if his purposes for entering Sivliére Castle were more conventional—that is, what if he were only there to steal jewelry or silver. Or gold? Like the two coins hidden inside his book.

When they first met outside Hoerlog, Morley armored himself with a half-lie: he and the archer were on their way to deliver a message to Earl Laisroch. Either way, Morley was no stranger to dishonesty. But that was all excusable, wasn't it? The lads must have believed themselves in danger, even if its degree were miniscule.

He wasn't lying, the ridder concluded. No matter how dizzying the coincidences, no matter how tangled the interactions. This lad was truly his half-brother.

"So," Morley piped up after finishing his drink, "you came here from the tower, then?"

"Yes," he answered absently.

"I suppose you passed through Olford on the way south?" The ridder nodded tiredly. The long day was catching up to him. And the interior of the mound was one of the more comfortable abodes he'd stayed in during his travels. He would have to be leaving it soon to make the trip back to Egainshir. "You didn't happen to see the archer there, did you? Sethan?" Morley queried.

"I didn't see him, no." He drained the last of the water from his cup.

"Any sign of him, maybe? His bow or cloak?" Willian shook his head "Must have gone off to Sylvan or…" He paused and got to his feet, then climbed up to the loft. He paced back and forth for a moment before ambling back down the steps with an oversized woolen coat on. "You can lie down, if you want," he offered, sitting again by the embers. Relieved, Willian gave back the cup, filled yet with the cryptic Simon's hat, and stretched himself out on the cot.

"Much appreciated," he mumbled. "That stuff is rather effective." He blinked once and his eyelids began to flutter in resistance to sleep. To fight it, he watched the apertures of the door: nightfall's dark grey.

Morley began to speak again, though his tone was low and unintelligible. He was moving about the house. In his tired stupor, Willian suspected the lad was preparing their gear for the next day's journey.

Their gear. Where did that thought come from? He opened his eyes a fourth time. How long had he been dozing?

"—hoping that he'll understand. The two of us went on quite a journey. And I'm ashamed I ended it so cruelly. Might even walk out to Westley if it's not too cold, try to see Yeva. I'm sure Seth would like to see his see brother, too. Anyway, there's probably much we can share of our lives. I might seem joyless, but I do like a nice walk and chat. And you *are* my half-brother, after all."

Willian fell away from the world again, fell into a scarlet dreamless sleep. The first he could ever recall.

*   *   *

Between Reineshir and the Temple of St. Berthe, Feofan took up a sizable stick and stomped down on one end to shorten it by a foot's length or so. As a result she broke off more than intended, but the new staff's crooked head was lowered to the exact height of her scalp. She took it as a sign—the fifth of that day alone—that she was in all the world's favor.

Red aeker thorn pricking blood. Cat mewling around the ankle skin. Pieces of a broken cup, all fitted together. What else? The all-together trio of shouting goats. Now this. A stream of symbols. What was it the old townswoman said, just this morning? "Been watching the aureole, haven't you? Been watching Haem and all his brood? You know what I mean, girl, I can tell. If you don't—well, that in itself is a sign I'm getting too old. I'm not seeing who's who." And then she offered that bit of cooked liver. That too could have been a sign.

When Feofan arrived at the church-house, the man in black and white was there, scooping away the already soggy snow. When she stepped up to the door with all the carved flowers and letters, the man was scratching his chin and observing the roof of the temple, maybe wondering if he should attempt the climb or if the shingles would hold out any leakage on their own.

Pretending she hadn't seen the robed man, Feofan touched the incomprehensible letters in the door and thrust her way inside, closing the board behind her. It was as black as the belly of a forgotten ship: no candles burned, no chutes welcomed the blanched day, no healthy fires crackled along the walls. Perhaps it was meant to be this way. She walked across the bald stones, waiting for the priest to pursue.

How many did they bury under these floors? When it is all done with, I must find out. Burn away this hideous, empty house, this blot of the big land. Catacombs or worm-ridden soil. Doesn't matter. It must be destroyed.

"Hello there?" came the man's voice at the opened entry. "Who is here? I can see you. Public mass won't be for another two days, but if you need a different blessing…" He came in without closing the door, though he had not yet looked in Feofan's direction. It was a bluff—he was unable to see through this shadow. She went to him, dragging the walking stick over the floor.

"Oh, it's you," he said of her once she entered the light. "Back already? I'd think you would be out in the fields for much longer. How much did you get?"

Expressionlessly, she reached inside the bag hanging against the small of her back, covered over by the mass of fur cloaks she'd recently collected. From it, she took out the box, cracked open its lid.

"Siklaz, you wanted?" she said, tracing the rim of a compartment with her fingernail. The priest, mishearing her, mouthed the word to himself. "You needed something for the cold, yes?"

"Ah!" he said, suddenly comprehending. "Is that what it is?"

Feofan took out two bunched roots, pale and twisted like dead spiders. "Yes, siklaz root." She placed them into the priest's hand. "Don't bend or cut them until you want to use them. At that time, it is best to chop to tiny bits. Then you put them in a steeper. Dropping it all into the water can work, but not always. Water needs to be as hot as you can possibly make it."

The man backed into the light and moved the stems about on his hand. "Odd little things, aren't they?" he said. Feofan smirked. "What will it do? The, eh, the concoction, I mean."

"If the water is clean enough, it will warm your insides up. Very simple." She cracked the joints of her hands and stepped closer to the exit. "What do you have for me? I am hungry."

"Come with me, then. I'll make a mash of oats and pour a cup of beer." He advanced around the corner of the temple after shutting the entrance behind them.

The woman walked out onto the road instead. "I do not drink that," she said impatiently. "And bread and whatever else you have will be good enough. Bring it out to me. I would like to get away from this horrid place."

The priest, now chafed and cheerless, crept silently back to the house, leaving Feofan on the road. Restless hatred trespassed her spirit once she returned to the lighted world—as she knew would happen. The island was infested by these unseen phantoms. They dwelled like fireflies, lighting the umbrae with their shimmer-bodies, vanishing before the swipe of one's hand. She wanted to beat something with that walking stick of hers. Maybe the man when he returned.

Hatred is the jewel standing out in the ford's stream, the rock the boy had dropped at the wrong place—interrupting the song of the river. It is the cough of the deer I cannot see, the one I can feel as it crushes through the underwood. The smell of that village and the slime that gushes through its people. The brittle-cold grass of the barren. That wagoner who cut poor Signy before his suffering. The staring, growing lust in the shepherd's pointed face. Younger man in the elder's house—who was it, really? One of my dream-brothers, but which?

The priest appeared with an old basket at hand and a necklace dangling from his opposite grip; he neatly placed the charm into the former then concealed it under the cloth within.

"Here you are," he said once close enough, holding out the gift. "I do hope to see you again one of these days. If ever you choose to come back down the south road, dear."

There was coyness in those last words. Feofan lifted the fabric: the necklace charm was wooden and flat, a circle with a smaller circle inside, held in place by a straight limb cutting through the core. The inner circumference was further held in its place by two other accoutrements, one at its top and one at its bottom, both connecting it to the whole: at the head, three smaller limbs, evenly space—at the base, two, both jutting from the same midpoint.

"What is this?" she asked, holding it up as if it were a soiled rag or some dead verminous creature. The priest, who had minutely regained his smile, lost his breath at this question.

"W-why, it's the Voss," he stuttered, conjoining his hands against a white portion of his dress, right up against his heart. "The mark of the Prophet Scribe, the mark of Merrenar. It's—it's a symbol of our faith."

Feofan concealed it again and began her hike up the northward road without another word. The temple was out of mind before it was out of sight.

244

She soon rifled through the basket: doughy bread, a square of 'cheese,' and mashed corn. Saving the better for later, she forced down the cheese, doing her best not to perpend its origin. After that she hung the carved amulet from her neck, rubbed it, and hooked the basket's handle to her elbow. She meditated as she walked, maintaining the rhythm of her walking stick and footfalls.

Voss, voss, voss. Mark of both Merrenar and the Prophet Scribe, whatever those are. Merrenar. I have heard of Merrens. The All-Being people—that's their god's name, or one of them. Prophet. I was called that once. By Savuer. Loving father—death on the ship to Taliorano. So who is the Merren prophet? A man—for it must be a man in this world—who said what he thought was true or right or good, and was accepted. Likely he thought all three were the same. Childish. I will tell you the truth: that birdsong bereft of name. The stem pushing aside the pebblestone. The brilliancy breaking through the dewy cockcrow fog. The sea stack under Wallenport's manmade mountain. And who can say 'this is the good,' who? Talk to the blind and use only colors—speak of the left and the right without touch or sight.

Night came and Feofan chewed on a condensed ball of brownleaf from her box. She then tramped deeper into the woods with an orb of fire hovering before her. She guided it carefully around the tree trunks, sometimes lowering it to the melting snow, sometimes making it shiver, making the shadows dance around her. Such was her austere sense of amusement.

Beyond the lake of dead frosted ferns were small hovels, each a mess of lush wattles or thatches: these were the houses of the wild folk, the rejects, the vagrants who had nowhere else to settle but the wealds along their island's midriff. Some had retreated from the continentals' settlements—in exile or by choice, there was no knowing—while others were surely true natives. Here they rested in a spellbound slumber, undisturbed by the light.

More victims of order. These need not be distressed. Viggdis is not here, she does not need to know. They can have as much time as they wish. They can dream their dreams and ride their nightmares. Rest, all. You will know when to run, when to swim, drown, float out to the infinite horizon.

The woman checked inside one breast-shaped hut: nothing but wet stalks thrown over the ground. Tiredly, she extinguished her flame and crawled within, fixing her staff against the opening. She set aside her bag and basket, then fumbled her hands through the dark in search of her box.

Upon finding it, she touched the contents of each small compartment, searching for the correct stimulant.

Drabber dust, not the dust needed. The chamomile from the other village man. I know this one has red aeker, not going to make the same mistake a second time today. Shreds of brownleaf. Ash of hahlixus. The somniferum. The somniferum, where is it?

It was as she dreaded. In the space where there should have been the crushed seeds of the papaver flower, there was nothing but loose grit. It had been twenty days since she last breathed its fumes. That was after she mixed it with the hahlixus—that was before the cold season arrived. The rest could have escaped to another section of the box or blew away with the wind when she last opened it. Or as she definitively guessed, she expended it all without realizing it. Unless she could build another fire, find a proper pot, boil water, and add the small amount of chamomile in her possession, she would have to sleep without an anodyne. The first time in years.

She woke six times throughout the night; at the sixth wakening, she had been roused because her swathing clothes were wettened from within. And before she could delve back into the miasmal pit of her self, the sour scent of urine came to her.

The sun did not yet reach for the dappled clouds, nor did it bestride the south reaches. It was early enough. Still unsteady from the lack of rest, Feofan gathered up her belongings and left the hovels behind, finding the main road just as the sky blushed.

She stopped twice along the route to rest her eyes—once under an ivied tree and again in an expired wheat field. There, she ate the bread given to her with the helping of cornmeal spread over it, then stuck a pinch of brownleaf in her mouth to warm her blood.

Not an hour after leaving the dull clearing and the emptied basket behind, she arrived at Olford. Much as it had been when she previously passed through, the margins of the Lightrun were hardened into lean plateaus of ice and, both up and downriver, the melting snows nourished streamlets and temporary ponds.

She leaned against a corner of the sleeper-house closest to the road and the creek, eyes shut against noon's blinding brightness. For a time she listened to the passing waters, the hissing trees, the chopping of wood, the low discussions between the bed-keeper and the grumbling tradesman; the whishing of a stick, a toy sword through the air, closer to the ruined house;

a crunching, a dissonant ring, and a song, hummed and forgotten and hummed again.

She looked across the road to the porched, mangled house. She did not notice him during her approach—that alone was testament enough of her exhaustion.

A young man in an oversized cloak sat on the house's patio, its raised and uncomely platform of stone. He had a messy beard running under his chin and over his neck; his eyebrows were inverted, suggestive of a recent distress. Held steady on his lap was a bowl, the contents of which were being lazily mashed with the blunt end of a dagger. This was new.

Who is this? Was not here last time—or was he? Is not familiar. Has a significant face, a canary among hawks.

Without comprehending the action, she had wandered to the base of his porch. The man stared dumbly at the top and sides of her head, then ceased his pummeling and put aside the knife. Feofan, having left her walking stick and travelbag against the sleeper-house wall, rested her elbows over the platform's edge, her chin against her clasped hands like a bull's head set on an altar.

"Hello," she said.

The young man gulped, pulled the bowl closer to him. "Ah'right?" he mumbled, leaning his head to one side so as to inspect one of her elevi ears—as she guessed. Most people did. "Can I—what can…" He tried again, shifting himself straight. "I'm Sethan. But call me Seth, if ye want. Ehm. What's yer own name?"

"Feofan. I am from Kamenin," she said, assured that he never heard of the place. Then with intended naivety, she added, "I have not been here before. Is this where I can buy poultices and the like? I could not find anyone in Wallenport who sold what I want."

Sethan peeked down at the bowl, then back at her, then up the north road, then back at her again. "Ehm. Not really. But I mayhaps have somethin' yer in need of. What're ye lookin' fer?"

Feofan nodded to the vessel by his thighs. "What is in that?" she asked.

The man bit his lip. "It's just a little, eh—it's a salve. Fer my mum inside." He drew out his words uncertainly. "She's been sick a long time now. Poor woman. I'm worried I don't have enough fer—"

"What kind of salve is it?" she asked with accidental seriousness, climbing onto the stone deck. She covered the stern slip with a laugh. "I make them too." Sethan's hand shot over his concoction, blocking it from view. They both knew how suspicious this seemed. He removed it.

"Well," he started. "The man I bought the add-ins from said they were, eh, rosemary. And fish egg oil. And a type of mushroom, I can't strike up the name."

Feofan laid her dirty, though gentle hand along his lower neck and drooped her head to the bowl: inside was a collective of black pellets, mostly smashed into a dry dust. From where she was standing the mixture didn't smell at all like rosemary or fish eggs, nor did it resemble either.

Rather, it was precisely what she thought it might be: somniferum. Seeds of the papaver head. What the Egainshir elder called 'uforian.'

A second later, Sethan sniffed. And Feofan, having forced away the sensations and memories of the night and all the imperfections correlating with it, relived the early morning. Her body still stank of urine. She backed away from him, imitating demureness or embarrassment. Such always seemed to work in this place, especially when luring horsemen off the roadway. One look and they would almost always follow—for whatever purposes they had in mind, noble or lascivious.

"Is there somewhere I can wash? I have been travelling a long time now," she stated. Sethan turned his head to the icy ford, then back to her. She smiled as nicely as she could. "Can you show me?"

The susceptible young man hid the bowl behind his chair and stood up, adjusting his enormous cloak as he did so. He pondered stiffly, then snatched up the vessel, hopped down from the patio, and dashed into his house, leaving the door cracked. There was a clatter inside as if he were sweeping a surface clear of sticks and pebbles. As the woman lowered herself to level ground, he slunk back out with an iron pot underarm.

"I can heat up water at the inn and you can clean yourself behind my house," he proposed. "Though it's damn stinky back there. Haven't had a chance to, uhm—never mind. Is that ah'right with ye?"

Feofan hid her arms inside the grey folds of fur draped around her. "How long will it take to warm the water?"

Sethan held out the pot and measured the volume as best he could. "A while," he admitted, searching the sky.

"Just take me downriver," she requested, inching to his side and taking his cold hand. The basin fell to the dirt with a hollow clang. Clumsily, he jerked his hand away and fumbled to pick the pot back up.

"I'll just—I'll just take this back in, then." He disappeared into the house again. Feofan wondered how much older she was than this fellow: eight years, nine years? If his voice were deeper, she would assume six years. She scrutinized him again as he stepped from the blackness of his abode. He had never once taken a blade to the patchy beard over his jaw, that much was evident. It was his first. Ten years, she settled.

"Lead on," she said, removing her immense reindeer coat and handing it over to him. Underneath the layer was a thinner cape of wolf fur from which the breeze-prickled skin of her arms was laid bare. Sethan turned away and led her down the creek beyond his house, the back end of which harbored several heaps of indeterminable debris. Once the ford was concealed from sight—or once he became aware of the ridiculousness of Feofan's plan to bathe in the freezing waters, he halted.

"The, eh, the water deepens there and there," he said, pointing blearily at two areas near the opposite bank. "Mayhaps we should've crossed at the ford and come down that way there. I'm sorry."

She took off the wolf pelt, proceeding to the small wool mantle under it. Handing them both to Sethan, she was singularly left with a dirtied gown that covered her down to the knees, snug with crudely sewn patches at the hem and torso. The black hairs of her legs stood on end. She shivered cheerily, watching her companion as he studied her.

"Won't ye…" he inquired, "freeze to death? I wouldn't want that— nobody'd want that."

With one motion, she pulled the long tunic over her head. Sethan made a sound which could just as easily have been an exhalation as an inhalation. She could feel him staring dumbly over her as she entered the flowing ice, submerging the bundled cloth at hand. She dipped under. When she resurfaced, expecting to catch Sethan's glimpse, the lad was facing the overgrowth. She stood and stiffened herself, focusing on the brownleaf she chewed earlier: all the moisture on her body puffed into a cloud of steam and wafted away. She proceeded to wring the gown.

"Why are you looking that way?" she asked. "Is there something there?"

"No. Well, mayhaps there is," he answered. "Yer makin' me shiver just by lookin' at ye. Dunno how anyone could do it. Ye'll need all the warmth in Olford if yer to live the night, I'd say. Ye'll catch a bad cold in minutes, I reckon." Feofan waded to the shallows. "Where'd ye say yer from?"

"Kamenin," she replied, touching the feather-shaped scar on her forearm. "Your people call it Albatross Isle. And they say it is an island of the Piiks, though I do not think they know who the Piiks really are. They call all the island folk by that name. But one out of ten thousand islanders is truly a Piik, I would say. One."

"I never knew." By his tone and by the latent evidence of his age, Sethan was likely oblivious to most things outside of his village. With this thought at hand, his succeeding words were as jolting as the passing waters: "Are there many other halfelevs where you come from? I've only known one."

Feofan stared at the back of his head. "Have you lived here all your life?" she soon asked, plodding back to the crystalline bank.

"At Olivien's Ford? O' course. Left fer a venture back a season or so, as I do. But I've been here otherwise."

"A venture?" she said, crushing a sheet of ice under her heel as she unraveled the wet tunic. She thought she heard Sethan gulp.

"Yeah. I went up to Wallenport, then Westley. All round the island, really."

Feofan crept up to Sethan and flicked his earlobe. He held the cloaks out to his side without moving. Amusedly, she gripped a side of his cape and dried her shins and feet with it. He did not protest. Once finished, she gathered up the furs, pressing the skin of her upper abdomen against his hand as she did so.

"What brought you to those places? Do you buy your ingredients there?" She latched on her short mantle and pulled over the wolf pelt.

"Nah, I pick my own flowers. As fer my reasons, it's more a case of *who* brought me to those pl—" He had turned to face her. Much was still exposed under the fabric and fur. He gawked up at her frigid face, then away past her head. "P-places."

"Go on." She started back for the ford, fitting on the reindeer coat.

Sethan attended her, keeping his distance. "Anyhow, there was another halfelev who came through Olford. Name was Fitzmorley—or just Morley, as he liked. And he needed someone to show him to the port, so off we went. It's really a real long story. Ended up in Westley at the end of it."

The weaving girl in the village— "I'll be making new gloves for Morley next week." What idiot needs guidance to Wallenport?

"Why did he need someone to travel with him? The northward path is tame," she said, giving voice to the thought.

Sethan was silent for a few beats. "Yer either lucky or dangerous, Feofan," he musingly stated. "Isn't common fer lone drifters to make where they need to get to without some harassin'. Ye weren't beset by any ridders or nothin'?"

First man—I waited. Did not speak a word before Signy speared him off the horse. Viggdis caught the beast, cooked it later. Man had the mantle and the money box. Sethan must not care much for these horsemen. Second man—Viggdis saw him first. Walked out, he halted, tried to escape before he could speak. Birgir knocked him, dragged off. Had only the mantle, a letter, and the sack of metal bits. Find out what he meant. Third man—

"Not that I know of," she answered. "Ridders. I am not so sure I know what those are."

"They're just men hired by the aetheling and others. They do things like carry messages, find outlaws. Largely, they steal from the smallfolk who walk by—the folk who don't have horses or protection or nothin'. Usually they're kinder about it—so to speak—and sometimes they take out their weapons. Not so fond of 'em myself."

Feofan nodded. The back of Sethan's house was in sight moments later: cracked and fragmented jugs were strewn along its wall. Closer to them was an elongated lump of soil shying out from under the snow crust. The lad muttered as he passed it by. When they returned to the main road, Feofan took up her bag, still against the inn wall opposite Sethan's porch. He came out of his house and offered her a plate of watery porridge.

"Is that all there is to eat around here?" she queried, moving the sticky lump around with two fingers.

The young man's face went red. "There's proper veg at the inn there," he said, pointing with a calloused thumb. "Possibly a bite o' meat, though Marion doesn't just give it away fer free. Might hafta work or help her cook."

Feofan thought back to Egainshir. She then reached to the bottom of her bag, pulled out the pouch of copper pieces, and tossed it to Sethan. It landed on top of his bile-colored meal. Taking it up by its stringed closure, his eyes narrowed. He shook the sack once. His squint swelled when he opened it.

"Where did...?" When no further words were uttered, Feofan's arm snaked around the young man's hip.

"Bring me whatever Marion has to offer and I will tell you anything," she whispered, nudging Sethan off the stone platform.

"She'll want to know where I got these," he protested, thumping down to the road. "She always asks me whenever I bring coin and I tell her somethin' different every time. She'll want to know who ye are—what should I tell her?"

"You can say it is for Feofan. I am a rich woman. Use it all." Sethan's jaw hung open for a time, then he trudged over to the inn. While he was gone, Feofan crept into his house, closing the door behind her.

Black beetle's blood—the stink and the dark. Empty bed with a mat atop. No mother, that was a lie to keep the papaver. Where is it—here. Enough to kill a giant, enough to last a year, enough to become the island. Take it and go? No. I will hold onto him for longer, take him to the tree, get rid of him later. Bow in the corner. Truly smells of waste in here. Like the swamp, like vodnik breath. Like Sjaman's bloated corpse.

She left promptly, setting herself down on Sethan's chair atop the stone platform. Across the river, the boy she spotted on her southward journey was inserting twigs into a glittering pile of snow. He often raised his head to stare back at her; she averted her eyes whenever he did so. When Sethan came out again, he bore a tall mug in one hand and a full handled pot of stew in the other. Two loaves of bread were held under his armpits. He raised the mug hand to the child across the ford.

"Marion says ye can have whatever else ye want fer the rest of the day, includin' a room," he mentioned, placing the items down on the even stones. "I've got here two loaves of brown bread, one old and one fresh, and this here is cabbage stew and this is wheat beer. I can mayhaps get ye wine if that's more to yer liking."

"The water in the stew will be enough for me," Feofan said, picking up the heavy pot and placing it down on her lap. She stirred its sunken contents with the ladle: carrots, beans, and strips of cabbage swirled to the surface. "You can have the beer if you want it," she added.

Sethan slurped down a mouthful without pause, then clambered up and seated himself across from her.

"Yer heart's too big fer the countryside. M'damme." He added the last word quietly and with juvenile reluctance, then handed her the fresher, softer loaf. She dipped the full end of it into the soup.

"Tell me about this Morley fellow," she said as she removed the soggy crust. "What happened to him?"

"Ah," he moaned before gulping down a quarter of his beer. "Not much more to say, really. Traveled around with him—first as a guider, then as a follower. Fought off a few vodniks, broke into the Sivliére's castle,

252

stole mead from some soldiers. Then I found out he's got royal blood in him. Well, *noble* blood I guess it's called. Whole rebellion started up when we were in Westley, though I dunno how. He might've had somethin' to do with it, I think."

As I thought.

"Anyhow, he disappeared back home to the south fields. No farewells, no promise o' return, nothin' at all. I would've gone after him as he was leavin', but..." He scratched at his dry lips. "In short words, it was between him and my brother. And he didn't wanna be followed, y'know? I dunno. I do hope to see him again."

He fell silent, looked up at the clouds. Feofan slurped her broth and intently chewed her brown bread. Once she was sated, she placed the pot down and continued picking at the porous dough, appreciating the new tranquility.

The shadow of the boy at the corner of the eye—he still watches. Born under Otron and Haem. Eye of Ianoch. Remember the old dreams—his death, his melting face, his drowned and pale eyes, his skull, the teeth chatter and chatter and chatter.

"Tell me about yerself, Feofan," came Sethan's voice. She steadied her breathing. The young man had been wanting to ask for a considerable span of time, she could tell. "Tell me about, eh, Kamena."

"Kamenin," she corrected.

"Yeah, what's it like livin' there?" He finished off the rest of his beer before asking, much to Feofan's disgust.

"For me?" she said, her voice grim. "Or for everyone else?" She could feel Sethan's mood shift with hers. "It is no different from the other isles. A big mountain peak rising from the ocean. And everyone there lives around its shores. Except me. I live far up in the rocks, where I built a house for myself, where nobody can reach me. I think the villagers all spend their days fishing and catching birds and sometimes farming where the soil is not so dry. They leave food for me every five days. And they sometimes call on me when the dancers come from Mavros, gliding on their catamarans, carrying with them a new feather.

"Most folk leave for the other side of the island at that time and the dancers storm through the village and call me with their horns. I hear them. I come to them and they praise my youth. The men touch themselves when they see me because I will not have them. The women meet me and decorate my body with new robes. And then I meet the new feather and the ceremony goes on until I take the girl or the boy away with me. The dancers leave and the villagers return. I let the feather go to them below. I have tainted too many and the villagers have hated me for it. They say I am a wiccha—do you know that word? They must use it here. Do you know what it means?" Sethan shook his head, confounded and disturbed. "Do you know why I left Kamenin?"

"W-why?" he stuttered.

"Sails of white and blue. Crossed bolts of lightning. Swords and bows and nets and chains. They came only once and my friends killed those who could not escape. That was not so long ago. Do you know why I came here?" Sethan shook his head again.

Perfect.

The corners of her lips stretched out. She slunk away from the chair, lowered herself, and stared deeply into his wide eyes. Her hands cradled the lines of his jaw, warming his face like coals against an ice-lacquered boulder. She spared not three blinks. "I know you have uforian."

"I—"

"And I know why you use it. But what does it feel like? What do you see, if anything? How do you consume it?"

The lad abashedly answered after a time. "I dunno how to describe it. I see what I see but the feelin' is like—like my blood's turned to steam and moves faster than time. It feels like a nice sleep. I know I can do everythin' and anythin', but I can't and won't. Because I see there's no point to life except to die. And death is still so far from my door and this makes me glad. I used to have a man in Sylvan make the stuff into a tincture fer me. But he's not there anymore, I'm afraid." Feofan broke away from him and stood. The lad seemed to be on the verge of tears.

"Everyone's left me. And they've all been leavin' me fer as long as I've lived. I never knew my papa's name. Then Serryl, Sieger. Morley, mum..." He wiped his nose and breathed for a moment. "I imagine ye'll be leavin' in a little while too."

The apothecary's words—"What's that? Uforian? Got none of that. But Semhren across the way has chamomile. The big folk say that's the infant of uforian. I'll take no more than a nickel for all this." Breath the hahlixus, suckle the blue leaf of beltreres. Crush the papaver with chamomile, use with hot water or hot wine. Take him. Take him along.

"I need you to carry out a task for me," she began. "And I will not leave you when it is done. I swear this to you. This will help."

As if enthralled, Sethan, his attitude now mildly sanguine, entered his house and retrieved the bowl of crushed papaver seeds. He gave them to Feofan, who took out her spell-box, then he splashed across the ford to a house half-hidden. While he was gone, she added the shredded petals of chamomile to the somniferum powder and grated it all together delicately. The other two anodynes were removed from the box as well: the beltreres was stored away in a self-made compartment at the cuff of her sleeve while the condensed ball of hahlixus was placed and preserved under her tongue. Sethan returned in due time, bearing a bulging skin of wine.

"Good," Feofan said. "Now we should be going."

"Going? Going where?"

"Into the woods, northward. We should be far away from here. There are things I must show you. And I do not wish for any of the villagers to hear us." Sethan gulped at these words, but anticipation still yet twinkled in his irises. "Cut up the rest of the bread, wrap it. I will keep it in my bag, you will carry the cup and the wine. But here…" She emptied the vessel of black and yellow dust into the beer mug, then handed it over. "We must be careful not to spill it out."

"Are ye sure ye…"

Feofan could tell his confidence was faltering but, after one glance at her, he relinquished his hesitation and fetched his bow, fixing a quiver to his crude belt.

* * *

Once all their equipment was at hand, they rushed out of Olford, the small boy watching as they went. The clouds lumbered over them in the accommodating air. The light followed them, burning through the canopy. Hours passed and they did not speak until Feofan took out the slices of bread. At that time they rested off-road, lying against a fallen trunk in the snow.

"How much further ye tryna take me?" asked Sethan, still catching his breath. "Fer that matter, *where* are ye tryna take me?"

Feofan tossed away a strip of solid breadcrust. "Not much further. It is closer than you might expect," she said. Birds tittered and distant deer huffed. "Tell me, Sethan. When were you born?"

The young man counted the fingers on one hand. "Bit o'er three and twenty years," he said after a few presumable miscalculations.

"During which face of the sky-turn?" she asked.

He scratched his chin, unsure. "I think Hetta. Not sure 'bout the exact time o' the season."

He does not know what I mean. Impulse to lie, yet he lacks brashness around women. Alleviation-bound. Quick to trust, though slow to show it. Adventurous. Had to be born under the blue-black of Rynria.

Sethan had finished the rest of his refreshment and was now gripping his cloak around him like a blanket. Feofan stored away the rest of the bread. After she pulled herself up and beckoned her companion to do likewise, they headed back for the trail.

"Do you know what the sky-map is?" she asked. The lad waited for her to continue, as if he believed he misheard her. "It was the calendar of the ancients, the revolution of the faces. I know so little of your kinfolk and your order, but I have heard you count only the seasons. This is now clearer to me. There is so much you do not know. So much the sky-map can tell us."

"What d'ye mean?" They strutted out onto the road. The monotonous thumping of Feofan's walking stick on the cold ground resumed.

"This night will be shining with the celestial Blanc, a world unreachable, a fibula for Haem's Halo and the Stars of Synesti—which will shimmer brightest at twilight. Come the morrow's dark, it will be as addled as the rest. But its milk—bleak and stinging as passing Death—will flood the shores and burn the trees. And I will welcome it. The both of us will welcome it together."

Seth was quiet for a moment. "What're ye tryna say?" he spoke eventually.

This time, the clandestine woman chuckled. "It is a portent. A fate. The stars and the celestials guide us, even when we do not know it, even when the heavens are not open to us. Blanc is the last luminous body to be seen before year's end."

"And what does it do to us?" Sethan, trying to observe the sky through the overhead web of branches, pulled up his hood.

"Nothing. We do what we will, as always. But the earth, the Real, which sees all who walk upon it and all that circles over it, controls our every thought. It has a life of its own, you know—a life that never ends. It dies and is reborn. Under the calling clarion of Blanc, the earth begins its new death. With it, we reflect on the cycle previous. All our rage, our sadness, our joy, our terror—they return to us a thousand-fold. They bring to us change, the destruction of our selves in living or dying. Yet it also ensures the continuation of *what is*. The mundane rapture. The love of what is. The hatred of that which is called truth."

Unimpeded silence pursued her final words. Sethan, as he had earlier, seemed to wait for her to give a definitive conclusion; that, or he ceased listening, his expectation of clarity now banished. They proceeded without speaking for another hour, until the sky was scantly lit by a hem of the sun's dress. At that time Feofan led him again into the wealds, over browned, wilted ferns and enormous hoofprints.

"There is a tree near here," she said, removing the beltreres leaf from her cuff, slipping it under her tongue with the unswallowed hahlixus grit. "We will drink under it and climb as high as we can. By then the night will be nearer. I will try and show you Blanc."

"If yer not fond of beer, why drink wine?" Sethan asked in a nervous murmur.

"I would prefer not to drink anything with useless poison in it. But this is a special circumstance, I think. I have you with me tonight." She smiled at him. He was busy glowering at the height of the trees surrounding them.

"Ye've, uhm…" He cleared his throat and tried again. "Won't it be dangerous to climb anythin' after eating uforian? I once rightly drowned 'cause I was led to think the Lightrun was only an underground passageway. What if I fall and…y'know." Feofan clutched his hand, dragging him close to her side.

"You will not come to harm while with me. I promise." She released his clammy fingers. "Now, add the wine to the cup. Stir with an arrow or a small stick."

He did as he was told, slowing his pace so as not spill any of the drizzling wine. The aforementioned tree was towering over them by the time their drink was ready: the chamomile was clustered around the edges of the cup as the cakes of papaver dust floated and bobbed near the center. Sethan took on a queasy countenance after sampling a taste.

"Are ye sure about this?"

The woman, still grinning, threw down her makeshift staff and removed her bag. Sethan set down his bow and quiver. She took the cup from the young man, one hand under its wide base, and took a gulp, washing down both the hahlixus and the beltreres already in her mouth.

"Hold your nose, if you must," she suggested, giving it back. Sethan did so, swallowing as much as half the liquid with a tight cringe. They soon began their climb.

The stomach boils in white heat—the fire runs through us in the oaken-arm cradle, branchlets grip and pinch. An air bath, a streaming space and corona of coming days. How we desire it. Pleasure. It does not sleep between pain and comfort as I know it now. It is in the heavens. And the heavens are in me as I am in the Real, as the white planet is in both the aureole and the dragon's gut.

Feofan broke from her meditation to hear her companion struggle beneath her. His cloak was caught against the split teeth of the tree's heaviest boughs. He called to her but already his voice was lost. She climbed on and found a pronged perch nearer the top.

The spirit, if it is believed in, can be pliant under another spirit's guidance. So few—I see—so few are able to guide their own. It is the guide itself, in them. It is the wildfire. How many days and nights could it take for the smallfolk to see the cosmos unending: beyond the Real is the Extant, beyond the Extant is Nothing, beyond Nothing is the Smallest Thing. And within that, there is the spark of Real, waiting to consume the emptiness already inside of it. The symbol from the priest was truer than I believed.

Sethan was now grappling the limb on which Feofan rested. Still unspeaking, she led him up to the roost which she previously warped: this had been done when she discovered the tree on her first trip to Werplaus. Its top resembled a hand lunging up to grope one of the twin moons, its branches perverted into twisting claws, its palm a bed of soft cracked bark. Altering it like this required two beltreres tears and a full hour of pained concentration.

And how will he know himself after this? What will he think of the body, the harbor of life—has he seen it before in a dream or a glass or a murky rill? To dwell outside it all is a curse to many—what is the word they use? Geister or ghast. I am sure he will think of this tomorrow as naught more than a wretched sleep. But he will remember what I have shown him. No one can ever forget it. They can only accept its possibility, like the sagittate patterns one sees through their own closed eyes, once they have irritated the skin. It is there—it is gone. And memory cannot capture its wriggling wet flagella.

"How could this get like this? Eh?"

Feofan saw Sethan's mouth move to these words. He was groveling under the gentle sway of the trunk, trying to hug one of the gnarled appendages within reach.

258

"Come to the center," she tried to tell him. Her mouth was numb and gave voice to a warbled speech. It was an immediate aftereffect of the beltreres. Either way, Sethan fearfully crawled in her direction. She leaned forward on her knees, opening her arms to him.

Come to me, sapling. Reveal your little life. Let me show you what I can know of the world.

She clamped her hands against the sides of his head.

Olford was there. And the child had a brother and a sister, both much older. An elm tree named Nanci—at the top looking down, a horseman was trotting through. A perfect shot: man fell to the dirt; and the boy climbed down and the two of them ran and ran. More horsemen, some without horses. "Ridders'll be ridders. But I'll do it different one o' these days." Then he was alone. Out in the underbrush, waiting. There! Strike him! No, it can't be done. Later: fury: into the eye! Mother has the swamp-sick—damn vodniks, I'll bet! It's that Sylvain man with the beard. Let him be, let him be. Been here all my life. "Morley, short for Fitzmorley. I'm on my way to Wallenport." Come up, come up! He's a halfelev, see? What think ye? "Trouble." He likes the lad, the fairest friend in years. The woman's name was Ranneka, beautiful and generous to the muttering drunk—gave him his only pair of shoes. Isn't so hard to figure out the way there. Morley, wait—Morley!

Hours had passed.

Feofan, now a spectre hovering above her and Sethan's collapsed bodies, moved the wisps of her hands. Their spirits were now one and the same, an invisible phantom above the island. But she was in full control. This was the only concern in carrying out the spell, she recalled.

It had been years since she attempted it with her sister. Then, she had failed horribly to conform their essences. This success came as a surprise— only because she had not known the young man until earlier that day. There was no knowing how volatile his spirit could be. But here they were, flying hundreds of feet in the air. Hopefully Sethan's body did not forget how to breathe in the absence of its owner. They drifted north.

Wallenport was below them. On this night it was surrounded by beads of fire, all lining the outer walls and sloping down to the edge of the wood. There were tents of white cloth and blue pavilions—large men in tunics and trousers, many wrapped up against the cold. There had to be hundreds of them, or even a thousand if more than three men shared a tent. Horses, though far fewer in number, were confined to a long post at the western

259

limits of the camp. Ships were anchored away from the docks, each swaying with furled sails. And the castle was dark aside from two open windows facing the sea.

The lower one—the middlemost of five identical portals, all lined up across the castle's mortared-stone head—glowed with the hellish blaze of brazier fire. Within the chamber a halfelev in a belted robe sat before a lectern, scratching feverishly at a cut of calfskin. His bed was empty. Four other strips of vellum were strewn at his feet. Every so often, he would cease his writing, rub his eyes, pace by the foot of his bed. This one often had trouble sleeping, she could tell.

He soon swept up the limp rag and, under his breath, tried to read from it: "On this date and eve of seventy-five Frysa in the All-Being's year of three-sixty U.R., I, Aetheling Felix of—deh deh deh. To the Damme—mmh—my mother, I bequeath the highest jurisdiction of all those properties and lands in the county of Westley, which run along the northwesternmost corner of the Crouxwood down to the—deh deh deh—including the stead called Michelhal and all its staff and all those who by right and by the justice of the kingdom are indebted and obliged to said staff—so on. To the Damme Anae, my wife and governess of the region of Sarcovy and sole inhertor—'inhertor?' Damn. In-hare-eh-tore—mmh mmh, that's enough. To Raul Chestervelt, chamberlain of the Sivliére estate—primogenitureship of the role of chamberlain and—however much we can afford, there it is. To Cato van Garm, cleric of the Church of St. Maguir and the household of the Sivliéres, yeh yeh. To Arnaul, manor of the Bertrisses. To Edma Iacob, all my chattels unclaimed by my wife, Damme Anae. Or if she should fall dead—amend that later. To the, ech…"

He dropped the parchment to the floor, took up a metal goblet, and upended its contents into his mouth. "Sanct's Bones," he whispered, noticing a pile of curled scraps and scrolls under the desk. He sat down at the edge of his bed, yawned, and rested his head against a fist.

"What in the black hell have I gotten into?" he said as he laid back on the mattress.

The second, dimmer light shone from a high room at the base of the castle's only tower.

"You could see it?" It was a youthful voice, not yet deepened with age.

"Even if there were clouds, it would still be clear." It was her mother's voice. She was in the same room as usual.

260

"I'll mark that down then. Other comments, damme?" There was a burnished table. Charts of the sky. Maps of the earth. Heavy tomes and stacks of unsewn papers.

"It will be as it usually is, but grander. Before the year's end there will be a shift." The robed boy etched the words on wax.

"I'll save that, then." Quietude.

"Have you no ink, Fien?" The chink of pottery.

"I do. Hard to see at this hour. Best to save it here then write it in the morning." He coughed. Another pause.

"There is a shade here. Not in this room, but here. I often sense it at this hour, though only during the recent days. Yes, I see." The legs of a chair rumbled against wood flooring.

"What are you saying, damme?" He picked up the candle and their shadows glided about.

"I see. There is a stranger here. And I believe the stranger has been on this isle for some time now. But now she is—or *he* is here. Both sexes. Watching us." Another bout of silence.

"Where?" Footsteps to the door.

"Nowhere and everywhere. That is the best means of describing it."

The rest of the castle slept peacefully, with some exceptions: one room over from the halfelev, another young man was in bed, naked under the sheets and over a much larger woman. Her head was visible against her partner's—it gazed up at the ceiling, lips closed, a hum whirring in her man's ear.

The woman was from a part of Sethan's memory. She gave him shoes as he stumbled through Wallenport, drunk on uforian. And he had run off, hooting gaily. Elsewhere, a man in wool with a drooping moustache circled the massive empty space of the tribunal chamber, his arms folded, his demeanor doomed. In the stables outside, another man removed a pouch of coins from under one of the hay mounds, emptied it in the corner of a stall, and began counting out nickels and coppers, often poking his head over the booth wall. Guards roved around outside, up and down the hillside steps, through the calm streets and alleys. They left it all behind.

The ring-castle slumbered as a shadow upon cadaverous titans. The satyrs tore the fur from a skewered buck, drooled over the steaming meat. Children rested in the warmth of the coastal column. Others yet crowded the hills and their valleys, drinking from the ice, settling the mountain maws.

261

Jutting from Westley's gate was a train of motionless hauling sleighs and wagons, their decks piled with lumber pikes, coils of rope, barrels, chests. Common thieves stalked the hovel grounds, waiting for the guards to finish their routes. Families, if they were still awake, orated scripture and prayed for safe returns. If they slept, they slept together, buried under silvery pelts. The snows were almost gone.

In the hall at the top of Westley's ascent, two lovers rested in privacy, both heaving, satisfied. The woman laid her head against the bare furry chest of the other, a handsome man of middle-age.

"You're pleased with me, then?" the woman said.

"Pleased?" he replied quietly. "About what?"

"About tomorrow. About marching with the foreguard."

"I don't think I'm pleased so much as I'm—"

"Nervous," said the woman. "I can always tell. You whisper when you're nervous."

"Women don't fight in the field," he articulated. "I know, we won't exactly be riding through the ranks. But have you ever seen a battle before? Even a small one?"

"There was a skirmish outside the gates of Lattaholm when I was twelve. A hireling affair. I left for Garm with my mother and sister right after it was over, before the corpses could be removed. Mennia cried, but I tried to stray away and see all the kinds of wounds the men took. I wasn't pleased by it all, of course, the smell was insufferable. I was fascinated, nothing more."

"I know what you're trying to say."

"Believe it or not, my sister and I both met young Michel when we arrived at Garm. And Mennia couldn't help but cry to him about the horrors outside our gate."

"What did he think of it? If you know."

"I don't." The woman shifted herself on top of the man. "But I imagine he cheered her up easily. He used to be such a delightful lad. If it weren't for his prolonged and susceptive ignobility, perhaps we wouldn't be here."

"I'm happy with where I am," the older man said, moving his hands down to his mate's waist. "Can't speak for you."

"You'll be even happier with where we end up come year's end."

"If we defeat him in the field, that is." The woman scoffed at this remark. "I'm serious. We haven't heard from Wallenport, we don't know how big his army might be."

"You really believe the continentals will have sent him aid?" she said. "Who would do that?"

"Your own family." No comment came from the woman. "And the Earl of Garm. And probably any merchant family who's trying to provoke the Bertrisses. At that, anyone who wishes to plant themself here in Westley. For all we know Wallenport could be overcrowded with ridders and levies as we speak."

"I don't believe it. Alherde says Michel is now Felix's diplomat. They're as good as dead if that's true."

"Fine," said the man, unconvinced. His partner began to peck slowly at his neck and face. "What about the aspirants?"

"Felix's?"

"I suppose."

"All-Being knows where they all are now. They might've gone home, might've gotten lost, might be on their way to better fortune here. Maybe they live now at Hoerlog, since you left it unguarded." She adjusted herself. The man let out a winded sigh.

"How do you know this and I don't?" he asked.

"Hamm came and went not a week past. You've been busy with the troops. Not with me." She bit his ear then murmured into it: "He's going to take charge with Amalic. Lead them into Wallenport. Through its opened gate. And Felix will be stranded out in the wood."

"Let's not talk about this anymore."

The woman paused. "Then what should we talk about?" she asked. The man beneath bit into her neck.

Something pulled their spectre away, down from the hill of Westley, down past the wells and shops and into the homely outskirts. Was it Sethan? How had he gained such control after so short a time? What did he want to see?

A disorderly barn. A grid of huts. One, just one in particular. There was a man inside. He bore the same face as Sethan though he was much taller, of greater brawn and bulk. He was hunched on a stool, sniffing a rag wet with oil. On his lap were two sword blades, grey-white and freshly forged, and a pair leathern gloves with buckled straps. Sieger. That was his name.

Behind him, a shape turned under the pelt atop his bed. He watched until it was still, then stored away his equipment in a small wicker basket. He stood and left, somewhat loudly.

The bedded contour rose, cast her tired eyes on the emptied hovel.. Then she saw them.

Blind white. The sheen of disbelief. Then oblivion.

"Yeva!"

Feofan woke at dawn with a scream and aggressively threw Sethan's sleeping body away from hers. She curled up, hands held over her long ears, tears already streaming, her arms and legs convulsing. Sethan, awake and afraid, reached for her halfheartedly. He was unable to lay a hand on her. Feofan could not tell why—she did not care to know—but he too appeared ready to sob. After a bout of uncertainty, he squirmed away.

"W-what's—what's happened?" were the only clear words to come from him. They were followed by a procession of subdued syllables. Feofan glared at him, hands still fixed against the sides of her skull. The clouds were heavy and congealed above them.

"Who was that with Yeva?" she stammered. "Your brother? Answer me!"

Sethan inched as far away from her as he could, until he was close enough to the trunk's edge. He glanced down at the mortal fall. Feofan jerked up to her feet, her hands now curled into pallid fists.

"Do you know her? Yeva, the girl in the bed? Why did I not see her in your memories—have you never met her?! Answer, damn you!" She took a step forward. The wind billowed through her many furs.

"No, I have—I have met her! But I—I don't..." He hid his face behind his hands. "Ye were the one watchin' it, weren't ye? Ye were the shadow behind me? The one throwin' me about like that?"

"Yes." Feofan turned away to the opposite edge of the tree. She had only been startled by the final visage, the unruptured scrutiny into the Real.

Yeva. Where have you been?

Abruptly, Feofan's anger returned and she charged back to the young man. He barely caught himself before she could grab him by the latch of his cloak.

"Tell me everything and I will leave you be."

He did so without ease.

Part III

Chapter VII – Convolutions on the Lightrun

It was now quieter than it should've been, Morley thought.

There were nearly five hundred men surrounding him, all of whom were either lined before the Lightrun's eastward bank on their side, placed within the elaborate formation on the road below, or scattered around the empty inn. Its roof was his convenient, albeit unprotected viewpoint. Ahead on the other side of the ford, even more men were positioned behind a sturdy tiered barricade of logs, its ends reaching from the furthest corner of Tomak's house to the forgotten ruin of Haarka's. From the dividing point of Larenta Creek further downstream to the bend beyond the millhouse and its garden of grapevines, the riverbed was littered with rock-filled boxes and barrels—lazy obstacles for the inevitable breakthrough.

"I still don't understand them," said Yeva softly. Like Morley, she rested prone against the short incline of the inn's roof.

"Understand what?" he asked, thinking she meant the hindrances in the current.

"Bitched battles," she said.

Morley narrowed his eyes. "Bitched battles?" Sounding it out himself was helpful enough, despite the quaver in his voice. "Pitched battles, you mean?"

Yeva rolled her eyes. "I guess that's right—it's hard to hear what anyone's saying when everyone's chattering back and forth, trying to be heard over the others. But like I said, I still don't get it."

"It's when two enemies, eh, agree to have a fight somewhere at a certain time," he explained, recalling the tractate in Semhren's compendium. His greatest regret of this new journey was opting to bring Geat and the claymore, but not the heavy text—which certainly would've been less hefty than the cask he stole over a season prior.

"Lots of famous battles were pitched," he continued, taking his mind off the other matter. "The Blood-week of Dennengroen. The Battle of Loren Lake, which was also fought over both land and water, like this one will be." He gulped. "In a way."

His stomach was like a sponge in the hands of a laundress. He'd only seen eight dead men before. And he'd never watched any of them at the moment of death or injury. Whenever Gale recounted the battles he was in, the old ridder avoided messy sketches and comprehensive descriptions of what it looked like, how the victim reacted, what the aggressor felt at the final stroke. He only ever noted how it began and ended. The important parts.

"Are you, uhm, frightened? At all?" he asked.

"I'd be more frightened if I didn't know they were on their way. Or if I was expecting something much worse to show up—but no, it's a nonsense *pitched* battle between naemas and only naemas. No beasts, no thunder. It could be so much worse, you know."

"I think I see what you mean." Morley said.

"If you're going to have a battle," she continued, "isn't it a better idea for the attacking army to not tell his enemy he's coming at a certain time to a certain place?"

"I suppose it's a case of politeness. The, uhm, the numbers on either side might be matched up, right? And Felix is sort of a gentleman from what I can tell of our only meeting." Feeling that the comment was expected of him, he added, "As much as I hate the bastard."

"Or mayhaps they're trying to trick us," she said, rolling over onto her back toward the wide fissure in the roof. She pointed down the road, past the alert horsemen and the emptied carts and sleighs on the Westley-ward trail. "Mayhaps they'll come from that way and get them all at their backs—what would they do then, Morley, hmm? What will *we* do?"

"We'll still run, I hope" he said without turning over. "In a different direction."

But first, he knew, they would have to charge back inside the inn to grab Geat, the sword, the coins—wherever they were hidden—and some amount of food they could carry.

"What if they come in every direction? What if they're lined up in a giant circle all around us?" The notion made his heart hop. Still, he analyzed the situation as best he could.

"That might not be a good move," he resolved. "Think about it. We have about five hundred men, they probably have about five hundred men, maybe. If they had all theirs spread out like that, Allesande's or Wortin's horsemen would just ride through one small side of their line and break through the circle. Then their whole stragedy...strategy—that's how I say it. It wouldn't work. I think."

Yeva rolled back over, bumping into Morley's elbow. "What *would* work, then?" she asked.

"I don't know and I don't want to think about it." He gulped down his nausea. "Not my problem."

"Think about Anae naked instead, that'll make you feel better," she offered. "Better, think about *me* naked." She ruffled his hair, giving a laugh he could only hope was forced. "Your head's turning into a tomato."

"I don't know what that is," he said, feeling his hot cheeks.

"They're soft fruits, we used to grow them on Kamenin. Guess they haven't been brought here yet." Neither spoke for a time.

Morley wondered again if Willian and the second man—the one called Sir Amalic—had eluded the army from Wallenport as it progressed to the ford. If they hadn't dodged the soldiery on their northward trek, the success of the rebellion rested only on Allesande's victory against Felix. If *they* failed...

As long as Morley and Yeva could get away from the bloodshed, there was nothing to be distressed over. Together, haunted by the circumstances to their own respective degrees, they would merely stroll their way to Reineshir, glide like lost spirits over the barrens of Werplaus, then disperse across the yard of Egainshir.

Still, where was Seth? Nobody knew where he'd disappeared to. Young Tomak could only say he headed north—not two days prior to Morley's and Willian's arrival—with a shape-shifter, a reindeer woman, a wiccha wearing the skins of a dream-beauty.

Morley didn't know what any of those things were. But he could tell well enough that the boy wasn't lying.

When Sieger arrived at Olford with the rest of Allesande's army, he wished for solitude in his family home. Later, on the morning of the following day, Morley approached him as he sat amidst the clay debris behind his house, watching over a muddy lump close by. He had been chiding any man who carelessly paced over it or defecated within his view, as Morley heard. Having entered Seth's house upon his arrival, days and days prior, he'd intimated an idea of the mound's purpose. He chose not to confirm it.

"I don't know where else he'd be," said Sieger morosely. "Not Westley, he'd have seen us on the road. Likely gone to Sylvan."

"If he did, that's not a good sign" Morley proposed. "I've been here waiting for him for over a week. I would think he'd be back within that time."

"Wallenport, then. Nah, he hated Wallenport." Sieger rubbed his lips in thoughtful reticence.

"Could he have gone to stay out with the wilders?" he asked without hope. "Y'know, to avoid all the ridders passing through?"

"Wilders don't play host. It's hard enough already for them to get by." Sieger stared darkly at the halfelev. "Of all people, ye should know that. Werplaus runt."

"I lived with a ridder for most my life," Morley replied calmly, standing. "He owned his land, same as you." As he strode off, another thought came to him: "Oh, is Yeva around? I haven't seen her." Sieger said nothing. And Morley peaceably returned to his room at the inn, the one he'd shared with his half-brother.

*　　*　　*

Whenever the name 'Willian' came into his head, Morley thought only of the long hat, the face, the coat and tabard. He could not for the life of him espouse the evidence of their brotherhood. In truth he was disappointed in himself, disappointed by the reaction he gave when Willian told him. If he'd waited at least half a year to share the discovery, Morley knew he would've shared fairer words.

From Gale's House to Egainshir, they listened to the wind's speech, Morley lugging the greatsword over a shoulder—an inseparable article, as he said—and, for the first time ever, pulling along Geat by leash. He was to stay with Minny, his old mate.

From Egainshir to Reineshir—and once they reluctantly allowed Geat to follow them onward—they talked of their curious mutual acquaintance with Semhren, the exiled scholar.

From Reineshir to Olford, however, they exchanged much more— scarcely any words on their pasts in Werplaus and Wallenport, but plenty concerning the walks of provincial and country life. By the time they reached their destination, Morley had exhausted his supply of subjects. Willian, on the other hand, after six days of lonesome contemplation and offered labor in Olford, brought forward another topic.

"I told you there probably aren't any radishes here," the lad was saying to Geat as his half-brother stepped inside the inn. "But you bloody insisted on coming along, didn't you? Now you'll have to suffer until we get back home, you stinker."

"I see you two are arguing again," Willian started, sitting across from the pair, snug by the hearth. Neither of them gave a reply. "I'd think you could buy him all the land's freshest foods from here to Reineshir. And more."

"Why do you say that?" Morley asked. The ridder peered to the other side of the common room, over the lone counter and back into the dim kitchen. Marion was out of view. Nobody was present but them. He removed his hat.

"Because of the gold you brought," he said, still quiet despite their privacy. "I'm only joking, of course, I don't think it'd be wise to show off gold around here. Hells, I don't even think it'd be wise to show it off anywhere on the island. Not Westley, not Wallenport. A single aureon could change a simple man's life forever. All he'd have to do is nab it from you."

"Well, anyone's welcome to try." He patted his tunic flap and the pieces jingled. "I meant to give them to Seth as an apology." In truth, his intention was to give only one to Seth and the other to his half-brother, just before they parted ways for good.

"Think he'll know what to do with them?"

"He'd know better than me." Morley stretched his arms. "Why, what would you do with them?"

Willian took time thinking up his answer. "I don't think I'd keep them either," he professed. "One would go to Semhren, I think." For whatever reason, he seemed to pity the scholar and his 'new' life away from civilization. "And the other would go to Mester Alherde. Imagine how lovely Reineshir could be with a bit of renovation. You know?"

This came as more of a surprise: while they were passing through the aforementioned town, resting for a short while outside its manor, they were met by Anae's old tutor—who was far, far younger than expected. Though they apparently knew each other well, Willian and Alherde did not seem all too close or comely during their brief rest. Why would his last piece of gold go to him and not to, say, Squire Hamm?

"Very well," Morley said conclusively. They watched the fire die for a time.

"You, ehm…" Willian soon started, "you mentioned meeting Ellemine in the upper floors of Castle Sivliére, yes? And she gave you the aureons. And shared other things with you, is that right?"

"It is," Morley said to the hearth.

"Then you came to Hoerlog, where we first met." They both waited. "You didn't know who I was at that time. Did you?"

"Nope," he confirmed.

Willian cleared his throat. "Did you even know you had another brother? Besides Felix?"

"Ellemine told me nothing about my siblings. She only said who my father was. And she verified that Felix is my brother. Our brother." Marion the Innkeeper brought him a small bowl of stew, smiled at Willian, then returned to the kitchen. "She doesn't remember me from my last visit," Morley muttered. "Probably because my hair's all cut down now." He slurped up a piece of cabbage and continued.

"Anyway, other than telling me about my father, Ellemine asked what I was doing there, so I told her. I would've pressed on with my questions. But imagine being in my place, running into your mother for the first time ever, finding out she's empathy-dumb and careless of her children's wellbeing. Finding out she's one of the most powerful people on all of Sarcovy." He sloppily sucked up more soup from the bowl's edge, dribbling the broth onto his massive wool coat. "I need not explain she was in control of the conversation. Given more time, I'm sure I would've pressed."

"I understand," said Willian. He watched Morley finish the stew quick and place the bowl down by the fire. "I ought to get a helping myself."

"It's warming enough, I'll say." He cleared his throat soundly and spat into the ashes below the fire. "Y'know, there was something odd about Ellemine. Other than the fact she was a pure-elev, the only one known to live within a hundred kalcubits. I'm sure you would have plenty more to say about it."

"What do you mean?" asked Willian.

"I don't know. There were moments when…" he gestured hazily, eyes shut in concentration. "It was as if she knew what I was thinking, yet she still felt the need to interrogate me. Did you ever experience that—if you've ever known her well, that is?"

Willian chuckled lightly to himself. Morley realized why quick: not once during their long trek to Olford did he permit Willian the opportunity to reminisce over his life in Wallenport.

"*Now* you ask me," grumbled the long-eared ridder. "Yes, I was raised in her hall for a long time, until about six years ago—or whenever the Bertrisses first showed up. That's when my father sent me to Hoerlog. Haven't been back since. And I never revealed my lineage to anyone other than Hamm. And Wortin, who knew who I was before I arrived. Most folk don't know what to make of the halfelev physique or don't draw the obvious connection to Ellemine but, just as a precaution…" He held up his crumpled liripipe.

"So you knew Ellemine well? Before your time at the tower?" Morley dug between his teeth. There was a loud bang outside. He dismissed it, assuming Tomak was playing another one of his lonely games of make-believe.

"Not as well as most sons know their mothers, I think. But yes. Neither she nor my father disciplined me or treated me as their child."

"Your father?" There had been no allusion to his patronage as of yet.

Willian carelessly tossed up a hand. "Roberrus. He wasn't my true father, of course, I never knew my true father. I only ever knew Ellemine and Roberrus, the unbreakable and unallied duo. And they were both preoccupied with…whatever they were preoccupied with. They left the acclaims and chastisements to Mester Semhren.

"Around the time Felix was born—which was around the same time Semhren left, actually—I spent most of my days away from the keep and the motte. I'd invade the castle pantry and buttery at the start of the week, hide the supplies in an old crate near the fishmongers, then go about my mischief. Stealing goods for cash, buying rounds for sailors.

"Anyhow, Ellemine caught me taking beer a number of times. And she always knew what I intended to do with it, whether I was planning to sell it off to an alehouse, share it with Alherde, or just drink it up myself. At first when I was still a young boy, I assumed she had eyes all over the town, so to speak. Once older I always made sure nobody was watching me. Still yet, she knew."

Before he could go on, the heavy door swung inward and a tall cloaked man stepped inside. As he surveyed the room, two others followed him, both adorned in surcoats and linens.

"Either of you the keeper?" said one of them through a heavy beard. As the words left him, he and his mate narrowed their eyes, heeding the half-brothers' elevi ears. Willian stuck his familiar hat back on.

"Uh," Morley blurted, "back there." He pointed to the kitchen with his thumb. The men strode further inside. Morley and Willian exchanged a blank look, then the former got up, stepped over Geat, and rushed through the closing door.

Outside, he froze: not twenty strides away, there was a halted line of sleighs and bull-yoked carts extending down the road to Westley. A crowd of men in plain wool sweaters were tiredly preparing to unload the supplies of logs, containers, and weaponry along the endless train. Around them, there were more horses than Morley had ever seen, each cantering about with armored men atop their backs. The men, ridders and workers alike, called back and forth to each other over the light din of labor.

Before he knew it, Willian was behind him under the splintered doorpost. He followed as Morley rounded the corner between the inn and Seth's house.

"Watch it!" came a sharp voice behind him. It was followed by a flash of black and brown, then the visage of a monstrous bay destrier with thick antler nubs trotting over to the ford, its sidesaddle driver bedecked in a skirt of chains over his—no, *her* leather breeches. Willian rushed to pull Morley out of the way, barely avoiding a second ridder's horse.

"Damme Allesande!" Willian shouted.

The riding woman halted and veered abruptly. Her hair was done up with a stripped bronze circlet latched through the braids and her face had all the hard memorable features Morley ascribed her back in Michelhal. She cantered to them, diverting the scattered traffic against Seth's raised porch.

"Sir Willian," she said before glancing twice at Morley, his shortened hair giving precedence to the unmistakable ears. "And Fitzmorley, harbinger of the rebellion." Already, the lad's mood was soured. "I would dismount, but I'm not sure where my pages have gone. All these pale-skinned farmer sons look the same when crowded together like this."

"Where's Wortin?" Willian asked.

"Somewhere. Likely closer to the back of the column."

She continued speaking—some words about the supply and the march from Westley—but Morley was distracted by the familiar contour of a man in an ink-black cloak rushing through Sethan's door. It was Sieger. That meant Yeva was probably near. Probably.

Sure enough, upon peering down the now congested southward route, there she was. Standing alone in a worn half-mantle. She did not see him. He thought of calling out to her, knowing well that his voice would be drowned. Or perhaps there was some other inhibition.

Measuredly, the young woman tramped her way to the door Sieger had entered. She tried the latch: it wouldn't budge. It seemed to clunk and clatter until she was forced to press her nose to the crack and call with gentle dignity. He never answered as far as either of them could tell. And Morley, embarrassed and nervous beyond reason, tuned his attentive mind back to Allesande and his half-brother. Or tried to.

"—around nine separate posts in the brush, like the points on a sundial's surface," Allesande was saying. "I don't take Felix to be a tactical genius and I know perfectly well that his war-mester—a damned tailor's son—has only seen skirmishes against Piiks. But we should be cautious. We had two spies, two aspirants, who both went off to check on Wallenport's garrison."

"And?" said Willian, too soon.

"Whereas the original plan was to crowd the woodlands and draw them out, force them to give chase, then send the others in through the unguarded gates—all a largely bloodless ordeal—we've since received some startling news." Her horse shifted restlessly and she scolded it with a sharp hiss. "The continentals answered Felix's call. Tenfold." Though Willian did not reply, he was not speechless. "It is entirely possible our men overestimated. But they did say the tent lights extended from the Crouxwood's treeline to the base of the palisade. That's quite a distance, is it not?"

"It is," he answered. Morley eyed Seth's door again. Yeva was not there. She was now headed for the river crossing, her drab mantle held tight around her. He observed until she was blocked from view by three men bearing bundles of spears.

"Ah!" he heard Allesande exclaim. "Here he is now."

Behind him, Sir Wortin's own white-speckled destrier stomped up. Willian pulled Morley out of the way again as a third horseman appeared, his mount scrawny and gentle compared to the other two. The rider himself was handsome, light-haired, and unremarkable in stature. The halfelevs were backed against the inn's wall with the trio surrounding them.

"Sir Willian," said Wortin, the grey kapitain. "Pleasure. You know Sir Amalic Pourtmann?" He gestured to the man beside him.

274

"I've heard the name," Willian stated with a short bow. "You're the—pardon if I'm making a silly mistake. You're the son of the hertog, yes? Eldest son of Aubin?"

The one called Amalic gave a kind smile and returned the favor of acknowledgement, but Morley again saw a shifting blot in the forestry across the Lightrun: Yeva was going deeper, further and further away. Then, once again, she was blocked from view: two cheery men stopped by the bank and began urinating into the river.

"Has she explained the plan on your end?" said Sir Wortin.

"I haven't," Allesande responded for him. "Though it isn't much different from the former plan. The only change is that you and Amalic are now in charge."

"In charge of what?" Willian inquired. Morley caught Wortin's gaze at that instant: the kapitain had only just perceived his elevi ears. They set him at ease, it appeared.

"The auxiliaries," said Allesande. Then, with an airy tone, she added, "The 'cave-men' up north. The men who dismantled The Stead." Willian grunted. "From what I hear, your squire has infiltrated Castle Chaisgott. That's good. It might be a useful position if we push the enemy back to Wallenport. The auxiliaries are all yours, as Wortin will be here with me. When and if Felix takes his force down the road to meet us, it's up to you to bypass his army and coordinate an assault on Wallenport's gate. Or harbor. Force the garrison to surrender by whatever means necessary, then build up the defenses in case the routed continentals make it back before we do. And if you deem it a fair enterprise, take the motte." Amalic and Willian gave trusting nods. "Well? You're free to go unless you have another inquest." Without ceremony, she began to veer away.

"I'm sure one will come to me," said Willian. Allesande's destrier started for the ford, Amalic at her tail.

"You'll have no trouble finding me on that occasion," was her last utterance.

The steed loped away and Amalic went after her. Wortin remained, snapped his head to a young man rolling a barrel. He ordered him to find two others to help with wrangling his destrier—or some related drudgery. Morley was heeding the wilderness across the river, trying his best to seek out Yeva over the heads of busied engineers and soldiers.

"I suppose the two of you had much to share, yeah?" he heard Wortin. The half-brothers searched each other for a decent response.

Morley piped up first. "Haven't found a comfortable opportunity," he said.

The two halfelevs, exhausted by the growing crowd, decided to go for a walk along the north bank—an idea suggested by Morley who, of course, hoped to encounter Yeva. They did not find her, nor did they speak much of the future or past.

By sundown, Amalic and Willian were on their way north. And an hour after their departure, Morley kicked himself: he'd forgotten to give his half-brother one of the golden aureons.

Yeva, meanwhile, was still nowhere to be seen. The lad's best and only presumption was that she came back and entered Seth's house while he was securing the warmest chair at the inn, now cramped up with hungry ridders and their favored levies. Assuming that his bed space was now appropriated by a gang of penniless recruits, he dubbed the chair his furnishing for the night. And even this expectation was challenged in due time.

A man in a padded tabard with a well-oiled hand axe at his waist thumped up to the halfelev. Morley, at the time, was tamping the charred logs with the flat of his greatsword. There was already another man, a large fellow, resting in the opposite chair.

The other, standing ridder spat a couple of demands and a threat, none of which were intently heard by the lad at the fire: he was far too absorbed by the blazing gems at the base of the hearth, too lost in the endless thrum of the tired Westleyans. The lad soon felt a hand grip his upper arm, then break away as if by another's will.

"He was there first," Morley heard Sir Wortin say. The mid-aged kapitain jerked away the unheard and neglected axe-wielder. "Go sit by Sieger's fire if you're really so cold."

The image of Yeva's flame-lit face came to him; he debated giving the brief antagonist his seat. However, before he could act on this option, Wortin was in his way, jabbing the sleeping man's breastbone until he was up on his feet, stumbling for the door. The kapitain sat in the vacated chair.

"I take it you had a room upstairs?" he asked, his deep voice rumbling through the commotion around them. Morley casually rolled his eyes. "You'll get it back. The keeper is having a few firm words with Allesande. She'll come through within the hour and berate her men to their tents. Which they have yet to set up."

"There are four rooms and as many beds," Morley said. Wortin leaned forward to hear him. "Who will get the fourth? If you get one and if Allesande gets one?" The lad didn't care much about the answer but, feeling somewhat indebted to the man, he thought it best to return the courtesy of conversation, even if it were single-sided.

"First person to pay for it. Or first person to make the highest bid— that's a better bet. The keeper ought to make a fortune for all the trouble we're putting her through. She the one who's in charge around here? Do you know?"

"I don't." It was actually a fair question. Egainshir had Elmaen, Reineshir had Mester Alherde—who was the head of Olford? During Morley's first arrival, Seth was the only resident he met and spoke with. The lad's unconscious belief, up until his most recent arrival, was that the archer had been the freeholder of all five buildings. Now, who else was there aside from Marion and Tomak?

"What about at Westley?" he added. "Who's in charge there now if Allesande's here?"

"Committee. A temporary gathering elected by myself and the stewardess." It was a telling answer, he thought. And perhaps it could've been the case at humble Olford.

He watched the fire awhile, fantasizing about leadership, the struggles of maintenance, the worries of leaving one's property in the hands of lesser folk. Or in nobody's—the case of Gale's house. He imagined Allesande and Wortin returning to Westley and having to go through the same episode his father had been put through, all in the same room and somehow with many of the same words. He disguised a laugh as a hiccup.

An argument about weaponry at the other side of the room cut through the general uproar. When its speakers could shout no louder, the dispute simmered into breathy cackles.

"You just as nervous as they are?" Wortin came in.

"They don't sound nervous to me."

"No, I suppose they wouldn't. You should hear them back in Michelhal—the ones who are allowed to live there at least. At this hour, if they're not snoring in their cots, they're chatting peacefully about their wives, children, intimates, their cows and chickens and goats. Is this one yours?"

He was pointing to Geat, asleep against the legs of his owner's chair. Morley had forgotten he was there.

"Yeah, he's mine."

"A nice breed." He looked back into the crowd. "You can tell they're nervous. There's been so much tension twisting inside them ever since we left Westley. Have to get rid of it somehow, right? It's either this or they can lie with each other, *heh*, pretend they're touching their wives back home, *heh heh*. That was how I used to do it—not with other men, of course! Piikish women, you know. I doubt any of these fellows have had that privilege. I know of only twenty other Westleyans who fought in those wars. And more than half of them are deceased by now, I think."

"That so?"

Morley had nothing to say about Roberrus' wars after The Acquisition. *Chevaliers of Bienvale*—the bulk of his historical knowledge—receded into denouement after the section on the aetheling's marriage to 'Allowyn,' the author's pseudonym for Ellemine as he later figured. After her introduction, the book sacrificed all its pertinent fantastical elements for an account on her beauty, wisdom, judiciousness. As a child, Morley tended to stop reading there, knowing it would cease mid-paragraph: "And though Rijk had done so much to steal and smote her pride, she bestowed to that flighted man a stretch of dirt in the lowlands south; and to Sturm…" This was the end of the book.

"—on Mavros and Telernon. Those were the strangest places I've been to and they were all in the same strait," Wortin was saying. "Before Roberrus ordered us to raid each village and take a share of prisoners, the war-mester—Dietrich was his name—was sent to visit the chieftains. I joined him on those excursions before catching the sick. Wish I'd stayed sick just long enough."

"Why's that?" Morley asked, lost to the narrative.

"There's a place we called Albatross Isle." The kapitain paused, listened to the men around him as if he heard his name called. "That's where I was sent. I'd show you my scar, but I'm rather comfortable at the moment. You'd never believe how I got it anyhow, nobody ever does. At times, I doubt my own memory of receiving it." He seemed beckoned by the fire for a short while. "I take it you've never been in a battle yourself?"

"I've never been invited to one, no."

"Ever see one from afar?" he followed up.

Gale and his nemesis, the man called Darry, came to mind. Then the bodies in the courtyard of Michelhal.

"Just the aftermath," the lad said.

278

"Some say that's worse than the start and middle." Morley disagreed, though said nothing.

"Were you here during The Acquisition?"

"The what?" Wortin questioned, leaning forward. He then solved it for himself: "The conquest, you mean?" Morley bit his lip and nodded. "I was here, yes. Though I was only a squire and had no place on the field. I stayed north and helped build Wallenport's bones."

"Who was your mester?" He expected to hear him say 'Sir Elmaen.'

"Sir Naugart," he said, much to Morley's disappointment. "He settled outside of Westley during its construction and entitled me into ridderstaat on his deathbed. I left the island soon after to join with Roberrus' next campaign. When I got back, I was made Kapitain of Hoerlog. The woman I was courting before I left did—"

Right then, the congregation fell silent: Allesande shifted into the threshold and pulled down her hood. It took only one man's apperception before all the others deadened their tongues.

"Call the wiccha-mother's name and thence she appears," Wortin muttered, pushing himself up.

In a course of minutes the whole inn was cleared out, upstairs and down. Allesande and Wortin retired expeditiously to their bedchambers— or single bedchamber—leaving Morley and Geat alone by the fire. Despite having his space back, the lad slept soundly by the hearth.

It was during the morning hours of the following day that Morley went to talk with Sieger about his brother's whereabouts. He hoped to find Yeva with him. But when the ridder did not speak of her, Morley expected only that she had gone back south. Thus, he brooded off to the inn.

Nothing significant occurred through the rest of the week—or if anything did occur, the lad was unreceptive to its significance. An 'avantgarde' came to report the movements of Felix's army beyond Castle Chaisgott on the first day of the new week. One of the nine watchers' posts to the northwest was found ravaged and devoid of its personnel on that same day. It was decided on the following morning that the villagers of Olford who hadn't yet left—Marion and Tomak—should be evicted with compensation to the safety of Reineshir or Laisroch County.

Morley and his goat were free to stay for a time, as the halfelev dishonestly vowed to head off west within the week. And with further luck, Allesande still yet protected his right to a bedchamber with benign imperiousness. He did however have to wait outside during her twilight councils with the lesser kapitains.

One night, wrapped in his wool coat with the naked claymore under his thighs, against the river-side wall of the innhouse, he studied the water as it broke and bounded against the dispersed refuse in the creek. He gripped the gold coins in one hand and rubbed them together. A dozen men conversed at the other side of the river, against the log steps of the roadblock. He watched three mailed soldiers try the door to Tomak's house. When they failed to unlock it by more ingenious methods, they fetched the axe-wielder who had tried to harass Morley on the first night. The man battered down the door with soft precise swings as his counterparts snickered behind him.

Distracted by the burglary, he failed to notice the young woman crouched beside him until a cloud of her hot breath wafted against his cheek.

"Not gonna do anythin' about it, are you?" she said. It was Yeva.

Morley, wanting to shout her name, squeeze her tight against him, kiss her—looked at the young woman and sighed with a shiver. Her head was an onyx oval against the dwindling snows.

"Nah, not much you can do anyway," she said, "that bastard's a bijl-ridder. And their lot's not to be reckoned with." Still, the lad could not think up the right words. "Speak, you long-eared git."

"Sieger won't be happy with them when he finds out," he heard himself say. This time Yeva was the one who couldn't answer. Luckily, Morley's mind was roused enough by his bland comment. "Where've you been? I've been looking for you ever since the Westleyans arrived. I had a feeling you went back to Egainshir."

"I didn't tell anyone where I was going—just told Sieger that I *was* going—and he didn't even watch me piss off down the road to Reineshir, if you can believe it. Anyway, what're you still doing here? At that, why'd you come here in the first place?"

"I wanted to see Seth. And spend some time with my half-brother," he said blankly.

"What—Felix?" she asked, confused.

"No, my—" He chuckled at himself. "His name's Willian, he's one of Allesande's men. I just wanted to travel with him on his way back north and stop here."

"Oh. So then what are ye still doing here?"

"Waiting for Seth." Saying it brought about a new feeling of uncertainty.

"Ah, not waiting for the battle."

Morley frowned: as odd as the statement was, there was truth to it. Of late, he'd been thinking more about the coming of Felix's army than the return of his good friend.

"He waited for you too, y'know," Yeva continued. "Back when you left us at Westley—though his first thought was to go after you and the goat."

"So why didn't he?" The words sounded foolish to him as they left his mouth. He stuck the coins back in his tunic.

"If you were given a choice between your brother and a friend you'd only met weeks before, who would you choose? Besides, you were awfully unapproachable at the time."

"Well, I'm sorry," he started facetiously, "it's just that I had, within that half-hour, met my father and then stirred the western side of the island into a rebellion that I still don't fully understand."

"That's your best excuse? Leaving us behind without any sort of ceremony or so much as a 'goodbye'—that's your excuse?" Her voice was firmer now.

Morley sighed again: it sounded to him like a good enough excuse. "I'm not going into an argument with you, Yeva. This is the first time we've spoke since *then*." He heard two men laughing across the ford and, for a beat, thought they were mocking him. "Is there anything nice we can talk about?"

"Not really," she moaned. "There's nothing nice to talk about in Olford, never has been."

"Then why did you come back?"

"Because I knew you were here. Because I'm a better person than you—I don't let my sadness and angriness take me by the scruff of the neck."

"I'm here now, aren't I?" he said, unsure of why he was grinning. "Waiting and waiting. Been here for two weeks or so. And I'm about to lose track of time."

"What have ye been doing, then?"

He recounted for her everything—too much, he later thought— between his return to Egainshir and Gale's House, his reunion with Willian, and their walk up from Werplaus. He was shocked: listening or not, Yeva was muted throughout the full recounting.

"So where's Geat?" she said at the end of it, as if Willian's influence on the story were less than a triviality.

Morley tapped on the wall at their backs. "Inside."

"He was invited to a meeting and you weren't. Allesande truly is as unappreciative as they say. At least, she is now."

"I prefer to keep him inside, is all. He can get nervous easily from sudden rackets unless I keep him leashed up. How'd you know Allesande was having a meeting?"

"Put my ear to the door, thought I'd hear you in there—or hear nothing at all. Woman's voice. Then instinct told me to circle the building and here you are. Doing your best not to eavesdrop." She nudged him and he laughed. "Yeah, somethin' about a ridder from Chaisgott and an announcement. There were two men speaking and Allesande interrupted one to allow the other a chance to speak. The man she quietened was talking about seizing someone while they had the chance and that it'd be easier now that they've let one come and go."

"No names?" he asked. He could see her head shaking. "Don't know why I'm curious about it anyway."

"Are ye sure you don't wanna head back home? I know you're worried about Seth and all, but his brother is here now. You can let him know you were waiting and maybe he can send us a message. Whenever Seth comes back."

"Mayhaps," he said, and left it at that.

"Still have a room upstairs?" Yeva inquired after a pause.

Morley's heart shot upward, then fluttered back down. "I do."

"Mind sharing the bed?" she said. The lad stiffened. And Yeva drained the tension with an additional comment: "Just like when we were young."

Less than an hour later they entered the innhouse, climbed its subvertical steps to the upper landing, slid into Morley's room, and clambered into bed. He laid awake for another two hours as Yeva crooned through her dreams and tugged away their blanket to her side of the matting. For a long while, he meditated.

How would she react if he held her? If he didn't, would she be less or more comforted? He stared at the back of her head through the dark. Perhaps she would notice her unconscious thievery of the coverings. Perhaps not. She was, after all, a very heavy sleeper. He drifted to sleep while waiting.

He dreamt of her then: she was walking about the room as if it were the space of a house, complete with a window and fireplace. She wore skirts instead of trousers, a shawl instead of a dirtied half-mantle. And her now lengthy butter-blond hair resembled Amarta's. She swept the floors, threw the balls of dust and rotted rushes into the stewpot. Then she tried to shake her husband awake.

When Morley snapped back to life, she was doing just that—and his own hands were clutching her strong arms.

"You need to see this," she said. Hairs of light shot through the uncovered sections of the ceiling. "Your brother's outside."

Yeva led him out to the west façade of the inn where a ladder was placed, its split lower side propped over the hearth's vent. They climbed with lacking caution. Sure enough, once they stood against the roof's low cusp, Morley could see the gathering across the ford: the road was overcrowded with spectating ridders, all adorned in their tabards, chainmail, assorted frog-helms and barbutes. Allesande and Wortin, both visible atop their warhorses, were stationary on the other side of the log roadblock. Strides ahead of them was a mounted tetrad, its flanking members holding up pennoned lances. One flag was blue and white, the other violet. Only one of the four was gesturing along with the subdued distant sound of a young man's voice.

"I can't hear a word of what they're saying," Morley muttered with a yawn. "How do you know it's my brother?"

"I was up closer while you were still asleep—I heard a ridder say it was Aetheling Felix and his 'emma' or something, but they wouldn't let me any closer." She hawked and spat off the edge. "What's an 'emma,' do you know?"

"I don't." The presumed figure of Felix hopped down from his horse and took a small tan cylinder from the man beside him. "Where's his army? Everyone's been saying he has an army from the continent." Then, in reply to his own question, "I guess he went ahead of them so we wouldn't be able to see how big or small it is."

"I guess it's small, right?" said Yeva. "If it was big—bigger than this one—wouldn't it be better to show it off? Give us reason to surrender and all that? Then we—*they* wouldn't have to fight. Or maybe he wants to murder us all for starting a rebellion."

"Doesn't seem like something he'd want to do," said Morley. "I've only met him once. But I guess his heart could've soured since then, considering all that's happened. And y'know, the island *is* at war and all that."

Felix had given the tiny object to Allesande. Unfurling it—it was a strip of parchment, Morley could now tell—she read it aloud. Through the wind Morley could only make out clusters of her speech: "...that consent is given...eighteen mounted men-at-arms for the efforts of...thus redrawing the county lines in provision of assarting grounds...by will of the Aetheling Felix Sivliére van Sarcovy, and his Damme, and the household..."

When she was finished, or possibly before, she held the paper above her head and tore it to pieces. The mob behind her chortled as the flakes drifted from her hands like snow.

"What did she just do?" Yeva asked.

"Something bold, I think."

Felix, having already started back for his courser, climbed onto his saddle and turned the steed around without a perceptible final word. His entourage followed suite. The rest of the onlookers began to disperse at Allesande's command.

"What else are you thinking?" the young woman asked.

"That we should get our things together and leave."

Already Allesande, Wortin, and the other horsemen were cantering back to the inn and the hitching posts installed nearby. The stewardess was glaring up at them like a fox at the foot of an elm, awaiting the descent of her bushy-tailed supper. Ignoring her, they ambled down the ladder, Morley snapping two rungs at the bottom. When he swung around, Allesande was there already, dismounted, breathing deep and slow. Three swordsmen beset her from behind. Wortin was walking in their direction from the still stationary train of carts.

"Expecting him?" she said.

"Who?" Morley returned, searching Yeva beside him. "Expecting who?"

"You were listening in on my meeting with the kapitains last night, weren't you?" she continued, her temper already faltering. "And then you took that information to your aetheling brother while all of Olford slept."

"I..." He couldn't think of where to start in denying her.

"I saw him look up to the top of the innhouse." She inclusively eyed Yeva. "Just as he was handing over the letter of compromise. A rather specific letter of compromise. Did you hear me read it?" Wortin was at her side now, likely piecing together her lattermost words.

"N-no," the lad stuttered, shaking his head.

"He offered six hides of land along the Crouxwood's borders. We only intended to request three before he presented the offer. More intriguing, if we were to accept, he demanded we surrender and restore Michel as earl. And give over two of our men. Specifically, Sir Willian 'the Bastard'—as he referred to him—and his younger brother, a certain Fitzmorley van Werplaus. The former is to be detained for his crimes, the latter is to be given a wardship within the castle."

Morley gulped. And Allesande saw his throat lurch.

"How must I interpret this exchange?" she concluded.

The halfelev, frozen in disbelief, could think of no answer other than, "I'd nothing to do with it." But Yeva spoke up before he could say it.

"You could call it an accident," she said. "A coincidence. Those things happen all the time in this place, y'know."

Allesande examined the young woman suspiciously. "And where have you been since last week? You're Sieger's girl, are you not?"

"I'm nobody's girl," she spat. At this, Wortin suspired and rubbed at his face with one hand. Though he wasn't sure why, Morley knew she chose the worst possible words.

"You wouldn't happen to know where he's gone, would you?" the man said softly. Nobody gave a reply. "He wasn't in his house this morning or late last eve. None of the sentries spotted him in the night. You were closest to him, in a sense."

"Tell us everything," Allesande spoke to them both, her teeth almost gritting. Morley began to fathom the issue at hand. With Wortin there to enhance the retrospection, he was brought back to the morning at Hoerlog.

"Not until I have my breakfast," Yeva defied.

*   *   *

The mystery of Yeva's past was what first attracted Morley to her, never mind her hard rugged features. And she was beautiful.

Morley didn't quite understand lust or love or all their inherent complexities, but he was no stranger to them. Serryl and Tommas clearly had a special bond, one which enabled them to have a child together and live under the same roof. Arrin and Ceridwen, meanwhile, had been engaging in a similar kind of relation—'courtship,' as Semhren referred to it. When not working at their own duties, they were together, hiding away and giggling in Serryl's house or maundering around with the sheep.

One evening, two years into Morley's tenancy, Arrin invited his young neighbor to join him, Ceridwen, and Yeva in his shack beside the varken-ox's pen. The herder then brought in a waxed thread, a cask of Reineshir ale, and a voluminous tankard he'd taken from Istain's wicker storage hut.

Over the next two or three hours they sat in the matted candlelit confines of his space and passed around the mug. Each drank deep, delightedly fogging their heads as Arrin guided their discourse.

"I got another one," he said, gesturing for everyone's attention. "If you got the chance to go anywhere in all the whole wide world—where, oh where would you go? Hmm?" Everyone quietly gathered their thoughts. Ceridwen spoke up as Morley gulped at his beer.

"I think I'd want nothing more than to go to Locqueshir and see the king there," she said, voice almost as high as Robi's. When they first met, Morley could not stop himself from staring at the strange reddish flecks across her face. Ceridwen at the time probably took it as a sign that the boy had fallen in love with her. As she later said with a laugh, she was partly disappointed to find out he was only intrigued by her skin.

"The king doesn't live in Locqueshir, you ditz," Yeva spat. "He doesn't live anywhere, that's the point of a king—they just march around their land and make sure everything's in order. That's the king's job."

"How 'bout you, then?" Arrin jumped in. "Where would you want to go, Yeva?"

"Taliorano, where they have pomegranates and olives. The sun is also brightest there and never hides behind the clouds." She slurped down a share of beer.

Morley only knew of Taliorano through the *Chevaliers* book: it tended to depict the people of that country as ruffians and liars—misguided men and self-gratifying women. Though the text also regarded Biens as infallible, an obvious fabrication on the scribe's part. Semhren was a Bien, as was Reffen, Gale, the watcher sisters—nearly everyone in Egainshir had been born on the continent. And they were all far from perfect.

"The symbol of Taliorano *is* an orange sun," Ceridwen said sluggishly in a voice of mock dignity. "And my uncle would always come back from there with browned skin. Arrin, you've gone there." The herder made a face as if caught off-guard, then took the mug offered by Yeva, upending its scant contents into his mouth.

Morley was tempted at times to ask more about Arrin's and Ceridwen's past on Aubin, but often withheld his questioning. He knew that they would mention certain things he did not fully understand, like sailing and star navigation. Normally this wouldn't be problematic with any of the adults. But with these three, ignorance was a vice worthy of ceaseless ridicule.

"I have, yes," Arrin answered Ceridwen, setting down the cup. "It's, eh, warm. Has lots of green hills, mountains in certain places. And they have fine ships. You'd enjoy yourself there, Yeva."

She narrowed her eyes and glanced at Ceridwen. "How did you get there, exactly?" she questioned. Before Arrin could open his mouth, she continued, "Ceridwen told me she saw you on Aubin every day for years and you'd both play on the beach—at what point did you go to Taliorano?"

"Oh, before I met her," he said, pouring more ale from out of the barrel's lipped spigot. "Long before. When I was only about, say, five years old."

Yeva scoffed as the herder drank more. Ceridwen, who had been bobbing tiredly from side to side, tumbled into Arrin. He spilled beer all over himself and her. The two giggled and the boy handed her the mug, saying in a bubbly voice, "You all right, there? You all right, huh? Clumsy lady."

Morley eyed the girl beside him: she was watching the other couple, a longing look in her face. He realized then that she was even more beautiful when she was sad or unamused—actually, she was *very* beautiful. So beautiful that he became conscious of his reeling head, of his swaying body and the cumbersome warmth of the shack. He was tempted to fall into her as Ceridwen had to Arrin, or touch the hand resting on her closest knee.

He saw her head start to turn in his direction. He looked away, feigning interest in the staff against the wall.

"If either of you," the herder started with a burp, "had to have a child with one person in the wide whole world, who would you choose?" Morley alone snorted a laugh at this.

Ceridwen had her head in Arrin's lap, eyes shut as if sleep had already overtaken her. Yeva's expression was unchanged, though there was a shadow of discomfort or budding frustration. She reminded Morley of Gale now. And he was no less attracted to her with this in mind.

"I still didn't answer the other question," Morley finally stammered. Yeva and Arrin gawked at him expectantly. He cleared his throat. "Well, I also need to think about it a little."

"No, you don't," Yeva muttered. "Just say the first place that comes to mind—the first thought is the truest." The contemplating boy balled up his fist, then stretched his fingers, then balled his fist, stretched. He truly didn't know what to say. He blushed under Yeva's gaze.

"I also would want to go to Taliorano," he said. "It sounds like a nice place. Warm and, y'know…sunny."

Arrin grunted his admission, unimpressed. Yeva said nothing and they all sat under the reticent metronome of Ceridwen's breathing.

Yeva soon stood up and cracked her legs with a sigh. "I'm going to bed," she disclosed with a near-groan. "It'll be chilly tomorrow so getting out of the blankets will be harder if I'm not well rested. See you all tomorrow." As she spoke Morley stood with her and, before he could make a similar announcement, the girl was out the door. The two boys watched her go.

"I'm also going," he said, swiveling back to Arrin. The herder smiled at him, then peeked down at Ceridwen and the beer stolen from Istain. "I can put all the trader's chattels back, if you want."

Arrin nodded tiredly and handed over the mug. "Did she seem upset to you?" he whispered, indicating the door with his head as he pushed in the spigot. Morley gave him a blank stare, which was then diverted to the exit, then back. He was stalling for a good answer and nothing was coming to him. His head was full of sludge. In the end he took the small barrel underarm and shrugged, leaving his two friends without another word.

Once he'd stepped outside and quietly fixed the door-board behind him, the boy searched his surroundings for Yeva, first eyeing Gertruda and Lunferda's house where she stayed. He continued his survey, stepping along the side of the cow pens toward Istain's adjacent house, the few chicken coops, and Lunferda's watching-chair.

After a moment of failed inspection he clumsily returned the items to the storage shed, stumbling once on the way in and once on the way out: when inside, he set down the cask and mug wherever was most convenient, realizing afterward that the trader would probably notice the misplacement in the morning. Morley drunkenly banished the concern.

Upon hearing a slight rustle from inside Istain's hovel, like someone shifting on a bed of rushes, he fled promptly to a safe distance, to a spot around the side of the baking kiln attached to Amarta's house.

There, he finally spotted Yeva: all the while, she had been leaning over the side of the well at the center of Egainshir's circle of houses. Her back was to him. But she must've known he was there somewhere—he would've been in clear view when leaving Arrin's. He stood still for a time, debating.

Approach her or head back to Elmaen's house? In choosing the former he knew he would have to come up with something clever to say—no, something genuine and heartfelt. But what if those kinds of words repulsed her? What if he stepped up beside her and said nothing, waited for her to utter the first sentence? What if neither of them said anything? He would be fine with that, as he only wished to stand close to her. But would she be just as comforted? No, surely not.

The other option, a more casual and less appealing one for certain, was to saunter back to his bed and drift into a much-needed sleep. But what if Yeva saw him as he walked back? Would she think he was ignoring her? Would she believe he hadn't noticed her there? Would she even see him moving in the first place?

Twenty minutes had passed and Morley was still leaning against the kiln, watching. At that point he was waiting for her to move, waiting still for a better idea to pop into his mind…

Nothing. Nothing but the thought of her downtrodden face, his own ineptitude, and the rising wind.

What is wrong with you? She's just as lonely as you are—lonely and beautiful— remember sitting on the goats' fence? That lonesome feeling? Go to her, go. Now. Go.

The voice was not his own. It came to him at times of irresolution— when he failed to act on his feelings, when he failed to understand what he wanted most or what he needed. It forced him to join Tommas on his excursion to the edge of the Crouxwood, the first time he was invited. It commanded him to push Robi when the child tried to hit him with a stick. It ordered him to run back to Gale. It irked him beyond his limits, impinged him with dread, confusion, even fear.

Arrin once tried to chase down one of the sheep during a rainstorm but refused outright to get his undergarments soaked. The creature strode over half a kalcubit away from Egainshir before the herder decided to unwrap his tight cloak and withstand the wetness for a moment or two. When he returned with the sheep in tow, he groaned: "I feel pathetic."

Pathetic. Now the word made sense to him.

Yeva pushed herself away from the squat wall, wiped her nose with a sniff, and marched off to the watchwomen's house. Morley sighed and shut his eyes, ashamed, weary, cold. "Pathetic," he breathed, partly as a reminder.

Rather than heading back to Elmaen's he made for the enclosure behind the cow pens, the stead of his two goats and all the sheep. He passed by Arrin's shack and heard nothing from within: the young lovers had gone right to sleep. Minny and Geat, meanwhile, were also curled up together inside the small shelter Lunferda had made for them. Morley climbed over their fence, sat against the nearest post, and wept.

The sobs grew heavier and heavier with each new thought: He would never see Gale again. He would never find a true companion, a lover. He would never know his mother or father, or why they gave him up.

Moments later as he choked back a loud wail, Geat stepped over and nibbled on the end of one of his soft leather shoes. When the goat chomped down on his big toe, Morley yelped through his tears and glared hard at the horned scoundrel.

Geat stared back with his odd everyday expression. The lad couldn't help but imagine him saying, "Better now?" He tried not to smile at the thought.

"Damn you," he said, opening his arms. Geat obediently stepped over and collapsed onto his lap. Not long after, as the goat returned to his comfortable spot in the shelter, Morley followed and squeezed himself between the two, breathing in the noxious scents of their abode. Minny grunted at him and he grunted back. And all three drifted to sleep.

*　　　*　　　*

Without delay, Yeva and Morley were sealed away inside the inn. They were given the oldest bread in stock and uncooked vegetables in cold basil broth. They sat in the middle of the floor with Geat between them.

"I'm sorry," Yeva muttered as Allesande and three other men arranged their seating away from the fire. "I assumed they would give us better food than this."

"It's fine by me," Morley assured her. "Better than raw radishes, I'd say."

For hours hence, Yeva's and Morley's entire past year was excruciatingly inspected, from their individual expatriations out of Werplaus to the moments before Felix's parlay. Morley's offered account was painstaking, reiterated until each of the inquisitors were able to tell the story of his misadventure just as well as he could. Yeva on the other hand was less compliant—not because she and Sieger were conspirators as the stewardess and two of her lackeys guessed, but because the events of her narration were of a more intimate freshly embittered quality. As Morley presumed.

For this she was moved to a room upstairs. A warden in full armor was assigned to her door; a second man brought all of Morley's belongings down to the common room where he and his goat were kept for a longer period.

"So," started Allesande once all of her officers were gone, "I've now heard the tale many times over—partly from Hamm, partly from Sieger, partly even from Wortin. And wholly from you. However, half of them are inconsistent with the other half. Sieger's and yours are the outliers. Nobody in my service can validate the existence of a 'Sir Gale van Werplaus.' Or an 'Elmaen van Egainshir.' In trusting Wortin as I do, this is all I can say for certain…" She kicked a chair closer and adjusted her kempt breeches.

"You and Sieger's brother appeared at Hoerlog, told the men there that you bore a message for Michel Laisroch from one of Felix's subordinates, then left the following morn with Hamm in your company. He guided you to Westley where you met with Sieger and Yeva. From that point forward everything is equivocal. Do you see what I'm saying?"

"I think," he said, though he wasn't sure if Allesande herself knew what she was saying. Her men had been whispering to her countless conjectures, each more twisted than the previous.

"We know nothing about Yeva, only that you two have a past. And that after she appeared in Westley and entered Sieger's household, the Olford ridder was spurned to action. He knew well, like many others in my service, that I planned to launch the insurrection by mid-Hosten. It was through his insistences and my trust that it started earlier. Quite hasty of me. Unlike Hamm's story and later Wortin's, Sieger's truth is the only one which lacks evidence from believable parties." Morley tiredly attempted to puzzle out her conclusion.

"Then, eh…you think we were working together to put you, uhm—no, wait. I just had it knocking about."

"You and the girl managed to convince him to serve Felix while functioning within Westley."

Allesande stood back up and walked past the lad to the counter before the kitchen door. The strands of her hair braids had been harassed into wild tufts of varying intensity. Morley was glad she was currently behind him, as he'd been having trouble holding her gaze.

"Ellemine coaxed Michel to have a child with her years and years ago, both to sustain his loyalty and to undermine his independence. Like a leashed goat. Bloody ingenious I must say, if all that was their true intent. Except they didn't anticipate that I, his sister-in-law, would exert myself unto his administration. By the time Roberrus passed on, I'd gained too much. Felix saw this during his inaugural tour I'm sure, and must have planned to survey me. He did so, chose to exploit one of my ridders. Sent Yeva to make him malleable. Then sent you, both to deliver his payment and to move me against Michel, to make me an open enemy. In doing that, he could take all the properties of Laisroch for himself. Make it seem like a fair acquisition. Exact his debt to the king."

Allesande continued with the mangled remains of her theory, invoking as many demented and often contradictory premises as she could: Felix's aspirant army was a decoy he intended to have destroyed—Alherde van Reineshir double-crossed and boisterously overstated the rebels' injustices at the hallmote of Aubin—Sieger, whose fealty rested only with his home village, hoped to get a cash compensation for the part he agreed to play, a worthy sum that could advance the wealth of Olford.

At this the woman tossed two coins down to Morley, still cross-legged on the floor.

Ellemine's gold. Geat stretched his neck over to sniff them and the lad curved back to see Allesande, still rummaging through an empty travelbag. Morley swept up the aureons furiously and got to his feet. The stewardess dropped the sack then, waited for him to speak out.

But what to say? The truth? Ellemine had given the gold to him out of groundless charity. Who would believe that?

"What about Willian?" he said eventually.

None of Allesande's speculations had incorporated his other half-brother, second-in-command to Sir Wortin—her own second-in-command. According to the stewardess, Felix's demands included Willian's groundless capture and imprisonment. Yet not one of the her wild assumptions involved him. As he hoped, she frowned darkly.

"Go on," she said.

Morley thought it best not to. Instead he chose far more distressing words. "I think you should ask Sir Wortin about it," he recommended. "He can say more than I can."

He believed he could hear the pacing of her heart increase, then slow. A moment later she rounded the side of the counter and stomped up to the lad, who shuffled back fearfully. She raised a hand to strike him and, flinching, the halfelev moved his forearms in front of his face. As he did this, Allesande snatched one wrist and dug her fingers into his closed fist, pulling out one of the gold pieces as the other rang against the stone floor. Startled or fascinated, Geat rose as the stewardess bent down to sweep up the coin. She went to the door, knocked on it, and a swordsman came in.

"Put him with the girl," she ordered.

The man prodded Morley to the stair. Before exiting he saw Allesande return to the counter with his gold. Geat looked back and forth at them. Losing interest quick, he slumped back down.

Upstairs the guard moved aside a set of benches resting against the lad's bedroom door. While being urged inside, Morley could hear the thud of sharpened steel plummeting against a wood surface downstairs.

"Yeva?" he said after the door was shut behind him, once the creaking of benches resumed in the outer hall.

"Over here," he heard her say. A boulderlike shadow expanded into a personable silhouette and came into the lance-light. There was a meek warble in her voice, the lad thought, as if she'd been crying or trying her best not to. "What happened there?" she said.

Morley paced reluctantly to the bed. "I think she's gone mad. Allesande, I mean. Of course." He sank onto the matting and the low disused bedframe made a splitting sound.

"Can we really blame her?" said Yeva, more carefully placing herself down beside him.

"What d'you mean?" he replied, though her rationale was implicit.

"Do you think she's ever done anything like this—led an army of hundreds against a proper enemy, against anyone? She must be terrified—

293

think what that might do to her. What was it that set her off in the first place, do you remember?" It had been hours since they climbed down from the roof after Felix's appearance on the road.

"Apparently Felix glanced up at us after he got down from his horse. Though I'm not sure how Allesande was able to tell that much. I couldn't see where he was looking, could you?"

She shook her head. The charming odor of her skin and hair wafted over him. A certain comfort followed from this, pulled him from the damp musk of their cell. In a matter of seconds, Morley was overcome by an unnerving impulse—a madness, a turbulence.

"It must've put her off balance," he said quietly, an attempt to take his mind off Yeva. "All that effort over the years and now it could very well get snuffed out like a candle. And it only took Sieger's sudden leaving. I'd bet it's the first thing to go wrong for her in a long, long time. Do you have any idea of where he might've gone?" Yeva did not speak. "Allesande thinks he's distressed over what we're doing to his home. So soon after his mother's death, to make it worse. But Allesande thinks he's been betraying her since the start of the rebellion. And that you were the one to—"

"I could hear everything she was saying, I was right here above you two." She tamped the floorboards with the leathery toe of her shoe.

"You didn't see Sieger on the road south, did you? While you were coming back?"

"No," she said with a ponderous heave. "But he could've left while I was sitting with you by the river. Or while we were sleeping. If he'd gone north—and there's no knowing why he'd go that direction unless he really was meaning to betray the Westleyans—but if he'd gone north I think someone would've seen him, even in his cloak."

"What about east?"

"He's not a moron, nobody should ever go east for any reason—you would know, if that one part of your story is true."

They sat in silence for a time. Morley made an attempt to slide closer to her, but the frame whined. He halted, wondering where her hand was, wondering if he should take it in his own.

"Y'know," she said, "when you left for your silly journey near the start of Hosten and when you didn't come back home for days, my first thought was that you'd been murdered in Reineshir. You know how much I hate that place—the brewers lay with each other's wives and daughters, and the shiriffs take whatever they want and strike anyone who tries to hold back.

And the butchers are the worst of them. Right before you and Istain left, I had a feeling you would jaunt off to Wallenport or something, but then Istain didn't come back either—at least not that night. I thought the both of you had been caught out. The sword is of dangerous value, as you used to say. Anyone could've taken it for themselves and killed you when you wouldn't let them have it." As she spoke, Morley tried moving again: their knees touched.

"Did you do anything?" he asked.

"I argued with Amarta, then Serryl. Ceridwen watched it all through her tears. I was scaring her, poor girl. Fear is the fastest disease to spread, as my sister used to say. Serryl told me I was in hysterics and I told her— oh, what did I say? 'I call it attention to detail,' or something. I've since lost the meaning I'd given the words but, after listening to Allesande downstairs, it's come back to me."

Morley placed his hand over her rough scabby knuckles. His thumb tip grazed a stitch in her trousers. She gave no reaction. He removed his hand, feeling silly, feeling a quiver rise up from his stomach, a shiver of dissatisfaction.

"Do you know why men don't have these sorts of reactions?" she asked. Yeva angled her head toward him.

Do it. Now.

Instead of moving to kiss her, Morley turned his head away. A tear formed at the corner of one eye and he did what he could to blink it away.

She repeated herself: "Do you know?" He didn't. "Because men give up far too easily. Sieger's father left his family behind, Sieger left his war behind, you left your friends behind—all have different reasons. And just now I can tell the thought of death has been choking you, squeezing harder and harder." Her voice was as conversational as it had been. "You wanna love me. Right here, your last chance. And you're gonna give up."

Still facing away from her, he cringed with embarrassment. "I'm sorry," he mumbled, his head heating up.

"See what I mean?" she snickered with triumph. "If you were like Allesande, you'd be throwing excuses at me." She got up and trooped about the empty space of the room as the halfelev wiped his face. "But Yeva!" she mimicked. "The soldiers dared me to do it for a few coppers, I thought it'd be a simple steal! But Yeva, the voices in my head took over and I couldn't do anything to stop them!"

"I get your point," he said without amusement.

"Oh Yeva, I thought my tender kiss could show you the truth of our bond—I thought you would take my love as a burdenless gift."

"Yeva…"

"Run with me back to Werplaus, where we can live together in a house of stone and wattle!"

This went on for a time, long after Morley ceased his pleading. Eventually her voice softened to the point of sincerity.

"…and we can have five little goats, a few sheep, a horse. We could ride the horse along the south beaches and grass dunes, let the old boy graze to his heart's content."

By then Morley was reclining on his side with eyes shut. Shortly thereafter Yeva joined him, wrapping her arms around him, nuzzling her head against the back of his.

"You're too good a friend, Fitzmorley," she said.

*   *   *

On the following morning they heard the blast of a cornu echo twice through the Crouxwood. It was followed by the deeper bellowing of a second signal horn, blown from atop Seth's porch.

Soon enough a rushing commotion flooded through Olford: kapitains shrieked their orders, horses roared and whinnied, footfalls pounded the earth, ridders tapped weapons and chains, steel and iron.

Morley tried the door, but an impediment of greater weight—a spare barrel or three, he figured—was now in place of the meager benches put there previously. Upon trying the latch a second time, he was certain their watchman had been called away from his post.

Accordingly, the lad threw himself against the stolid wood until both arms ached. Yeva conceived of a better plan while he did this: she threw away the bed's mat, took up the frame at a lengthwise end, and battered it against the low ceiling. It took less than ten pummels for her to break through the slate-work. Once the hole was large enough, she threw away the now broken casing.

"Now, if anyone watched the roof break," she said, "let's hope they're distracted enough not to care."

They climbed out. Rather than fleeing, however—and much to Morley's heightening fears—Yeva laid herself flat along the roof's incline and watched the opposite side of the river, the dew-drowned woodlands.

"I think we've lost our chance to get away unseen," Morley groaned many minutes later.

It was a true enough conjecture. If it weren't for the superfluity of visored caps and helms on the arranged men below, they likely would've been detected right as they climbed through their self-made crevice.

At the yard-side of the inn where the broken ladder was affixed, arbalesters and archers in padded dresses were strewn under the pines, some crouching and shifting from trunk to trunk, some endeavoring to scale the obscured boughs. On the road a mixed block of destriers, geldings, and their mailed riders waited restlessly. Allesande and Wortin were at their center, Morley saw. In front of the horses and before the ford were two lines of troops: spearmen at the waterline—the same breed of shield-holders were formed up on the other side of Seth's house—and an alignment of axe-wielders and swordsmen behind.

Strangely, Morley could distinguish the galloping of hooves from the southward road which, as he now saw, was clogged up with overturned wagons.

"D-do you think we should hide?" he asked.

"We are hiding," she replied, louder than he wished.

"I-I mean somewhere better? Back inside maybe? That's where my sword is. I think."

Yeva sighed and put her hand over his. "The door's blocked, dummy," she reminded. The young woman's lacking fear instilled a brief confidence in him—so long as he kept his mind on *her* and not the awful potentialities abounding through his head. All of Olford continued waiting.

Half an hour passed.

Shouting. It came to them from far ahead, from an invisible host in the befogged brake. Morley thought of the wolf, then of Gale and Darry. The cries became rhythmic, loud. Two trumpets blared. A thousand distant men chanted over it: "Dode, dode, dode," Morley heard. It was an empty intonation, one made no less horrific by the chorus of champing boots and the chinking of metal bits. Though he could not see their faces, he knew the tabarded men behind the barricade were in a dire regretful state.

Then came the first thuds: the soft pattering before a rainfall—a deluge-worthy one—and the crackling of twigs, branches snapping in the wind or under a heft of snow. A plop. Then another—toads hopping in the Sylvan swamp water—then another.

One word, shouted by an arbalester not twenty strides away: "Arrows!" It was repeated through Olford. Everyone who held a shield, large or small, held it low above their head. The archers, meanwhile, if they hadn't yet sought the protection of the pines, fled behind the nearest vacant trunks. Morley watched the hundredfold black needles rise high above the treetops and plunge down on the village—and it had only been seconds since the first ones landed. A horse screamed. Commotion followed. And two shafts bounced simultaneously against the other side of the rooftop, clacked their way over the edge.

"I'm getting out of here," Morley determined as the words left him. On his hands and feet, he fumbled over Yeva and, before dropping back down into the bedroom, he again recalled the blocked door. Without warning, the young woman pushed him down through the fissure and hopped after him.

"Take an end!" she demanded, returning to the skeletal bed. He did so and, like with the delicate ceiling, they slammed the broken case against the door. It took over a dozen strikes before the rusted stakes rang against their hinges; not after a dozen more did the door snap from its supports and tumble against the hindrance on the other side. It was another bedframe from another room, now propped along the width of the hall. They squeezed through the new opening and descended to the main room below.

Geat was standing on the counter, an ear twitching. He bleated to his longtime mate.

"I know, I know," Morley replied as he rounded the board. Allesande's knife stood lodged in its surface.

"Do you hear that?" said Yeva, and the halfelev was astounded that he hadn't yet: there was a continuous rumbling outside, much like the collective of voices at the aspirant feast in Sivliére Castle—but this squalling and battering whirred through all the world. There were singular shouts, shatterings, and boisterous death bawls—the drub of split planks, stomping horse hooves that circled them on every side, hollowly thumping bowstrings and lathes, the heavy jangling crash of bodies against bodies and fists beating away enemies or friends. Above it all the marching knell of Felix's army continued like a rapid presumptive heart.

Gale's stories. The Battle of the Lightrun. The Death of Sir Olivien.

"What are you doing?!" came Yeva's voice from the kitchen. "I didn't say stop moving—let's go! I'll get food, you get whatever else we need!"

Morley searched the shelf under the countertop. The claymore was there, diagonally jammed in place across the full length of the compartment. Underneath the lifted blade was a stack of nickels with two larger coins beneath them. The gold. He swept them and the nickels into his hand, took the goat's leash, and continued probing beneath the shelf, clearing out whatever items remained—water jugs, a ruined basket, wads of spent wax.

"I don't see any food in here—if there's any at all, I can't find it!" Yeva shouted.

"Sod the food, then!" His belly whimpered as he said it, having been empty for a full day. Removing the sword with his free hand, he stumbled back against a wall and panned over the rest of the room: it had been stripped of every last chair, every log for the guttered fire. Again, he listened to the clamor outside. Time, flowing lucid as the space between sleep and discernment, jostled on. Something clubbed him against the chest.

"Come on," Yeva insisted, slinging a half-filled travelbag back over her shoulder. Morley set down the coins, tied an end of the leash to Geat's neck, tied the other end around the waist of his trousers, retrieved the coins, then followed Yeva to the door. She kicked it open and sprinted out.

Seconds after they left, a disordered line of seven horsemen flashed by, their spears held either underhand at their chain-skirted knees or overhand by the skull of their frog-helms. Archers fled against the reigned tide— some without their bows—as the wave of beasts broke through the trees, trampling heedlessly into those in their path.

The rest of the arbalesters and longbowmen retreated to the carts, following their few comrades who had already escaped into the far distance. There was a crunching impact and a grunt from the horsemen's route: a man, cloaked and coated in blue linens with a rounded steel cap, was skewered with a spear. The clothing below his ribcage darkened as he propped himself against the nearest tree. Other men with shields and axes in their hands were dashing between the trunks, garbed either in blue cloaks or weighty grey linens. The mounted ridders rounded on them. Two of the men in blue threw their weapons at the horses.

Yeva yanked at Morley's arm. And he in turn yanked at Geat.

Before rounding the corner of the inn, they could see no life on the road—only the weapons deserted by the numerous routed ridders and a dead gelding stuck with three arrows shafts. But once they stood upon the beaten bolt-plugged dirt, they could see all.

The carnage at the ford was of paralyzing severity. The groupings of spears, swordsmen, and bijl-ridders had advanced into the stream as a crooked semicircle, the open interior of which was filled up with the most ferocious men Morley had ever seen: even when still they bellowed a perpetual fury—their helms were deserted, their wet hair matted against their brows or sopping like clumps of seaweed—several were missing their boots, others their gloves.

With synchronous agility they leapt against the backs of their brutish allies. They knocked over the barrels and boxes into an expedient palisade, a miniature dike to retain space between them and their onrushing enemy, all of whom were pouring out from around the abandoned houses, past their opponents on either side. There were too many, it seemed.

On one front, the soldiers in blue and grey were clustered to the space between Tomak's house and the mill; on the other, downstream toward the prong of Larenta's Creek, a limitless swarm stretched down the bank from the broken wattle-work before Haarka's croft. There were helmeted heads as far as Morley could see, though they injuriously diffused their ranks when wading into the body-cluttered, darkened rapids of the Lightrun. To better corner and hold them off, the center of the rebels' arc broke, its defenders spreading to the edges of the ford stones and the houses close by—the section of road between them maintained still by the levies at the barricade ahead. There, more men were grouped than anywhere else within sight.

Again—and evidently for Yeva as well—time oozed like silt into a cellar. Not even Geat's nervous yammering could rip them away from the devastation.

Another gang of horses galloped behind them. Yeva spun about. Quickly, she hurled herself against Morley's back and they fell to the trembling ground—the halfelev felt something brush sharply against his calf, like a hoof landing a hand's span away from his leg, then lifting again in propulsion. Instinct urged him to crawl forward from under Yeva, but the young woman hopped up and clutched the back of his tunic with both hands. She heaved him up. Three or four riders were still behind them.

"The arrows have ceased!" said one, an older man. It was Wortin, judging by the voice.

"Halfelev!" shouted another, a woman. Morley and Yeva spun around to see Allesande—unkempt as ever—with her second-in-command and two other kapitains. "Get out of here!" It would've struck him as a benevolent order if she hadn't proceeded to spur her destrier past them, flying with such aggression that he was again flung to the turf. Geat's tired leash unfurled itself from his hip as he rolled into the ground. He raised his head quick: Allesande raced over the ford to the mass at the adverse shoreline, her men following suite. Yeva called to him as she took up the claymore from where they had first plummeted.

"The gold!" Morley gasped. He'd forgotten all the coins were still in his hand after they left the innhouse. He had to have thrown them away when Yeva shoved him.

"Forget the g—there! By the shield there!" she cried out, pointing. Without glancing twice at her finger Morley was upon the blackwood disc and the now conspicuous piece. The nickels were also strewn about with the arrows and lost weaponry. But the gold's twin was yet hidden from view.

"I can't find the other," he shouted, upraising the shield. Before he could search any further Yeva had him by the scruff of the neck, had again drawn him up to his feet.

"Forget it!" She thrust the sword's grip into his hand and retrieved their sack.

"Where's Geat?!" Looking south he saw the horned grey blur of his goat fleeing through the wagon train.

"We'll get him later!" said Yeva without hearing or seeing either of them. "We should head for…" She let go of the travelbag, dumb with sudden alarm.

The fighting raged on as it had been. But Yeva stared past it, past Morley and the dying men. The halfelev, beguiled and remarkably afraid, tried to master his tongue. His insides felt as though they were shrinking. He wheezed and panted; his legs wobbled at the knees as he tried to brace himself for yet another fall.

Cautiously, Yeva held out her hand as if warming it in a hearth. Morley went deaf. Sparks of white light swirled before his eyes. He went to his knees, propped himself up with the greatsword. He tried to scream, "What's going on?!" but neither his lips nor his ears permitted him to do so. Yeva fell forward as he did. The soldiers still hacked at each other—two horsemen raced by to the ford—a dark wind howled in his head.

301

It all returned with a great clap of thunder, a sustained concussion that quaked the earth like ten thousand destriers. The conflict, the rattling of blades and the outcries of all—everything ceased.

"It wasn't a dream," Yeva respired.

Then, it came.

It was like the distant shouting they heard before the assault, magnified into a song of misery. And the cloaked army of blue was pushed onward, their intent forgotten, their vanguard crammed haplessly against the rebels. Beyond, a tower of flame. It swept the treetops with unnatural burning wings, only to dive down to the forest floor and crash like the waves of the sea, over and over until the trunks were blackened twigs, unburning and meek. The bodies of men beneath them had to be naught more than ash or bone.

Morley was the first to come to his senses this time. He hooked his elbow around Yeva's and, as efficiently as he could, dragged her back to the open innhouse.

"She's been here this whole time," she muttered. "She's come for me, after all these years…"

By the time they reached the inn's open door, every last man who yet had the will to move was racing south—tripping over shields, dismantling chainmail shirts—some were even clawing and stabbing at those in their path.

Inside the inn, three rebels sat against the counter: one was holding a torn rag to another's eye, the third was asleep or dead. Releasing Yeva, Morley closed the door behind them. Turning back to her, she was already well out of arm's reach, heading for the steps. He mindlessly followed, calling her name, pursuing her back to their chamber and its broken ceiling.

He peered out before climbing back through: she stood at the cusp of the slates. And Morley was reminded again of the previous morning—of a time when the world wasn't ending. Cursing, he tossed up the sword, mounted the roof, and crouched beside her.

The Crouxwood across the river, beyond the dead trees, was burning.

Felix's army, a horde of hundreds, ran in all directions away from the chaos—over the ford, upstream, down. Before long, whole gangs of burning men and horses leapt screaming into the alleviating Lightrun. Without end, they poured from out of the unfed flames.

The *unfed* flames. The torrid sourceless heat. Indeed, the wildfire seemed to billow forth on its own accord, charring timber and flesh without satiation—as if a monstrous creature spread its heat from bowels of flint and oil.

And thus it came: from over the smoke and its lapping blaze, an umbral titan loomed.

Its faceless head was covered over with a black cascading mist which, upon meeting the height of the exhausted trees, ignited into hellfire. It moved and swayed, yet did not come closer to them—or didn't seem to. Rather, it raised its arms, bony limbs of the same nightmarish fog, and outstretched fingers like sleek lacerative knives. From the undersides of its arms, a raincloud—dusk-dark as beaten coal—shimmered down over the destroyed forest and the road cutting through, its closest spans covered with scorched bones, red-hot blades and buckler plates.

Then it all faded from under the titan, disappeared in a cool fog, grey and smooth as an egg. The woodland was now a colorless copse of raven-feather spikes.

Morley had never imagined jotuns to look like this. Gale always referred to them as icy elders, bearded, white-haired, indistinguishable from immense naemas. He stared at this behemoth drowsily, unable to speak or move, unable to conceive of what stretched ahead of him. Unable to wake himself.

Yeva uttered a word, though Morley could not tell what it was.

"Feofan!" she cried out again. And the halfelev at last fell away from consciousness.

Chapter VIII – The Vertebrae

So it ends, Felix thought as he watched Allesande and Wortin confer between two old trees. But *how* did it end and who was the victor? Those few rebels who still lived? If they were of any wit they would be fleeing back to Westley with all speed, back to their wives and children, never to set out into the open world again. A pity he himself was so far from that base sect. Perhaps it wasn't too late.

But as for his own army, his borrowed legion from Lattaholm and Garm, they would find Reineshir if they kept running south. The bolder Lattamen, once they formed into a large enough herd, would most likely veer back north before nightfall or the following dawn. The Garmites, conversely, being unused to fights in the field as Michel had warned, would be indefinitely disseminated. He would give them two weeks to get back to Wallenport before evicting their ships from the harbor. As for the hertog's ships, those would be sent back to Aubin with all haste.

Felix's rump was getting sore. He stood from his rock and waded his feet through the Lightrun's bony shallows, wincing whenever a jagged stone pressed against his soles. He hunched down to test the cold stream with a finger again. The pain was sharp still, even just below the nail, but it was no longer intolerable.

After three deep breaths he plunged his glistening burnt hands into the water. He clenched his teeth and gave a throaty squeak. Poor Iacob, he thought. Such a fate for an edma.

Glancing up, he caught Allesande as she averted her eyes back to Wortin: he was stalking slowly away into the deeper woods, halting at every couple of steps and staring out in any direction. Felix lifted his hands from the river and reached for the remains of his cloak, dabbing his knuckles and palms with the unblackened parts of it. Once finished he tossed it back over his boots and kept his back turned to the incoming stewardess—or whatever she was now.

"How are they?" he heard her say from the middle of the river. "Your hands." He caressed his joints and gave no answer. Her voice had reignited his frustrations.

When she and her ridders found him down the river, not half a kalcubit away from the ford, they led him further into the Crouxwood—and with no negligence for rough abuse and slander. At one point Allesande even accused him of plotting some mind-numbing conspiracy, an intrigue worthy of the false histories and one he knew he could never fully cognize. Part of it insisted he had sent a girl—a certain 'Yena' or 'Yevha'—to seduce a ridder in her employ, Sir Sieger. He of course never heard these names before and probably never would again.

Further than that, the scheme was so baffling he couldn't bear to listen to another word, not even to the unamusing mention of his half-brother, Fitzmorley, and his 'obvious' cooperation in carrying out the plot. Such a bizarre incident. That bumpkin among the aspirants, that familiar-faced lad with his iron twin, summoned alone to the aetheling's table. Another half-brother, an exile-at-birth.

Why did their mother hide this truth—why cast him out as she did their older brother? Because he, like Fitzwillian, was not spawned of Aetheling Roberrus the Cold, the careless father of Sarcovy. Perhaps they were the lucky ones. Roberrus did whatever he could to escape the duties of family. Felix was a hinderance to him—this was forever clear. He so often noticed this, greeting the man upon his many returns, watching him pace through his gallery, listening to his rare conversations with his wife. He bore a sightless love for Ellemine only. His singular mistress. His tormentor.

"Did you hear me?" Allesande said.

Felix turned his head, not far enough to see her. "What did you say?" he quietly jested.

Allesande splashed over to the bank, into his line of vision. She looked strange without the chainmail skirt, with only muddied calfskin trousers and a loose-fitting tunic, the hem of which sagged over her waist.

"I asked if you'll live through the night," she said, almost as a sigh. "Or if your blemishes will be the death of you. I have no ointments to pamper you with."

Felix chuckled. "Surprising," he said. "I thought you a decorous woman."

She glared awhile. Truly, the stewardess was a fearsome woman even without her armor. "What are we to do with you, Felix?" she said.

"And what am I to do with you?" he countered lazily. Far behind, Wortin hollered to them, though his words were lost. To him at least.

"They went west!" Allesande yelled back. "Look for them west!" Wortin said something back and Allesande groaned privately.

"How long do we have to wait?" said Felix.

This time Allesande was the one to withhold a reply. She stepped back to where she left her mail dress spread out over a root-gripped boulder. Felix's gut grumbled.

"It's just," he started, "unless you want to eat cold mushrooms and drink water that two hundred men died in not four hours ago, we should get moving. Anywhere but here." His dark mood returned, bidden only by his frustration. What had happened? Why did he grow so faint near the end of the fighting? How did they spread those flames? Then, as if the stewardess were listening to his thoughts...

"What was it?" she said in a nervous snarl. "That—that thing. In the trees—that daemon. The giant."

Felix stared at her. "I don't know what you're talking about," he said, sitting back down beside his boots.

"I suppose not." This concession surprised him. "It tried to destroy you too. And all your men. So many men—we never would've…" She seated herself, he could hear. "Wortin talks about this all the time. The kinds of abominations out there. Out here in the uncivil world." Felix nodded. Neither spoke for a time as they wallowed in their respective pities.

He knew precisely what she was talking about. He hadn't fought in any battles during the last invasion of the Piik Islands, but he sometimes heard stories of particularly bizarre forays: inlets guarded by water goblins, lakes filled with three-headed eels, goat daemons who walked only on their haunches, winged naemas who could hide inside the cup of a tulip. He brought the tales back to Wallenport with him, shared them with the prettiest of the scullions—even upheld the truth of it all with his own descriptions of these beasts. And all of his fun ended when Cato Clerici and War-mester Herman received the rumors of young Felix's journeys across the southerly isles. After that he was forced to find new lies.

He thought over his staff back home. What to tell them once he returned to the court? Who would be enraged by the results of the battle, who would be indifferent? What would Anae think if he found her there, if she'd returned from Chaisgott with haste? She would be a dear as always, a loving wife. "You tried, Felix," she'd say, "and that's all you ever need to do." Hot-headed Arnaul would go on about the Sivliére debt, now plummeted beyond repair: their only hope, he might say, is to bestow the lordship to another, to chicane a family of merchants into purchasing the region, then flee for the coast in the guise of clothiers or silversmiths or horse sellers.

Better yet, they could travel to Taliorano and sell the island to a wealthy family there. Then, wrathful as a storm, King Hugon would probably do them the unintended service of crushing a few Talioran bones. All for the sake of regaining the territory for Bienvale. The Sivliére staff could disband throughout the kingdom—everyone's satisfaction preserved! Except for Anae's. And Chamberlain Raul's. And especially not his mother's, as she was never satisfied by anything.

And what about his cleric? Cato Clerici was a woman of the All-Being: did this not insinuate her pleasures were always complete as long as the sun burned? He supposed she could stay and watch over the church while the rest of the retinue disbanded. Though, without money to pay for its conservation, the mortar and brickwork would crumble within ten years. Unless she gave up her station, she would be forced to sell the relics of the apses in order to pay her stonemasons—that is, if the relics weren't already stolen away by a mob of angry Lattamen or starving fathers. Or Felix himself.

He thought of his father, then of his father's death, then of his flagship. Cato as usual had been most reasonable on that morning by the piers when they waited for Roberrus' body. He had always judged her as the least valuable of his advisors until then. Now, somehow because of his taproot choices on that blustery day, one of those advisors was now deceased, the other missing—though probably deceased as well. Cato would no doubt sail back to the continent with Arnaul in tow within the week, Felix thought. Most reasonable indeed.

No. It hadn't all been his doing. The aspirants had been honored, dignified in their vocation. Those sons, brothers, fathers of craftsmen and sea-folk. True enough, they resembled levies—pike rabble and fodder for the vans—but this resemblance went only as far as the depth of their purses. They would have been much more outstanding. Instead they received less than a season's worth of training in the field before being cast out of The Stead, disbanded to every corner of the island.

Such disappointment wracked those multitudinous groups who returned to Wallenport. If they'd been given more time—half a year or more—their enthusiasm alone would have made them of finer character than even the landed ridders of Westley. Those manipulable bastards, slaves of Allesande's treachery.

307

Felix thought back to his tour, the ride through Sarcovy at the start of his rule, the visit to Westley and Michelhal, the first words he imparted to the earl and his stewardess, later his proposal of war. Michel Laisroch had his own response of persuasive dedication; and the exact words were lost to a smog of apathy. But the woman, she gave no voice. She only watched the exchange with a pout. Had it not been hanging down her face from the moment of his arrival? Had she been envious of all their grandeur from the start? Possibly, at least until her moments of pride, her exposition of the shining Westleyan ridders.

"Why are we here, stewardess?" he said to the seated woman nearby. Her head had been resting against her folded hands. Now, her back straightened. And once again it were as if she could read every impressionable speck on his face and, thusly, every modicum of his meditations.

"Because of your gratuitous plans for war," she said. "Because you sought to purchase prominence with the lives of my people."

"*Your* people?" he questioned moderately. "If I'm not mistaken, the people of Laisroch County are not *your* people. Is your surname Laisroch? No, it isn't—it's the surname of your brother-in-law and your sister. And you threw them out the doors of their own house." Saying it aloud was like tasting its preposterousness for the first time. "Why?" he asked.

Allesande stood. "Because they were cowards," she said. "Because for you alone, Michel would've ordered me to give away over half my ridders. Just so you could carry them off to their deaths in your vengeance war."

"You mustn't have carried much faith in them, then! If you think they would've met their deaths in my service. If you had, say, beseeched me in person, offered yourself as an obedient kapitain, we wouldn't be here now, would we? No, no, that's not what a *strong* kapitain does, no! Rather, a strong kapitain like you takes it upon herself to resist any order she doesn't approve of. Isn't that right?"

"We would've bested you," she said, searching under her limp armor. "Yes, I made one or two mistakes. But failing to appeal to you was not one of them. This is how I see things: if I had the spine to storm into Wallenport—mere weeks into the rebellion, still when the leaves clung high—and if I had the stomach to slaughter husbands and fathers as they stood at your gates, spears shivering, I'd have no errors to live with. I'd only have regrets. Bloody hands, the hatred of the helpless. Nightmares and deceptive dreams." She removed a knife from under her chainmail and sat back down over the tree roots. "I had no intent to take your place, you know."

"I find that hard to believe, stewardess," Felix scoffed. Without wanting to, he began to pity the woman. Insufferable as her intervention had been, she carried herself with a heartrending appeal. Even as she tested the point of a hilted dirk against her fair blistered fingertips.

"But do tell me anyway, what was your intent?" he asked. "Or what *is* your intent, if you still hold it?"

She artfully twirled her dagger at its tiny crossguard. "I sought to force your surrender," she said. "Afterwards we would come to an agreement and I would allow you to live on as Aetheling of Sarcovy."

"And Michel would be welcomed back to Westley as its true earl?" Felix asked. Allesande tilted her head unsurely. Or disapprovingly.

"That would be counterproductive on my part," she said. "He wouldn't go so far as to have me killed, but he and my sister would send me back to Triume tied in a sack. Thence I could never return to Lattaholm or Garm with honor. Mind you, I'd take no serious issue with the debasement."

"I suppose you recognized the men in my army, then." The woman nodded at this, her lips thinning. He wanted to remark on Michel's duty as a continental envoy, his surprising success in mobilizing the Lattamen. But Allesande possessed an uncanny ability to intimidate. Principally so with a knife spinning between her fingers. "So you believe I would've given you, my recent opponent, a near-third of the island's land. And you think I would've resumed trusting you as an even higher official than you were before?"

"No," she grunted. "I never said that. I would continue as a stewardess of the household. But under a new earl." She looked out to where she so recently spoke with Sir Wortin.

"Let me ask you something else," said Felix. "What would you do if I were more craven than you first expected? That is to say, what would happen if you encircled the palisades of Wallenport with your three-hundredfold band, then found out later that I had fled for the coast of Bienvale without organized decree? What would you do then?"

Allesande took time to deliberate. "Depends," she finally answered.

"Depends on what?"

"Many, many things. But one choice remains above all others. I would not take the lordship from you. Knowing our king, my role here would not be tolerated. Better to seat a more likeable youth. Like Fitzwillian." Felix felt an ache of anger throb above his heart. Allesande continued before he could speak up: "Do the people of Wallenport admire your mother? Damme Ellemine? The purekin woman, the precursor of the island's rule?"

"Those who know of her. Those who believe she still lives. Yes. I'd say so."

"Do they admire you?" she asked.

Felix felt obliged to pause. "Yes."

"Even after all that's happened?"

Again he feigned reflection, but chose a different return. "What is your point?"

"Did they love your father?"

"Yes, they admired my damned father—what is your point?!"

"But did they *love* your father? As you loved him?"

Her inflection struck him like a war-mallet. He thought back to the silent processions around St. Maguir, the ceremonies following his return from the southerly islands or Triume's coast. He had been with him during three of those cavalcades. Not once did he behold a glowing face; not once did he meet the eyes of the small people. All of them—women, children, and men alike—searched the passing ranks without a step forward or back. Others yet strode alongside the rumbling column, wading through and repeating one or two names. All their heads were cold and pale as if they'd been living under the stone streets. Every so often a cry would sound out, but only once did he manage to trace its source: an old mother, a tightly cowled and shrunken thing, fell into the arms of a stern young man who shifted out of his line and into the crowd. A friend of a son, he guessed.

So then why were the aspirants so glad when Felix invited them into his hall? Why did they bother to come at all? Why did the women and men at Cato's sermon wear their nicest garments and happiest faces? Did they not assume the training of five hundred young and middle-aged men would lead to war sooner or later? They were proud to have Felix as their aetheling, they had to be. Proud to see their boys begin the journey to grandeur. Why else would they have saved their tears for the start of the migration west?

"You held potential, Felix," the stewardess said, tapping the side of her dagger against her shoulder. The aetheling got up from his rock and roved closer to the center of the stream. "If only you left Roberrus' legacy alone. If only you hadn't made plans for sailing to Taliorano. If only you hadn't dipped your—"

310

As he hoped, her voice was mostly lost under the tinkling of the rapids. Something then caught his eye up the river: Wortin, he was sure. Or even one of the pages who went back to investigate the far-off outcry, to see if it came from one of the lost rebels. The figure was as bland as the taupe underbrush blocking it from view—and a second crackling traipse resounded not much further. It had to be the pages, then. He pivoted away from them and Allesande called out to the distant shapes, her free hand cupped to her mouth.

"Anything at all?! Who's that?!" She joined Felix in the water and gazed up the current. He could hear her begin to call again, then stop. A crescendo of stirring, swirling water advanced on him—

Felix was knocked down, thrown onto the riverbed with a hard splash. The front of his face, as it submerged into the depthless current, scraped against the smooth stones. As speedily as he could—and with no shortage of resentment—he hustled himself up to one knee.

"What are y—" Felix spat the words as he tried to whirl about. Allesande snatched the collar of his wool coat and brought him to his feet. The point of her knife scraped against the corner of his jaw as he turned his head. He stumbled, faced downstream: a crooked pole floated by and tapped the scalps of surfaced rocks. Elsewhere, a man called out. His voice was overtaken by a braying animal. Allesande muttered, frightened. Felix oriented himself behind the woman.

Just over twenty strides upstream were two devils, hunched down to the height of a man and shrouded in heavy rags. They had horned heads, thin and elongated as a horse's, with swaying tassels hanging down from their throats like the braids of a sailor's beard. Both were armed: the brown one, the furthest beast, held a load of staves or javelins bunched in one talon-like hand, with a single pole pinched in the other between its claws. The grey one held a staff of its own, the end of which was affixed with a curved blade like a sickle's.

This fiend advanced with terrible speed. Within the four heartbeats it took for Felix to fathom this sight, he could see it was missing an eye—a filthy socket at the midpoint of a carnation-pink scar.

Allesande backed into the young aetheling until he once again lost his balance and fell rearward into the water. The stewardess, still moving away, soundlessly held out her dirk as the closest beast sloshed to them, readying the hook of its weapon. It snarled, its pointed tongue protruding straight out from behind its contorted teeth. Felix, his whole body shaking, squirmed and wriggled off down the river. The moment was lost to him, to his unconquerable fear.

By the time he made it to the dry edge of the bank, the devil had struck Allesande's head with the butt of its staff. She swung around with a howl, landing face-first in the water, the dagger escaping her hand—dinging against the point of a stone—plopping into the freezing silver water. As the stewardess attempted to stand back up, the daemon planted a cloven hoof at the middle of her spine and swung the blade down to her neck, halting the crescent around her head. She did not call out, though she struggled with gritted teeth. It reached down with its free hand and clamped its sickening fingers over the whole of her head.

Felix watched her, deciding that he was in a nightmare.

This effluvial passage of time bore no resemblance to the paces of Reality, the beating seconds of heart's blood, the true moment whereby a true belief is consummated, the hours who watched the sun or passed as eyeblinks to the All-Being. Now as the movements of all things ceased in consideration of their siblings, Felix could feel everything: the trees and their patience, the melting snow, all the birds as they fled overhead.

Over them all he felt Allesande's breathless daze, her new and piteous desire for death, for release from the hellion. And he had never known such disdain. And he now treasured this woman more than all his possessions. Alas, he adjudged, this *was* all a dream.

The young aetheling leapt for the knife, tore it from the waters, and charged for the devil. A spear shot by—less than a hand's span from his ear—and grazed his shoulder. He kept wading, lifting his feet high. The creature over Allesande showed its jutting teeth, shimmied its ugly throat braids in animal mockery. Another javelin flew over its head, missed the mark utterly. Felix upraised the knife and screamed—and the beast thrust the curved blade over the young man's head and pulled. Its sharp point bit into his back just as he was flung forward, down to the devil's hoof.

He saw the fur-matted cleft rise: it pressed firmly down on the top of his skull. He heard sloshing footfalls even as his head submerged. Then a warm ichor dribbled down onto the back of his neck and the monster receded. Felix rose from the water slightly. Riding boots now stood before him.

"You remember me, yeah?" It was a man's voice. Wortin's. The daemon huffed nearby. "Yeah, how could you forget? Demented bastard."

The kapitain strode after the creature. And the unmistakable whooshing of a sword followed, its steel rarely meeting his enemy.

Felix crawled to Allesande. Her hands trembled by her face as he attempted to pull her and himself up.

Then he stopped: blood was cupped in both her palms. It dripped rapidly from her chin—far too rapidly. He released her and shifted onto his back.

Wortin swung his sword like a madman. Over half his cuts were deflected by the beast—now standing upright, a full ell taller than the kapitain. As he slowed, the devil made several jabs at his head, hooked it with the blade, then pulled back just as it had done with Felix. Like an alley cat Wortin shied under each attack and anticipated the returning blade deftly. He launched himself forward after a swift bout of dodges, sword tip straight as an arrow—a soft fleshy sound and the cough of a hunted deer followed.

The fighters froze. Then Wortin was lying face-down under the creature, who bled continuously onto the man's cloak. The kapitain's sword was stuck above its groin. It dropped its staff, collapsed onto its side, breathed without rhythm.

Relief surged through Felix until the other creature stepped to them, its cloaks parted to reveal limp udder-like teats at its abdomen. She removed another lance from her cluster. Once close enough she gripped Wortin by the shoulder, tore him up from the stream like a child's linen doll, raised the tip over his head.

Felix covered his eyes with an elbow. A wet thud followed.

The dream was coming to an end, he knew.

When he removed his arm, the last devil seethed over him. Felix averted his gaze: Allesande's dagger sparkled by his thigh, its tip poking out from under the water's surface. He took it with one hand, held up the other. The daemon leered at him. Sour hot breath came out her snout. Felix gawked down at his legs, unable to bear the haunting mien above him.

As this was the worst kind of nightmare he knew, the kind that followed him through the streets and halls after a night of drinking, he knew well enough that there was only one way to bring it to a peaceful end. He'd tried to cut the devil before, he'd tried to run, he'd tried to get it to speak his tongue. Nothing ever worked. Always, there was one solution for waking himself.

"I'll do it," he told her, bringing the blade's tip to his neck. The devil reached out to him.

Anae would be beside him when he woke, her bare skin warmed by dawn light. And he would slip closer, kiss her awake. He would tell her, as he had so many times before, that she must never leave the sheets above them. And she would smile, as she had so many times before, and hold his head close to her.

Chapter IX – Axiom and Eidolon

Morley woke on the softest, loveliest bed he'd ever been on, then went right back to sleep.

When he woke again, a door was booming shut at the other end of the room. He kept his eyes shut and turned over onto his side, away from the sound. As he did so, it felt as though someone swept a serrated blade down his back. He winced at this and, all of a sudden, he was entirely awake. He opened his eyes: the bedroom's light was softened by a protracted length of heavy parchment hooked against the open window above him.

The rest of the room was much smaller than he had thought while half-wakened—though during many of those feverish dreams, he conceived of himself resting on a cloud in the endless empyrean. Other times he was on an altar beneath a tree, a chamber with walls made up of enormous roots. And for few other instances, he was cradled in Anae's arms.

"Are you alive now?" she said. Morley looked slowly to the door. There she was. "Can you hear me?" Was this another dream, then? Set in a weaker version of Ellemine's solar, perhaps, hence the impossibly comfortable bed. Was she going to berate him again for coming after her—*had* he gone after her again? Was this actually the first leg of his first journey, and the rest was all a dream? Was Seth still waiting for him at the inn down at the foot of the motte?

"I suppose not," the young damme said with a sigh, reaching for the latch of the door behind her.

"Wait," Morley wheezed with a dry cough. His mouth was so parched that his tongue stuck to the surfaces all around it. Ignoring the pain, he squirmed up to the headboard and seated himself upright. As he did so, Anae adjusted her skirt and glided to the mattress.

"Morley. Are you really awake now?" she whispered.

"Can I…water? For this?" He pointed to his mouth.

Sitting down at the bedside, Anae reached to a tall cup on the stand beside the headboard—which, the lad realized, was more conveniently in his reach than hers. She made no fuss about it, naturally. She was the most graceful woman in the entire world. She handed him the cup and he poured its cold drink down his throat, letting it dribble in streams down the sides of his mouth.

"So," she said, "what do you remember?"

Morley finished off the water and returned the cup to its place beside a long-expired candle and a wood bowl. He noticed a bitter taste at the base of his mouth. "That's the first thing you want to ask me?" He intended for it to sound comely and confiding but, as he spoke, his gravelly voice lent his tone to dissatisfaction. Thus, he attempted to rectify: "Not, eh, 'How have you been?' or 'What in Being's name did you do to start all this?'"

"I know more about how you've been this past week than you do, country boy," she replied. "Believe me. I've been talking to you for days and you've said nothing back. You've been a rather inhospitable guest."

Morley wondered now if *her* statement had been aimed as a joke, conducted as a sneer. More importantly, his curiosity was tickled. "How long have I been here?" He felt the furry sheets wrinkled against the wall. "I feel it's only been a night, maybe two."

"Seven days," she said flatly. "Seven nights. I've been trying to force you awake for the past three. You were found outside the gates in the early morning, unconscious. Alone."

"Wha—how? What happened?"

"I would've told you already if I knew. It would've been the first thing to pass through my lips."

Morley was reminded of a particular dream he recently drifted through. Rather absently, he changed the subject. "Did you kiss me while I was asleep?" he asked frankly.

Anae tried not to smile. "No, I didn't."

"Are you sure?"

"Yes." She had seemingly returned to her serious self.

"When I dreamt it, I think—I thought you were trying to bring me back to life. Like when—"

"Like Damme Heilwig and Sir Gilbert," she said. "After they were hunted by the royal falconers. After Gilbert was stung by their birch arrows."

"Yeah. That's the one." He rolled his tongue around in his mouth. "Oh well. Can you tell me what happened, eh, say, eight days ago? Not concerning me, just…around here? The last thing I remember was the battle ending. The one on the Lightrun. And I was with Yeva." He knew there were more details to divulge, but the whole event was indistinguishable from his deluge of dreams and nightmares.

Anae stood up, clasping her hands together by her waist belt, and proceeded to step about the room. "Eight days ago. Nothing really. Over two weeks ago, Felix passed by with an army in tow. I expected him to camp them outside for the night, but they all just kept going. South, they went—but I guess you know that. Nobody won the fight, from what I heard. And you were found before anyone could bring that news to us, strangely enough. They were about to throw you in a cell with another—he was also found outside right where you were. I watched as you were carried in and it nearly made my heart stop. So, the castellan's nephew put you in here instead." She gestured up at the narrow space. "As per my request. Therefore if it weren't for me, Morley, I would say your long slumber would've been spent in the gaol. And it would've been far less cozy there."

"I don't know, Anae," he said, recalling Allesande's distant comment about Willian and Amalic storming inside Wallenport. "I have a familiar face. Well, *head* anyway." He itched behind an ear. "And I've got plenty of good friends throughout the island. I'm sure someone would've come to my rescue soon enough." Anae's face darkened, though not out of anger. "I'm sorry. Thank you for the bed. And for watching over me." Silence entered the room and stooped between them.

Morley used the interval to assess the missing or incomplete pieces of his memory: Geat had retreated with all the other men at the end of the battle at Olford. And Yeva was there with him the whole time. At what point did she disappear? And why? Most mysterious of all, how did he manage to lose consciousness and stray inside the aether of his mind for such an unbelievably long time? And who brought him to where he was— wherever he was.

"Where, ehm—where are we, by the bye?" he asked.

Anae again sat beside him. She did not meet his eyes. "Upper floor of Castle Chaisgott," she said.

"Huh," he buzzed. "Never been here. Only saw it from outside once, earlier this year. After I left Wallenport. Speaking of which, why are you here and not there?" She did not answer. "You mentioned Felix marching by without halting. Does that mean you came on your own?"

"It's been hard for me to live around Felix of late," she sighed. "And still worse, it's been hard for him to live around me. Ever since the hallmote. It's as if all the dignity I once saw in him has been rubbed away. All because a handful of old men were able to snuff his pride in public.

317

See, that was my obligation up until then. I was the one to question each of his actions—usually in private—and Iacob was the one who abutted his plans with faith. But we couldn't prepare him for the hallmote, not sufficiently."

Morley had heard this term before and did not know what it meant: was it a ritual? A gathering of some sort where elders yell their voices hoarse and spread gossip like a band of brewers or weavers?

"Why can he not be around *you*, then?" Anae did not answer as she played lazily with her streaming hair, as she motioned her innocence. Or guilt. She used to do this whenever one of her parents called her away from 'that waif with the ears' and scolded her for making Mester Alherde wait on her.

Morley had met Alherde while passing through Reineshir with his half-brother. As Anae often stated in the past, the man was showy and inflated with vanity, hardly giving Morley a second glance even after hearing about his relation to Willian. The tutor seemed a fitting alternative subject, a topic of derision—as neither of them were in the mood to talk about Aetheling Felix.

However, before the lad could bring up the scholar, he perceived something: a man outside was yelling very loudly, pausing as if to wait for someone's retort. None came, so the man continued his tirade. He was sure Anae could hear it, too. She might've even been listening more attentively.

"Who is that, do you know?" he questioned.

"I don't know his name. But I know he's a Lattaman."

"And what's that exactly?"

"Someone from Lattaholm," she said. Morley cleared his throat quietly. "Lattaholm is a city on the coast of the continent. They sent seven hundred men to help Felix fight the rebels." She huffed with a concealed displeasure. "They evidently lost the battle. Both sides lost as far as I can tell."

Morley tried to think of how they could've failed with so many men. "What's he yelping about out there?"

Anae shook her head. "They've had the castle surrounded for four days now," she muttered. "Some are calling it a siege, but I don't think they have enough men for a proper one. Besides, they don't have any engines or equipment aside from axes and swords. They just claim to have Count Bertram captive—he's the man who oversees this place regularly. But

318

whenever Sir Matten bids them prove the count's confinement, they bring out a man with a bandaged head. He doesn't move or anything. But he does wear Bertram's clothes, there's no mistaking that." She paused for a deep breath.

"Some went to Reineshir, I know," she went on. "Two of the men out there have Zondottir and Credence—I know it's them. No other bay horse in the world has a white blotch over her left haunch." It took Morley a moment to recall what she was referencing: the steeds that once belonged to her and Alherde.

"What do they all want?" Morley's feet were beginning to get clammy under the sheets.

"Their request is senseless. In exchange for the alleged Count Bertram, they want the castle. Probably so they can ransom it further for—who knows what. Some price to make up for their casualties. Maybe a ship or two. That'll all be up to me, I imagine."

"Not Felix?" Morley asked. Anae did not speak. "I'd think he would be in charge of all that, right? Like money and bargains and all—"

"Felix has been missing since the battle." She forced out this truth as if she were pressing a splinter from her thumb. Morley, somewhat glad to hear it, kept his mouth shut. "That means Damme Ellemine is in charge of absolutely everything until I return. And I'm not sure if she knows it."

This struck the halfelev as odd. Why was Anae not in charge now, despite not being in Wallenport? Did this mean that Felix, whenever he was out on the road or the open sea, could not act as though he were in charge? Is a lord only a lord when he's sitting in his castle, supervised by his supervisors?

"—take weeks for Felix to get back to Wallenport, he's horrible at navigating land by himself."

"Luckily," Morley added uncertainly, "he's always got at least three men standing beside him. I'm sure one of them lived through the battle."

Anae slanted one eyebrow. "What do you mean?"

"I can't really remember. But…" Something came back to him: heat, stench, ash. A jotun? No. There was a bedroom with Yeva in it—how did they get out of it? Door had to be unlocked. Maybe the inn was burned down around them.

"Yes?"

"I can't remember. I'm sorry, Anae. I know I was there in Olford but can't tell if I dreamt the battle or—"

"You were in Olford?!" She leapt back up to her feet. "When? What happened?"

"Like I said," he confessed.

"What's the last thing you can recall, then—give me anything, an image, a sound."

Yeva, their bed, her musty scent. In toying with the idea of fabricating a sturdy illustration, he was prodded by another picture: a gold piece, a broken roof, a heavy sword, a fire. He promptly forgot Anae's insistences, jolting upright.

"Did I have any chattels? When I was found outside the gates here?" The young woman shook her head. "Not a sword? Nothing?"

"Just you and your clothes."

His heart sank. Gale's sword and the gold coins—even Yeva! How could he have lost any of them? Furious, he threw away the bed covers, flung his legs over the side of the mattress, and got up. He then fell immediately against Anae, who lowered him back down to where she had been sitting previously.

"It's Gale's sword you're talking about?" she asked. Morley did not answer. "I suppose it was. Of course. I thought something was missing. I don't think I've ever seen you without it."

Every problem that entered his head upon waking returned. And still yet he could solve none of them. He needed time to contemplate, needed a more recent face, a bowl of hot stew, a place to walk, another cup of water, a tree to piss under.

Anae brushed her hand across a side of his face—a brief meaningful sensation. He needed to stay with her, to protect her. Wherever she went. Or wherever *he* went.

"I need to get back to Olford," he said. "I need to see what's happened there."

"You can't," she said. "Not with the Lattamen out there. They have no reason to take you as their prisoner but, if they see anyone coming through the portcullis, they'll tie your hands and put you with the rest of their captives. If they have any others at all."

"Then what am I to do?" Morley's voice caught halfway through the query. Yeva was gone, Geat had run off, Seth disappeared without a trace. Now Ellemine's gold and Gale's sword. Hopelessness drifted over him like a blanket tightened about his head. Anae watched as his knuckles whitened; she then silently stood up and moved toward the door. She

320

turned back her head, lips parted, ready to speak: she rescinded her thoughts, rotated away. This occurred once more. Finally, she swung back around, her intent solidified at last.

"I must leave too. For Wallenport," she said. "I should've left days ago, right when the troops showed up outside. But I needed to see you wake up."

The halfelev eyed her suspiciously. "I thought you sai—"

"There is a tunnel," she interrupted. "It leads northeast to the quarries, within three kalcubits of Wallenport. I don't know how long it will take to pass through—nor do I know if it is entirely uncollapsed. Under less bothersome circumstances, I would say you should stay here and rest. But…" She turned an ear to the shouting Lattaman outside the castle.

Morley continued eyeing her. "You were about to leave me here?"

Anae shook her head. "You were—you started to leave not a moment ago but kept turn—"

"I was reasoning, Morley," she interrupted again, her face hard and serious. "It's something I often have to do as the damme of all this land, something my old mester tried to train me in. Something you failed to do a season ago. Do you know what I was thinking just now?" Morley remained still. "I was deciding whether or not it would be prudent to bring along an impetuous young halfelev who, after sleeping for seven days straight, tried standing up just now and had to be caught and laid back down. By me. I was wondering if, in the likely chance that you will lose strength and be unable to continue on—if I will have the heart to leave you behind. I was wondering if you will be an aid or a detriment, both within the tunnel and beyond it—if we pass beyond it at all. And I was wondering if I should attempt any of this at all, if I should even tell you what is my mind."

She sighed and Morley's stare softened.

"I realize now what you might not have realized a season ago, country boy, before you went on your misadventure. Reason can be bested by uncertainty sometimes. And that desperation plays a greater part than I thought." She laid a soft hand against Morley's cheek. His heart thumped as it had during the battle: images and sensations of it all returned to him with each beat.

"I won't leave you behind," Anae said at last. "Try to stand again."

Morley obediently did so, wobbling back and forth. Anae gestured for him to approach. He took three steps, pausing before her. His legs were sore and felt as if they were encased in tight metal boots, but the pain had already begun to subside.

The young woman sighed indecisively. "I'm not going to force you to follow when I depart. It might be a day or more to the tunnel's egress at a steady pace. And I assure you it won't be a steady pace the whole way. Most of it is roots and stones in complete blackness."

Morley leaned against the stone wall. Though he was drowsier than ever, he knew he would follow Anae anywhere—into the ocean, into the skies. "It's better than a swamp, I'm sure," he said.

A loud bang resounded outside the chamber and the two of them stared at each other. Another followed soon after and a group of men sprinted down the hallway. Anae yanked at the door's latch and rushed out. Morley followed at his own sluggish rate.

The corridor was timber and stone much like the one in Sivliére Castle, though this one had a lower ceiling and level iron-barred windows overlooking a central yard. Without scrutiny and in thinking back to the structure's shape after his march with the aspirants, he determined the whole place to be in the shape of a ring.

Anae was searching through the nearest barred window. "Wait here," she then urged, running off down the hall as fast as her skirts permitted.

"Piss on that!" he called after her, pursuing. After eight strides or so, his knees began to buckle and sparks floated and vanished before his eyes; but he pressed on past banded doors, vacant sconces, and decorative quilts hanging down the outermost wall. "Anae!" he called out. Seconds later, she charged back down the hall, flustered and irked. Two men brushed past him from behind with empty quivers belted to their hips.

"What?" the young woman called.

"Wait for me, please!" he cried. Anae scoffed. She then flew to the door closest to her.

"Come this way," she insisted. Morley joined her in a cramped stairwell lit only by the natural light at its bottom level. "They've opened the machicolations over the gate," she said as she stomped down. "I couldn't get a good look—but the Lattamen are battering at the grid, probably with a tree trunk. I don't think they'll get through in time—the archers will get them to fall away while others boil up water or fetch oil. Either way, there's no better time to get moving."

The halfelev didn't understand most of what she said and soon forgot the words entirely as they stepped out onto the courtyard's circular walkway, an amply pillared perimeter directly beneath the upper hall. At the heart of the open court was a man carved of stone, encompassed by a sea of opened boxes, targeted quintains with ripped sides, purposeless racks, boards, and other debris. The statue—his plain stocky features made plainer by his hood and dress of mail—stood upon a block of stone, the bottom sides of which had grates installed, vents to a hidden abyss. Looking away from this oddity, Morley could see only five or six other men throughout the whole space, each bearing a load of some sort, each undoubtedly busying himself with the gate's fortification.

"Come on," Anae ordered, dragging him by the wrist to the other side of the ring. "The cellar is accessed through the kitchen, right after the gaol. I need you to wait there while I go find a few wrapped torches." All of this sounded so familiar.

Before he knew it, he had passed through another short hall and another door—rather, Anae had launched him through this latter passage, throwing the dingy lath closed behind him. He was now in a room of faded brickwork, complete with the abundant and distinct amenities of a rich man's cookery. Starved, he took up a slab of white cheese from the room's most crowded table and chewed on one of its corners. He then scavenged the rest of the surface for unfinished bread loaves, finding only old scraps of bacon and dry ham.

As he rummaged around the stacked eating-wares, a clay bowl slipped off the edge and shattered across the floor. He winced and heard an exclamation somewhere: a grumpy old man being torn from his midday dreams. It came from a passage beside the largest of the kitchen's fireplaces, from the throat of another descending stairwell.

Morley waited for a successive sound. A voice then rose melodiously from the stepped chute. Somebody was singing, likely one of the prisoners—if the stairs did indeed sink to the gaol. The lad went to the top of the long descent. The song below was dissonant though easy enough to follow. Slowly, one dim step at a time, he treaded downward, speeding up once the lyrics and its voice were less reverberant.

"And in going north, the silver then saw
A herd of old men in a mountainous maw;
To make them much worse,
She threw them a curse
So they'd stand up as tall as the skies;
Then she cast them below
Where forever they'd grow,
Where ponds'd pool up from their cries.

And in going east, the silver did ken
A nasty white folk in a horrid black fen;
They spat and they hiss'd
As she stood in their midst
But she raise'd up her paw with smile;
They turn'd grey 'n' green,
Got a poisonous sheen,
And were furthermore wicked and vile.

And in going west, the silver did hear
A timid young tribe that quiver'd with fear;
So she beckon'd them out
And show'd them the route
To the leaf woman's wonderful tree;
Then they went in its trunk
And they came out all drunk
And were thereforth allow'd to go free."

Morley didn't need even a flicker of light to know the singer was Sethan, lying like a grey skipping stone on the floor of a cell. "Seth?" he said, then tripped over a hollow object like a bucket.

"Knock it off, ghost! I'm still not in the right mood. Won't ever be, as I said." Sethan spat and sputtered as if he were trying to be rid of a foul taste. The halfelev got as close as he could to the voice until he could feel the obstruction of metal bars.

"Do you recognize my voice? It's Morley. I can't really see you and I'm sure you can't see me."

"I've seen everythin', Morley. And yes, I know yer voice, it's a hard one to mistake. But I don't know why yer appearin' back here again. How'd ye find the hole without Matten, eh?"

The halfelev didn't know how to respond. Seth sounded as though he were inebriated or in a trance, uttering the first words to come into his head; it were as if he shouted in his sleep, though listened well to the sounds of the wakened world. Morley wondered if this were how he himself had been when in his deep slumber.

"Are you awake, Seth? You don't sound all too well."

"I'm feelin' better than I've ever felt in all my life—what kind of addlehaired, idly, cankerous question is that? Ye keep askin' it and I keep tellin' ye. I'm feelin' better than I've ever felt in all my life. Ye gettin' mad about it too? I dunno what else to say to it."

"Where've you been?" Morley pressed. "I've been living in Olford for weeks, waiting on you."

"Hope ye didn't go in my house," he said with a discordant tone. "Mum's in there. She can't have any sunlight else she burns up."

"Seth, something's happened. In Olford. Felix marched there with an army and, and—remember Sir Wortin? And the rebels? They were all there. There was a big fight but I don't know what happened during it or who won. But I was there. And I can't remember anything at all."

"Neither can I," he said, surprising Morley with his supposed lucidity. "I keep sayin' it to Matten. Though he doesn't care much. So I keep chewin'."

"I know there was fire and that I had Gale's sword and Yeva was with me. And—" Before he could divulge another detail, the lad heard his name: Anae was shouting it in the kitchen above. "Down here! I'm dow— ach!" He stumbled again over the bucket while making for the stair. "I'm down here, Anae!"

"She'll never come down, Fitzmorley," said Seth. "No matter how often ye call to her, Matten never lets her come down. Not even when she insists herself. She's a kind girl, I can see why ye tried to go after her."

A lambent orange glow warmed the steps up to the kitchen. As it came closer with the tap of Anae's feet, the filthy gaol was revealed. Rotted straw was clumped up to the walls of each cell—and once the shadows of the bars settled, Morley could tell there were only two confinements, each taking up a full side of the aisle. A black niche opened at the end of the lane. And once Anae brought her dripping torch into the room, Morley saw that Seth was curled up without his cloak, facing away from the light. He shared his space with two rats, one of which might've been dead.

"I think I mentioned this one to you, right when you woke," Anae said of the prisoner. She held a damp strapped sack of torches and a second pack swayed from her shoulder. "I thought I heard him yell your name once but, each time I tried talking with him after that, he would only speak nonsense. So I let him be." Morley opened his mouth to speak, but she continued, "We need to keep going while the garrison's occupied. Right down this way." She marched to the crevice and Morley saw she had torn off the hem of her dress, shortening it to her calves.

"I know him," he pressed quick. "His name's Seth. He's the one who brought me to Wallenport." Anae froze, one hand already against the wall of their exit. Seth was murmuring in imitation of the both of them. "Where's the key?"

"You're serious?" she said. Morley couldn't tell if she were unamused by the proposal or simply shocked. "You can barely hold yourself up— how are you going to carry him out?"

Seth began to unfurl, his trousers and tunic clinging like a second skin. His face came into the light: much of it was swollen, bruised, and glistening. A grubby though relatively short beard was wrapped around his jaw. His hair was clumped and matted down in certain places. And the worst of it all was exposed when he raised his arm to block Anae's torchlight.

The fingers of his nocking hand were each severed at the middle joints, bandaged over with dark vermilion cloth. Morley was speechless.

"That fire there really stings," he said. "Really stings. And that's really strange because…I'm not *really* awake, am I?" He straightened, brought out his other, unharmed hand and inspected it, bringing it into the light. Tiny azure leaves were stuck together on his palm. "I'm awake as the sun at noon!" At this he sprang to his feet with unforeseeable stamina. "And yer here, Morley! Yer here now, yer here! Morley with short hair!" He slammed his hands against the bars. "Yer gettin' me out, eh? Like I said ye would, just like I said ye would? Right? Come on, then!"

The halfelev stared on in disbelief, knowing his friend's delirium had not yet burnt out.

The archer swung his head to Anae. "I was gonna help him rescue ye! From the clutches o' the evil Aetheling Felix Sivliére!" Seth piped up with no lack of enthusiasm. "But then ole Fitzmorley had to make a fast escape when ye couldn't be found. Had to swordfight a few men, had to leap out a window—right from an adventure story! Told me everythin' over breakfast the next morn. Whole trip was fer naught in the end, though he did find out about his parents. So we went off to Westley and, and…"

Morley's face had reddened, but he still peered over at Anae. She very much believed everything Seth was saying: her deadening stare made this plain enough.

"And then ye left, Morley," Seth said with confusion. "And I didn't see ye ever again till now—now! Yer here now with yer lady love. And *she* can rescue *me*! Yeah?"

Anae pointed upward. "Matten's spare," she said. Morley looked up: a single brown key was placed across two tiny hooks overhead. He took it down, feeling its corroded skin. "It's this way."

With that last unconcerned offer, she strafed into the parted wall, leaving them in almost total darkness. The halfelev, upon taking down the iron rod, poked the lock repeatedly in search of its keyhole. Seth gabbed on about their escape as he did so. Once he was freed, he fell onto the aisle's stony floor and seemed to kiss it—though it was of course the same floor he'd presumably been sleeping on for weeks. Once he was back on his feet, Morley could hear and vaguely see him scraping at his undamaged palm with one of his blunted fingers.

"Had enough o' that fer a life, I'd say right." he grumbled. Morley, groping in the black, found Seth's shoulder and drove him forward to Anae's vanishing beacon. They then struggled into the cramped valley of stone.

"Seth…" the lad started, uncomfortable with his impending query. "What happened to your hand?"

"Oh. I guess the leaves got stuck to my skin. I was holdin' them fer days and days and days. I think I got 'em off now, nothin' to worry over."

Morley shook his head, flustered. "I meant the other hand. What are these leaves you're talking about?"

"I've had them as long as I've been here. Dunno who put 'em in my hand, but I think they've been there this whole damn time. Every night I woke in pain I stuck one in my mouth—just as she urged—and felt much, much better. But I feel I've been asleep fer a year."

"Beltreres tear," said Morley, thinking of the deep black-blue mark in Seth's one hand, faint in Anae's light. "You've been eating beltreres tear. And it's a miracle you're alive if you've been having as much as you say."

Reffen had often talked about the medicament, sometimes with curious affection: it nullified all pain and all pleasure, addled one's sense of what is real and what is solely imagined. It was used most often, as the apothecarist said, to soothe a dying body. If Seth consumed a leaf before the severing of his fingers, it was possible he felt no pain. However, if he continued to ingest the amount given, his body would soon forsake his mind.

"Who gave you the leaves?"

"I've always had them, I think. Can't remember the last time I wasn't holdin' them." Morley considered the possibility of this for a very brief interval, then dismissed it.

"You mentioned a 'she.' Who's that?"

"Huh?" he buzzed. "When'd I do that?"

"Not a minute ago. You said your habit was to put the leaves in your mouth, 'just as *she* urged.'" Seth gave no response but soon began to hum. It were as if he'd forgotten Morley's words right as they left him. "Did they take your bow?" he soon questioned.

"Eh? Eh. Someone did, yeah. And my shoes. But I never use either anymore."

"What's the last thing you remember?" Morley tried. "Before I woke you in the cell, that is." The passageway constricted around them, giving way to natural rock.

"Waking in the cell alone," he admitted. "And the stars only know when that was."

"What about befo—" Morley missed a step, a short drop down to earthy ground. Somehow, the half-conscious Seth had managed it without hazard. "What about before you woke here? Do you remember where you were before coming here?"

"Olford," he offered hazily. "Then the Crouxwood. Then I was here." Ahead, Anae was stopped in an open space, her torch held steady.

"And you can think of nothing else? Why did you go out into the Crouxwood?"

"Went to find papaver flowers, I think. No, I went to see Sylvain again. Him and all his house is gone. Only a stack o' rubbish left behind. That's when I went to find papaver, all on my own—no, no, that's not right at all. I got the seeds all on my own, then went back to Olford and I was there, and…" He slowed as the tunnel widened. "What happened to my shoes?" he asked himself.

Before Morley could continue his interrogation, the brightened aisle yawned open. They stood with Anae on a wooden platform overlooking a grotto—its walls of uncut rock, its base a depthless pond from which slabs and monoliths protruded. Along the rim of this watery pit were boulders and bald tree trunks, all buried and haggard. Above, a beam of wet light floated down: the openings beneath the statue in the courtyard. This then was the belly of Castle Chaisgott, a gutter for all its rainwater and waste. That would explain the smell, at least. It reminded him of Maud the Innkeeper's forbidden cellar back in Reineshir. Gentle vibrations rumbled occasionally throughout the well; wisps of grit and dust floated down with each quake, ignited by the gleaming shaft. Seth collapsed to his knees despite Morley's quick effort to keep him steady.

"I'm dizzy," he said. "The air is cold."

"The Lattamen are still battering at the gate," said Anae in a careless uncharacteristic monotone. "If either of you want to keep following me, I'm going down there." She directed her weeping flame over the edge: a set of steps drooped from their platform past a yet unobserved scaffold and pulley, part of which had rotted away into the central basin. At the bottom of the stairs was another shadowy tunnel much like the one behind them.

"I've got enough light to last me a few more hours," she said. "If you don't want to be groping in the dark and if you don't want to be falling over every few steps, I'd recommend you stay close. I'm in a hurry." She started off.

"Anae, wait!" Morley called to her once she was near the muddy landing. She kept moving.

"She's the one ye wanted to save?" asked Seth as he attempted to stand. "Bit of a nasty one, if ye don't mind my mindin'. She probably was the one who took my bow, I'd bet."

"She's just…" He wanted to say it had something to do with what Seth blurted out earlier, his disclosure of Morley's first mission and the contrived conclusion he'd been fed in the motte-side inn. Perhaps it had to do with the crude mention of Felix. Either way and without a doubt, the archer had surely forgotten the exchange. All those long minutes prior. They started after her cautiously.

"I think we're more of a hinderance than we might think," Morley stated.

"*We*? What d'ye mean *we*? I'm the one who's been poisoned." Morley recalled the taste in his mouth as he woke, the days and days of slumber.

329

"You might not be the only one. Like I said, I don't remember much either. But I've been here for a while. According to Anae I've been here for seven days now. Just sleeping. I was found outside the gate, same as you."

"Found outside the gate, ye say?" As Seth spoke, Morley missed the ledge of a step. Neither fell, though both slipped and landed with a heart-piercing thud. "Didn't know that's where he got me."

"Who?"

"Matten. King of Chaisgott. Didn't know I knew him till he said so. He's the one who beat me bloody and cut me up. He's a loud one too. Only got one eye too—I dunno who put him in charge. I'd guess he took my cloak. Awful bastard, can't do one rightful thing, can he? It was a nice rag, y'know, better than the pelts these ridders like wearin'."

The halfelev thought of his own coat, the woolen one Amarta had made for Gale. Yet another lost memento.

"As fer the bow," Seth went on, "I'll bet they have plenty more in Wallenport. 'Twas only a bow and I didn't use it much, like you and your sword. Quite a pair we must've looked back last season. Like two little boys playing pretend."

Morley wondered about the claymore, whether or not it could still be found in Olford with all the rest of the dropped weaponry. Though if the Lattamen had returned north over the ford crossing, they certainly would've taken time to restock: Gale's blade was now in the grimed hands of a stranger, a continental. Unless he left it up on the rooftop, still well hidden. The rooftop, he thought—what rooftop?

"Oh. This must be where the jotuns were buried."

Morley stiffened.

Ahead of them, strides away from the lower burrow and Anae's dwindling blaze, was what he had dismissed as rocks and trees, all remnants of the hollow over which the castle was constructed. As Seth uttered the word 'jotuns,' Morley saw them for what they truly were: bones. Massive blackened bones—ten thousand times the size of the dove bones he so often snapped during childhood suppers, back when he himself pretended to be of jotun kin. Fingers like tree trunks poked from out of the water; the empty eyes of an ebon skull gaped from under a layer of mud across the grotto, its spine snaking into the pond, its ribs rising like pillars from under the filth. Though it had sunk down over the many decades, the body had apparently been cramped into total discomfiture before its death by starvation or injury. Or fire.

And then it all came back to him.

"Seth," he said. "Jotuns are real."

"I'd say so, yeah."

"No, I mean there was a jotun at Olford. After the battle there, I'm sure of it. It was no nightmare, no dream. I was up on the inn's roof at the time. The forest was on fire—and so were the men fleeing for the river. Then I saw a jotun there. And flames and shadows poured down from its arms. Then, it shrank down. Disappeared." He looked to his friend: his eyes were tired and misty, two grey pebbles in the dark.

"Yer sure it wasn't a dream?" At that instant, Morley's convictions ebbed away. How could he know? Who else could support him? "Ye wanna get closer to it or should we be off after yer girl?"

"I was with Yeva," Morley went on. "She sensed something—we both did. There was heat. Then she ran off back to the inn and I had no better choice but to follow." He heard Seth mumbling the name as if he'd forgotten who it belonged to. "She was the one living with your brother when we got to—"

"I know who she is, I'm not bloody lost. But she—I saw her. Recently, too recently. Where was that? Not Olford, not Westley, not the wilderness."

Morley eyed the tunnel entrance beside them: through the dislodged stones and tilted supports, Anae's torchlight was no more than a sliver of red flitting away from the channel's foremost curve.

"We should follow before Anae's too far off, come on." He pressed his friend onward through the ingress. Before following, he stared again at the colossal skeleton, thinking of everything its sunken body implied, every truth hidden away in the vault of its head. He left the cavern behind.

"Mayhaps that was also a dream," Seth spoke later on, after they found their footing. The tunnel floor had once been fitted with wooden cart tracks as Morley guessed, but they'd long since rotted. Every other step forward met a hard impediment or snagging gap.

"What was a dream?" Morley asked.

"Seein' Yeva in bed after Sieger left her alone. Alone? She *was* alone. Couldn't have been if I was floatin' there, right? I must've dreamt I was a geister." He knocked his head on the corner of a beam for the fourth time. "Does she have a sister or a mother who lives round the island? A wilder of some kind? An apothecarist?" The lattermost word fumbled its way out his lips.

"She has a sister, yes. I've never met her. But Yeva used to talk about their childhood on Kamena."

"Kamenin, it's called," Seth corrected. Morley then fumbled into him, as he was poised still along the path.

"What is it?" he asked.

"How in the name o' nothin' did I know that?" Seth said.

Three hours and over four hundred vexatious stumbles later, they had together organized a groundwork for their respective experiences. Still yet the unaltered problem remained with them: where did Dream diverge from Reality? Likewise, on which of those two courses were they still venturing—how could either of them know they were now awake? Or if the courses never truly diverged, if they were now in some new part-Reality, how could they tell apart the unproven truths from their own disguised ideas?

The circumstances were equally strange for the both of them, Morley assumed. But there were still clues they could share. For one: if they were asleep, how could they be so conscious of their present state, their movements through the inky black underground? Morley, his eyes already wide open, tried to enlarge them further, tried to open them to their soft middles in an effort to wake again. He could not.

They tried calling out to Anae, but no voice returned to them. If they were awake, where had she gone and why did she not answer? Were there multiple turns they missed—were they going in the wrong direction? They cried out, more desperate, began charging and tripping across the tracks. Eventually, they stopped to rest. And in doing so, they felt more and more as though they were trapped in a nightmare, an evil fantascape. Thus, they splayed themselves across the girth of the passageway, reassessed what they knew until their tired heads were lightened by the fogs of sleep—or whatever waits beyond sleep, if not death.

"And then she tried to accuse your brother of siding with Felix in secret," Morley was saying of Allesande's twisted assumptions at the innhouse. "All of it is so vivid now, out of nowhere. It's like one memory—one tiny remembrance—is a key to another thought, which is itself a key to a number of memories. She barred Yeva inside the room I was sharing with her. Then, later, I was thrown in as well. Everything after is questionable, I'd say. We woke in the morning to the sound of horns. Then there was a battle—a wild one. There were men in bluish cloaks and grey cloaks and men on giant horses. Blood seeped into the Lightrun, bodies floated in it."

"Then, as ye keep sayin'," Seth came in, "a fire jotun appeared over the heads o' Felix's troops. And all men, friends and enemies, ran off together t'wards Reineshir." They again weighed the premise in quietude. "I dunno, Fitzmorley. Vodniks are one thing—meanin' to say I can believe they live where they live. But don't ye think someone would've seen this monster before, even if it was out walkin' the highlands where nobody else lives?"

"It had the power to vanish. Or it had the power to grow to its greatest size, then shrink at will. Maybe it wasn't a jotun at all but a person who could become one—unlike the poor fellow back in the big cave. Maybe this person never left Olford or the brush around it after you were brought to Chaisgott."

"Who?" the archer asked.

Again Morley attempted to conjure a rational answer, a personage who could fit into both their accounts. "You said earlier you weren't sure about your encounter with Yeva's sister, about most of the day before her arrival. Yet, and even I must admit this, it all sounds much more believable than my own story."

Seth chuckled. "Ye believe a beautiful woman came to my house, took me downriver, bathed naked in front o' me, then later led me up a cursed tree? Then from its height—which was shaped like a big hand—we together flew off over the island and watched a thousand lives as they walked and slept and coupled in their beds?"

"No," said Morley. "But I believe Yeva's sister is the key to what we don't know. Didn't you refer to her as an apothecarist?" He could sense Seth nodding, though his body was imperceptible. "Why is that?"

"She looked like one. Whenever I think back to her, all I see is a bald-haired…" He interrupted himself to yawn. "Furry wild creature. A wild woman. Someone who collects poisons and herbs."

"Fine. But whenever I think back to *Yeva*, back to when we were trying to escape the battle, all I can see is the jotun. And Yeva standing before it, confronting it alone as all the fighting men run by, screaming and fearful. Why else would Yeva stay? Even if all that was part of my dreams, why did I imagine it like so?" A lull came over them. Semhren came into his mind: the two of them once had a conversation pertaining to this, he thought. The ex-scholar's exact words, however, were lost.

"I was once told that all dreams and nightmares are forced on us," he continued. "I mean, the things we see in them are from wakened life, they're—what's the damn word he used? They're pressed or pushed on us. Like when someone writes letters on a strip of paper. The people and things surrounding us always invade our heads when we let our guard down. When we fall asleep. You get it?"

"Mmm. Mhmm."

Morley could tell his companion was drifting. The beltreres was assuredly still in his body and would be for another day or so. Though he was still groggy as well, the halfelev had no intention of stopping. As Anae said, it would take days for them to reach the other side. And above all, he needed to catch up with her. Wherever she now was.

"Mother's gone," Seth mumbled. Morley perked up, held his breath. "The sick took her finally, I forgot to tell ye. Happened while we were away." His words were slurred and unsteady. The delirium was once again restored, Morley assumed. All the same, he hung onto every word. "Olford's done fer. Was like that even before ye got there fer the first time. I tried to hide it—I hid it well. And since, it's worse now. Damn Haarka, ye got no faith. Tomeson's been gone, left his poor boy all on his own. Jaasper the Miller, All-Being knows where he went—probly went and died somewhere. It's just me and Marion if she hasn't left yet. And Tomak. Then the wild woman. Now it's me, it's just me…" Silence. And quiet exhalations.

"Seth?" Morley murmured.

"Mmm."

"Are you ready to keep going?"

His companion gave no reply. They both breathed softly and metrically in the cave's heavy air. Soon enough, Morley's conviction began to slide away from him. He crossed his legs behind one of the rail's bricks, rested his hands against his chest. He did not close his eyes. Instead, he bided his time, waited patiently for Seth to wake back up or for some other sound to come.

He thought of Willian. On the first night after they met at Hoerlog, he'd overheard him talking to Sir Wortin about his dreams. Then, after their reunion outside Gale's house and just before their subsequent journey north on the following morning, he had commented on the surprising emptiness of his sleep during the night. Morley attributed it to the mushrooms he strained in the water, but the ridder rejected such—as if he

334

believed dreams were something more than simple reconfigurations of experience, visions unaffected by medicine. It was no wonder he got along so well with Semhren: they probably argued over the origins of the imagination long before Morley was born.

*   *   *

Elmaen and Semhren had been the only ones to try and snap Fitzmorley from his childhood stubbornness: the former was the first to mention the function of myth and outdated truth—how they differed from fact—and the latter had attempted to drive this idea into his heart. Fitzmorley, however, had deflected Semhren's reasonings with sound naivety.

The older man had too few minds to exercise with over the years, Fitzmorley guessed. But all the same, he enjoyed listening to people—or absently hearing them at the very least, as so much of his life before Egainshir had been lived in silence. Discussions with Semhren were pleasurable in moderation, an amusing clash of logic and imagination. But the elder's recent tendency of leading the lad into a territory of overcomplicated words—eventually ending with an assurance of his own validity—was cheap and often aggravating.

As he himself claimed, Semhren had been exiled from Bienvale after a decorous affair with the king's daughter. Elmaen insisted it was actually because he once made inappropriate advances on the woman; Reffen insisted that the lonely scholar came to Egainshir out of his own volition. Fitzmorley didn't understand or care about any of the cases. All he knew was that Semhren thrived on believing he was the cleverest man on the island, often sharing self-indulgent and largely puzzling propositions followed by his 'veritous explications.'

"This statement is false," the man had announced one day near the end of Fitzmorley's first year in the hamlet. At the time, the lad was helping him with housecleaning, one of his typical duties. It was a means of escaping outdoor labors on particularly cold days during Frysa, if anything. In reply to the elder's sentences, all Fitzmorley had to do was say 'true' or 'false,' though he could rarely pass up a comment or two.

"Which statement?" he asked, strafing behind the scholar with a box of emptied clay inkwells in his arms, glancing over Semhren's shoulder to see which part of his book he was reading from. Fitzmorley moved on unsuccessfully and tried to find a spot for the box somewhere on the man's junk-crammed bookcase.

"That is the statement: 'This statement is false.' Thoughts?" He took up his cup of beer at the other end of the table, stretching feebly over his tome.

"Oh. I suppose it's false, then," Fitzmorley said without thinking. He ambled by a tight space between the table and the bookcase. Semhren's house was somehow even smaller than Reffen's, he thought.

The man clucked at his young friend's presumption. "But if it's false, would it not then be true?" he asked into his cup, dribbling its contents onto his trimmed white beard.

"No." Again, it was an absent response.

"If it is true that the statement, 'This statement is false,' is false, then it would be true."

"But what's the statement?" Fitzmorley asked again, blowing the dust off a stool's underside and wincing at the consequent flurry. "There's nothing there. If it was followed by, I dunno, 'Sheep have blue wool,' then yeah. It'd be true."

Semhren chuckled. "Good, you see it is insoluble. Since its content denotes nothing more than the asserted nature of truth and falsity, it is an undisprovable sophisma." Fitzmorley shook his head privately. "Here's another: 'The following statement is a truth: the preceding statement is a falsity.' Thoughts?"

"Sounds like the same thing but longer," the young man muttered, setting down the crate of inkwells on the freshly undusted stool. "Find one that's more interesting, Semhren."

The scholar looked up from his book, unamused. He slammed it shut, took up his beer, and leaned back in his chair.

"You're starting to sound like my first pupil," he said. "Why don't you try a few on me, then? Since you're so clever today. I'll wait." Fitzmorley cracked a smile and thoughtfully swayed his head from side to side. "And wait. And wait." The elder began to hum an old road rime.

"Gale is Amarta's child," Fitzmorley soon said, recalling both the general structure of Semhren's puzzles and a conversation he recently had with Egainshir's baker. "False or true?"

"Ah, that is a good one, fast and familiar. Well done." He rested his head back against the height of his chair. "Given that there are no children with the name 'Gale' under the guardianship of a person of the name

'Amarta'—elsewhere, that is—then the statement is, in point of fact, a potentiality. Though, it is dually a falsity at this time, and in two separate regards. Amarta—that is, the baker of Egainshir on the island of Sarcovy in the Daarkan Sea—has a child, an infant child, though his name is not Gale, for he has no name as of yet. And if the name 'Gale' is here used in reference to the man who was once the housemate of Fitzmorley, then that is an outright impossibility. Ergo, a falsity."

Fitzmorley had ceased his work for a moment to rest, pretend to listen, and think up another sentence. He then remembered the perfect proposition, one he was ready to debate—one which came to him after an exciting dream.

"Jotuns dwell to the north."

"False, of course," Semhren stated. "A very basic assertion, that one. 'Jotun' is a word that significates a non-existent creature, a myth, so it therefore means nothing—or better yet, it states that 'nothings dwell to the north,' which—"

"Have you ever seen a jotun?" the young man interrupted, crossing his arms; Yeva always made the motion whenever Arrin or Robi uttered a rude joke.

"No," said the scholar. "They do not exist. Nobody has ever seen one."

"I saw one in my dream the other day," Fitzmorley said. "It was all white with a great big icicle beard and it left snow wherever it stepped."

"Dreams are not the stuff of Reality."

"Then what are they, Semhren? Hmm?" He grinned victoriously. "Can you answer me that? Gale couldn't even think an explanation for them and he thought up a lot of things. Or so you would have me believe."

The elder frowned. "Dreams are the perversions of that which has been impressed upon the soul," he murmured slowly as he walked into a contradiction. "They occur when the body's spirit abandons the confines of Reality. The soul must be in a constant state of being and experiencement, so it conjures up, ehm, images. Unreal images."

"But where do the images come from?" Fitzmorley tried. "I mean, how does the soul—whatever it is—manage to make them up? They have to come from somewhere that's real. Besides, that All-Being thing—"

"Here, how about you check this chapter of the *Conjecture*," Semhren speedily proposed, bolting up to fetch Gale's book from an adjacent shelf.

Fitzmorley's last reference to the god of the continental faith—an entity known to exist despite being unreal—was a viable proof, a 'virtuous exemplum' as Semhren would say. Supposedly, the scholar had never considered such a logical blasphemy. It being a blasphemy though, the scholar was quick to dispose of the conversation, opening *The Divine Conjecture* to a chapter on the capabilities of the imagination, knowing Fitzmorley would still fail to grasp its meaning in his effort to decipher the old words.

Even so, the lad smirked as he joined Semhren at the table. The fact that the man had to refer his young friend to some other source of knowledge instead of sharing his own usually meant the answer was out of his reach. The elder additionally covered over his ignorance with the excuse that he had to go gather up more kindling from Tommas, whose house was right across from his in Egainshir's circle. Victory, Fitzmorley thought.

He did not read the prescribed text, though he did reflect further on his recent dreams. Whenever the Frysa snowdust blew over Egainshir, it carried away his sleepless spirit to lands both beautiful and perilous.

The island of swaying folk who circled about their bright bulbs of flame, its smoke drifting up to the twisted sea stack mountains and their high houses. And in these houses, he knew, there dwelled horned things with long snouts and claws. On and on the people danced and sang to their gods. He often danced with them around their hearty fires.

Then there was a place of stone and intrusive roots, its shadows blue and black like the canals flowing backwards and forwards along its endless floor. Dark things wandered its chasms, searching for mice, rabbits, doves—tending their impossible lightless gardens. There was at all times the hum of a restful jotun below.

Most piquant were his dream-journeys to the Swamplands of Sylvan: there, a dome of yellow vapor concealed the thick wet fields and their consumed monoliths. On closer inspection, each of these grand stones had columns of text dripping down, quite literally, like rainwater on an ashlar block. Above it all, there floated a house and its bearded tenant, who screeched and bawled like a hunter owl. Fitzmorley always awoke with a start when the mad creature swooped down to him.

*   *   *

There was a moan in the dark, like a dry tree swaying in a breeze. It came from below. He felt the ground at either side of him, dug his fingers into the terrain of dirt-caked rock. There was then a hum, this one like an old man dozing in his chair—though magnified dreadfully. His wonderment seeped down the cracks and soon he beheld what could've been the Inferno. There were no flames here, only an endless forest—no, it wasn't random enough to be a forest. It was a grove of lined trees, their sizes uniform but ultimately indeterminable. Bearded jotuns walked between these trunks, each carrying greatswords against their backs. One, its eyes yellow and burning, turned to him. He shuddered.

"Morley, is that you?" There was a shaky thin hand touching various parts of his face, measuring the lengths of his nose and ears. He reached out and felt a soft lump of fabric. Moving his hand up, he found the warm base of a neck.

"Anae," he said. "Is Seth still there?" He felt her leaning away, rotating, then she was back at his side.

"Yes. He's asleep. I think he was the one who frightened me a moment ago, when I was walking."

"How did you get here?" he asked absently.

"I walked." She set down one of her bags as she sat next to him, curling up close and gripping his shirt, her tremors subsiding. "It took a long while without a torch. They all burnt out faster than I expected and then…" She rested her head against his shoulder. "Then I was cold. Alone. And no longer sure what I was doing."

Morley said nothing as he basked in her perspired robust scent. He feared offending her now—the wrong words, the wrong actions, the wrong inactions maybe. The best he could do, he felt, was breathe through his noise.

"Have you ever felt that?" she asked.

"Yes," he said. "But I'm not bothered much by the cold. And I like being alone sometimes. If I'm out walking, that is."

"I see. I like walking alone too. Out on the beach before nightfall, just below the motte and the castle and its sea stack. But I also often wish another would come along the shore and stroll with me. Though, in truth, if I saw a man from the harbor coming towards me, I'd be afraid."

"Does—did Felix not walk with you? Not ever?"

"Yes, he did. Mainly around the keep itself, sometimes down to St. Maguir's Court. I think he prefers to go where people can see me with him.

And he hates getting sand on his clothes and in his boots, so he avoids the beach as much as possible."

"That's a shame," said Morley. Anae was quiet for a moment. The halfelev suspected she was trying not to cry. Just like on those occasional evenings in Reineshir when her mother's criticisms were markedly harsh during her family's supper. She and Morley would later cuddle up in the stable loft and, without speaking, without the help of encouraging words, her coat of bitter self-loathing would thaw.

"I really have missed you, country boy," she said. "Really. I'm sorry about what happened last time we met."

"Ah. I'm sorry too," he replied. "I know you didn't want to have to say what you said. And I should've known better from the start."

"Yes, you should've. You truly, truly should've," she stated without a change of tone. Morley grunted. "And after I left you on the beach, I couldn't help but meditate on why you would ever make such a plan—actually, the plan itself is what I was trying to first discern. Where would we go, back to Werplaus? It's not a very large island, you know, we would be found within four or five weeks. And you would've been punished harshly, even if you didn't take me by force."

"Is that so?" he said, not believing her. "You'd let them torture me?"

"No, Felix would never go that far. And if I admitted to my willful cooperation—in the event that I *did* cooperate—my role in his house would've diminished. I would have to lie and say you kidnapped me. Then your punishment would end up being worse and I would have to live on with the guilt."

Morley gulped. Then he recognized the voice she was using: she was merely jesting.

"Would my mother let them do it?" he asked. "If she knew it was me?"

Anae lifted her head at this as if in reflection, then replaced it. "I hadn't thought of that. Rather, I'd almost forgotten you two are related. Strange."

"What?"

"If your birth wasn't illegitimate…which means if—"

"I know what it means," he murmured.

She placed her hand over his heart. "If you and Felix were both of the same father as you are of the same mother, and if I were to proceed in marrying him, thus rendering you my affine, and if you were to persist in making advances on me—let's pretend that part of the story has been kept—and if I were to persist in welcoming and satisfying those advances, we would be committing an incestuous act."

"You've lost me," Morley said. "What is that?"

"An incestuous act?"

"Sure."

"It's when two members of the same bloodline lie with one another. Like a brother and a sister."

Morley hummed at this. "And that's bad, I suppose?"

"The church says it is and so do most common people" Anae said. "Priests govern the rules of matrimony."

The lad had never seen a marriage and didn't know what it entailed. A ritual of blood-mixing? A spell and a sacred talisman? "So then are you trying to say you and I will never be together again?" he queried unhopefully. "As we once were?"

"I shouldn't think the answer bears repeating, country boy."

"I thought so." In truth, he felt as though a daemon had taken a bite of his innards. "I've found another anyway," he heard himself say.

"Oh? Who's that?"

"A Werplaus girl," he bluffed. "A goat-tender."

"Is it Yela, your old friend?" Anae asked, and Morley caught a trace of joy in her voice.

"Yeva. And no. She would never. She likes ridders. Or men who resemble ridders."

"Why would she not fall in love with you, then?" Anae nudged. "Ah, that's right. Because you lost your sword."

Morley's stomach turned and he immediately felt tears welling under his eyes.

"I'm joking," she followed, patting his chest. "Even without armor, even without a horse, you're more of a ridder than any of my husband's vanguards. True, a ridder is nothing more than a man with each of those things. But there is a spirit, I believe. Something that makes a ridder a *chevalier*, a hero. Something passed down through all those stories we used to read. When one carries only the image of a chevalier, an image molded out of our romances and fantasies, one carries pure inspiration. Like a soul defined. The wish of nobility in a person who has no wealth is much rarer than you might think, Morley. You're the only one of your kind."

The lad tried to summon an eloquent response. He gave up.

"You still prefer life in Werplaus, is that correct?" she asked. Morley nodded, rubbing his cheek against her oily scalp. "Even better. There are some mornings where I yearn for a simple life like yours. You might not see it as such, but I do. I wake and think of all that must be done by the end of the day—Felix does the same. Go to the chapel with Cato, check on the staff, sit at court and listen to favors and pleas if there are any to be heard. Only after I return to my bed do I realize how fortunate I am. Still, I never know if I deserve it.

"All the comfort, all the servants, the respect of our people. At least I'm no longer cursed with voracious want, as I was in Reineshir. You taught me how to overcome it, I think. Selling your sword would've made you the richest man in the island's south—before my parents, that is. You could've had a stack of silvers in exchange for it, enough to become a ridder. That would never cross your mind though, no matter how much you wanted to fulfill those dreams. The blade meant too much to you. A precious reminder of what's been lost, what can never be regained. That is real nobility."

She took his hand and placed a fragment of cold chained metal into it—a pendant with a design of circles and lines on its face, he felt.

"My mother gave me this on the day Felix came to take me from Reineshir. I thought it was hideous at first. Then when I found out my mother and father left the island, when I received no letter, no messenger, no warning…I cannot now dispense with it. If I am ever to see her again, one of us must now risk the waves of the Daarkan Sea. She won't, I know that for certain—she hates sailing. I would in an instant. But I can't until all of this rebellion foolishness is done and forgotten."

Again, the halfelev wanted to impress her with his speech. As before, his head was thick with exhaustion.

"Morley," she spoke. "Your involvement with the rebels. It was all an accident. Right? You didn't do anything to start it. On purpose. Did you?"

"No," he said. "Wrong place, wrong moment. Wrong words, wrong company. Only thing I did right was leave it all behind before I could be kept. And still yet I think I regret doing so." He tried peering through the dark at Seth. "What's going to happen when we get to Wallenport?"

"If you still wish to join me all the way there, I'm sure I can have a room spared for you two. Normally, you'd be rewarded for your service to me. But I'm not sure if we have any substantial recompense left to offer."

342

There was movement across from them. "I could get you a new sword, a smaller one. Or an axe, a spear. Whatever suits you."

"We'll figure it out when we get there. Perhaps my mother—*our* mother has something nice to offer." As he spoke, he could hear Seth shifting upright, his breath unsteady or absent. "Are ye awake now, archer?" No answer. "I'm still a trifle tired myself. Might as well rest a bit more."

Still, he said nothing. They could feel his air: punctual motions like spasms or nightmare throes. Morley tried to guide his foot over the rails and onto one of Seth's legs without luck.

"Seth. What's wrong?" Then, a brief stillness.

"Where am I?" he said. "What's happened to my hand?"

Chapter X – The Adventure

Ten days after the shadow-jotun took over Castle Sivliére, the survivors from Olford returned.

As per Willian's insistence, Sir Amalic took full control of the rebel infantry and the subdued garrison of Wallenport. His ploy in gaining the guards' cooperation, as Hamm offered, was to convince them of the danger in allowing the defeated continentals back into the city. Allies or not, the Lattamen and Garmites were without a leader—a series of winded couriers announced as much—and they had surely not acquired what Felix promised them before the march: a victory, then the typical spoils.

Further, according to one of Willian's mounted avantgardes, Castle Chaisgott had been encircled by many of the Lattamen. Upon first sighting of the avantgarde, two men amidst the besiegers had begun lobbing arbalest bolts. And their fellow footmen did little more than cheer the pair on. Therefore, as the outrider windedly proposed, these men were now no more than untrustworthy strangers, born-again barbarians.

But after the giant burned down the city's palisade with a tidal wave of fire, none of this was of much concern. Nobody had any inclination to investigate the castle—where the mysterious beast now dwelled—or replace and watch over the cindered wall. Nobody had any inclination to stay on the island, in fact.

Within minutes of the shadow-jotun's sudden arrival, all the populace was scurrying for the docks, overcrowding its piers. All sought to board the mainland cogs. Of course, they would've been long gone if the shores hadn't miraculously frozen over into white blocks of ice. Fervent prayers of salvation thus filled the air.

So, the Westleyans were no longer of any use to anyone. And those who remained in the emptied port city, like Willian and Hamm, could do little more than wait for a conclusion or reflect on their failed plan and broken aspirations—or particularly in the duo's case, debate their next destination.

The long-term success of the rebellion had relied upon Allesande's victory at the Lightrun's ford, which swiftly became a fool's hope as Willian, Amalic, and the few hundred others filed little by little into Wallenport: the grounds between the gate and the edge of the Crouxwood were muddied with thousands of old footprints and wagon tracks, littered with droves of ruined fabric and circles of stone with burnt grass cores. Unless the army from Bienvale purposefully spread its assets over this grand extent in order to seem much bigger—an intricate and unlikely conclusion made by the hertog's son—Allesande and Wortin were in terrible danger. If it hadn't already passed over them.

Then, everything was forgotten. A grossly unexpected new threat came to the port.

Willian could not get away from the image for days and nights after: the monster, its head of flowing pitch and body of flame, rising from the Crouxwood, holding high its talons as it invoked the sun's fire, as it growled lugubrious curse-songs. Over the black field it lumbered, through clouds of stinking soot, all under an undaunted blue sky. With three steps it surmounted the motte's slope, vomiting a torrent of flame until not a spark was left to spew. At that time, its body dispersed into a storm of ash, blanketing the city and the beach with pale flakes. Then, as Hamm later averred, a young man accompanied by three strange creatures emerged from the distant burnt brush of the woodland and ascended the hill. Nobody else could verify this—as nobody else but him watched it all unfold from the roof of an insula house.

Willian, when he first spotted the daemon giant, raced to an old basement beneath a tavern he often frequented in his youth. Once again the stuff of his dreams had crossed into Reality—and violently so, this time.

Like so many others, as he soon found, Willian began to question the consistency of his world, the shared existence of all, the All-Being everyone claimed to praise; and at the end of this inner tirade, he, like so many others, thirsted for a strong cup of ale.

Before dawn on the following morning, in the privacy of The Motte-side Inn's parlor, Willian and Hamm shared a cask they'd secured. By then, and despite constant warnings made by a select few, most of the citizenry had begun their exodus west down the road to Laisroch County; others, more receptive to the consultations, went south along the beach to Debois and Sylvan. Everyone else—that is, a fourth of the Westleyans and an assortment of hopeless and hapless locals—went about their business of stocking up on their neighbors' goods.

"What do you suppose is happening up there?" said Hamm as he tightened his new, though oversized cloak and leaned forward on the table.

"Up where?" Willian replied softly into his hands.

"The keep," said the other. "You know, where the daemon went. Before it disappeared. Where the boy and those beasts went after the smoke faded."

"Daemon," the ridder repeated. "Is that what everyone's calling it now?" He rubbed at his eyes weakly.

"What would you call it? If not 'daemon'?" The squire spoke without inflection or cadence as he glared into his cup.

"I've been partial to 'shadow-jotun.' But names are names. I'm not in charge of them." They both uplifted their tankards.

"Shadow-jotun," the squire repeated. "Isn't that what you called the thing from your dreams? Well, one of your dreams at least. Unless you've seen it more than once?"

Willian nodded. "I've seen it in four dreams to be exact. And they all came to fruition, more or less." He finished his drink and began pouring a sixth. "First, it was rising from out of Chaisgott's courtyard. Then it was crawling through the caves, dragging away young aspirants as they screamed. Then it was floating down the Lightrun, which was then impossibly deep though I stood on its surface. Then, in the last one, it strode out into the ocean, never sinking no matter how far it went. I dreamt that one the night after I left Olford with Amalic."

"Strange," said Hamm after a deep gulp of beer. "What's the word you often use? Perdition—no. Premonition?" Willian nodded again. "You have the gift of premonition."

"Doesn't have much use, if you ask me. Never mind the number of times my nightmares have prepared me for that thing, why would I ever expect to see it in my waking life? Have you ever seen anything as staggeringly unreal as what you saw yesterday?"

"No, I haven't," Hamm said. "I've only listened to Wortin's stories about the Piik Isles. Believed them, too."

"As did I for a time," Willian muttered into his cup. Hamm poured another for himself. "Fables aren't meant to be preparations for the unwieldy. They're meant to infest the imagination. Those're Morley's words, believe it or not." He sighed. "I guess he was telling the truth about the vodniks in Sylvan."

"Did you have any dreams last night?" asked Hamm, as if he missed everything his counterpart had just said.

"No." Before the squire could exclaim his surprise, Willian added, "I didn't sleep whatsoever. Might not be able to until I drink myself into a stupor. That'll be the case for several days hence, I think." This time, Hamm nodded. Willian took a heavy draught and spilled beer on his wool coat. "That reminds me, I never answered your first question."

"I've forgotten it, to be honest."

"You were wondering what's happening up at Castle Sivliére, right?" Hamm buzzed in confirmation. "Do you have any ideas? Imaginings? Anything?" The other said nothing. "Neither do I. But I intend to find out soon enough."

The squire coughed into his tankard. His presence during the infiltration was implicit. "How soon?" he asked, clearing his throat.

Willian finished his sixth beverage. "Once I've drank my fill," he said.

*   *   *

Seven days passed.

They woke together in the vacant house of Hamm's father and sister—both of whom had joined with the southward exiles—then went for a walk by the frayed walls. They heard one of the men near the gate yell for Sir Amalic: a crowd of Bienvalians, all garbed in blue and grey, were advancing eastward along the Crouxwood, barely more than half a kalcubit away.

Hamm and Willian, swathing themselves in their tabards and respective cloaks, thus made for the beach below the castle. Each carried along a sword and a pair of clean carving knives from the tannery. As Willian mentioned a week before, Roberrus had kept in place a portion of the scaffolding for the motte's earthwork as a means of escape or unceremonial reentry; the elevation, though aged into disuse, led up to a clever postern in the castle's buttery.

Hamm was familiar with it, oddly enough. Though he'd never accessed it himself, his sister Enriet had utilized it frequently during her long-term affiliation with Felix. Not knowing what horrors awaited them in the aetheling's courtroom, both men were partial to this approach. And Hamm, excited and unnerved as ever, referenced a tale of Sir Cadmael no less than three times on the march there.

After hopping down from one of the piers and crossing over the glacial shores, they found the hidden entrance and removed its driftwood barricade. Without ease or grace they squeezed through the burrow to the other side, to a crepuscular well of patched sunrays.

A flood of fond memories seeped through the ridder; his companion, meanwhile, was utterly awed by the structure. For so many years, as the squire said, he gazed over the rough rock and the keep above as an immutable image of might, a mark of civilization's power to subsume Nature to its own uses. Now, seeing it from within, seeing it as a shoddy and incomplete mess with no chance of standing for another century, his faith was again swayed. So, minding both the broken and unbroken planks, they scaled the framework, splitting numerous boards beneath them.

They reached the top unharmed and entered a gigantic hollow barrel stuck into the wall. Willian tested its head, pressed his hand smoothly against the unhinged end. To his surprise it creaked open without strain, revealing the cellar beyond: it was far gloomier than the chasm behind them. The brazier stands had all been knocked over and no light shone from the stair opposite them. The big round barrel-door groaned a second time once fully opened. And something large scurried away behind one of the nearby racks, tripping over an out-of-sight brazier and swearing faintly. A strained silence followed.

Willian unsheathed his broadsword slowly and Hamm did the same. Together they stalked into the dark, Hamm throwing a corner of his new cloak over a shoulder, raising the enlarged hood. Once they were midway to the dusky outline of the stairwell, the naked footfalls unhurriedly continued toward the secret entry.

"Is somebody here?" Willian ventured, stopping and holding out an arm in front of his companion. The other steps ceased as well, waiting. "We're two ridders of Hoerlog, we mean no harm." At this, Hamm's head turned; this had to be the first time anyone ever referred to him as a ridder, Willian guessed.

"Right, then," the halfelev said decisively and with moderate volume. "My name is Fitzwillian. I'm the son of Damme Ellemine. I grew up here. I'm acquainted with the aetheling's staff." He hoped this latter statement was still true. Whoever he was talking to probably knew the buttery as the best hiding place in the whole castle. "Curator Arnaul. War-mester Herman. Cato Clerici. I'd say other names, though I don't think they still reside here. You can come out now, we're here to help."

"Maybe it was just a rat," said Hamm.

"There are no rats down here, trust me." Finally, the footfalls resumed without suppression.

"He's right," came the whisper of an older man. "Not one rat has ever been found in here." Around the side of the closest rack, a squat lineament appeared. The figure came closer to them until the paleness of his skin pervaded the cellar's darkness.

"I take it you're the same Fitzwillian who lived two doors down the hall from Damme Ellemine, just above the kitchens?" the man questioned. "I only know this, mind you, because I manage the surveys and records of this plot."

Willian tilted his head. "Chamberlain Ounstadt?" he inquired, putting away his blade.

"Raul," the other murmured. "I replaced Ounstadt two years ago. Poor fellow died of 'swamp-sick,' as they say." Once close enough to the duo, he leaned against one of the few remaining barrels in the rack. Though Willian could hardly see his face, he could tell the man wore the same style of velvety robes that Arnaul was once accustomed to wearing.

"I'll tell you anything you wish to know," he continued, "but not here. I've been trapped in the staffroom for over a week now. Only just got the confidence to sneak out, you might say. But I need to get out of here now—the whole place has gone mad. You won't believe anything I say until it is right before you. And by then, you'll wish you hadn't been so curious—really. If there truly is an All-Being, it has forgotten this land."

"Tell me," Willian demanded quietly.

"Only once you've gotten me—"

"Just make it quick," he said. "I'll even give you a damn knife for your troubles. You'll need it, I'm sure—the city itself isn't much safer now that the continentals are back." Willian removed one of the two skivers from his belt and thrust its hilt into the man's chest.

"Fine. Fine," Raul conceded, almost dropping the weapon. He sighed. "So, the rebellion is over? What's happened to Aetheling Felix?"

"No one knows," Hamm said. "But the Lattamen are on their own. And I doubt they're satisfied with their state of affairs."

"They were routed, then?"

"One can only presume," the squire confessed.

"Mercy," Raul murmured. "This land truly is lost."

Willian grunted at this. Though it sounded to him like a simple-minded assertion, the cynical gripe of a craven, there was a sincerity in the man's voice that plucked a foul note. Indeed, the ridder thought, there is nothing left here for anyone—other than myself.

"Go on," he said. "Tell us what's happened here."

The chamberlain held the knife against his chest with both hands. "Believe me or don't, it makes no difference," he said. "There is a wiccha here. A wiccha and two satyrs. Goat beasts, horrible brutes—like the ones that wander the Piikish archipelago, as some say." He seemingly waited for them to speak out, to scoff at his claim. Neither did so. He continued.

"She called a storm of fire when she first came and burnt away the front doors and every man guarding it. I'd already started retreating to my room by the time she was inside, calling for Ellemine. I looked back down at the court once I reached the second floor. And everyone just watched her, spellbound. Then the satyrs came in. I fled to my quarters and forced its door shut. Once I heard the screams, I knew I'd be trapped there for a long while. Longer than two weeks perhaps." He paused to catch his breath. "She taunted me, that horrid woman. She beckoned me out for days, every time I stepped near the latch. I could hear her in my head." He searched the ridder and the squire again, expecting incredulity. "Today, it finally stopped. I crept out not half an hour past—haven't had much to eat…"

Most surprising to Willian was the fact that he wasn't surprised by the man's account.

"You missed the worst of it, then," said Hamm. "Unless you saw the fire giant burn away the palisade before stepping up the motte."

Raul straightened, ready as ever to leave them. "Is that a jest?" he said.

"Afraid not," Willian verified, treading back from the chamberlain. "I recommend you stay on the strand until nightfall. There's a large tavern near the base of the motte, do you know it?" Raul groaned to himself, evidently knowledgeable of the type of people who once frequented it. "I unlocked the door to its cellar last week. You can find it if you go around the back side, around the empty crab traps there. The bread and cheese might have mold. The smaller boxes on the shelf have dried fish. Just pray the Lattamen haven't cleaned it all out."

"If all else fails," Raul moaned again, "might as well take a boat down the coast."

"Yeah," said Hamm. "If the ocean's thawed out." The chamberlain had no comment to give.

They walked with him over to the open barrel and offered advice for the descent: stick to the edges of each plank and test them at their centers to be sure the next step hasn't broken entirely. Several beats later, they closed the barrel head behind him, then made for the stairs. Neither of them dared make a sound thereafter. As they climbed the steps one by one, weapons drawn and backs to the wall, they listened for the slightest scraping, the subtlest trace of a voice.

Nothing. Not even once they reached the kitchen at the top of the stair.

At first sight of that room, Willian was flushed with a series of reminiscences—some poor, some pleasant. There had been only four cooks when he was a boy: his favorite was Ingomar, a mester of custard and ham, a man who'd traveled thousands of kalcubits from the heart of the continent. Another was Ashien, the later proprietor of the Motte-side Inn, a fair fellow who came to the island during its first conquest. Less favorable here were his memories of scrubbing the crocks and cutting boards as a regular punishment for his disobediences. The lesser ones, that is.

Now, the kitchen was almost as dark as the buttery—and something pungent, like rotten meat with a disconcerting floweriness mixed in, hid from their view. Two of the tables were overturned and the legs of a third had all been snapped off. The overhanging hooks for meats, radishes, and garlic braids had all been unburdened; the hearth at the far end was filled up with untouched, finely bleached logs. Everything else—pots, utensils, bowls, boards, and stools—were strewn over the floors. Willian pinched the latch of the closest door, angling his ear to its hands-width opening.

Just then, a loud series of bangs and rattles sounded out beneath them. Willian pushed the door shut again, peering worriedly at Hamm as the castle quaked, as the littered clayware rumbled at their feet. When it ceased, they breathed their cautious relief.

"Raul," the squire said with a low voice. "The scaffold."

Before Willian could make any remark, another noise came into the outside hall: the clopping of two hooves. The halfelev gestured to the open pantry across from the stairwell. They both ducked inside, striding cautiously over its unhinged door. It took no more than two beats for them to notice that the smell was strongest here—that its source, at the very back of the room, was a pile of stained blankets and rags thrown over a pile of crumpled waste. Willian, too fearful to cast his eyes back over the mass, assumed the worst. As Hamm crouched beside an opened chest of rags and tablecloths, Willian hid beside the door's vacant outline. He placed his head against the edge of the frame, allowing one eye to peek around its corner.

The door to the outer hall inched open. A grotesque hand was clasped over the latch, its gaunt appendages tipped with black blade-sharp nails.

Upon first sight of its snout—nostrils flaring, teeth jutting like a horse's—Willian shifted back around the corner, breathed steadily through his nose. The monstrosities of his nightmares had again breached the curtain of sleep, transcended into Reality without one accessory amiss. Unless it were the contrary: unless he were trapped inside his slumbering mind. Or within an illusion composed by the unnamed wiccha. The thought made him dizzy.

The satyr thumped into the kitchen and issued a contemptible gurgling belch. Willian swallowed air to relieve his twisting stomach. He wanted to run out and kill the bastard chimera, to cut away its hideous head.

Once again, and out of pure impetuosity, he glanced around the corner: the creature was receding down into the buttery, wobbling with one hand against the spiral wall. The tap of its hooves became more and more remote with each step.

"Is it gone?" whispered Hamm.

"For now," the ridder said through partially gritted teeth.

"Was it like my description?" he asked. "And Raul's? Was it some sort of…goat?"

"As far as I could tell." He rubbed his face with his free hand, then beckoned his companion to him. "Let's go before the other shows up."

They left the kitchen for the outer hall, which was by far the only area of the castle still lit up with brazier light. At its end—right outside the kitchen door—another set of stairs led to the upper gallery. They took this route quickly and quietly.

When they reached the grey corridor above, with its five doors on one side and its overlook of the court on the other, Willian was assailed by another string of memories.

One of the oldest images stored at the nadir of his consciousness was of himself, running back and forth down the hall, back and forth between two smiling faces. Roberrus and Ellemine. An extreme rarity, in retrospect—perhaps that too was dreamed.

Two other memories located him at opposite sides of the hall. In one, he stood on a footstool, watching over one of Roberrus' raucous feasts with strange long-haired men; in the other, he stretched for the handle of his mother's bedroom door, yet unable to reach it, whimpering like a newborn bird.

There were other pictures, other senses, the provocations of which were conditioned by the weather, the time of year—other such arbitrations. Whenever it rained and water seeped down the stone walls, it dried into a rich flavored scent of sediment. On clear or cloudy days this was often coupled with the laugh of gulls. Now everything was unnaturally cold, as if Frysa were only just beginning instead of ending.

There was a door within arm's reach. Willian toyed with the whim of opening it, the portal to his old bedroom. Quite a reminder. It was on a day similar to this one. He and Alherde, dismissed from Curator Arnaul's lessons early, thought to bide their remaining afternoon in the young man's chamber. They'd had too few chances to speak ever since the mutual confession: meeting and walking along the beach was out, as Alherde always tracked sand back into his father's house, and the tavern was too public even when they secured the private parlor. A finer opportunity was unforeseeable, they agreed. Not long after they blocked the door and drew the baldachin, they heard a servant knock.

They both heard it. But their affections—and effectively, their attentions—were doubly consumed by the ardor of freedom. One day, one careless adventure. One rich rumor. It was no wonder Roberrus wanted him out of the castle and out of the county so quickly, out where nobody could see him. And at least, Willian now thought, he had been noble enough to repurpose Alherde. The Bertrisses needed a seneschal and tutor, and Roberrus needed an extra set of eyes on them. He had the perfect man for the job. But the other, Fitzwillian the Fatherless—no, he had to stay on the sightless coast. Sir Wortin would set him right.

Already, Willian knew: he would not be leaving this place. Or otherwise he would never return again.

"Willian," Hamm murmured near the window to the court. "You hear that? Someone just came in." Sure enough, a young woman's shouting voice echoed up to them. Hamm crouched by the window's ledge, pulled down his hood. Closer and closer the voice came, as though the speaker were marching from the furthest end to the aetheling's chair. The words were elucidated by the time Willian reached the overlook.

Earlier, he had envisaged the doors to be unhinged and burnt coal-black, splayed across the floors. In truth, they were stretched and obliterated along the length of the hall as long irregular shadows, blasted into the stone and scarring the walls. The entry was now a naked archway. And through it the young woman had come.

She bustled on to the center of the hall, where a cone hut was curiously situated. The material of this structure was oddly recognizable, the ridder thought: it had a fanciful doorpost—a feature unbecoming of such a wild misplaced design—which he swore was composed of the legs of Roberrus' feasting table. The whole hut, in fact, was made up of finely sawn strips of scrubbed wood. Closer to their end of the court, where the aetheling's chair was commonly positioned, there was an accumulation of abused décor, from the embroideries of his parents' room to the once hanging scutum shields of the lower hall.

"Did you hear me?!" shouted the young woman below, now blocked from view by the hut. A figure ducked out from under its low inscrutable truss. Another woman. The one from his dreams, the one he met in Egainshir. The bald halfelev.

Who else would it have been, Willian thought, what would have truly surprised me? This was probably how Morley felt when they met outside his hill-house. Unamused. Apathetic. Perhaps even distantly perplexed.

"Yes, I did," the dream woman responded—or so Willian heard. Her voice was low and of a bland tired tone. She was still garbed in her superfluous pelts but now bore a staff with a forked end. She leaned into the support exhaustedly. "What of it?" she asked, louder.

"What of it?!" the other yelled. "You burned away the front door— what're you going to do when they realize everyone is gone? Are your stupid goats going to protect us?!" She appeared around the side of the hut: she wore trousers and a ripped-up cloak. "Look at you! Your face is sagging, wrinkling—you look like bloody Sjaman. And you can barely stand—what have you done?"

Slouching forward on her staff, the dream woman mumbled a few unheard words: names, a list of things, it seemed. The other gave an exasperated huff. "That's not what I meant, you know that's not what I meant." The dream woman chuckled at this. Another satyr lurched into the light of the open entrance far ahead, a hornless silhouette dragging a heavy strip of metal behind it.

"It is almost over now," the fur-laden wiccha wheezed. "I am stronger than I look. You will see soon."

The other woman was speechless, still as a statue. "What are you doing to yourself?" she said, quieter in her advance but still audible. "Why are we

still here in this place? There's nothing here, you've looked everywhere."
She now stood by the dream woman, who muttered a few words up to her.
Willian nudged Hamm with the tip of his boot. He tried to move his lips to
'What did she say?' but the squire only stared dumbly back.

"I've told you," said the short-haired woman, still with a low voice,
"she would've showed herself by now." Then they were both silent, fixed
on each other. This went on until the woman in trousers broke away,
pacing back around the hut. "Stop that," she growled, loud enough for all
to hear. "You look like a crone when you do that."

"She is here still, Yeva," the wiccha called out. "That sense you feel
when I reach out to your thoughts. I have been hearing it all this time. If it
is only a trick of hers, then she means to keep us here for a reason." The
one called Yeva scoffed. Such a familiar name, Willian thought, a pair of
syllables he'd undoubtedly heard together in passing.

"So that when the soldiers come back from wherever they've been,
they can take the castle back and kill you! Why would she show herself to
us willingly, look at what you've done to her home! You're not ev—"

"This is not her home!" the wiccha tried to cry out. Her voice failed
then and led into a moderate coughing fit, during which she gagged and
spat. By the end of it, she seemed fifty years older. "I will show her our
true home."

"And what're you going to do about the men below?! They'll start
marching up the hill soon—are you going to kill them all, one by one?!"

"Birgir and Signy will be enough for them," the wiccha answered.
"They need only spread the entrails of five men or more, hang their bodies
over the entrance."

Yeva, standing motionless at the center of the courtroom, did not
speak. Hamm then poked at the ridder beside him, pointed to his own ear,
then down the hall: hoof-falls. Both panicked, breaking indiscreetly away
from the window and scuttling for one of the niched doors. They each
took one, waited. As the steps came closer, Willian tried the latch behind
him—the door to Ellemine's room, he recalled. Locked.

Then, he halted. Upon noting the progression of the hoofbeats, he
glimpsed out of the alcove: they were not heavy, nor were they bipedal as
before. A shadowy head formed at the head of the stairs, a horned head. A
small grey-white beast.

It was Morley's goat. Geat. He waited at the top step, watching the
both of them. Willian separated from his niche and Hamm followed suite,

casting a befuddled glance over his companion. The ridder turned to the overlook: the young woman called Yeva, still at the midpoint of the grand hall, was squatting down with her head buried in her arms. The wiccha was nowhere in sight.

"How long did you think it would take?" came a voice in his head.

He whirled around. The wiccha's face stared at him from the center of Ellemine's door, her skin and flesh as wooden as the board surrounding it.

Hamm barked in surprise and stumbled backward onto the hard floor; Geat investigated without urgency. Willian went cold with fear and dropped his sword. The wiccha pushed through the obstruction, her naked body creaking as it passed through the oak, as it oozed back to its creamy paleness, glistening like a newborn infant's. Once the wiccha's entire body was through the door, staff and all, she faltered, swayed breathily in place with a haunting grimace. Her furry clothing followed her from under the door—slithering across the floor as rags, snaking up her legs and covering over her emaciated frame again. Within three eyeblinks her garb was renewed, draped amply over her.

"I heard you both treading over the sands and climbing the castle's bowels," she said. "'Wiccha,' that man called me, that lonely survivor. I will miss him."

Before she was finished, Hamm drew his sword and jerked up to his feet. Willian, dumb with fear and disbelief, watched the squire as he lunged for the woman, as she raised her staff and jabbed the young man's throat. Hamm's shortsword flew from his hand, singing as it struck the wall and floorboards. He lay where he had first tumbled down, rubbing his neck as Geat sniffed at his hair and cloak. Beyond them, the satyr who descended into the buttery was shambling up the steps. Willian paled as the creature lurched toward them, its horrid udders and tassels swaying like mangled excess skin.

"Signy," said the wiccha, "take them down to my sister."

The monster snatched up Hamm by his hood. Then, dragging him along without struggle, it approached Willian, who made no motion of resistance as the beast wrapped its claws firmly about his lower neck and pulled him effortlessly along. It towed them back to the stairwell as both Geat and the wiccha waited in place, watching them go.

So this is how it will end, the ridder thought, eaten or gutted or tortured to death by a devil. If the terrors that plagued his sleeping mind were good for anything, it was preparing him for this doom.

I am ready, he realized.

The men shared no words as their captor hauled them roughly down to the lower gallery and out into the singed court. They were dropped to the ash-covered stones. The girl called Yeva stepped over, her eyes irritated and red. She examined them both in turn from where she stood, then leaned closer over Hamm. Something in the movements of her face—the scrunching of her brow, maybe, or the way her mouth began to gape— suggested a previous encounter.

Beats later, the wiccha rose out of the ground nearby, this time with her clothes still encumbering her small body. Her legs buckled and she adjusted her stave, using it to buttress herself upright. The satyr she called 'Signy' came to her, holding out its forearm as an offering of support. The wiccha swiped at it. A silent tormenting moment of inactivity followed as Morley's goat rejoined them.

"Who are you?" Willian finally managed to say through the surreal hush.

The woman turned to him with some struggle. "I thought you would ask me in that village we first met in," she answered, then coughed breathily into her hand. "Were you too alarmed? I know the other man was, the one with the same face as our younger brother. He did not have yours, though. But you knew him all the same. I will guess he was your mentor once, back when you lived here in this castle. For he once resided here as well. A servant to Mother Ellemine, an intelligent friend. A lover once, I think. Am I wrong?" The ridder continued staring at her in stark disbelief. "Of course not. The connections have become so easy to make of late."

Now, Willian thought, he absolutely knew how Morley felt when they met again in Werplaus.

"So," she continued, "now that I know who you are for certain, would you care to tell me your name?" The ridder heard her say the words, though they were all bereft of their meanings. "You do not have to tell me, I can find out on my own. But it is an unsavory method. And hearing you speak will save us both from fatigue. What is your name?"

"Willian," he stated. The girl called Yeva snapped her head in his direction. She had likely heard the name before; 'Yeva' was itself familiar, after all.

"Who was your father, Willian?" the wiccha asked.

"Roberrus Sivliére," he lied. There were shouts of panic outside. The second satyr guarding the front entrance picked up its weapon and scampered out of sight down the motte's gravel path beyond.

"Are you sure of that?" Her tone suggested she was better informed than he'd hoped. Or worse, she could see through him, sniff out the truth like a hunting hound. "I know his face well enough. He came to our home twice." She gestured to Yeva, who turned away. "I do not see him in you, not at all. His life was of fair consequence. If it were not for him, Ellemine would have lived in perpetual peace. And I would have lived with her, the only daughter of the purekin. The Wiccha of Sarcovy."

She leaned reflectively into the prongs of her stave. Willian clambered to his feet. Hamm did the same and the satyr nearby growled at them both. Yeva left them all for the hut.

"Who are you?" the ridder asked again.

"My name is Feofan," the bald woman said, "though you may know that already." Willian shook his head. "No, I guess not. I have gone by many names throughout my life. And 'Feofan' is the gentlest of them." She shut her eyes and touched her face with one hand.

"What do you want?" Willian spoke. "Why are you doing this—whatever you're doing?"

"I am doing what I was born to do," she moaned, "what Ellemine wished of me when she spread her legs and forced me from her body." She glared stiffly at Willian, forcing him to step back. "Now it is my turn. What do *you* want? Why were *you* born?"

"I..." the man started, unsure of how to continue.

"You did not know your father. Why is that? Did he not want you, did he conceive you out of hate? Mother wanted you—why else did she keep you around? Her first son? Boy of an evil ridder." Her face curled suddenly in anguish as she spoke the words. "She saw something in you. She knew she could use you, but how? Felix had a purpose, though it was pointless in the end. Even our youngest brother had one, from what I have heard. But I do not always believe what people say when I listen, when I float above them and invade their discussions. Sometimes it is the stuff of dreams that I see and hear." She held her head again. "What did she see in you?" the woman whispered, possibly to herself. "What was your purpose?"

"I didn't have one," the ridder murmured. "My life is an accident. The result of an evil deed."

The wiccha tried to straighten her back with a cringe. "Was I ever in your dreams?" she spoke. Willian's heart sank into a pool of viscous dread. "You were in mine, though not so often. Not as often as Felix." Another discomforting pause. "Well? I asked you a question."

"Yes," he said. "Every single one as far as I can remember." Feofan seemed both unsurprised and disturbed. "Why? Why are you there—why have you been haunting me?"

She ambled closer to him. "I have not been haunting you," she said. "Not at will, at least. What do I do? In your dreams, I mean." Willian shook his head again: her nightmare visage didn't do anything at all besides watch him, follow him into the morning. He was unsure of how to say such. "I remember seeing you once. You were amidst the hills of this island, the high ones to the west. You ran from me but could not escape. Then I felt I was not myself, not even one person. And I did not know who I was. I was everyone *you* have ever known. Following you and watching you. Have you ever had a dream like that?"

"Many times, yes." The detail was almost correct: he was always with Alherde when the crowd showed up.

Subduedly, Feofan hacked into her hand. "Have you ever seen me kill Felix?" she asked. "In the horse stalls beside this place?"

"No," he said. "But you sicced a ball of fire on him. And it chased him down the motte."

"He is dead now," she said, and Willian's heart quavered. "Or so I assume. Viggdis and Signy went to find him after I ended the battle at the creek. Signy returned to me without Viggdis or Felix in her company. So yes. I do think they are both dead and gone."

The ridder recalled the last moments he spent with his half-brother before being sent off to Hoerlog: Felix was five and ten years old at the time and didn't act as though he knew Willian was leaving for good. The boy merely asked his sibling where he was off to. And before the stripling ridder could give a reply, one of the scullions passed by with clean linens at hand. Felix stalked her out of the court and Willian left without bidding anyone else farewell.

"So that was your goal, was it?" said Hamm.

"To kill the Aetheling of Sarcovy?" Feofan sneered at the squire. "No. I do not care about aethelings and ridders, I do not care about Sarcovy or the northward continent. I do not even care about you or any of my half-brothers. I only want my mother. And my sister. And I want everyone else to leave us be, else I will purge them from this unnamed land."

She started for the rubbish pile at the end of the courtroom, hobbling like an elder. Signy followed her close, ready to catch her if she fell. Once she neared the back side of her hut, she bent over a plain sack crumpled against the woodwork and pulled out a flat box—the one she carried into Semhren's house. She checked its insides with a shaky hand then stored it away again. Willian knew, with a sudden curious instinct, that the case had something to do with the shadow-jotun, the warped wood, the frozen shoreline, the satyrs...

"Where are you going?" Yeva said from inside the hut. Both were blocked from view, but there was frantic hushed muttering on the other side. This ended with the satyr's growl.

Hamm prodded at Willian's arm. "What do we do now?" the squire asked.

"Whatever we want," his mate replied. "I don't think we're of any concern to them." He glanced back at the open entrance: the other satyr was returning to its post there, dragging its blade across the turf. "That loud racket we heard below the kitchens..." Willian said, probing his friend's face.

"I was thinking the same thing," he replied. "Raul. He broke some of the scaffolds."

"Yes."

"Any other posterns out of here?" said Hamm.

"No. But we truly do need to get out of this place. I don't know what this wiccha intends to do, but this castle may not be standing by the end of the day." Hamm made a questioning face. "The town's foundations have been here since the first landing, since the first day the Biens came to these shores. By the time Roberrus claimed all the island for their kingdom, there were already walls, some roads, several neighborhoods. But the castle took years and years to build, twice as long as the harbor and thrice as long as the church. Though I was only an infant, I remember seeing the scaffolds before the hill was formed. In a way, this is only half a motte, a hill leaning against a face of weak eroded rock with an open chasm in between."

Before he could conclude his explanation, a squat blur at the corner of his eye provoked him to turn: Geat was watching them as the girl called Yeva rubbed her knuckles between his horns.

"Where did you find that goat?" he said to her abruptly.

"He found me," she muttered without facing him. "He came back for…his best friend. But it was too late, as Feofan said, so I took him. I don't trust anyone else to watch over him." She placed her brow against the goat's.

"He belonged to my half-brother," he said. The woman looked to him. "At least, I think. I haven't seen many other goats with horns like hi—"

"Morley," she said over him. "You're talking about Morley."

Willian bowed his head. "Did you say he—"

"He was alive the last time I saw him, but my sister—*his* sister—and yours…" She seemed to lose her point.

"Yes, it's, ehm…" he tried. "All very strange, I know." They stared at one another, acquainting themselves with the stuffy air of kinship about them. "What happened to him? My—*our* half-brother?"

"We left him outside the big castle over the Crouxwood. She said he would be safer there." Hamm wandered to the hut to inspect its alien design. When neither Willian nor Yeva continued speaking, he voiced his interest.

"What is this here? This shed thing." Yeva left Geat and the gentle awkward beast plodded over to the solitary ridder.

"When Feofan and I were young," she explained, stepping over to him, "she was ordered by her old mentor to go up into the mountains and live alone for a season and practice what she'd been taught. She did for a while but, once she taught herself how to leave her body, she flew back down to the village and forced me to come join her. It was horrible. Terrifying. Even after I saw it was only her. I helped her make a hut—it wasn't as nice as this one, but she hadn't yet learned how to break and rebuild things in her special way. Afterwards, she made me stay for the rest of the season. Kept turning into a spirit, too. She'd visit each of the villagers and demand them to bring food to a certain height. And make them swear not to let Sjaman find out." She sighed, seating herself against the back side of the structure, next to the sack. "I can't say why she bothered to build another right here. Mayhaps she was trying to convince me she's still the same."

"Why did you come to this island?" Willian asked. Hamm sat down next to the woman as she pulled up a sleeve: on her forearm was a scar the shape of a feather.

"I was chosen by the dancers. They would sail from Mavros during the hot season and bring all sorts of people with them. False shamans, conquerors, thieves. I guess they're all thieves when you think about it.

361

Feofan used to say that." She concealed her arm. "They discovered I'm her sister, a perfect sacrifice. They marked me as I descended her hill one morning. When Sjaman found the brand they gave me, he didn't know how fresh it was. He thought Feofan already agreed to the ritual. So, the next night, he brought me to one of their boats—didn't tell me why or what we were doing—and then we left. We came here to Sarcovy, made a house in the swamp. Then he let me go when I wanted to live in Egainshir."

Willian felt urged to embrace Yeva, this girl with whom he suddenly shared so much. In a way, this 'Sjaman' was her Wortin, Feofan her Alherde. And Morley was shared between them almost perfectly—a brother left behind. She glanced up at him with watery eyes. And he was then committed to his impulse, taking a single step forward.

"Who was your true father?" she said. He ceased his movement. Hamm looked to his companion with fearfully knitted brows. Perhaps he was afraid to be disappointed, Willian thought.

"I don't know," he answered. "But Roberrus raised me as his own until…" He could not bring himself to mention his lost Alherde. "Until he no longer needed me. What about you? Your father and Feofan's?"

"A fisherman named Savuer. He told me once that Ellemine had called him to her across all those leagues of ocean, but I think he was just lost at sea. He happened upon Sarcovy, the barren shore, the glade where Reineshir now stands." She bit at a fingernail. "He also told me that Ellemine warned him of the coming Bienvalians after their time together. And she begged him to take my sister away to his home. Somehow, they made it back to Kamenin. I was born about ten years later. My mother—she was called Yeva too—died right after."

The court was quiet then. Outside, the other satyr hunched down, feeling the length of its weapon with a grotesque hand. Willian thought of Morley, of how the men of Chaisgott were treating him; then, he wondered what had become of the ring-keep itself. If all the Lattamen had to march past it in order to reach Wallenport, did they find time to break open its gate, to storm inside, to plunder all the unvalued trash thrown about its inner courtyard?

Was there any hope left for this place, any reason to leave or stay within the eye of the storm? What was stopping him from taking up the skivers he still carried, from advancing on that new guardian of the castle—besides, of course, certain death? But as he noted earlier, the potential for death was hardly lesser if he stayed right where he was. And so, just as it was with Alherde and all their shared affections, all the dangers at the heel of their pleasure, Willian knew well that misfortune awaited him at the end of his many trails.

"My father's name was Kabb," Hamm chimed in. Willian and Yeva stared at him. "He dyes leather and makes shoes for a living. Made a fair sum from it over the years."

They waited for him to continue. He scratched at his neck.

A thunderclap shook the castle.

Chapter XI – Wallenport

"A swift-quick sit-down," Seth panted. "It's all I ask fer."

"Just to the top," Morley reminded him once again. "Just to the top."

With blistered feet and sore knees, the trio out of Chaisgott mounted the tall hill above the northern coast. A huge column of cut rock stood at its grassy scalp. From there they could see all of Wallenport below. Its incinerated walls, its frozen shore and dozens of broken ships, its scorched motte, its littered waste, its yet-bustling populace—all of whom lugged crates, barrels, and sacks into the streets.

"Sanct's Bones," Anae breathed. "I'm too late."

Morley eased Seth to the ground beside the abstruse pillar; the latter had been the first to lose his will to continue on, or so he confessed with a joke about his toes falling off. He now rested his eyes and cradled his severed fingers. Anae, countless times throughout their journey, had proposed he was sick with a fever. Seth, on the other hand, rejected this with an assortment of excuses.

"What is that?" Morley piped up tiredly, pointing to the pale white shoreline. It looked like a short bluff covered over with ice. Anae sunk to her hands and knees, heaving her breath as though all the exertion of the past three days finally caught up with her.

"What is this?" she breathed. "What's happened here? Burnt earth, ice…" She continuously shook her head. "The damned shore is frozen solid—it's frozen. This is madness."

As the word left her mouth, the head of the castle's tower exploded into swirling seaweed-green flames. The turret's stones flew through the air, each trailing a sickly smoke, smashing through the roof of the court or down onto the humbler houses beside the motte. A haze lingered over the faceless tower and, above it, the weak ceiling of clouds curdled into umbral fumes—the same shadows that seeped off the jotun's head. As the fog faded, Morley could see a single figure atop the high turret. A cloaked shape with a walking stick in its raised hands.

Anae stood back up, speechless.

The sky above the ships soon blackened into the same miasmal smoke—or rather, from the headless tower, it flooded forth and clotted the already thickened air. Then, with a random precision, eight gaping maws formed within the cloud mass, eight black pits in the heavens, each floating above one of the seaward cogs. And from each of these holes, there descended ten or more bright tethers, tendrils of rose-colored flame that writhed down like fern sprouts, every one of them unfurling as they reached for the hulls of the marooned ships. Synchronously, the fire-fingers navigated all about the vessels: some snaked across the broadsides, some wrapped themselves about the masts, others yet dipped below deck, scavenging down into the cogs' empty guts. As the ocean behind the white stage of snowless ice began to roil and crash against the ships, the centers of three stuck cogs exuded heavy fumes. Oily flames dripped and slid across the shallow waters beneath them.

By then, the waters beyond were flowing over the surface of the ice, directing the now unrestrained smaller ships—fishing vessels and the like—into the continuing surge. This flood, as the moments passed unbidden, swelled and frothed, sometimes sidling into the rootlike tendrils and coughing the steam of their flagrant tips.

Once the waters were streaming fast over the beach and the crooked piers, a fishing ship rammed into the side of one of the burning cogs, its bowsprit piercing the ember wound. It was followed by several of the other small boats—of which there were seven, as far as Morley could tell through the rising smoke—all of them crashing against the occluded sides of their larger cousins.

Soon enough, the waterline was nothing more than a mangled smoldering wall of hulls, burning masts, and the sourceless limbs of a daemon god. The flames spread quick all across this ruined barricade as the tendrils tightened their grip. A quarter of the supposed citizenry was crowding by the edges of the docklands, ducking away whenever a new wave broke over the jetties and down the streets; the rest, all men and all bearing heavy luggage, fled west toward the Crouxwood.

Morley then caught the visage of Anae, trampling and sliding down their hill toward the dismantled wall and the motte's steps.

"Anae!" he cried out. "Wait! Where are you going?!" She did not reply. Morley reeled back to his friend at the pillar. "Seth!" he called. "Seth, get up!" The young man did not move, as expected, but opened his eyes and peered at the chaos ahead. He turned his head away, shut his eyes again.

"I can't," he said. "I simply can't." The halfelev glanced back down at Anae: she had already reached the rocky base of their hill. The choice was made. "Go on without me," Seth mumbled. "I'll meet ye in the mornin', somewhere."

Morley charged after her, flying deftly down the slope, ignoring the sores under his feet. By the time he reached the bottom, Anae was struggling over the hedge of crisp timber that once served as the city's only bulwark. The cobbled street beneath and before it was submerged in a nail's length of cold salty water. It streamed between the rounded stones and pooled along the distant curbside. There, a heavier torrent flowed from the direction of the church and the sea, carrying an assortment of ragged unidentifiable oddments out of the city. A large group of men struggled down this stream, each with various goods underarm or overhead.

"What are you doing?" he wheezed at Anae, slouching down and wincing over the fallen logs. Anae swung her head back: her face reminded him of the stone man in the courtyard of Chaisgott, the one above the jotun's pit. Her eyes were dark and furious, like Yeva's after a provocation—her hair was rumpled with knots, like Allesande's during her tirade. While lost in these images, Anae finally removed her beaten shoes and threw them away, progressing over the blackened splinters.

"Wait! Please, wait!" he called, stumbling on. Once over the demolished wall and into the road's endless puddle, Anae made straight for the castle's hill.

At its twentieth step, three quarters of the way to the top, she again fell to her knees. Morley halted two steps behind her. They were surrounded on all sides by bundles of forgotten clothes and other gear, loads of materials probably left behind by those who retreated from the castle...

Or, as Morley quickly noticed, the sprawled leavings *were* those who retreated from the castle. He sprinted up to Anae.

"They're dead," she stated with a firm plainness to her voice. "These men are all dead."

There were less than thirty of them but all were spread out, their cloaks splayed about the steps as though someone had dragged them down from the keep. Blood dripped across the few exposed faces and hands; their weapons, all drawn and some still held, were unstained. Anae, as Morley presumed, had tripped over the cold arm of an arbalester, his weapon a mere foot's length out of his reach, still cranked and loaded.

"W-who are they?" he asked, gagging as he caught sight of an open wound across one man's belly. "Did you—did you know any of them?"

"They're...they're..." she muttered, shaking her head. "No. I've never..."

366

Led in by a chorus of panicked shouts, another powerful din shook the earth beneath them. Morley, spotting its origin, snatched Anae by an arm and hauled her up: a tidal wave had smashed into the docklands, carrying with it the line of broken ships, directed still by the strings of flame. Tiny men fled around the courtyard of the church—some even ducked inside—and the foremost deluge swept the rest away toward the western egress. Together, the largest of the ships battered a path through fisheries, homes, workshops, and warehouses—all the way up to the city's heart, where the once cumbersome wave had already decayed into dozens of nimble, frothing streams.

As several of the fishing ships continued on past the church and broke into irreparable rafts against the insulae's facades or along the castle's artificial slope, the burning cogs—all barely keeping afloat over their separate districts—each overturned onto the drowned clusters of buildings beneath them. Steam burst from these sinking, breaking hulls as their guiding tethers snapped and fizzed, crackling thousands of golden sparks and ebbing back into the heavens. By the time their heat had fully dissipated, most of the water was spilling beyond the city limits, seeping down to the Crouxwood as shorter, gentler waves continued coursing down the lanes and alleys.

Morley and Anae, nearer the final steps of Castle Sivliére, again collapsed to the pebbled ground. From there the halfelev assayed the destruction below: the broken, sunken port, the fantastical ruin of Sarcovy's regime. He wondered, how long would it take for this incredible circumstance to become known, then fabliaux, then outdated truth?

"What's happening to us, Morley?" said the young woman beside him. "Why is this happening?" The lad shifted closer and wrapped his arms about her. "What is this spell we're under—this awful nightmare? Why can't I wake from it? I feel so sick."

She buried her face in Morley's tunic. Though she did not weep, she began to ramble and shake against the soiled garment. The lad placed a hand against the back of her head and gazed back over Wallenport, a vaporous boneyard of flotsam and jetsam, ocean detritus, the carcasses of once proud crafts and, at the center of it all, the largely unharmed church. How lucky for the latter, Morley thought.

Behind them came the huffing of a horse. Morley did not attend it; he hadn't embraced Anae since their first day in the tunnel and, ever since, he wanted nothing more than to hold her close and comfort her. She had

367

nothing left, he realized. Her home was now a wasteland more harrowing than the flats of Werplaus or the dreaded slime-fen of Sylvan. Where could she go—and how could she get there? Perhaps Allesande would take her in at Michelhal. Perhaps Alherde would let her return to her father's manor in Reineshir. Perhaps she could be persuaded to stay in Egainshir...

"Anae," he whispered without complete intent. The horse nearby grunted again, this time closer, few paces up the motte from where they sat. Morley twisted to examine the beast: it stood upright on two fur-matted legs and had a worn cloak clasped about its shoulders, between which was a head like a goat's, its teeth protruding and its horns sawn short.

It wasn't a horse, obviously, but a satyr. If Yeva's description bore any truth.

And it wielded a claymore in one hand.

*   *   *

The youngest of all Egainshir's residents was Robi, the son of Tommas and Serryl. He was tough, yet tiny and fragile. For the most part, Fitzmorley knew toughness to be a fine quality in people: Tommas was patient when dealing with a splinter or sore and Serryl could spend hours out in the cold without so much as shivering.

Robi's toughness was peculiar. It was more agitating than admirable. He reminded Fitzmorley of the man who came to Gale's house, the supposed ridder called Darry. The child was prone to using provocative words and, when those failed to stir any emotion in his opponents, he settled with thoughtless actions.

When Fitzmorley first arrived in Egainshir, he was the only person the child targeted. One day, barely a year after he was taken in, he sat alone with his goats—since named Minny and Geat as per Ceridwen's insistence. As he straddled their fencing, he suddenly felt a blunt jab against his outer thigh. Snapping his head to the source, he saw that it was Robi, armed with a kindling stick. When their eyes met, the boy couched his weapon in both arms and lunged it at Fitzmorley's head. He dodged, swiping it patiently away with the back of his hand.

"I challenge you, Fizz!" the younger boy exclaimed, holding the stick as if it were a heavy club.

"Why?" Fitzmorley countered. "First of all, I don't want to fight you. Second of all, it's pronounced like 'Fits.' Third of all, I—" Before he could finish, Robi made a lateral swing. Nearly toppling from the fence post, Fitzmorley hopped down inside the pen.

"Will you quit it?" he tried, a phrase Tommas once used to calm the boy down. Robi stabbed at him again. "Please?" The word never worked in this situation, but it was worth a try.

When Robi made another slash, Fitzmorley caught the stick by its end and pulled it away. The younger boy watched in pretend shock as his adversary gripped the stick with both hands, snapped them in halves, then quarters, then tossed them into the mud by Minny's hooves.

"Run! Run!" the child cried, charging back to his parents' hovel and the lean-to where all the hamlet's firewood was kept. Fitzmorley shook his head without amusement and returned to his seat on the sturdy bars.

Sitting in silence this time, he could hear Robi as he raced back. He had a much larger bough at hand, the branchlets of which were untrimmed.

"Put it down, Robi," Fitzmorley demanded before the child had reached him. "I'm serious this time."

The boy rushed onward, gripping his weapon as high overhead as he could. Fitzmorley hopped down and waited, his frustrations simmering as his attacker bounded closer. Finally, once at proximity, Robi swung downward. Fitzmorley sidestepped as the bough thudded down against the fence.

"You're done, Fizz!"

The halfelev's thoughts spoke to him through gritting teeth.

No more.

In a flash, Fitzmorley clutched the end of the unmoved stick and shoved it into Robi's chest, pushing him to the ground. His messy long hair fell away from his eyes and face, which bore a genuine look of surprise bordering on brief trauma. After a few silent beats, the boy clambered up, his face curdling in anguish, and he fled with a whine, calling for Ceridwen. Both of his parents were preoccupied outside the hamlet.

Still new to the place, still immensely timid of the people around him, Fitzmorley regretted the action. Again he resumed sitting on the fence, debating with himself: go find the boy and apologize, compensating with a game that didn't involve pretend swords, or wait out the inevitable consequences.

The best possible result followed moments after. Elmaen limped over to him, walking staff at hand, beard swaying in the breeze. He had been the one to take Fitzmorley in, both as an inhabitant of Egainshir and a resident of his house, granting him a cozy niche beside his fireplace. He was the oldest man in the hamlet and possibly all of Werplaus.

"I was hoping you'd do that," he grumbled with a toothy smile. "The kid needs a bit of a kicking sometimes. Isn't so right for someone my age to do it—might kill him." He laughed breathily. "Tommas and Serryl will understand, don't worry. And I'll vouch for you anyway." The elder then hobbled off, humming a song.

As it would later turn out, he was right. Robi told his father of Fitzmorley's roughness as soon as he returned from the Crouxwood. And Tommas said nothing more than, "He'd never do such a thing unless ye deserved it, boy."

*　　　*　　　*

Without reaction, Morley parted from Anae and stood up, advanced to the next step of the motte. The monster before them went as far as the edge of the earthen landing, where it drove the claymore's point into the ground beside it, blocking the path forward. Morley's heart galloped. His hands, squeezed into fists, began to tremble.

"That isn't your sword," he said, more to himself. He heard Anae behind him, scurrying up to her feet in alarm. "That," he tried, louder and through barred teeth, "isn't your sword."

At the penultimate tier, the satyr removed and stuck out the blade, its tip half an ell from the Morley's heart. He heard a muffled cry from Anae, then his name—shouted pleadingly.

The halfelev kept his eyes on the beast, then wrapped his hand around the topmost edge of the blade before him. His scar, nearly forgotten, tickled. The satyr made a face: it reminded him of Geat's whenever someone rubbed at the back of his neck. It then began to extend the sword forward, even closer to the lad's torso. But Morley kept his hand in place. His lip quivered as he felt the skin opening, gushing warm blood down the metal strip. Its point scratched at his chest through the threads of his shirt. Anae called his name again and, judging by the monster's wandering flat-pupiled eye, Morley knew she was mounting the platformed stairs behind him.

The satyr made another push and Morley stepped back. Anae gasped. By the length of a fingertip, the blade tip had entered his chest. It stung in its slight movements, tingled wherever the blood beads drizzled. He clinched his other hand along the downward edge, immediately feeling the flesh tear. But by then, the pain was all commensurate. They stared.

Then, between the beast's legs, Morley spotted a figure bounding out from the open entrance to the keep. And he leapt aside.

The satyr was shoved forward as Geat butted against the monster's haunches, stabbing its thigh with a horn. Before Morley could make a run for its clawed hand and the hilt of the claymore, the satyr swung around, dislodging the tip and slicing at the open air as if it expected a full-grown man to be standing behind. Geat continued charging around in wide circles, faster and faster. Morley, taking a cue from his lifelong friend, threw himself forward and butted against the satyr's other haunch. This time, though, it snorted and reached down with its free hand, grasping Morley by his shirt—ripping it with the terrible claws—and throwing him onward to the castle's opening.

He rolled several paces on impact and landed on his back. In trying to scramble up, he slapped his hands down on the dead turf, forgetting about the open bleeding cuts across his palms. He collapsed forward onto his elbows. Geat, in the meantime, raced cunningly around the satyr as it chopped and jabbed, hissing.

A figure stepped out of the court: it was Hamm, the squire from Hoerlog, gawking dumbly at the dueling goats. Stranger yet, he wore Seth's unmistakable black cloak. And behind him, the halfelev felt the presence of another.

"As I live and breathe," came Willian's voice.

Morley straightened up and clambered to his feet; and two burly hands helped him up. It was indeed his half-brother, wearing the long liripipe and an exhausted face. With a pat on the arm, he glanced at the satyr. "We're in it now, brother."

He strode forward with the squire, a dagger in his hand. "Hamm, stay as close to its back as you can—I'll stay in front. And watch out for the goat." The squire looked over at his companion, frightened and partly confused, then drew out his own dagger. Before Morley could join the duo, someone grappled onto him from behind. A somewhat slender comfortable frame.

"Don't do it," Yeva said. "Not as you are." She hauled him over to the stone frame of the castle's vacant entryway. "Wait here," she ordered before running off around the closest corner, toward the overlook of drowned Wallenport. Disobediently, Morley moved to join the armed pair closer by, wiping his bloody hands on the sides of his trousers. None of them could get within three strides of the beast, as it repeatedly swung the greatsword in long impervious arcs.

"I'll get around the side of it," Morley announced to the others. Closer to the edge of the motte's summit, he spotted Geat, now planted further down the steps in front of Anae.

"Don't get too close!" Willian bellowed. "You're unarmed!"

"We all might as well be!" Hamm replied, holding out his knife. Soon enough, the trio was spaced all around the satyr, Morley taking the steps between it and Anae; Hamm and Willian were positioned above. And yet, despite the soundness of their placement, none could get within eight paces of the creature, as it frantically slashed all around itself. Only once could Willian get within reach of the steel: he cantered sidelong toward the satyr while the claymore's tip was pointed fleetingly at Morley but, right as he was preparing to lunge, the monster pivoted, the strong of the greatsword striking Willian's shoulder and his feeble shivering weapon. He backed away and Hamm moved up—only to be held at bay yet again.

Suddenly, Anae, having ascended to Morley's height, grabbed him and pulled him off the gravel. A bolt flew over them and punched into the satyr's back, pinning its ugly garment to its spine. It snarled and bent forward to the ridder, who took his chance to strike. Instead of countering with the sword, though, the creature seized Willian's wrists with one hand and yanked him about, with the claymore directed at the squire. After his weapon fell away from him, Willian was flung over to Hamm, who immediately offered his spare dagger as he helped the man to his feet. The satyr progressed upon them. Geat charged again, bucking his horned head into the back of the beast's knee. Morley got to his feet and helped Anae to hers. As he did so, he saw another man climbing the stair.

"Seth," he blurted. His friend was slouching tiredly with an arbalest in his arms. He tossed the mechanism away and casually sat down. "Seth?" Morley said again.

"There," Seth murmured. "I got up."

The satyr screeched. Above its arrow wound, the haft of a pitchfork dangled loosely—then fell away, head and all. Yeva was opposite the ridder and the squire, plucking a second pitchfork from out of the ground and holding it over her shoulder, ready to throw. The beast turned and stomped to her, hissing, its head lowered like a stalking cat's. As Yeva brought down her weapon defensively, Willian dove for his dropped blade. Yet again he sprinted for the satyr's back, Hamm following behind—and yet again the satyr whirled around, swinging the blade. This time, Willian ducked under its sidewise cut, stumbling to his hands and knees right below the monster. He plunged the knife into its abdomen. The satyr yelped again and the ridder fled through the gap between its legs. As it batted the ground before Hamm and Geat, frustrated and uneasy, Yeva moved up and jammed the pitchfork into its tailbone, then pulled it out. The creature spun, Geat took his advantage—and so on.

Without warning, as the others continued their fight, Anae stood and rushed for the keep's entrance. Morley made a grab for her, barking her name as he pushed himself to his feet. He watched her dodge behind Willian as he sliced into his enemy's haunch—then she disappeared into the bleak interior. By the time Morley reached the top step, the satyr had resumed its maddened thrashing. The fighters procedurally distanced themselves.

Not long after, failing to prop its body up with Gale's sword, the beast exhausted itself and fell abruptly forward, squirming slowly and helplessly on its belly. The claymore's hilt rattled down within a stride of Morley's foot.

Hesitantly, as if he feared the habitation of some cursed taint within the steel, the halfelev placed a bleeding hand on the crossguard. He glanced up: the satyr's head hung off the topmost stair, its tongue obtruding over its crooked teeth and its eyes unfocused, one half-closed. Further ahead, Willian and Hamm, both breathless, watched him with blatant unease. The latter tossed away his dagger and bent over; the former nodded darkly to his half-brother. Yeva, on the other hand, was no longer present.

Morley heaved the sword up. Forgetting its weight, he staggered back. Geat ventured to his side and Seth joined them.

"I wouldn't do it," said the archer, his mouth dry and voice low. "When I first went off on a hunt, I wouldn't do it. Kept making that face, it did. Made me sick." He sat back down clumsily, cross-legged. The satyr shut both its eyes but continued to breath. "I think it's almost done now. Can't ye hear it?"

"Hear what?" Morley asked, knowing the answer would be no less cryptic.

"The shouting, the echoes?" he mumbled. "Women, it sounds like."

As he spoke these words, Morley heard tense voices emanating from inside the court. They were cut off by a shriek—much like the satyr's though of a higher pitch. The halfelev stared over their downed adversary, into the open castle. Though they were both scant contours, he could see Yeva squeezing Anae's upper arm, holding her in place as she thrashed and kicked. Two other shapes were present, one of regular size, the other of a height and form comparable to the beast's.

Morley moved forward. Inside, Yeva wrenched Anae away, leading her back to the open door as the second satyr marched after them. And the furthest shade glowed orange. And fulminated into an unreal misted fire.

It expanded, churning into a storm of sick purple, enveloping the whole of the courtroom. Right as Yeva and Anae made their escape, the flames consumed their bestial pursuer and spurted over them, licking the entry's massive stone frame, roaring like ceaseless thunder. Everyone fled from the stinging heat. Anae and Hamm both cried out in agony; Seth yelped and sprang up.

The fire soon dissipated. And revealed the jotun, cramped under the timber ceiling of the castle, moaning with its clawed hands against the confining walls. It attempted to crawl forward through the inferno.

The roof collapsed over it and the outer stonework shimmered. A haze boiled the air around them. Its draped head halted before the crumbling portal. And a face like a pyre, a womanly mirage, furious and afraid, glowed through the curtain of searing amethyst. Then dripped away into smoking globules of petrified stone.

And the world blazed into blind white.

Chapter XII – The Culmination

I've died, haven't I?

"No."

It was Ellemine's voice, clear as the mid-mornings of Hetta. Though she was not before or behind, above, below, or at either side of his invisible body, she was there in the silver-white glow. He was inside an orb of reflective metal, it seemed. And somewhere, a smaller orb of plain light floated around him. Black specks like inverse constellations appeared and disappeared under the roving radiations, like sunlight manipulated by a convoy of flowing clouds.

Where am I, then?

"You would not comprehend it if I told you. All I will say is that you are safe here with me. You and all the others."

A memory bloomed in him then, an image he had never seen in wakened life. This then brought forth a storm of other memories—some entirely known to him, some altered, and most as foreign as the lands across the sea. But the stem of it all was clear still…

A colorful grove, apple trees and grapevines and bunches of red-eyed berries, women draped in white himations all plucking the delicate leaves, all smiling, beckoning the bright world. And Ellemine watched them all.

There was a tingling below her stomach. Four shades came into her mind, a girl and three boys, their beginnings conflicting with their ends.

A boy, unloved even before birth, who wanted nothing more than to love all others.

Another boy whose future held the profoundest promise, whose life was surrendered in accordance with personal prophecy.

A girl who sought to rise above Reality, succeeded, and, when there was nowhere left to go, fell away from her triumph.

And the last boy, the youngest of them all: did he know what he wanted most? If he did, would he go after it all on his own? So much trouble would come of his desired course. And of his undesired course, so much misery.

What is all of this you're showing me?

"I am not showing it to you," came Ellemine's voice again. She strode through the floor of mist, Morley felt. She continued: "Or perhaps I am. I have brought you here, after all. But what you see is what you wish to see, is it not? You may have forgotten it all, though you still wish to see it."

I don't know what it is I'm seeing. It's a paradise, I think. But I can feel things through it. I know things without pictures and words.

A girl stood on a dock of stone, watching a barge as it was pulled upriver. Then she was in a harbor—the familiar stench of salt and slippery fish—and she was watching a ship unfurl its sails and waft away. Over these memories were imposed the signets of Excitement and Dread.

"Yes," said Ellemine. "Their truth is the clearest you will ever know, I am sorry to say. But even so, it will be impossible for you to know exactly what this truth foretells, what it follows from."

Why show me? Why now?

Three children sat along a crick. The smallest stepped into the water, frightened. As the two others spoke their big words, the youngest splashed them, laughing. And the largest entered the stream after him, lifted the youth over his head and spun him until his joy ached. The seated one spoke: "Don't do nothin' bad, boy. 'Less ye know ye can get away with it." Their mother used to say those words.

"It is not my choice to show you what you see, as I mentioned." Ellemine raised a hand: a pattern of dots overhead was conjoined by vibrating strings. It resembled a sequence from one of Mester Semhren's maps, the chart of stars and their navigation. It was called Synesti. "The only choice I made was to save the few lives I thought worth saving. The lives of my children. And their companions. My power permits this, among other things." She was in front of him now. And she was completely formed of silver, like liquid steel come to life. "Do you want me to show you?"

There was a simmering bay at the island's northmost corner. Few treetops waded over it, still abiding the winds, and the inland slopes of the coastal cliffs dipped their toes into its gaping runnels. A church poked its triple-apsed head over the surface, as did the necks of ship masts, their ragged shawls hanging about their timbered shoulders, floating gently along with the debris below. All of it was so recognizable—even the lone sea stack and the mountain of stone, wood, and earth hugging its one side.

Wallenport, he thought. Its remains.

And you say I'm not dead?

"You are not dead."

A boy sat at his father's table in the dark. His sister, sick with a Hosten cold, rested in a niched room within the boy's reach. His father rambled by the window. To himself? To the boy? It didn't matter at the time, as his son listened nearby, clutching his belly. "He's going back to the Piiks again, I'll bet. As if he didn't slaughter enough of those folk last year—or the year before. Won't stop any time soon, I'm sure. Ehhh, shouldn't leave the field for the sea, she said. And I did, didn't I? Shouldn't leave for a piece of Roberrus' land. Madman." Then he lifted the stewpot's lid and dipped a bowl into the tepid water. The boy took it to his sister.

How is that possible? Did you carry us?

"In a sense," she said, "I did. Is it really so unbelievable to you, after all you have seen? The drowned giant, the destruction of the port? Your sister's second aspect?"

My sister...

The man's turf and the hump of grass. And the land was so wide, so long. There were many strange creatures inhabiting it, small, large. And though he was safe with the others, safe behind the chewing wood, a beast stalked the land. They saw it before, walking in the black. But now it was safe, safe with the food-udder and the grass and the excitable others. He saw Fitzmorley, the little boy, sitting at the hilltop.

Who is she?

A vicious rainstorm battered the girls' mountain hut. They could hear the water dripping in rapid streams down through the uncanvassed roof— but this was all outside the blanket, under which the sisters huddled close, unspeaking. She was so young, so afraid of the older girl, like a stranger. How long had she been out here? Almost two seasons? She could only bear one season alone before sending her grey spirit back down to the village, demanding her sibling to leave the cozy stead of their earliest days and venture up, up, and up further. As another snap of lightning and thunder shook them and their breaking house, the eldest squeezed the girl tight: "I love you so much," she whispered. "Really, I do. Don't ever forget that, no matter what happens to us."

Ellemine, still statuesque and argentine, swept through the aether wisps. "I am afraid you know her as little more than a titan. The 'jotun,' as you called it, that creature who came to the Lightrun, who obliterated the castle and its motte. You and all your other siblings felt her before she showed herself at the battle, for she drew from your individual spirits so as to end the fighting. She is very good at her art. But far too careless. Indeed, before I brought you all here, she too was in the embrace of death."

Two young men sat behind the stables, watching their home city against the shifting leviathan of the ocean, a moon-kissed surface like ebony under candlelight. The bay-haired one touched the other's hand, slid his fingers underneath the palm. They tried to gaze into each other through the shadows. No luck. A head rested against a shoulder—the steady pace of breath. "We need to be careful," said the blonde lad, "or else we're not going to last long in this place." The other replied: "Then we'll be careful. I promise you." The first boy spoke again: "The All-Being will have no mercy on us. They say it isn't the natural way." And the other replied: "I'll give the celestial bastard three days to show me why love isn't natural."

Why would I want to see any of this? I hardly know what it is I'm seeing.

"Then what would you prefer to see?"

Anae watched his approach through the brush south of Reineshir. Gale pointed up to the buzzards flocking over the horizon and called it 'a dance before dinner.' Yeva smiled during their walk with Geat and Minny. Anae touched Felix's face as he wept and sputtered, his nose dripping. Seth walked into the Crouxwood with Feofan, a bald-headed woman with reindeer fur. Anae slept against his chest in the gazebo behind her manor.

I don't know. Maybe I don't want to see anything. Not now, anyway.

"We are outside of time, my son. You can see as much as you wish within certain limits."

The woman and her three satyrs had a long-decked rowboat they had taken from the villagers. The ocean was still one day—so still they could see a marlin swimming under them. Signy raised a spear and was stopped quick by the woman. They waited for it to get closer. Feofan had been chewing brownleaf all morning, waiting for this precise opportunity. When the time came, she placed her hand barely above the surface of the water. A cloud of hot steam roared around them and the boat trembled. Later, the marlin was too big to bring on board, so they cut it into their desired chunks, seared them over a ball of flame, and ate. Twenty more days until they reached Sarcovy. Hopefully the anodynes could last her until she found Sjaman.

What limits?

A thousand faces blinked before him.

"The limits of what one person knows. Or the limits of what a hundred people know. Or a thousand people or tens of thousands. Despite what one might think, people do not yearn for material, for wealth and comfort and all its cousins. Their meanings dwell in the open crypt of our experience. People yearn for feeling. Think of the culmination. A thousand truths, a thousand-fold Reality presented to you outside of time. What more could you want?"

Fitzmorley's third year was almost upon him. He stood at the top of Gale's hill-house, staring out north at the slight rise of land—a hairy endless patch of bushes. How many doves fly under those branches, he thought, how many goats chew at their trunks? Gale came up beside him, having finished his work with the garden below. "What do you see?" he said. The man had never before asked him a question. So, the boy didn't answer—he didn't know what an 'answer' was, or a 'question.' He hardly knew how to speak, in fact. He stared up at Gale. Then one of the old goats belched. "Tha-that a goat," he replied.

You said the others are here with us now. Do they know about this? Have you offered it to them?

"I can show them if you wish. I will leave that choice up to you, my son."

A swirling and colorless eye opened before him and burned away the black constellations of Synesti and Haem. Something mingled in its beatific core—more images, perhaps, or a living being. It waited for him to decide, he felt.

Why me?

"I must ask you, what will you do after I have freed you?"

The eye was closer, its heart yet obscured.

Return home. I live in the hill-house. I live undisturbed and disturb no one.

More moving images, their figures leaving traces as thick as the aether mist, the unburdened and willful ephemerae.

Anae, as she strode into a cloistered garden, a dining room for the gathered gentry, was welcomed by shocked and frozen faces. The man at the head of his square table stood.

A wolf stepped close to the bottom entrance of the hill, its head low and eyes focused—and the goat watched from atop the loft, ready for a last fight.

A finely adorned older man rode his horse through the Crouxwood— he looked like Seth if he rubbed his hair with ash and fashioned it with a comb—but his ride was short-lived as the steed reared and flung its rider head-first onto the ground.

Hamm, after a week in the highlands, was ready to head back to Westley; but an arrow skipped clumsily along the ground near his feet and a man behind called and pointed up the slope to a dim childlike figure receding into a hollow.

In a colorful and crowded town, Willian found a man who sold lavender—but before he could request a trade, his friend called him over to a side street where a much older man sat alone. The figure pulled down his hood fondly.

Yeva remembered Sieger suggesting they return to Olford, where his brother had somehow gathered more men to assist with the renovations. She had no intention of leaving Egainshir but knew she could be convinced—no, certainly not.

Another boat landed over another shore: the passengers, two women of significant appearance, abandoned it and headed for the untrodden paths into the mountains, where the disciplines would be etched anew into the younger's mind, where she could meet her potential, the nature of her art.

Morley walked to Gale's house with Geat by his side—and someone, he could hear, was following close behind. A faerie barefooted tread.

"I believe it," said Ellemine as darkness settled. "This is only for you. You, my son, who always carried such purpose in your heart. Even when all seemed lost." A dull open blackness hung over him. "I will be with you still. As I always have been. I promise."

"I suppose this is goodbye, then," he said aloud. A coolness brushed through his hair.

"Did you hear that?" came a girl's voice. "He's awake!"

*   *   *

The gold piece sat numbly in Morley's twice-scarred hand. He traced the squashed markings on its face—the profile of a man with a robed torso and a face like a crude charcoal drawing, above which was the word 'Hugon' and the numeral 'IV.' It weighed more than it did when he last carried it. Or he had become minutely weaker.

He wondered first if there were any others in the entire world with an identical imprint, perfect in its imperfections. Then he wondered if there were anyone else on the island who had but one gold piece, similar or dissimilar to his own. Probably someone in Westley. If anyone of notable wealth still resided there, that is. Everyone else felt it, or so they said: without its incumbents, its ridders and its earls and its aetheling and all his retinue, Sarcovy Isle was a tree without its limbs, without its salient bark. It was a gold aureon without its oddly contrived depictions. He put the lonesome coin back into his trousers.

Quite wisely, Yeva had taken it off his unconscious body just after the clash at the Lightrun and the arrival of her sister—allegedly *his* sister as well; but when she awoke after the complete destruction of Wallenport, she found it squeezed in her clenched fist, its insignia imprinted into the skin of her palm. And she found herself and all the others resting on a forest floor with little purple-petaled clusters of lilies sprouting around them—glories-of-the-snow, they were called. She claimed she was the third to wake, the first being Feofan and the second Geat. The goat had slumped down on Seth, waking him, then moved over to Morley and did the same. But the lad stayed asleep for four more days.

Yeva said nothing more about the instant of her awakening, to Morley's fleeting discontent. Nothing at all. Not one mention of their sister, Feofan. She was with her mother, he knew, somewhere. He abstained the detail, yet unsure of its truth. Or yet unsure of how Yeva would react.

With Geat at his side, Morley rested against a slanted elm, facing away from 'New Wallen' as the seven of them had begun to call it. Its builders and dwellers had not yet given it a name. They were all of mixed origins: some still donned their burnt blue wrappings and others were dressed in simpler, greyer clothes, largely the older men and more than half of the women and young girls. Otherwise, a select few were covered over with pelts, as if they had already been living as wilders for years now.

As far as they could see, there were no hovels or huts as of yet, but a series of broken deserted shacks and one expansive pavilion built up of brambles, rope, and cloth, an open-air shelter that stood only two heads higher than Morley himself. The twelve-legged canopy, bordered with stones like a makeshift firepit, was situated from end to end within a flat glade, around which a long fence was being erected.

It was considered a temporary abode, some said, a place to stay until Westley's condition was made clear, though each week saw a fair number of departees, trios and tetrads of impatient elders led forth by a generous, albeit aimless Lattaman. Others yet expressed no interest in leaving the fair pavilion, at least not until they could secure a means of getting off the island entirely. Morley quietly wished them luck and kept the notion of Werplaus to himself.

The seven of them had been in New Wallen for nearly two weeks. They'd reached a simple agreement to leave on the tenth day and head southwest for the road to Olford.

Hamm, however, would be traveling elsewhere. As he and Willian had discussed with Hanz—one of the settlement's four overseers—the aspirant youths, the 'survivors' of the attack on The Stead, were still inhabiting the highlands, or so it was rumored by the men of the Jotun Cave sometime before Felix's march out of the city. Many of the women in New Wallen supported this, claiming their sons and younger brothers never returned home after the start of the rebellion. Thus, it was decided: a search party would set out to find and bring them back to the relative safety of the Crouxwood, to the comfort of their families' arms. Morley wondered, staring up through the foliage, if the expedition had already left.

"There you are," came Hamm's voice. The goat raised his head and the halfelev leaned around the trunk—straining the bandage wrapped about his chest. The squire's face was bright; without Seth's cloak, he was dressed in plain sodden threads much like Morley's own. A bag was strapped across his chest. "Was looking about for you and the others. I'd hoped you would be with Yeva and Seth. You know where they are?"

"Hunting," he replied, sitting back against the tree as Hamm rounded it. "I think. That's what I heard from Willian." Silence fell. Hamm's cheerful glow began to darken. Morley gradually became aware of his own countenance: a somber, almost pallid languish. "Are you leaving, then?" he asked, slightly louder so as to remedy the discomfort.

"In an hour or so. Think those two will be back by then?" The halfelev shrugged.

Ever since he'd woken, he felt a profound sadness clotting within his heart. For a short time he tried to resist it, tried to gaze thankfully over his friends and siblings. But there was something he saw in the lost mist of images. A set of unconnected premises or portents. Yes, 'portent' was the right word, he decided. A collective of truths, some incongruent with the present procession of time.

"Are you feeling unwell?" Hamm said. "You woke days after the rest of us. And both Damme Anae and Willian seem concerned."

It occurred to Morley then that Hamm had never seen him in a pleasant state: when they first met and ventured to Westley together, the thought of Anae's rejection was still fresh on his mind; when they crossed paths a second time, right outside Castle Sivliére, they'd started a fight with a goat daemon. If there ever were a chance to try and rectify this pattern, it had to be now. Half-reluctant and partially nervous, the halfelev stood. He took up the greatsword, which he had been sitting over, and Geat stood with a groan.

"Have you said goodbye to either of them yet?" Morley questioned.

"I said it to Anae, yes. Lovely young woman, I hope she makes it back home soon." At this, Morley's heart sank. Anae hadn't made clear her plans or intentions for the future since he woke. Rather, she took to flavoring their discussions with the sweetness of retrospection. "But anyhow, I haven't seen Willian yet. Was thinking he'd be present to see us off, but I haven't seen him at all today."

"Let's seek him out, then," Morley proposed.

He rested the flat of the blade on his shoulder and the three of them set off over the fresh tufts of grass, minding the bunched snowdrops and a broad patch of immature hyacinths. Three young girls in the distance stopped picking the flowers for a moment to watch them go by. As Hamm stared back at them, Morley sifted about for something to say, anything that could dissolve his pretense of displeasure. If it really *were* a pretense. Before anything came to mind, Geat broke the silence with a belch and Hamm successively spoke up.

"Been through much since Westley?" he asked. It took Morley several beats to figure out what he meant.

"I'd say so," he said. "An unexpected adventure, if you could call it that. Or misadventure."

"How's that?" They stepped beyond the glade. A line of men and women carrying bundles of sticks marched by unattentively.

"How's what?" Morley eventually replied.

"How was it all a mere misadventure? You got out of it alive, no? Unhurt for the most part? And the things you saw before it was over…How many other people in this world have seen what you've seen? Daemons, obliterated cities—"

"I have no idea what other people often see," he murmured morosely. "I've never been across the sea, you know. I've been all around this island—one of the dullest places in all the world as I've been told. For all I know, fire-tentacle storms could be commonplace in Triume. Jotuns might be as easily found as an innhouse and good-mannered goat daemons might walk the streets of a hundred cities." At this, Geat grunted. A group of men were chopping logs somewhere nearby, as he could hear.

"I've never been off the island either, you know," said Hamm. "But I'm very sure none of those are typical. Before, the strangest sight I'd ever encountered was a big black shadow swimming below the cliffs of Hoerlog. Then it got to a certain spot where the waters were roughened and an army of fishes flapped out of the water. That went on for a few minutes. And after that, about two years later, there was the day at Michelhal. That was a strange one, for certain. I'd never seen a dead body until then. And I'm still not sure *why* there were dead bodies—I mean, why they had to be. Never mind." They walked on. A sustained creaking echoed through the wood, then a shout of "Watch!" and a soft splintered crash. "Have you ever seen anything as bewildering as that shadow-jotun? The thing that destroyed Castle Sivliére?"

"Yes," Morley said. "When I was a child in Werplaus, I saw a silver wolf." He immediately realized how silly the response sounded, but Hamm waited for him to say more. "I didn't know there were other living beings in the world up until that moment. I thought there was only me, Gale—he was the man who raised me—and the goats we kept. Gale went and got his sword, this one here." He knocked on the pommel and was very briefly set off-balance.

"Nothing else happened," he went on. "The wolf just went away, left us alone. That was it." He shook his head. "I remembered this when I went back there for the first time in years—this was before I left to see Reineshir for the first time, just last Hetta. I went to find old goods to sell to the traders there. Couldn't bring myself to take the place apart, couldn't find anything of great value but our old books, a helm, and his sword— which I kept. As you can see. Then later that day Anae saw me with the blade all sheathed up. And she chose to approach me. I continued my visits to Reineshir for a year after, just so I could be with her. Then Felix came about and…"

He quietened. To continue speaking would be to divulge everything that transpired over the past two seasons: the joys and sorrows, the fears and furies. It could all be done quickly, of course, as was the case for all stories. But could he resist the inevitable digressions? The claws of the vodniks, the flames flowing through Olford, the bones beneath Chaisgott.

"What were we talking about?" he asked Hamm. The squire pursed his lips. Geat belched again.

"Something about the shadow-jotun," he said. "But never mind that. What were you saying?"

Morley cleared his throat. "Have you ever seen a water goblin?"

They circled the pavilion for just over a half-hour. By the time the lad reached the part of his story concerning Willian's revelation outside Gale's house, the ridder himself appeared before them. He too was dressed in haggard clothes, part of which was once the upper section of his tabard. He carried two hefty wedges of wood underarm, freshly sawn.

"I heard you're going with Gavfred and the others into the highlands," he said, dropping the heavy chunks and amicably knuckling Geat's head. "Did you change your mind? I saw them gathering up closer to the road, over where they cut the first trees."

"I'm on my way there now," said the squire. "Went to say my farewell to Morley here and got caught up. Sounds as if he's seen both the worst and best of it, eh? What did I do? Sat around in a cave and a castle, stole a cloak. Did my fair share of daemon-fighting when the occasion called for it. Meanwhile, it sounds to me like Morley's seen it all. As if the world offered itself to him."

Morley gulped. Somehow, after telling Hamm of everything that excited or troubled him through the last half-year, he'd left the story open to interpretation. For whatever reason, the squire seemed to think the misadventure—or adventure—was all an improvised tall tale, a fiction worth fitting into *Chevaliers of Bienvale* or some work of greater absurdity.

"You'll be back in Westley, I assume?" said Willian to Hamm.

"I imagine so," the squire answered. "Who knows what's happened there after the Lightrun incident. It's like the whole island is buried in a fog. Maybe Allesande survived and made it back—maybe the same goes for Wortin. Who was next after those two? Next in line for the rule of Westley, I mean. It isn't Sieger, is it?"

"Worried nobody will be left to officially anoint you as a ridder?" Willian chuckled. "You know, in the old days, ridderstaat was passed on in patrimony. It wasn't duplicated as it is today by the ruler or his stewards."

"What's the use?" the squire replied, much to Morley's surprise. "I first swore my vassalage to Michel Laisroch and Felix Sivliére, then Damme Allesande once she took over. Where are any of them now? Michel ran off back to the continent, back to his family's old estate. If Allesande made it back to Westley, she's little more than the lone baroness of Michelhal—or Allehal, as she'd probably call it. And wherever Felix is now, he's as powerless as a clam. Who's left? Hertog Pourtmann? What use is he now that the aetheling and all his earls are gone, eh?" The two halfelevs exchanged blank glances.

"Y'know," he went on, "I'll bet I'm the only squire left on this entire island. And something about that idea is very pleasing to me. I could go on with being called The Squire—and all my notes could enlarge the 'T' and the 'S'. The Squire. Charming, yeah?" The brothers looked to each other again.

"Indeed it is, Hamm," Willian said. The Squire snorted a laugh and adjusted the bag across his back.

"Care to join me for a last walk?" he requested, turning toward the unseen road. With a nod, Willian adjusted his two wedges of wood and headed off with Hamm at his side. "Take care, Morley!" the young man called over his shoulder. "Until we meet again!"

Morley waved back, profoundly unsure—as always—of how to say farewell.

Once the pair was hidden by the pines, he and Geat set out to find Anae. Since his recounting of her departure from Reineshir earlier in the hour, the urge to check on her festered. Worse yet, he was reminded of his dream from the night before: a manifold vision of her life with Felix. Surely she had forgotten him already, Morley prayed.

With the help of the flower-pickers he'd passed earlier, he found her sitting alone against the moss-soft face of a boulder, trying her best to weave three viable branchlets into a wreath or crown. He heard her struggles before rounding the side of the rock; at first sight of her, one of the sticks sprang out of place and flicked her on the wrist.

"No, no, wait," she said hurriedly, "I'm not done ye—" She peered up. "Oh. It's just you." Morley twitched a side of his mouth into a fractious simper. Anae was dressed in the likeness of the New Wallen folk, with a threadbare gown and a trimmed shawl of reindeer fur.

"I was going to show the girls there how noble ladies wear their hair during Skonhet festivals," she said, "but I forgot I've never had to make my own wreath. And I never watched my handmaid back in Oxhead while she made them." She examined the mess at hand. "You, eh—you wouldn't happen to—"

"I'll give it a try," Morley proposed, sitting down beside her. Geat roamed forward into a grouping of bushes, sniffing at their various low-hanging leaves. Morley took the twined sticks from Anae and turned them over. "Maybe you need another one in here. And this one looks a bit too thick to twist easily. Where did you get the sticks?" The young woman pointed outward arbitrarily and rubbed her face with her other hand.

"Most of the ones I found on the ground snapped in two, so I started wrenching them from the branches. But I don't have a knife or anything sharp, so it's hard to break them off." She sighed. "The girls probably know how to do it without struggle. But I sent them off to get the flower petals for me and, well, I haven't seen them. Perhaps they forgot or found something else to distract them."

Morley recalled the girls' pile of purple and white flowers, and how they so quietly delivered him to Anae's hiding spot. If anything, he thought, they knew of her tedium but chose graciously not to embarrass her. They were likely watching them now.

"We could make one that's especially large," he said. "Then give it to Geat." This elicited a giggle from her.

They listened to the breeze: it had great character, he thought, like air fostered only by the earth, its favorite cousin, all throughout its intransient life. Anae rested her head on Morley's shoulder. He forced himself not to gulp, focused on the surprising softness of her fur shawl. She seemed much happier than he would've originally expected.

"What's on your mind, Anae?" he asked. She did not speak. "I mean, are you contented at all? So much has happened over these few weeks. And I feel as though everyone has forgotten about...y'know. Everything."

She moved away from his shoulder. "I think we're trying our best not to speak of it," she said, "lest we lose our minds to the madness of it all." A mockingbird sang above them and they listened for a moment. "Why do you ask? I suppose it was especially strange for you, country boy. Living with Ellemine over the past half-year, I think I was more prepared for the sight of monsters and fire from the clouds." Morley pondered this implication, then chose to save his questions for later.

"Did she prepare you for life in the wilderness, though?" he asked.

"Reineshir was enough preparation for that."

"And yet you chose to stay in Wallenport when I came for you." He had conceived of the statement as a jest, but a stifling quiet followed. "Staying out in the woodlands wouldn't have been so bad after all, see?"

"You didn't think that plan through, Morley." Her tone had fallen into vacancy.

"I didn't think I had to," he countered moderately. "You loved the chevalier tales as much as I did, or you claimed to. I thought only of the excitement. Hiding away from the ridders on the road, hunting and scavenging for supper. I never would've expected you to fall in love with the evil aetheling."

"He wasn't evil," she said sternly.

"I know, but I just meant—"

"Far from it," she pushed. "He was actually very gentle. Sensitive. He was hurt by the disapproval of his subjects. The lordship wasn't right for him, he was nothing like his father." Morley hummed his displeasure.

"So, I guess you really were in love with him, then," he said, lowering his voice.

Anae scoffed. "It should be of no concern to you. Especially not now. He came and took me away from Reineshir, away from that awful house, from my mester and my relentless mother."

"He took you away from me," Morley said.

They were silent again. Somewhere behind the obscuring shrubbery, Geat tugged at the trees' drooping needle clusters.

"I'm sorry," he soon followed. "You'd warned me enough times, you tried to prepare me. And I couldn't accept it no matter how many times the truth was repeated to me."

The young woman beside him crossed her arms. "He wasn't evil," she said again. "Despite everything I said of him before I left for Wallenport. I thought he would be a storybook aetheling—cruel, desirous, unfeeling, implacable. But he was generous and kind, he only wanted to make ridders of the little folk. You should know, you were there at one of the feasts."

He thought of the expensive display and the conversation he'd overheard in the upstairs hall just after ducking out of the courtroom.

"Fine, fine. I trust you," Morley resolved for Anae's sake.

The only interaction between the two unheeding brothers was charged by Felix's compliments. And indeed, the feasts he hosted, regardless of any controversy, did well in getting him recruits for whatever endeavors he'd planned. Endeavors that dwindled and blinked out before they were even remotely close to their fruition. Thus, another inkling came to mind.

"But," he began, "how do you justify the rebellion against him? All the lives lost for his security?" Anae scoffed a second time, spitting her breath as though it were thick with a rancid poison.

"Why don't *you* tell *me*?!" she demanded. "You were much closer to it than I was. Sanct's Bones, you were there at the Lightrun, weren't you? Why don't you tell me about their war cries and their speeches? All-Being above, what kind of ridiculous insistence is that?! For all I know, you're the only one left around here who can say *anything* about why the Westleyans chose to defy my husband." The mockingbird resumed its playful singing.

"Tell me something, Morley," she said quietly, "and be honest. Why did you go to Westley after I left you on the beach? What was your goal and what came of it?"

The halfelev sighed. She would never believe him, he thought. "I only wanted to see if it was true. That Michel Laisroch is my father. But someone else...tried to use me as a tool for a righteous uprising. It had something to do with Felix's campaign against the Piiks or the Taliorans or some other people—I don't remember the name anymore. None of it mattered near the end. Some wiccha with her own vengeful intent swept through and put an end to everyone's squabbles. For the time being." He sighed, already regretting his petty spite. The breeze brushed through their hair. It bore the pungency of the wakened trees.

"Everyone thinks they're doing the truest good, I suppose," he went on. "Maybe everyone's really doing evil, especially when they assume the role of an aetheling or earl. Like Allesande. Her intentions and beliefs were all muddled near the end, take my word for it. I'm sure Felix faced the same problem here and there."

"Nobody is truly evil," Anae murmured. "Except for the goat beasts. And that fire daemon." Morley tilted his head: she very well could've been wrong in this assumption. "Felix was just paranoid, even before we were married. And Allesande didn't help her people much in challenging him, pressing him to stand down and give up the plans that he put so much effort into." She sniffed and shook her head. Then, she stood up.

"I believe you, Morley, I don't think you meant to help Allesande or any of her brood—no offense to Hamm or Willian. But you have some thinking to do." She started back for the glade. Morley got up and leaned meekly against the boulder. Geat trotted over.

"What do you mean?" he called after her. "Thinking about what?"

"About why you're still jealous of your dead half-brother," she answered without so much as a glance back. "For one thing."

He spotted the three flower-pickers then, fleeing away from behind several trees nearby. Ashamedly, he sat back down. She had finally accepted Felix's death. Or otherwise, it had somehow been proven to her. For a while he sat with Geat. And did precisely what Anae had insisted of him.

Yeva, Seth, and the other hunters returned at sundown with four dead reindeer in tow. The carcasses were left with a pair of butchers in a secluded nook of the forest, where the meat was prepared for a late-night roasting. Elsewhere, closer to the pavilion, cooking fires were built up.

Morley found Seth alone by the edge of the hyacinths, polishing his crossbow with a cloth he had drenched in some dark oil and wrapped about his maimed hand. He faced away from the bright sun, the light of which drifted through the trees like a translucent yellow frock. The archer—or arbalester, as he now preferred upon hearing the elaborate name—grinned earnestly up at his dear friend.

"Good Sir Fitzmorley," he said. "I hear Hamm left a few hours back. Shame I didn't see him off." Morley settled beside his mate. "Guess we'll see the lad one of these days, knowin' our luck. Mayhaps make a little trip out to visit Sieger and such. If he's still there, that is."

"You remember my words in the tunnel, then?" During their escape from Chaisgott, the halfelev had mentioned Sieger's disappearance from Olford just before the battle.

"I do. Hard to forget words of my family's whereabouts, y'know." He paused for a moment. "I remember a lot of things now—things I'd never remember unless I was reminded by...well, reminded by myself." He rubbed his nose with a sniff. "I've heard it said that a dying man's life is shown to him just before he falls. I saw mine well enough, as did Yeva and the squire."

This was not the first time Seth referenced the silver dreamscape. However, his idea of it was far detached from Morley's. And Yeva's, Willian's, Anae's, all the others'. Seth seemed to think, simply enough, that the men of New Wallen had miraculously appeared before the motte collapsed under the crumbling castle and its imprisoned titan. Hamm had challenged him for an explanation: the arbalester could only conclude that their rescuers were fleeing from the deluge below, then happened upon the seven of them—or eight, as Morley knew.

For whatever reason that Seth could not rightly uphold, the altruistic Lattamen elected to carry them off to the safety of the deeper Crouxwood. Hamm ridiculed the theory and asserted an equally miraculous one: that they all merely survived the destruction while unconscious, that they were recovered later by the returning citizenry. All the others kept their mouths shut.

"You know what our plan is for tomorrow morning?" Morley asked, itching to change the subject.

"I imagine we'll get our portions o' venison fer the road early as we can, then head out fer Olford." He stopped wiping down his crossbow again. The halfelev had a fair assumption of what he was mulling over.

"Afraid to see what's become of it?" he asked. Seth made no reply. "You're not alone there. Lately, I've been more afraid than ever before." A lark chattered above them, waking the arbalester from a reverie he surely didn't know he was in.

"Of what?" he said.

"Of finding out that it's not over," Morley answered. "Of waking up in a soft bed in a sinister place and finding out the worst is yet to come for us. Though I'm not sure how that could be possible at this point."

"Really," his mate said with a laugh, "what could possibly top it all off fer ye? Discoverin' the island itself is only the scalp of a sleepin' water god who's about to wake and rub its head?" Morley shrugged. "I guess there could be worse things than a jotun made o' fire and a pair of satyrs. Could be wicchas, tree beasts, pale serpents. You ever heard o' the cyclops?"

"The tale of Sir Baelah," Morley said. "He fights one who steals away the mothers of outer Locqueshir to make marrow stew. He then rescues the women and jabs out the beast's only eye with the branch of an elder tree. The mothers are thus restored to their children." Seth was quiet for another moment.

"I thought it was a wind spirit," he said. "Five women who circle round their victims and steal the breath from their bodies." Morley shook his head.

The concept, however, evoked a smile from him. "I've never heard of that," he said.

*   *   *

As planned, the six woke before the sun on the following morning, gathered up their provisions in two heavy sacks, and headed southwest, reaching the main road as the first bright flecks of light dribbled onto the overgrown dirt trail. Every now and then, Geat disappeared into the dense brake for a time, only to canter back out with a mouthful of moss. Once or twice, Yeva went with him and brought back palmfuls of the lush wet clumps, then squeezed out their water over her open mouth.

On her second excursion, Morley joined her and brought back enough for Seth and Willian to try. For hours, the two men were submerged in a discussion about their respective courses through the past two seasons— the Great Accident, as they called it.

Morley soon offered some moss to Anae who, without dispensing her dignity, rejected the moist patches with no more than a wave of her hand. She had been inordinately reticent during their hike, much to Morley's discomfort.

By the afternoon, everyone was too exhausted to speak or continue on, so they chose to rest off-road on a sunken collective of stones. There, Willian and Seth continued their conversation, which soon faded into the arbalester's hopeless speculation on their survival outside Castle Sivliére. Discomforted equally, the other three distanced themselves.

Morley peered carefully at Yeva: she too had been largely speechless since Wallenport. And rightly so. Did anyone else—namely Willian—know about their shared relation, about Feofan, about her secret powers? This dissolved again into the repetitive question that only Anae was presently capable of answering: If he and Feofan both shared a mother and if Feofan and Yeva both shared a father, was he then Yeva's half-brother?

He thought of Semhren and how the old scholar most definitely knew how to define it. Perhaps he was only a quarter-brother or third-of-a-brother. Perhaps their lack of shared blood meant they had no relation at all. But what was it Anae had said in the tunnels beneath the north cliffs, about how the two of them were brother and sister by law? Was he and Yeva bound by secularity? Did any of this matter now that the island was essentially lawless? Did any of it ever matter?

"What did the three of ye see?" came Seth's voice, interrupting the steady thinkers surrounding him and Willian. Anae, Yeva, and Morley all turned to face the duo; Geat made a sound in reply before tramping off to find a sixth lunch. They all eyed each other. Clearly, none of the three caught any trace of Seth's question. And still, none of them were willing to request a more complete illustration.

"They haven't been listening," said Willian. "We're talking about our *visions.*"

His emphasis on the lattermost word insisted disbelief—as though he were playing the role of a skeptic who'd slept soundly in blackness all throughout their rescue. But he of all the others, a proper son of Ellemine, would've possessed a better understanding of the dreamscape. Probably even a better understanding than Morley or Anae, if she hadn't seen any of it before.

"They *were* visions," Seth attested. "I saw all manner o' things through them, things which haven't happened yet but are bound to. And I saw the past just as well! Not just my own past, but other ones. Like yers!" He pointed to Yeva, who narrowed her eyes. "I saw the very second when ye met my brother. Ye had Geat on leash and he stood to the left of ye. When Sieger opened the door, ye fell in love with him—I felt that very feelin' right at the moment ye saw him, but it wasn't *my* feelin'. It was all through you."

He then pointed to Anae and blushed. She received him with the coldest stare Morley had ever seen, so he shifted his finger to the awaiting halfelev.

"I saw the climb to Sylvain's house and the vodniks below, then I felt it when ye caught the sword and it cut up yer palm. And ye were so afraid at the time and ye kept climbin'."

Morley balled up his scarred hand. He wondered, did Seth really see the future as he claimed? Ellemine had told him, her youngest son, that she would be there for him and *only* him. Why? And what did this mean? The portents—the pictures he saw before waking—were thus far assumed to be the impartation in question, the ideas Morley was trusted with containing. But if Seth also had visions...

"What did you see of the future?" Morley asked his friend.

"Of yer own future?"

"Sure. Let's start there." He allowed a wry smile.

"Well," Seth started with a fidget. "Eh, mayhaps I ought to tell ye later. Yers was a bit, er—it was a bit personal. Y'know." His pupils shifted toward Yeva, then Anae.

"You're not doing too well so far," Willian jumped in. "I only insisted you try and convince me, but now you've dug yourself deeper. Now you have to convince all of us. So go on, at least whisper it in his ear."

Seth gave Morley a semi-imploring shrug. The halfelev answered with a similar motion and an inward sweep of his hand. Seth crept over, lowered himself to one knee, and muttered his vision.

"I saw ye with Anae. Ye were both in a barn with lots of hay and, y'know. Ye were both naked and all."

Morley nodded reservedly and Seth broke away, returning to his previous spot. The halfelev cast his eyes down to the sword across his lap in blatant avoidance of the others.

"Well?" he heard Willian say. "Was it your future or past? Or neither?"

"Hard to say. I'll leave it at that," Morley answered.

Willian chuckled. "How about you share one you're not afraid to share aloud, Sethan?" the ridder challenged. "Like mine. What did you see of me?"

The arbalester rubbed his nostrils. His confidence was now openly wavered, as Morley could see. "I saw ye in a nice house out in a barren field. Ye were with a woman and a child. And ye looked rather happy." Willian snorted at this.

"Anything else?"

"Nothin' I kenned. Mayhaps ye'll take off for the continent soon and get yerself a nice strip o' land and a fair lady. Mayhaps the vision wasn't yers at all and I couldn't tell a difference." Seth leaned back against a green elm trunk with his heavy crossbow over his chest.

"Likely," said Willian. He exchanged a look with Anae, then returned to Seth. "Who showed you these images?"

"Eh?"

"I heard a voice all throughout my dreams. Didn't you?"

"Sure," Seth replied. "I don't bother with voices like that, though, I hear them enough after havin' my uforian brews. 'Twas a woman's. Kept sayin' my name, tryna get my attention. But I kept on watchin' what I was watchin'. And I knew it was the future." He cleared his throat. "Why, did the rest of ye hear a woman too?" He searched each of them in turn. Morley followed suite: Yeva nodded slowly and Anae turned her head away to the woodlands.

"Yes," said Willian. "My mother's."

They fell into a cozy silence. Morley wondered on: had Willian never been shown the dream chamber? Not once during his many years in Wallenport? Did he really know so little about their mother's capabilities or was he putting up some pointless feint?

"Well, I certainly didn't hear *my* mother," said Seth, resting his eyes. Willian and Morley gawked at each other, both satisfied by the arbalester's lack of extrospection.

Four slow days passed on the road.

By the final night, they came to a stretch of ashen ground covered over by slouching black trees, most of which were branchless and starved though still standing upright; others splayed their defeated, tired bodies over the seared earth and their equally seared cousins. This, as Morley could tell, was where the fire giant first woke.

They could hear the drizzling Lightrun ahead. And soon enough, the silhouetted houses of Olford shaped themselves against a bulbous glow on the Westleyan road, the light of a finely oiled torch or lantern. The tiered barricade set up by the rebels was cleared away, though its larger half-burnt logs were rolled meagerly up against the ruin of Haarka's house. Across from that, they could see Tomak's old abode through the dark: that too was now a partly collapsing heap. Seth was deathly silent all throughout their approach. Yeva, on the other hand, announced quite casually the thoughts which she and Morley speechlessly shared.

"The bodies are all gone—and the weapons and everything." Evidently, not one of them could think of an appropriate or astute reply. Once at the edge of the river, a soft cindery fog wafted past them and bore the smell of warm embers. Someone still resided in the innhouse.

"What should we do?" Anae whispered, her first words since that morning, when she quietly asked Willian for a second strip of salted meat. Ignoring their caution, Seth waded across the shin-high waters, his crossbow underarm. Morley lifted the claymore back to his shoulder and followed suite, beckoning Geat along.

Midway across the current they met another smell: a sweet, yet unpleasant aroma coming upstream from the divide of Larenta's Creek. When the two of them reached the bank, they turned to see the others' advance, each of them more careful about preserving the dryness of their clothes.

Seth continued on to the front door of his house. Yeva, right in the middle of the stream, halted and raised her head. Through the dim lights of the silver moon and its receding bronze brother, Morley could see her head turn east toward the unseen source of the stench. A moment later, all three were back on dry land.

Seth seated himself on his porch. "Someone's in my house," he moaned, exhausted. "Door's locked and I can hear snorin'."

"Why not knock?" Willian inquired. "Wake the idiot up? It's your damned house, no one else has a right to reside there. Not even in your absence."

Seth huffed and shrugged. "I'm not all too attached to the room anymore. If ye wanna liberate it, be my guest. I'll be cozy enough out here."

They then heard faint laughter from inside the inn. Listening further, they could descry the droning of low voices.

"Sounds like there are others still." Morley said, sticking the sword's tip into the ground. "Should we check it out?"

"I'm not opposed to the idea," said Willian. "But you should let me borrow the sword. I don't want to take any chances." Seth laid down along the edge of his porch, sliding the arbalest away with one arm and rubbing his eyes with the other.

"I'd rather not hand it over to anyone else from now on, Willian," Morley avowed, hugging the strong of the blade close. "We should walk inside without posing a threat to anyone. The war's over, finished. Really, what's the worst that could happen to us? What would they possibly take—our clothes? A few hunks of dry meat?"

"What if they're guiltless killers?" Yeva came in bluntly. "Or cannibals? Or torturers?"

"And what are the chances of any of those being true?" the lad grumbled.

"They're all more likely than you think," she followed. They focused for a moment on the hum of voices coming from within: they heard a woman's, then a man's, then another deep intonation belonging to a much older or gruffer fellow.

"Think about it," Willian spoke again. "If there are any Lattamen or Garmites in there, they must know what state the island's in. They must know they're essentially outlaws no matter where they go. Even if they're well-meaning at heart, they must want to get back home to Triume as soon as possible. Bandits don't always lack reluctance, you know. And looking at your sword, I can think of at least two general reasons for why any of them would consider taking it. Same goes for Seth's crossbow." There was another short bout of laughter coming from inside. A woman's mature pitch commingled with it.

"At least they're not of the worst sort," said Yeva, "if they *are* bandits."

Before Morley could continue ridiculing their paranoia, he heard the light tamping of feet on the grass beside the innhouse: he then noticed Anae was no longer behind him. The inn's door clattered open and the men gathered inside were immediately hushed. Morley gulped as Willian and Yeva rounded the building's corner.

"What's goin' on?" Seth asked, sitting up. "I wasn't listenin' there fer a beat." The woman inside the inn gasped and spoke a few rushed words.

"I'll find out." Morley placed the greatsword beside his friend on the stone porch and scurried for the inn's open entrance, leaving Geat to wander at will.

Yeva and Willian stood inside, right in front of the open entry, and the lad pressed past them lightly. The interior was particularly damp, hazed by the gloom of the hearth flame, and brimming with occupied benches and tables, furnishings that survived their alternate use during the battle. The men sitting on them, their combined aspects fading into the darker corners, had all turned to Anae, who stood within Morley's reach. Dirks, warped swords, spearheads, and arrows covered over the tables' surfaces wherever there wasn't a resting elbow or tankard.

A woman closer to the back counter—Marion, the lad soon realized—was jostling through the cramped space toward them. Few other men stood in surprise as she did so, allowing her passage. Once close enough, Marion froze and examined the trio who followed Anae in. She recognized each of them with some shock, mouthing their names in turn.

"Damme Anae," Marion whispered, wringing her hands and panning over the gathered men. Some turned away and handed off or drank from their cups. All of them were cloaked modestly, though the colors of their garb ranged from mildew-grey to the all too familiar blue of the Lattamen.

"You're unhurt," the keeper continued. "W-we all expected the worst. W-Wallenport was destroyed, we heard. Flooded and drowned."

"It's much worse than you'd ever think," Anae murmured in reply, offering her open hands. Courteously, Marion took them in hers. Willian sidled over to the borders of the fireplace, where the standing space was most ample and where he could dry his wet feet; Yeva stepped after him. More than half the men watched their movements with suspicion as the other near-half resumed their quiet discussions. But soon enough, disinterest further disarmed them and the peaceable buzz continued in full.

"You've been there for me at the strangest times, Marion," Anae said. "My first journey south to Reineshir, my first journey north to Wallenport. And now…" Morley saw the girl's hands begin to shake. Then, abruptly and somewhat awkwardly, she fell into the keeper, embracing her. The lad stood by the door, fixated on the women, ignoring the men against the back wall as each tried to subtly point him out to their surrounding mates.

"Yer in good hands now, damme," Marion said, much to the Morley's irritation. She meant it only as a comforting remark, surely, or a courtesy intended only for a woman of higher birth; but something about the words stiffened him, made him feel as though all his efforts over the past weeks were irrelevant. "I haven't forgotten yer kindness the last time ye were here. Yer aetheling husband…is he still with us, damme?"

Morley was out the open door within seconds, sealing it up behind him. In making his way back to the road, he could see Seth, still seated upright at the edge of his porch. He was repeatedly flicking a flat stone over his head—likely a chip from one of the many crumbling ashlars beneath him—and catching it with a swipe of his hand. Geat, meanwhile, was drinking from the Lightrun.

"Well?" he asked, tossing the stone again. It glinted in the moonlight upon reaching its peak height, then fell away and landed in his palm with a remote thud. At the same time, Morley heard the innhouse door opening and closing again. "All's well?"

"Marion is back," he said, listening to the brush of feet behind him. "And the men she's tending to don't appear to have any bad intent." Seth tossed up the piece again and caught it, yawning as he did so. "What is that you have?"

"Dunno," the archer said, holding it up unhelpfully. "Caught its sparkle pokin' outta the ground right down here." With his foot he tamped a spot where the soil met the base of his patio. "Might be a pendant or a broken brooch or somethin'. Or the end of a necklace. I can't tell. Here, check."

Without further warning, he launched it forward with his thumb. Morley made a grab for it, missed, and watched it thump down on the dirt. As he bent down to pick it up, he froze.

Its circumference. Its shadowy etchings and unnaturally rich color. He raised his hand to the flap of his breast pocket and felt the outline of the coin Yeva had preserved for him. He'd lost the second one here, just before the end of the battle.

"I guess we're amidst friends here," Yeva said behind him. "Or at least amidst men who won't try to kill us within a breath."

Morley plucked up the aureon and weighed it in one hand, feeling its face and markings with his thumb. It was precisely the one, undiscovered—miraculously undiscovered—until now. Yeva joined Seth on his platform. Through some curious instinct, the halfelev folded the coin up in his fingers and hid his hand behind his back.

He'd already accepted the loss of his coins by the time he entered the tunnel under Chaisgott, weeks prior. In fact, he had almost forgotten about them entirely until Yeva returned the one she'd taken off his unconscious body. Why did she return it—why not keep it for herself? Probably because she wasn't one to steal from her closest friends. And being a woman of Egainshir and flat Werplaus, she had no use for such a magnificent item.

So then what use did it bear for Morley? A memento of his mother's kind, fantastical—and perhaps criminal—generosity. A token to be traded for the possession of anything.

Now, Sethan, yet unaware of Morley's previous possession of this treasure and of its incredible value, happened upon the aureon while it was embedded in the turf of his land, his property. Morley wondered what he could say: "Ah, this is actually mine. I lost it while trying to flee from the battle here. Don't believe me? Well, look here. I have another piece just like it. I got them after attending the feast of the aspirants, my mother gave them to me. Yes, I was carrying them the whole time after we left the port. I just didn't think to tell you about it—I would to get around to it eventually. I kept forgetting." Beyond all that, he would be lying. And what about Yeva's reaction, right at the present moment, if he were to give the coin back to Seth, if he were to admit to its true worth? Never mind the claymore or the arbalest or whatever other possessions they had. Thieves or not, the men in the innhouse would undoubtedly try to filch the piece.

And what of the vision? What of Seth's demise? If it truly did portend the future, would the archer really use part of his gold to buy a horse? He didn't know how to ride one, as far as anyone knew—of course he would fall headfirst off the beast and crack open his skull.

"Ye hear me, Fitzmorley?" came the archer's voice, brushing through the crowd of conjectures. Both he and Yeva were watching him, their faces blotted in shadow. "Toss it back over."

The situation would resolve itself well enough, Morley decided as he underhandedly hurled the coin back to his friend and headed off to the soggy riverside nearest the inn. Before the others were out of sight, he heard Yeva's voice but discerned no words.

He planted himself against the stone wall and stretched his legs. Geat trotted over and reclined at his side. The Lightrun tinkled by, warping the egg of the bronze moon's light into an incandescent puddle.

His mind wandered. What of the other visions revealed to him, other than that of Seth's fall? He saw Hamm walking though the highlands, stopped by a crude arrow. When he woke up in New Wallen, he was surprised to see the squire still present. And upon speaking to him, the young man expressed concern for the lost aspirants, introduced his plans for recovering them and bringing them back to their families, the people of New Wallen.

Thus, Morley's conclusion was duly at hand: somehow, while asleep, he had been sent into Reality's future as a spectre—a spirit, now returned to its flesh, that could henceforth alter the flow of time at will. Or perhaps not. If he chose to take the aureon from Sethan, would the young man still come to possess a horse? A comb? Would he still grow a prim greying beard if Morley did everything in his power to prevent him from doing so?

And what of the other images still? Anae in the cloister and all those shocked faces, those finely adorned court folk: she was not yet done with the nobility. But where was that centerless table and that square fresh-aired chamber? It was nowhere on Sarcovy, nowhere that he knew of. It would be of no surprise if she chose, eventually or without delay, to return to her home in Bienvale. Oxhead, the city was called. That's where her parents were according to Alherde, the new steward of Reineshir, Anae's old mester, Willian's closest friend.

What of Yeva's future? He could not recall the image, if there were one. It was pure sensation—no, a deliberated sensation, one which came to her as she dozed into the night. Why did Ellemine give him this knowledge? Or why did he so distantly choose to see it once given access? And why did Seth, days previous, have the presupposition of seeing the future? "This is only for you," the silver sprite promised. "I will be with you still."

"Morley." It was Yeva, rounding the corner. "I called your name three times. What's wrong?" She sat down beside him. He thought of the night of her return, during Olford's occupation under Allesande and her rebels. They'd sat in this same spot.

"Why'd you call?" he said, clearing his throat. Geat rested his head on the lad's lap.

"That little bit of metal Seth found," she began. "It's the other gold piece your mother gave you—remember when we were trying to get away from the battle? You tripped and threw it somewhere." Morley hummed dismissively.

"Did you tell him that?" he asked.

"I did, yeah." A thoughtful pause followed.

"How did he reply?"

"He wondered why you didn't say anything to that point. And I'm wondering the same thing now. Why give it back to him—it's yours, isn't it? And it's real valuable."

The halfelev rubbed at a side of his brow. "I'll talk to him about it tomorrow."

If anything, the discussion would focus on all the reasons for why Seth should avoid horses, Morley thought. There were far better projects to spend the gold on. Like the renovating and rebuilding of Olford. This line of thinking then prodded the lad towards the unfathomable, almost hated question: What could he do with his own aureon?

"What're you thinking about?" Yeva asked. It occurred to the lad that he hadn't yet engaged her in conversation since they were imprisoned together. Up in the bedchambers of the innhouse.

"Are we brother and sister?" he blurted.

"What?" she replied with a single flustered laugh.

Morley felt a flush of embarrassment. "Feofan and I both share a mother. And you and Feofan both share a father, right? So, does that mean we're related?" Yeva did not answer. "It's just Anae told me recently that, since she was married to Felix, with whom I shared a mother—by law, she and I are brother and sister, I think. So, I—"

"By law, you say?" she interrupted. "I don't think that should matter for a long while. No, I don't think we're brother and sister. We're not related by blood as we are with Feofan." She fell silent again, hugging her legs to her chest. Morley now yearned to know what she was thinking, though he had a particularly fair assumption.

"Do you think she's alive?" he asked. "Our...your sister?"

"I know she is," she said under her breath. "I saw it with my own eyes, right after we were saved. I saw it in the dream we all shared. The dream we all entered together." Morley shuddered at this. More so than the limitless connotations which poured forth from the dogma of an almighty All-Being, more so than the unknown and terrifying mysteries of the satyrs,

401

the vodniks, or the jotuns—the idea of a controlled and tangible realm of dreams, an impossibly enormous crossroads of inalterable circumstance and potentiality…all was as dizzying as his discovery of multiple languages, back when he first learned to read.

"What did you see?" he inquired. "Was it the future?"

"No. The present," she murmured. They could hear warm laughter lulling through the common room on the other side of the wall at their backs. "Seth didn't see the future. It's impossible to see the future, though Feofan did what she could to find its truth—not that it has a *real* truth. The future is the only thing that changes with every bump of the heart, you know. That's what she used to say after coming back down from the mountains on Kamenin."

"What did she do there?" he asked.

Yeva shook her head. "She slept. That's all she would tell me and that's all I saw—I followed her up once to see what she was doing. I know now what it entailed, of course. She consumed a leaf of beltreres tear and drank a bowl of soup, then went to sleep on a bed of soft grass. I watched her as she rested for a time, then went back down to the shelter we built. She didn't come back for another two days."

At this, Morley cleared his throat. "That's what she gave me after the battle, isn't it?" he said. "Just after all the men retreated south."

Yeva nodded. "She gave Seth even more, she told me. They met while she was on her way back from Werplaus—she went there to look for me not so long ago, but I was in Westley with Sieger. The two of them drank a tincture she made, then she led him up a tree and became a geister with him. Beltreres is not meant to be overused. She told me she gave Seth ten leaves of it, hoping it'd offset his soul or something."

"But why did you allow her to give *me* a leaf?" Morley asked. Yeva said nothing. "Why did you let her leave me outside Chaisgott, just as she did with Seth?" Still, the young woman stayed quiet. "Yeva?" At this, she sighed tremulously.

"I'm sorry, Morley," she murmured. "I truly am. If I had the choice, if I could return to the past and correct myself, I would. But see it this way: our lives were in danger, yours and mine, when we were fleeing from this place. Then Feofan appeared. I hadn't seen her for years and years— imagine that. And she suddenly shows up as this…giant thing. She'd managed to assume that aspect before but could never grow to such a tremendous size. I suppose she never needed to. Draping herself in shadow was enough for the people of Mavros and Kamenin." She huffed again. "She didn't want you with us. Not even after she recognized you from her dreams or visions or whatever she saw."

"But you let her dispose of me still. Why didn't you protest?" His throat ached. And his eyes began to sting in the cool air.

"I did. Not nearly enough, but I did. She assured me—another proof from her visions—that you would live and we would see each other again. That came true. But it didn't do her much good in the end. Unless destroying Wallenport was the only goal at hand—and I know it wasn't. She just wanted to find your mother. Her mother." She inched closer to Morley until their shoulders touched. She grasped his hand. "I thought Feofan and I were going to go home. Go anywhere. I thought everything could go back to the way it once was. Before I came to this place."

"What's wrong with living here?" the lad questioned. "You're surrounded by people who all love you dearly."

"That's not how I saw it at the time."

"*I've* always loved you," he said. "You'd have to be blind as a rock to not see that. And everyone in Egainshir loves you." He thought then of including Sieger in his short list; and quite suddenly, her rationale and her sudden desire for leaving was all too clear.

"I know. And I love you and all the others just as much. As I said, Morley, I regret what I did." Yeva released his hand and rested her head against his. Through the slight pause that followed, they could hear the low rumble of Willian's voice around the corner, no doubt conferring with Seth.

"Imagine this," she continued. "What if Sir Gale rode into the battle on a giant horse, slicing through anyone who stepped or stumbled into his path? Imagine if I was the one to faint and not you. And Gale halts his steed between me and you. And he demands you to get on, to leave me behind. Wouldn't you—"

"Gale has been dead for years," he interjected. "I watched as he was being put into the ground."

"Would the appearance of his geister be any less believable than the appearance of a titan made out of fire?" Morley said nothing. "Imagine if you left with him. And he rode you back to Wallenport, where he planned on kidnapping your mother and sundering the whole of the city."

"But Feofan never died," he said, "you never watched her fight a man to the death. You never saw her take her last breaths, never listened to her last cries or watched as she was sealed away in a box. If I saw Gale again, I would know it wasn't him. It couldn't be him. Feofan...she changed. And she'll change again, I'm sure." Yeva lifted her head from the bony ledge beside his neck.

"What're you talking about?" she asked in a whisper.

"The dream we were in. I saw things, same as all the rest of you. But before I woke, I saw other things. I saw Hamm in the highlands with Gavfred and Hanz—though I didn't know their names until I woke and met them in person. I saw Willian in Reineshir, which was all ruined and abused. I saw Seth riding a horse and wearing a colorful tunic." At that very second the arbalester made an odd sound from his porch, like an exaggerated yawn. "And I saw Feofan. Stepping out of a boat with Ellemine." Yeva did not speak. "Maybe I only saw an idea of the future and nothing more. But I believed it was the truth. My mother...that silver sprite told me as much."

"What silver sprite?" she asked. Before Morley could answer her, she added, "The one in the white dream?" He nodded. "I see. I recall dreaming of a creature like that. It spoke to me, same as you, but I didn't answer. It told me I was very brave, braver than most. But I was more afraid than ever before." More laughter quaked inside the innhouse.

Yeva sighed and stood up. "I thought I was going to die," she said. "Or stay in the mist forever." A figure rounded the nearest corner, softly startling them both.

"Everyone's well?" came the voice of Willian. Morley and Yeva nodded in unison. Geat perked his head up then rested it back on his mate's thighs. The young woman began marching slowly upstream along the bank.

"The smell is unbearable," she said abruptly. "I'm going to go find somewhere pleasant to rest my head. Somewhere with fresh ferns."

The two brothers quizzically watched her fade into the dull grey treeline past the inn. A hush drifted through all of Olford.

"I suppose not," Willian said, slouching against the wall. "There's no sleeping space left in the inn, according to Marion. All the men in there are mostly from Garm, though four are from Lattaholm and three are Westleyan. The Lattamen are allowing Anae to take their room."

"What're they doing here?" Morley said, deciding against silence.

Willian sniffed the air. "Burying their comrades. Recovering abandoned chattels and weaponry. Nothing vicious. Though I wouldn't get too comfortable." He cleared his throat and spat, again causing Geat to raise his head. "Some of the sword blades were melted when the shadow-jotun came, then cooled after being coated with ash. A few men want to sell them off as artisan-craft—or say they were deformed in dragon fire. I'd be lying if I said such wasn't a charming plan. The merchants of Aubin drool over nonsense like that." Willian took a deep, tired breath. "What's this I hear about you dropping gold in front of Seth's house?"

"I lost one of my aureons while trying to flee from the battle here," he answered.

"The ones Ellemine gave you?"

"Yes." At this, Morley absently reached into the flap of his tunic and pulled out the second coin, offering it for Willian's inspection. The ridder took it, held it up in the moonlight, then gave it back within seconds.

"I was thinking about it recently," he said, "trying to figure out where she got two pieces of gold." Morley thought of the daisy head, how Ellemine had inexplicably converted it into the twin coins. "Could be forged. If our mother is capable of transporting our souls and bodies as she did, why should we be surprised of her ability to alter, say, a dish of solid gold into a few pristine aureons?"

"Or the head of a flower," the lad muttered. "But where would she get a golden dish? I thought gold was rare, a royal specialty."

"Every so often an earl comes across a brooch or a buckle of gold, an heirloom of sorts. Or a foolish investment. One worthy of spurring rebellion maybe." He sniffed and broke from the wall. "I'll see you in the morning. I'm going to go find my own bed of leaves."

"You react to things strangely, Willian" Morley said as his brother took a step away from the corner. "I wouldn't care any more or less if Ellemine was a daemon or faerie or wiccha-mother—I didn't know her until last year's Hosten, didn't care to meet her. But you lived with her for almost half your life. And you don't seem affected by any of this. Why?" No reply came. Willian was gone.

Morley removed the goat's head from his lap and scooted to the corner of the innhouse: his brother was fading steadily into the dimness, his arms crossed in front of him. Little distance away, meanwhile, Seth was lying flat on his back along the edge of his platform, unstirring.

The halfelev stood up straight and cracked his back, deliberating where he should rest his head for the night. Across the river? No—his feet had only just started to dry entirely. West down the bank? He'd probably trip over Yeva or disturb her, wherever she was. East down the bank? That was where all the bodies were kept, judging from the breeze...

Morley seated himself back down against the wall. He slumped onto his side, rested his head on Geat's belly, focused on the trickling river, the broken rushing streams. Cold as a cave, it dripped and flowed until, soon enough, the lad forgot himself and his locale.

After a while, he thought he was on the floors of the inn's kitchen, where Marion slept in her cot with Anae by her side. Then he saw he was in the kitchens of Castle Sivliére, newly repaired—or never destroyed. Someone in a gown stood by the oven, a hollowed portion of the wall as big as a burial coffin. She removed twenty loaves of bread from a long rack within it, placing them within a wicker basket. Ellemine, he thought foolishly. It was Amarta, holding her child close as she peeled out the bread with her free hand. Morley got up and called her name; she turned before the words left him and offered the first golden brown bun.

No. It wasn't Amarta either.

He woke in the early morning to the visage of a young man, nearly his age, crouched by the side of the Lightrun. Geat was next to him, slurping up the stream. The man was wrapped up in a filthy oversized cloak that barely resembled those belonging to the Lattamen. His hair was shortened to the point of near-baldness and the skin on the back of his neck was bruised and rough. He rubbed water against his unseen face and over his scalp for a time, shivering from its briskness.

He stood and turned a minute later: as their eyes met, Morley saw that a large section of his face, perfectly delineated from the inner bridge of his nose down to the opposite corner of his mouth, was cracked and scarred a greyish red. With a dissonant pace, the unknown figure promptly strode away toward Seth's house. Curious still, Morley followed, stepping out onto the road.

Anae, seated beside the arbalester on his porch, held out a cloth for the marred stranger and tried a kind smile. The man took it and dried his face; as he did so, Seth waved Morley over to them.

"Good morn to ye," he mumbled tiredly once his mate was close enough. He then averted his eyes with subdued guilt.

Anae—to Morley's utter surprise—grinned, hopped down from the stonework, and clasped herself to his rigid torso. "Good morning," she said. The lad caught a whiff of the foul air, then Anae's pleasant odor. A line of six men grimly exited the inn and made for the ford.

"Ehm," he said. "Good morning." The scarred stranger dropped the cloth down on the porch and sat beside it. Anae broke away and placed a hand against the man's back. He glanced up at Morley, then continued glaring down at the ground.

"Thought I recognized you," he said, his voice incompatible with his appearance. "Fitzmardy, was it?" Both Anae and the halfelev corrected him at the same time: the latter gave the name 'Morley,' the former gave 'Fitzmorley.' The scarred man issued a weak chuckle.

"I imagine you don't recognize *me* too well. Only time you were around me, you were scared pale. Not to mention this…" He pointed at his face with a thumb.

"This is Iacob," Anae said, seating herself next to him. "He was Felix's edma. His closest advisor."

"Closest friend, I'd say," Iacob said. "I was seated near him during the feast you attended, remember? He called you over to see the claymore." With the other thumb, he gestured behind him: the sword and arbalest were propped up against the house. Iacob lowered his hand and leaned back, using both arms to buttress himself. Morley remembered then. He and Felix had been identically dressed at the aspirant feast. And identically complimentary.

"I see you've made it as well," the burnt man continued. "Bit of a nightmare we've been through, eh?" The halfelev nodded, wondering how much of the madness he'd been exposed to. Clearly, enough. More men left the inn, these ones carrying loads of shovels and axes.

"So…" Anae started. "You haven't found him yet?"

"No. A third of the bodies recovered were burnt worse than mine. Burnt beyond familiarity, really. But Felix was not among them. Trust me. I made sure of his safety.

"How…did you survive?" As she spoke, Morley spotted Yeva stepping along the opposite riverbank. Her short hair seemed dark and wet. Geat splashed across the ford to meet her.

"The rebels—well, the *Westleyans* returned here several hours after the battle. And they found me moaning in the middle of the road. There were so few others who survived the burning, fewer still who yet live today. They were all carted off to the west—those who could be saved, at least. But I stayed, found some balm inside." He began to point a thumb over his shoulder again and froze. Seth made a tightlipped face. "Sorry again, Sethan."

"No great loss," the arbalester replied, sticking a hand into his trouser pouch and hopping down from the porch. He headed for the innhouse, patting Morley's upper arm as he passed. The halfelev took his place at the edge of the ashlars.

"How many died that day?" Anae whispered cautiously.

"Nobody bothered to count," said Iacob. "Many were buried privately by their friends, out in the deeper wealds. Westleyans and Garmites largely. The Lattamen regrouped somewhere further south. Reineshir, I'll bet, as they came back through this place with loads of food and drink and other things. At that time, we outnumbered them, urged them to continue on their way without hassle. By 'we,' I mean the Garmites and Westleyans who returned and made peace. The majority went back west last week, as I said."

"I see," Anae mumbled. Morley, gawking drowsily down the cracked road, noticed Willian's tan attire just past the split in the road: he appeared to be urinating on the base of a pine trunk. The lad prayed that nobody was buried too close to it; and this thought, like a fly against the sun's orb, brought forth a morbid consciousness of the surrounding dead. His stomach shrank.

"We're now burying the unclaimed, unknown bodies downstream," Iacob went on. "Lattamen mostly, based on their clothes. Hopefully, if the weather is fair, we'll be finished by next week. Speaking of which…" Iacob lowered himself down from the platform and headed sluggishly for the inn. "I should eat before following the others out. Please, do come join me. Good Marion tells me there's more food here now than there's ever been. All thanks to the Westleyan council." He glanced back at the two of them and gave a quick half-smile.

"Wait," Anae pleaded while he was still in earshot. The young man turned back to her. "I've never had a doubt about your integrity, Iacob, not once. But you were my husband's edma, you still have influence. It seems so odd to me that you've taken up this duty. As a gravedigger. Even if you're only overseeing the work—"

"Have you been near death?" he asked blankly, searching between the two of them. "I mean, throughout this whole bizarre ordeal, has there been a moment where you believed you were dead or about to die?" She did not answer but, by the way she held her breath, Morley knew what she was thinking.

"After I stopped feeling the pain," he continued, "I thought I'd already passed on. I imagined—vivid as can be—that I was looking down at my body. All I could think was that there was nothing left for me to care about before ascending into the All-Being. Except one thing: how pathetic and disgraced I looked, splayed out right here." With his foot, he traced a line down the center of the road. "Pathetic because of *why* I died. Why all the other men here died. What they gave their lives for. You mentioned influence—this is all I'm good for now, I'd say. The least I can do is lend a hand, as I can't sleep soundly until we're all completely at peace."

He veered back toward the innhouse. "Come on. Marion's got country frumenty left over."

*   *   *

By noon, the six resumed their southward journey, again embracing a somewhat melancholy quietude as they left behind the smell of tainted earth.

Anae strode beside Morley for the entirety of the first day—so close that their knuckles often brushed. Willian took the lead, admittedly anxious to see what remained of Reineshir; Yeva, too, walked alone with a large basket of bread and cheese. And Seth—whose reasons for continuing on with them were obvious yet unspoken—took the rear. It rained in the evening, though not heavily enough to keep them off the road for long.

Few days later, on a bleak misted morning, they reached the familiar grounds of St. Berthe's Church, more crowded than ever before. Huts, much like the ones they saw being built around the pavilion of New Wallen, stood like fresh lean-tos against the church's outer walls. Only seven of their denizens—and an additional four goats—were awake and in plain sight, each sharing food and drink. Three of them, two young women and an older man, rushed forward to Anae at first sight of her. Likewise, she sped on toward them with open arms.

As per Morley's insistence, Yeva, Seth, and Willian continued on down the trail without delay, each hoping to reach Reineshir by the early afternoon. The lad then joined Anae and the three others whom, to his own surprise, he identified only seconds later: the old man was Byraon the goatherd, the first man of Reineshir he had ever met, and the two girls were the youngest of the Ornhatter sisters, Serra and Sofra. The latter, the youngest of the sisters, couldn't take her hands off Anae's fur-heavy clothes.

"Reineshir's in an ugly state, for sure," she said in answer to an unheard inquest. "The bluecloaks came in and went away like locusts. And they took whatever food wasn't hidden away and emptied out the brewery— and that caused the most fights. But Chaplain Jahn saw them coming down the road here and raced to warn us all, so Mester Alherde called everyone into the manor and closed up the doors and—"

"Slow down, slow down," said Serra. "You're telling it all out of order again." Morley peered at Byraon, who was then returning from the other side of the church with a thin slab of dry meat. The goatherd was eyeing him from head to toe, from the sword's point to its hilt, chewing at something as he did so. He ripped two pieces from the toughened meat and distributed them.

"Yer friends en't hungry?" he asked gruffly, nodding down the road at the vanished trio. Anae shrugged and broke her portion into smaller slivers.

"I think they just want to reach town as soon as possible," Morley answered him, breaking apart the meat in like fashion. The old man tugged at his beard.

"Well, food might be scant there," he said. "Alherde's the only one sharin'. The rest are all hidin' theirs away—the 'rest,' I mean those who en't here and en't out in Westley. Too few a number..." He began smoothing his long beard again. "I've seen ye before, haven't I? Istain brought ye that one day. I'd remember yer blade if nothin' else. Ye had sloppier hair, yeah?" The halfelev touched a greasy lock at the back of his neck.

"Let him be, Byraon," Anae scolded. The goatherd grunted a laugh and the Ornhatter sisters snickered. "Anyhow, none of you have explained why you're all out here. Wouldn't Westley be the better option in any case?" Byraon harrumphed at this, though it sounded no different from his laugh.

"Father says he trusts wilders better than he trusts rebels," said Sofra. "And everyone knows there are wilders right around here, so off we went into the woods."

"And I en't bringin' a single of my goats round that den o' thieves," Byraon jumped in as he scratched at Geat's head. The goat left him to investigate a pair of females lounging beside a chopping block.

"Everyone has their separate excuses," Sofra added.

As they spoke, a woman had emerged from a hut against the furthest side of the church. She was dressed in profoundly revealing rags and carried a dense head of knotted, ratty hair. The woman stretched, then made for the deeper wilderness. She was soon followed by a man of equal stature and uncleanliness, who stepped out from their wattle shelter and near-copied the woman's routine. Morley recognized him as Gerry, one of Reineshir's woodcutters.

"But you can't all stay here forever," said Anae. "What happens when you run out of game? What happens if Jahn's soil goes bad?"

"We're prepared enough for now," Serra chirped, pointing in the direction of the chaplain's stockade. Morley was then reminded of when he stole bread and cheese from that quaint store while on his way north for the first time. The memory made him blush.

"Father says it won't be long now before the Biens come back again," said Sofra. "That is, not the men from Lattaholm and Garm, but the uplanders. The king's men." There was an unnerving pause. Byraon left them to fetch Geat.

"Ah," Anae muttered. Her face had whitened.

"They'll set everything right and we'll be able to go back home and fix things up," Sofra added. "I can't wait! Everything will be all better!" The ex-Damme of Sarcovy said nothing.

They stayed for the better part of an hour, Anae trying her best to retain a cheery mood as she was reunited with the townspeople both familiar and unfamiliar to Morley. Soon enough, they left the encampment behind with promises of return. And as the three of them marched down the yet-befogged roadway, they nurtured a ponderous lull. This persisted through a canto of lark songs and an eventual refrain of cawing crows. Their three companions were still nowhere in sight after more than an hour of walking through the grey forest. Nonchalant as always, Geat broke the quiet with a belch.

"Something's troubling you," Morley said to the young woman at his side.

"Yes."

"Was it word of the king's men?" he said. "I wasn't so sure what that meant. But I saw how upset it made you."

Neither spoke for a fleeting moment. Morley listened to the circuitous resonance and dissonance of their steps.

411

"Yes," Anae soon repeated. "I'm scared, Fitzmorley. Terrified. I haven't felt like this since my mother spoke of leaving Oxhead for this place."

"Well, what're you afraid of?" he inquired. "Coming here turned out fine. After a while. Didn't it?" Again, Anae held her tongue. "You fell in love—maybe more than once. You gained more power than your mother. For a time." Still, she said nothing.

Morley sighed. "You have to leave the island," he said. "Don't you?"

"I've got nowhere else to go." Two squawking crows flew overhead; Geat sped moderately after them.

"You can come with us to Egainshir," he offered. "I promise you, it's much nicer than all the other places we've been to over these recent weeks."

"I believe you," she said with a forced smile. For the remainder of their walk, they kept their thoughts to themselves.

Hours later, they saw the open ground of Reineshir ahead, flanked by Maud's inn on one side and the imperious walls of the Bertriss manor on the other. It seemed no different. Further within, however, the distinction was prominent yet eerily well disguised: it was peaceful. Quiet. The only racket throughout the whole clearing, somewhere down the main road, was the hammering of nails or thinned metal on wooden boards. Otherwise, the heavy air remained rich with the echo of birdsongs, the swaying of pines and young leaves, the rare creaking of wood or rust.

The buildings around them, once besmirched by the dirtied staring faces of drinking bystanders, all putting off the day's work for a few double-pints, were now ghostly. There was a haunting naturalness to them, covered over in the copious grey clouds. As they stood before the manor's closed gate and glared down toward what used to be the venders' grounds, the distant hammering stopped. And Morley wondered if it had been imagined.

Anae rapped on the solid gates to the estate's toft, though she called no names; Geat, more curious than his travel mates, left them to investigate the grazing pen past the inn. None of them had said a single word since the town was in sight before them—neither of them could bear to interrupt the domineering hush. And neither of them needed to: not long after Anae knocked, a door whined open.

"Hello?" came a feeble call from somewhere inside the toft.

"Alherde?" Anae answered. "Is that you?" There was a rushing patter and the clunking of a crossbar, then the door opened inward. Without observation, Alherde—bearded and generally unkempt—flew through the gap and hugged Anae tight.

"Good Being above!" he exclaimed, his voice muffled against the girl's neck. Willian appeared behind him; he widened the fissure between the doors, motioning for Morley to come inside. He did so just as Alherde broke from his old pupil and issued an unheard greeting. The two of them remained outside as the half-brothers entered the manor, exchanging the events or non-events of their mornings.

Morley was overcome by a peculiar feeling of ignorance as he trod through the manor's front entrance. During his numerous liaisons with Anae, he had occasionally been invited and guided into her bedchamber via a postern at the back corner of the manse. Not once in his whole life had he stepped in through the main entry. Often, he'd imagined doing so, imagined what sort of magnificence awaited within…

Now, having seen the airy resplendence of Castle Sivliére's court and the burnished bright majesty of Michelhal's foyer, the house of the Bertrisses seemed utterly inadequate.

It was dusty, drab, and poorly lit, its lower corridors hidden away by moth-eaten curtains, its high ceiling opaque with cobwebs. A beaten, bare-surfaced, and splintered table stretched along the central aisle—perhaps an eighth the size of the Sivliére courtroom. A dozen people sat about, some at the table's benches, some sitting along the walls; every one of them stared at the halfelevs until they passed through to the back door and out onto the croft.

From there they ventured into the woods, where Seth and Yeva sat within the gazebo, around the block of bland concrete. Not long after they took their seats against the wood rails, the sun punctured the overhead clouds and illuminated the vapors of afternoon mist. For the first time since the start of the new year, it felt like the Skonhet season had come.

"I must say," Yeva announced, "Reineshir is outright pleasant without its people wandering the streets and leering from the alleys, don't you agree?" The question was left open to each of them.

"Dunno," said Seth absently.

"The first time I came was after the rebellion had started up," Willian added. "I'm not one to speak of how populous it once was."

"What do you think, Morley?" said Yeva. The only terrible memory the lad possessed of the town pertained to the day of Felix's arrival. Otherwise, Reineshir was a refuge of indulgence and fair romance. Now, it seemed a hopeless husk, an irreparable mass with the singular promise of ruin.

"Think we can make it to Egainshir before nightfall?" he heard himself say. All three of the others turned their heads to him dubiously. "Sorry. I'm just itching to get back home. We're so close now and…"

"I'd walk with you," Yeva confirmed. "Though I'll need more of a rest before setting my feet on the ground again." As she spoke, Morley saw Alherde and Anae through the trees, both slowly exiting out the manor's back door. "If only Istain was in town today, we could ride with him and Nudd without having to traverse all the overgrowth. Though, I wonder who he buys from now that there's no one left to trade with around here."

"I hear there are dockhands who sell goods from Aubin somewhere on the channel's shore," said Willian. "That's where the Westleyan traders go. That's where Alherde and I are going, first thing tomorrow morning."

"Really?" Morley muttered. "Why's that?"

"Well…" He too glanced over at Alherde and Anae, now strolling down the perimeter trail of the wood, evidently speaking with a tenderness yet unfounded in their long tedious relationship.

"In short, the land's in a bad state," he continued. "And Aubin is the only place left for us to make a proper assessment of our options, being the home of the hertog and the center for hallmotes. The councilmen of Westley will be there, he says. Alherde must go, as he's the acting steward of Reineshir. I must go too, I suppose, as I was once a child of the Sivliére household. And as I'm sure Anae knows by now, her mother and father have also been summoned to it."

Morley's heart fell into his stomach. He thought of the vision: Anae in the cloister, the gathering, the surprised faces. She would be there, he was sure of it.

"I see," he said. "Anae is coming with you, then?"

"She's welcome, of course. Though the Westleyans—and in her case, the hertog—probably don't know that the two of us are still alive."

"I see," he mumbled again, unsure of what else to say. Alherde and Anae disappeared from view behind the meager line of blueberry bushes. "I heard the king may send men back here." Willian bobbed his head ambivalently. "Not mercenaries or anything, but his own soldiers and captains."

"Alherde told me as much. Word of Wallenport's destruction will reach northern Bienvale in no time. I imagine some refugees of the flooding will reach Westley—if they haven't already—then the traders of Westley will bring the news to Aubin, then the sailors of Aubin will carry it back to the continent. Then, at last, interested barons will send off their couriers to the king. And I'm sure the finer, truer details will be lost to skepticism. The firestorm and…and all that." Willian scratched at the back of his head and Yeva fidgeted.

"What will happen after that?" she inquired.

Willian shook his head. "Order will be returned to the land," he guessed. "Or the island will be abandoned, its people carried off back to their first homes."

"This *is* my first home," said Seth, standing to stretch his legs. "Once those troops piss off from Olford, I'm goin' right back to mum's house to fix it up."

"That's all fair enough. Alan Pourtmann will stay in Aubin, I'll bet. Though I doubt he'll continue as hertog if there aren't aethelings for him to host."

A feeling of nervous impetuousness came over Morley then. He stood and left the gazebo for the cool floating moisture of the wood. Seth followed him, leaving Willian and Yeva alone in the gazebo. Looking back, they saw the young woman standing with arms folded, though she did not move away from the block-table or the ridder, who sat in silence.

Once Morley and Seth were at the edge of the nearby pond, still a generous distance away, the arbalester held out his fist.

"Here," he said. The halfelev gawked dumbly at the hand.

"What—"

"It's the gold I found, ye numbhead," he said. "Yeva over there tells me it's yers, that ye lost it when runnin' outta Olford." He chuckled. "Not sure where ye got it or when or why I never knew ye had it. Wasn't even really sure what it is or what it does. But I've got no use fer it, I'm sure. And if I hear from a friend that it belongs to ye, it probly belongs to ye. Here, bloody take it."

He took Morley's hand and pressed the aureon into his open palm. The halfelev looked at it: as he'd assumed, nights before when his mate tossed it to him, its rich sheen was faded with rust, its letters emboldened with caked dirt.

What if he joined the others to Aubin? Paid for their ship, paid for their rooms, their breakfast and supper, their new clothes? After all of that, he'd likely have coin left over from the purchases—in fact, the other piece of gold would probably go untouched.

The prospect was followed by a counterweight of ideas: What if the second aureon was stolen from him after he revealed the first to a devious vendor—what if all of Aubin was in a state comparable to Sarcovy—what if their ship crashed against a sea stack like Gaeshena's Rock?

As he balanced the coin over the tip of his thumb and the curve of his pointer finger, he knew. He was sick of adventures.

He flicked the gold up into the air toward Seth. The young man caught it with a start.

"Just promise me one thing, Sethan," Morley said, slapping a hand against his mate's chest. "Don't ever buy a horse." The arbalester agreed with a hidden grin.

*   *   *

On the following morning, Morley woke glumly and walked out the manor's front door. The sun had not yet risen and the lad knew he had at least another hour to rest up, but he quickly reasoned there was no point to it: the floors of the manor were foul and uncomfortable, and somebody in his shared space snored with an exhausting metrical profusion, like waves against the beach. And besides, he hadn't seen Geat since the day previous, since he left them knocking at the Bertriss gates.

Much to his tired joy, Willian waited by the toft walls.

"I hope you didn't go to sleep last night thinking I wouldn't see you off," said the ridder. "I couldn't rest much myself. I suspected you and Yeva and Sethan would be off at first light." He looked up at the clearing pale blue sky. "Didn't want to miss you."

"Wasn't all that comfortable in there anyway," said Morley, taking his place against the gates' bar.

Willian took a deep breath. "You know," he started, "if I could travel back through the years as a ghost and speak with myself, a young and cynical outcast adjusting to life on the high coast..." He scratched at his head. "What would I say?" Morley couldn't tell if the question were being posed for him.

416

"Have patience?" he suggested. "Keep faith? I'm not sure. For how long would you be allowed to talk?"

Willian shrugged. "For as long as I wish. Or for two minutes."

Morley, oddly stimulated by the scenario, pursued this idea. "Would you tell yourself about everything yet to come? Or would you just impart the promise that good things are yet to come?" He pressed on without giving Willian a chance to deliberate. "What if you spoke of last year? What if you mentioned my arrival at Hoerlog and the rebellion and the jotun— what if you looked forward to all these things? Think of that. Wouldn't everything turn out differently?"

Instead of the expected nod, Willian tilted his head, unsure. "I saw many things in my dreams," he said. "And I thought them all to be real until my moment of awakening." He waved a hand. "I just meant, I wonder what my past self would think. Ah, I'd think it all a dream, an elaborate one. A strange and vastly peculiar one." He tapped at his lower lip. "What would you do? If you could do the same, I mean, and visit yourself while you still lived in Egainshir."

"I'd..." He was prepared to say that he would share everything: the romance with Anae, her inevitable marriage to Felix, the escape from the vodniks, the meetings with his parents, the rejection, the losses, the fears and discomforts...

It then occurred to him that the future was only so recently offered to him. And though it was given as a series of vague truths, he knew they were set. He knew he was cursed to believe in them.

What would life be without its endless surprises and coincidences? What sanity was there in spoiling the life to come; and what madness in following the idylls of prophecy?

"I'd tell myself to look out for a man named Willian. My brother." The ridder's face tightened with shock. He blinked until his eyes stopped glistening. "Imagine all the messes I could've avoided." At this, they tiredly laughed.

A moment later, after they resumed their discussion, Willian nodded towards the manse. Anae was groggily exiting the immense house with a bag underarm. She was dressed in a casual cloak and gown, much like the one she'd been wearing on the very first day they met, out by the warehouse's corner.

"I spoke awhile with Alherde before the two of you arrived yesterday," murmured Willian. "He said it'd be easy enough to convince her. One more day with Fitzmorley van Werplaus. Aubin can wait."

Morley gulped. "I do hope we meet again," he said. "You know where to find me. And I know where to find you."

*   *   *

Once Seth was roused and once Yeva returned from her long morning stroll with Geat, the five set out for the flatlands of Werplaus. The sun never emerged through the heavy duvet of clouds, though its brightness shyly soothed the earth, warming its drab dew-wet hairs. Anae and Sethan, both in awe of the immense land and of the heavy sky above them, often paused in the tall grass to take in the world's lonesome enormity. Geat did the same, though only to chomp down on a mouthful of weeds.

"So…" Anae started after an hour of windy quietude, turning her head to Morley. "You walked all this way once every two weeks or so. Just to be with me?"

Yeva piped up before Morley found the chance. "Ye best believe it," she said brusquely. "All on foot, too. Unless he was with Istain." Anae did not look back at the young woman. A pause followed. "Better yet, think of where Wallenport used to be—think of the days and days of travel from here to there, carrying a heavy sword over his shoulder. He did that all for you, my dear."

"And now I'm here," Anae said, "walking back with him."

"And now you're here," Yeva continued, "walking back with him. But will you stay through the night? There isn't much space, you know—you got lucky in Olford. Also, it won't smell much better. Two cows and a bull."

"That's fine by me," Anae tamely replied. "I've been to plenty of villages."

Yeva gave a subdued snicker. "Well, Egainshir isn't really a village. It's a hamlet—have you ever been to a hamlet?"

"I don't know," Anae said honestly. "What's the difference?" And Yeva, who clearly expected more from the dignified Sivliére daughter, said nothing.

"A hamlet grows all on its own," Morley offered. "A village belongs to an aetheling or damme or earl and pays regular tribute. And a hamlet is a piece of land that belongs to one person, who usually shares it with others who help with work and such. I think that's the difference." It had been an incredibly long time since he heard Elmaen's explanation. Perhaps *he* could tell Anae all about the dynamics of a hamlet. Perhaps not. The wind swept past.

"Holy, bloody hell," Seth said abruptly. "I'm going to see my sister!" This was enough to set everyone back into a tamer mood.

Hours later, the humble circle of Egainshir was in plain view before them. Closer, they could see Gertruda sitting upon her red oak chair, drinking from a tall wood cylinder. She stiffened and leaned forward upon noticing the four. Then, she leapt up.

"Good great bones o' Being—it's Morley and Yeva and Geat!" She shouted the words in announcement to the whole hamlet.

Seconds later, Ceridwen and Amarta cantered forth from between Semhren's and the watch-sisters' house. As they threw themselves on their two old friends, Lunferda, Elmaen, Tommas, Istain, and Reffen came into view, their pipes lit at hand. Istain headed straight for Anae and hugged her tight; likewise, Tommas slapped a heavy hand against Seth's back. He proceeded to introduce his old neighbor to the cheered faces surrounding them. Two others soon approached to observe the small crowd: Robi and Tomak.

"Yeah, it's rightly unbelievable," Morley heard Tommas say to Seth, his strong voice rising through the mild cacophony. "Tomak here said he was kicked outta Olford by some Westleyans, so he headed south and stayed at Reineshir—then he was kicked outta there! *Ha ha!* Only after that did the kid decide to come south—where me and Serryl live, as he said ye told him. How did that go, Tomak?"

"Ye'll never let me bloody forget it, will ye?" said the young boy.

Tommas chuckled. "Istain and I found him shivering in the grass on our way up to Reineshir. Lucky him."

"Where's Semhren and Serryl?" Morley heard Yeva ask. He moved closer to her.

"Ah," came Amarta's soothing voice. "Serryl's out with her brother, Sieger. He came here weeks ago. He said he'd heard about this place from you and from his brother, though he didn't say much about how he knows you. He's a very nice man—distant at times, but nice. Serryl couldn't believe it was really him. In fact, she outright denied it until he was in front of her."

419

"I see," said Yeva.

"And Semhren left for Aubin some time ago," Ceridwen spoke up. "He said he made a fair sum of money after selling chamomile to a strange woman who came this way. And he wanted to spend it on something nice over on Aubin. Very suspicious, if you ask me." After she finished speaking, Morley noticed Arrin stepping past Semhren's house. He froze, wide-eyed, and sprinted for the halfelev with open arms.

"Fitz, you mischief-monger!" he cried, throwing himself onto the lad. Geat cantered over and nudged the back of his leg with a horn. "And Geat, you beautiful ugly beast!" He rassled with the goat for a moment, then spotted Yeva between Amarta and Ceridwen. "And Yeva! You cold-headed hard-hearted wiccha—where have you been?!" He lunged for her as well.

"So," Elmaen said quietly to Morley, "the girl over there wouldn't happen to be your damme, would she?" He pointed his thumb at Anae: Istain had his hand wrapped about her upper arm as he introduced her to the watcher sisters. Ceridwen bashfully stepped over to them and Anae half-smiled at her.

"Yeah, that's her," Morley confirmed.

"You finally brought her back, eh?" said the elder.

"What'd it, ehm—how'd you manage it?" Reffen asked. Morley wondered where to begin—or if he *should* begin. To his luck, Yeva joined them.

"Well, well," Elmaen began, "the wayward girl of Werplaus returns. We heard all about your little adventures from Sieger, y'know. He came weeks ago and—"

"Yes, I've heard," the young woman interrupted.

"I'm, eh, I'm sure you've had enough of the lands abroad by now, eh? Won't be going back to Wallenport any time soon, no?"

"No, probably not," she answered. "Not unless they rebuild it in a year or two."

The two old men gazed dumbly at her. And Morley, seeing his goat retreat into the hamlet's circle, decided to follow. Behind him the voices of his fellows—of his family—receded with the gliding air.

"I won't be stayin' fer too long," said Seth somewhere, "mayhaps a week or two. I'm gonna head back to Olford and see what can be done about fixin' it all up. Yer welcome to come along, y'know. Marion's the only one left."

"If we could, we'd offer you a house all to yourself," came Gertruda's voice elsewhere. "A noble damme like you shouldn't have to bed with us humbler folk. Hells, to think you agreed to come all this way in the first place! You're a special type, you are—no wonder you caught the lad's eye."

"Serryl's youngest. I can see the resemblance," Amarta spoke. "You three must be starved half to death if that's all you've been eating! Well, I'm sure your siblings will bring in a good catch, as they have been lately. I'll get to work on a few extra loaves right away."

"A jotun, you say?" Reffen questioned.

All else was lost as Robi raced up to Morley, slapping his back as his father did to Seth.

"Thought ye were gone fer good, Fitzy! Who's the girl ye brought?" They walked together into the circle.

"Her name's Anae," he said. "She's my friend from Reineshir. Remember? I'd always talk about her."

"Wasn't she the one who was stolen away by the aetheling a while ago?" The halfelev shook his head. "Guess that was someone else, then. Are ye lovers?"

"No, we're not," he replied with a forced laugh.

"Ah, so I'm allowed to swoon her, then?"

Morley shoved away the cackling boy. "It's too bad Semhren's not around," he said. "Do you remember when I used to argue with him about jotuns and whether or not they're real?" Robi nodded. "Well."

As expediently as he could, Morley referenced the many bizarre creatures he'd encountered through his journey: the vodniks, the satyrs, the destriers. By the time they reached the goats—both of whom were eager for the fence's gate to open—Robi was begging to hear more. However, and quite conveniently, Tommas called to his son; looking back, it was clear the man wished to properly introduce the boy to Sethan, his unmet uncle. Robi, fascinated by the strange arrow-shooting device in his father's arms, urged Morley to save his stories for later, then scampered off.

The halfelev, alone at last, opened the pen's gate. Geat charged in and greeted Minny, his well-fattened wife. Morley latched the door closed and clambered up onto the ageing pegs, watching the two as they lovingly sniffed at each other. Stretching his arms from side to side, he breathed deep the nearby scent of fresh dung. And beyond the long stinking shelter for the cows and the bull, the chatter of Egainshir reached him with surprising clarity. Occasionally, he'd hear his name conjoined with an inflection of inquiry: he was, after all, entirely hidden from their view.

Ten minutes, he pleaded with the heavens. Ten minutes to think. Ten minutes of isolation.

The unseen forces complied with his request.

"There you are!" Yeva's voice soon emerged. Turning, he saw her and Seth advancing towards him.

"Ah," said the disarmed arbalester, "so this is Geat's beloved. Charmin' abode, they have." He and Yeva mounted the fence, seating themselves on either side of the halfelev.

"Everyone's been asking after you," said the young woman, resting an arm around him. Seth hummed with fascination at the living pool of white fluff in the near distance. Arrin soon appeared in view, charging back to his flock.

"I needed a moment to think," Morley said. "And rest."

"Hardly a rest! Balancing yourself on a fence like this." She shifted backwards and forwards unsteadily. "And besides, you have all the time in the world to think now."

"I…" the lad tried. "I suppose I'm just nervous. Restless or something."

"Nervous o' what?" asked Seth. "All the lovin' folk around ye? Afraid they'll smother ye to death with kisses and hugs? I wouldn't mind that so much, considerin' everythin' else that almost killed me of late." He looked over a shoulder. "Death by the kisses o' Cerwen…" Morley and Yeva looked distastefully over the arbalester. "That's her name, right? The wheat-haired one?"

Yeva shook her head. "I understand you, Morley. I'm feeling something similar."

The halfelev knew precisely what impinged the feeling upon her: the arrival of her old lover. Their consequent and eventual resolution. He was tempted to ask, to verify this idea.

"Well, I'm feelin' right and well," Seth announced. "I'll be eatin' well tonight in the company o' my family—together again after years and years! Just wait'll they hear what we've been through, eh?" Again, Morley and Yeva looked over their mate unsurely. He noticed their angst. "What?"

"Do you think they'll believe us?" said the lad. "Any of them? Besides Robi?

"I already mentioned a thing or two to Reffen," Yeva noted. "He was more confused than I've ever seen him. He even stuck a finger in his ears, tried to clean them out. Old sod."

"Mayhaps we'll draw the story out, eh?" said Seth. "Make it more interestin' at the parts where it's dull?"

"How would we do that?" Morley asked, scratching the back of his neck. "And how would that make any of it more believable?"

"Easy…"

For an indeterminable time they sat on the pegs, wandered the pen, then sat again, discussing the fine points of their journey—the parts worthy of greatest explication, the scenes that could be sacrificed and forgotten. By the time their 'performance' was devised to a reasonable extent, they heard Gertruda's call at the other end of the circle: Serryl and Sieger were almost home. And Sethan, more joyous than ever before, charged out of view. Yeva, on the other hand, moaned and rested her head on the halfelev's shoulder.

"Not ready to see him?" he said.

"I'm as ready as I'll ever be. And I'm sure he is, too." She got down from the fence. "It'll be fine. Are you coming?"

"In a moment," he murmured. Yeva did not move away, he could tell, and a quietude came over them. He stared out at Arrin and the sheep, waiting for the receding footfalls. Instead he felt her place one foot on the lowest peg of the fence, lifting herself. She kissed the side of his head And wordlessly, she headed back for the hamlet proper.

Then it was Morley, Geat, and Minny, finally at peace. The two goats receded into their shelter, sturdy as ever before, and tiredly collapsed on each other. The folk of Egainshir all buzzed behind him: pleasant laughter, discussions and stories, offers of bread and beer. The hamlet had never hosted so many guests in all its long years.

He thought of Gale's house, what state it was now in after weeks and weeks of dereliction. Perhaps the legendary wolf had moved in, as was its right. If only he could pick up the turf and the rooms buried beneath and carry it all closer to this center of life. Isolation had its charms, he found, its lacking frustrations, its delightful boredoms. But why live if living alone? He had Geat, of course, someone he could care about with the fondness of a father—though, similar and somewhat dissimilar to life with Gale, all his conversations would be one-sided and empty.

No. He needed the amity of friends, the commune of the untroubled.

"Morley," Anae cooed, paces away from him. Before he could turn to address her, she was clambering up, perching beside him as best she could. "What is it?"

"Look at those two," he said, pointing to Minny and Geat. The latter's head was swathed around the other's body, eyes closed. He could swear there was a smile curving along his snout. "Hard to believe they're still as healthy as they are. Really, I remember when they were kids, hopping around and braying for attention. I was a kid myself then, so to speak." Anae did not respond. "I'll be going back to Gale's house tonight. If you want to come with me—I mean, if you would like to see it and spend the night there…"

"Istain is leaving for the channel docks tomorrow morning," she said, much to Morley's fear. "Wouldn't it be a longer walk if I had to leave from there in the morning?" Morley nodded. "Then perhaps I can see it when I…" She paused. "Well, *if* I get back."

"I see." He traced his thumb around the aureon in the flap of his tunic. He removed it without reluctance.

"Here," he said, holding it out for her.

She did not move a muscle. "How di—"

"Don't ask how I got it," he requested, placing it in her hand, folding her fingers. "It shouldn't matter anymore." She made a series of exasperated noises, as if she were attempting to contest the coin's existence. Finally, she gave in with a sigh.

"I have no words anymore," she said, a whimper hidden in her voice. "I don't know what to say." She was either about to cry or break out into hilarious laughter, Morley guessed. He placed his arm around her, attempted to think of an elegant response.

What would Sir Olivien say? What verse would Sir Tornau spin? Sir Haubauld? Sir Cadmael?

In the end, Fitzmorley said what Fitzmorley would say.

"Neither do I."

Appendix

[If you jumped straight here before reading the story, know that nothing will be spoiled: rather, you will be better equipped to understand the trivialities—in regards to the plot, generally—of the measurements, religion, and other norms of the time.]

Measurements – In the middle realm, the annual calendar is comprised of 400 days evenly split into four seasons, beginning with Skonhet (the fertile season), followed by Hetta and Hosten, and ending with Frysa (the cold season). The changing seasons are indicated by the twin moons and their distances from the planet: both moons are closest during the Frysa season, for example. Each season is comprised of 20 five-day weeks. The days of each week are Enaday, Devaday, Triday, Stiriday, and Fimmday (the day of rest). Each day has six liturgical hours that occur every four hours: Maudin is early to mid-morning, Sendons mid-morning to noon, Vosses noon to afternoon, Spaken afternoon to evening, Tierles evening to midnight, and the "Unholy Hours" are midnight to early morning.

The calendar era, U.R. ("Ure Rekf"), means "new- or now-time" in the scholarly language of Triume. It was established by a council of prominent rulers in the early 4th century (U.R.). They further determined that the years past should be grouped into epochs as a tool for framing the truth of their historical discourse. The first 262 years are thus the "Age of Majesty"; the following 70 years are the "Age of Chaos." The year in which the U.R. calendar was instituted, 332, was the first in the "Age of Renewal."

Units of spatial measurement are—from shortest to longest—a pace, a stride, a kalcubit, and a league. A pace is equivalent to a shuffling or "thinker's" step while a stride is a marcher's step, about three paces. A kalcubit, with similar arbitration to the pace and stride, is considered the average distance a person can walk in an hour. A league is predominantly a maritime unit of measurement roughly equivalent to four kalcubits. An acre, meanwhile, is little over four thousand square strides of land; and a common hide is at least twenty acres in Bienvale.

Places and People – Triume, the continent due north of Sarcovy Isle, is several hundred times larger than the small island of this story. Triume is made up of three realms: from west to east, they are Ka-Zsani, Daedor,

426

and Ishune. Sarcovy is within the demesne of Bienvale, the second-largest country on the southern coast of Daedor.

There are many strange creatures in this world but, as it is with our own, the strangest of them are the "rational animals," of which there are recognized four different species or "breeds" (during this novel's time period): they are naemas, elevs, garves, and oruxes. They are each naturally distinct. For instance, oruxes have leather-tough skin, sharp teeth, and black eyes that grant them superior vision; and garves are robust and skillful at communicating with animals, which greatly aids them in their uncontested engineering endeavors. They respectively hail from the deserts of Ka-Zsani and the underground deep-cities across all of Triume.

Most prominent in this story are naemas, who are thought to be related to (or descended from) naiads, a supposedly extinct species of semiaquatic river-dwellers. Characteristically, naemas are the most diverse across Triume because of their aptitude for hypermutation. They have a peculiar way of reflecting their environments through time: a group of short naemas who live in a forested area will grow taller over a decade or so; a naema who lives among garves will become stouter and hairier. It is believed that they can even be transformed into beasts called therianthropes.

Elevs are particular because of their natural attunement to Venei (exposition below). They live for many centuries and are not frequently found beyond the realm of Ishune—at least not as "purekin," or those whose forebears never mixed with the other breeds.

Heredity and Sexuality – Through their coexistence, the four breeds have inevitably mingled and progenerated "dualkin" throughout the millennia. Strangely, not all couplings can successfully produce offspring: a child born of a garve and an orux is unheard of and believed an impossibility, but men of both those breeds can have a child with a naemal woman; further, it is less common for a naemal male to procreate successfully with a female garve or orux, though it is not impossible.

Elevs and naemas have generatively mingled most, even to the point of transparency in some regions. Male and female naemas can produce offspring with purekin elevs, though purekin women can birth no more than four children in their lifetimes. These offspring are called "halfelevs" (or "halfnaemas" in certain places) and they share the qualities—including the purekins' natural attunement to Venei—of their parent breeds evenly.

Beyond them, the offspring of a halfelev and a naema is often called a "common elev": they bear the distinct physical features of elevs, like long pointed ears and sharp eyes, but their connection with Venei is far more diminished.

Meanwhile, discrimination towards homosexuals has occurred since antiquity: they were denied the right to marry in Daedor and Ka-Zsani, as marriage was traditionally viewed as legitimate only if children could be borne of the union. But homosexuality was otherwise acceptable during those times—even conventional among the wealthy.

It wasn't until the Age of Renewal that homosexuality was deemed a vice by the new authorities, who primarily sought control through religious, administrative, and social unity (instead of might, as was ordinary in the Age of Majesty). It was associated with the decadence of bygone heathen emperors, who were held responsible for ushering in the seventy years of Chaos; and on the other hand, the heterosexual family unit was pushed as a balanced idealism, one that ensured fortune for long family lines and big litters of children.

Venei and Merrenar – There exists in this world a crypto-element (known as a "spirit" or "magik" through most of history) called Venei. It is considered an essential force of nature that is inscrutable to all breeds but the elevs and halfelevs—and sometimes naemas who have lived among elevs for many years. Its manipulation was once a widely-practiced art. In fact, the U.R. calendar begins with the founding of the Communio Venei, a school of "philosophers" who attempted to study and systematize the element in isolation; the ensuing Age of Chaos, furthermore, begins with the Communio's mysterious annihilation.

Purekin elevs can utilize Venei at will and to countless ends: they can turn air into fire and water into ice, they can alter the physical features of any material, they can hypnotize armies and mobs, and so on. Halfelevs, though, require the aid of anodynes, natural supplements that are specific to the faculties one may wish to access. The anodynes can be organic—ingesting beltreres leaf can enable a kind of telepathy in the user, for example—or mineral—meditating on an aventurine gemstone can turn one invisible.

The continued study of Venei was, however, overshadowed with the swift emergence of Merrenar, a dualist naemal religion proliferated by the followers of Merr, the Divine Scribe (writer of *The Divine Conjecture*, among others), throughout the Age of Chaos. In short, its adherents worship the All-Being, the prime mover and creative force of Existence that stands opposite the Abyssal, the primary destructive force.

The religion's history is mostly irrelevant to this story, but the brunt of its influence is yet observable, mainly in its churches and local hierarchy. Church-building (to the Merren official) is an act of legitimizing a district or space as sacred and, thus, within the subliminal territory of Merrenar. Their commissions are dispatched by the clericus, a regional head in Bienvale, to their subordinate chaplains, who then oversee the construction and management of the new temple. Lastly, each church or chapel is dedicated to a sanct, a deceased Merren of notable fame who has been consecrated by consensus of church authorities (much the same way emperors and war heroes of antiquity were deified for their deeds.

Char Leshess resides in southeast Pennsylvania and is the creator of the (forthcoming, July 2021) podcast Field of Fields. This book, written in 2018, is Char's debut novel and first professional self-publication. It is, in other words, like a wad of gum spat onto the sidewalk long after losing its flavor.